FAR FROM OVER

Sheila O'Flanagan

HEADLINE

First published in Great Britain in 2000
by HEADLINE BOOK PUBLISHING

10 9 8 7 6 5 4 3 2 1

British Library Cataloguing in Publication Data

O'Flanagan, Sheila
Far from over
I.Title
823.9'14 [F]

ISBN 0 7472 7575 0 (hardback)
ISBN 0 7472 7107 0 (trade paperback)

Typeset by Palimpsest Book Production Limited,
Polmont, Stirlingshire
Printed and bound in Great Britain by
Mackays of Chatham plc, Chatham, Kent.

HEADLINE BOOK PUBLISHING
A division of the Hodder Headline Group
338 Euston Road
London NW1 3BH

www.headline.co.uk
www.hodderheadline.com

That the birds of
Worry and care
Fly above your
Head, this you
Cannot change.
But that they build
Nests in your hair,
This you can prevent.

Chinese Proverb

For keeping my hair nest free even though sometimes it seemed impossible, love and thanks go to:

My agent Carole Blake
Anne and the entire team at Headline
Patricia – a friend indeed!
My family
Colm

And to all of you who part with hard cash to read my books, thank you so much – I hope you enjoy this one!

Chapter 1

O n the day that David Hennessy married the tall, thin, flame-haired
bimbo bitch, Gemma went on a major spending spree. By the
time that David and the bitch were exchanging vows, Gemma had
amassed a bright orange jacket from Pia Bang, three silk tops from
Airwave, a denim skirt from Principles, two pairs of shoes from Nine
West and an outrageously expensive leather handbag from Brown
Thomas. But it was at the Brown Thomas cosmetics counter – where
she hadn't originally intended to buy anything at all – that everything
went horribly wrong.

The sales assistant, Monica Coady, smiled brightly at her. It had been
a quiet day so far – the weather had kept people out of the shops
and on the beaches – so this sale would help her commission figures
considerably.

'I'm terribly sorry, Ms Garvey,' she said as she looked at the
machine, 'but authorisation has been refused. Maybe if you left out
one item . . . ?'

Gemma looked at the Christian Dior cleanser, toner and moisturiser
package in front of her, as well as the foundation, lipstick, blusher and
bottle of Dolce Vita. She attempted to calculate how much might be left
on the card after all her previous purchases were taken into account.

'Oh.' She tried to look nonchalant. 'I must have got a bit carried
away.'

Carried away was an understatement, she thought. It had been
absolutely wonderful to walk into shops and simply buy things for the
sake of it. She'd got a buzz every single time a purchase was wrapped in
tissue paper and slid into a bag. The sales assistants had been smiling and
cheerful and helped Gemma feel as though she should be smiling and
cheerful too. And every time she signed her card she felt a little better.

Now she simply felt embarrassed.

'I think I'd better forget it,' she said, much to Monica's consternation.

'I'm sure some of it would fit on the card,' said the sales assistant.

1

'There's no need to leave everything. Or you could use your store card if you have one? Or cash, of course.'

Cash! Gemma grimaced. 'Not right now,' she told Monica. 'I think that I've done enough spending for the day. I'm sorry.'

'OK.' Monica tried to look friendly but it was difficult when she thought about the commission that had just disappeared. 'See you again perhaps.'

'Sure,' said Gemma and walked out into Grafton Street. Beads of sweat had appeared on her forehead. Partly because it was in the full glare of the sun and partly because she was reliving the scene in the shop. She'd tried to ignore the curious glances of other customers as the sales assistant had taken back the cosmetics. But it had been humiliating all the same. She should have known how close she was to her card limit. She usually tried hard to keep track of any purchases she put on it. But she hadn't kept track today because she hadn't wanted to.

She gritted her teeth and pushed her way through the crowded street towards St Stephen's Green. She needed to sit down and take the weight off her feet. Besides, she could feel a blister beginning to form on her big toe because she'd worn her leather shoes with no tights today. They were beginning to chafe at the heel too.

The park was thronged with people – men with no shirts and women with skimpy tops or, in some cases, nothing but lacy Wonderbras. Gemma wished that she had the nerve to take off her plain white Calvin Klein T-shirt and sit in St Stephen's Green in nothing more than her bra and skirt. But it was one thing for a girl of eighteen to sit practically topless in the centre of Dublin, it was quite another for a woman of thirty-five to flaunt her sagging boobs in public.

There were no park benches available. Gemma walked across the grass, past a group of laughing students, and sat down in the shade of a chestnut tree. She arranged her packages around her and closed her eyes.

Thirty-five. She wondered when, exactly, thirty-five had started to feel old. Maybe it was when she realised that no exercise in the world was ever going to give her back the body she'd had when she was younger. The slim, taut body of someone who could eat as much as she liked and not put on weight. It wasn't as though she was fat, exactly, now of course. But ten years and two children had changed her shape more than she would have liked. Sometimes, when she looked in the mirror, she felt as though she'd turned into someone she didn't even know.

She was quite sure that there were hoards of thirty-five-year-old women walking around the city who looked as good as they had when they were twenty-five and who felt as young as ever. Even worse, she'd opened a magazine today and seen a dewy-skinned Goldie Hawn smiling out at her. The woman was in her fifties, for God's sake. A wrinkle or two would have been nice. Gemma sighed. She dreaded to think what she'd look like at fifty given how much her body had let her down already. Especially when she compared it to that of the eleven years younger, flame-haired bimbo bitch.

She'd always thought of her as the bitch. From the moment she'd heard about her. It was stupid, really, she didn't even know her and it wasn't as though she cared any more. At the time when David had first met her, he and Gemma were already in the process of getting a divorce so it wasn't as though the bimbo had broken up their marriage. She hadn't swooped in and lured David away from his wife and family. But it had bothered Gemma when she heard about it. David was seeing someone in the office, she'd been told, and the girl was young, red-haired and absolutely gorgeous.

When, one day, she finally met her, Gemma had almost choked. She'd seen Orla's smooth, clear complexion, her riot of tumbling red-gold curls and her long, long legs shown off to such advantage by her short, short cotton skirt and she'd wanted to scream with rage that he'd found someone so lovely. She couldn't help feeling consumed with envy that the young and beautiful Orla was in his life while she trundled towards middle age on her own. Except for the children, of course. David's children. Yet, much as she loved them, they didn't make it easy to start all over again.

She told herself that it wouldn't last, that David would get tired of Orla's wide, beaming smile and irritating manner of clearing her throat before she spoke but it was hard to be sure. She'd seen the looks that they'd exchanged, the same intimate glances that she had once shared with him, the unspoken belief that they were the only people in the world who mattered.

She sighed as she buried her toes in the grass. It was funny how clear in her memory the day she'd met David Hennessy was. It didn't seem like almost fifteen years ago. She smiled faintly. A true sign of age, she told herself, that fifteen years seemed like a short time.

It had been late on a Friday afternoon. A day almost as warm as today when the air was heavy and oppressive. Gemma was hot and tired and her back ached. There had been a constant stream of clients into the busy city centre hair salon where she worked and most of them had appointments with Gemma because she was a naturally gifted stylist and was always in demand.

3

At six o'clock that evening she still had Stephanie Russell's cut and blow-dry scheduled. But Stephanie had phoned to say that she'd be a little late. Only fifteen or twenty minutes, Stephanie promised. She had to wait for a phone call from their US office. Half an hour at the most. It would be OK, wouldn't it? It was only a cut and blow-dry. No colour or anything like that.

Stephanie was a regular customer and a generous tipper. Gemma told her that it would be no problem. Besides, she was glad of the break.

She sat down on the black vinyl settee just inside the door where she could get a hint of fresh air. Although all the fans in the salon were on, it was like a sauna and the smell of ammonia and hair spray lingered.

Then he walked in. He was at least six feet tall. He was tanned, square-faced and very attractive. He was built like a rugby player, with broad shoulders and muscular legs. Gemma could see he had muscular legs because he was wearing dark green Bermuda shorts. He also wore a beige T-shirt which said Be Nice to Me I've Had a Hard Day.

'Haven't we all?' Gemma grinned at him. 'Can I help to make it better?'

'I need it cut.' He ran his fingers through his hair. 'I want something less casual and more business.'

She smiled. His hair was almost shoulder length and jet-black. She couldn't wait to touch it, to allow it to slide through her fingers.

'What kind of business?' she asked.

'Suit business,' he replied. 'I need something that looks good in a suit.'

'OK.' She looked at her watch. Plenty of time to do this before Stephanie arrived. And if she wasn't finished, Stephanie would have to wait. Gemma wanted to be the one to cut those thick black locks.

She led him over to the basin and handed him a gown.

'I don't need this,' he said.

'Of course you do.' She held it out for him. 'You don't want to get splashed, do you? Or get hair all over that T-shirt?'

'I'm sorry.' He smiled and the edges of his eyes crinkled endearingly. 'It has been a hard day!'

'Why?' asked Gemma.

'Because this morning I decided that I should stop fooling around with my life and get a decent job.'

'And did you?' asked Gemma as she turned on the water.

'Well, yes.' He looked abashed. 'I did. With the proviso that I get my hair cut!'

4

She cupped her hand across his forehead as she began to wet his hair. 'What sort of a job?'

'A personal investment adviser,' he told her.

'What on earth is that?' Gemma tipped some shampoo into her hand and began to massage it into his hair. She worked slowly, allowing the shampoo to build into a dense white foam, enjoying the feeling of closeness to him and the sensual pleasure of her fingers against his skin.

'Actually, it's life assurance and pensions,' he said. 'But we're supposed to call ourselves personal investment advisers. It sounds better than insurance salesman.'

Gemma giggled. 'It sure does. And when do you start this job?'

'Monday.' He sighed. 'I can't believe I've done it. Until now I bummed around, worked in bars, travelled – you know the sort of thing.'

'I've heard.' Gemma had never bummed around. Her mother wouldn't have approved. She'd started her apprenticeship as soon as she left school. She'd made quick progress from sweeping the floors to cutting hair herself and had looked forward to the day when she'd have her own salon and be her own boss. It had been her dream ever since the day she'd hacked the hair off her favourite doll to give her a more trendy look. Gemma had the interior of her salon mapped out in her head. And she'd already chosen the name – The Cutting Edge. All she needed was some time and experience.

'Where have you travelled to?' She rinsed his hair and rubbed it with a towel.

'All around,' he told her. 'Europe, the Far East, the States – everywhere.'

'Lucky thing,' she said. 'Torremolinos is as far as I've got. And Santa Ponsa.'

'Travel is good for the soul,' he said as he sat in front of a mirror. 'You learn a lot about people.'

'Probably,' said Gemma. 'Look, can you keep your head still? I don't want you to end up lopsided. Or worse still, stab you in the neck.'

'Sorry,' he said.

She snipped at his hair.

'You don't think you're being a bit radical?' he said doubtfully as a lock slid down his gown and onto the floor.

'A cut for suits, you said. We get a lot of suits in here. I know exactly what you need.'

Afterwards he looked at himself in the mirror and nodded. Gemma had applied gel to his hair and combed it back from his forehead. She'd cut it tight at the back of his neck.

'My God,' he said. 'I look like some whizz kid.'

'Maybe you are,' she told him. 'Maybe you'll be a very successful personal investment adviser.'

'I look the part,' he said. 'I didn't when I came in. Now you'd think I was born to it! Thanks.'

'You're welcome.'

He followed her to the till and paid her. He tipped her a pound.

'See you again,' she called as he walked out into the warmth of the evening.

'Sure.' And he waved goodbye.

'Nice butt.' Stephanie Russell, who had been waiting for the last five minutes grinned at Gemma.

'Nice bod,' said Gemma as she led Stephanie to the basins. Even as she washed and cut Stephanie's hair she was thinking about him.

It truly didn't seem that long ago. Gemma could even remember what she'd been wearing – white jeans and a white top with huge shoulder pads and a sequinned lion on the front. Her own hair had been long, bleached blonde and piled up on her head so that she looked much taller than her five feet four inches. She'd worn her tomato-red sandals that day. She'd looked good. She'd been a size ten.

She ran her finger round the waistband of her skirt. She was a size fourteen now. Her pot belly had come after Keelin was born and all the exercise in the world hadn't shifted it. And her hips had widened along with breasts that had expanded too. Her hair, though always well-cut, was now her natural, unexciting light brown with occasional threads of grey.

David had said, at first, that he liked her better when she put on some weight. That she'd been too skinny when he'd first known her. That it had been strange to feel the bones in her body when he'd held her to him. And that he'd never really liked blondes anyway.

But she hadn't quite believed him. And, of course, the flame-haired bimbo bitch, though not a blonde, was a lithe size ten.

Size ten and not much older than Gemma had been when she first met him. Did any man ever go for an older woman after his marriage had broken up? she wondered. Did they ever pick on someone with greyer hair and wider hips and saggier breasts? Or someone with a couple of quarrelsome, exasperating but always lovable kids?

And what was it that made a perfect size ten twenty-four-year-old marry a forty-year-old bloke who wasn't exactly the Diet Coke man himself?

6

Surely sex was enough? Gemma shivered despite the heat. She didn't regret divorcing David. Marrying him had been the mistake. She'd been taken in by his easy charm and his relaxed manner and his chat about bumming around the world. She hadn't realised that, in cutting his hair, she'd cut away that part of his life too. She'd married him for the man she thought he was, only to find that he was someone quite different. She could see now that divorce had been inevitable. But she hadn't ever imagined him marrying someone else. She hadn't for one second ever believed that anyone would force him up the altar. Or, in the bimbo bitch's case, into the registry office. She hated to think that it had all worked out so neatly for him while she couldn't help feeling a failure.

She rubbed her temples. She wasn't a failure. She really wasn't. She'd done her best. Everyone told her that. But no one had been surprised when they separated. No one except David, who'd been shocked when she asked for the divorce. And Frances, her mother, who'd been (as Gemma had expected) utterly horrified. Neither of them understood how she felt. Frances had said, grimly, that David was the best thing that had ever happened to Gemma. Gemma, she told her, would be lucky to find someone like him again. When Gemma retorted that she hoped not, Frances had sighed and called her ungrateful. David had always wanted her to be grateful too – for the house and the holidays and the luxuries he provided. Despite her love of beautiful things and her enjoyment in spending money, Gemma could have gone without them if only he'd been home before ten every night.

Now she'd learned to cope by herself. Her life, though unexciting, was lived by her rules. She'd brought up the children well. Her best friend, Niamh Conran, who'd worked with her in the city centre salon and had since opened a place of her own, had offered Gemma a job with flexible working hours which Gemma had gratefully accepted. She almost had it all under control. Except the finances, of course, which she knew she'd never completely get under control. Money management wasn't her strong point. David had been the money manager in their marriage.

Now he was married again and she felt hurt all over again. She hadn't expected to feel like this. She hadn't expected to feel shocked, and stunned and – somehow – betrayed. Because she'd always expected that life would go on pretty much as it had for the past few years. Even if they didn't love each other any more she knew that they were still joined by their cares about the children. David cared about the children. He saw them regularly, he never forgot their birthdays (although he'd never

7

remembered when he'd been married to her) and he always took a keen interest in what they were doing.

She sighed. Now she felt as though he had succeeded in truly rebuilding his life while she was merely living. He'd moved on while she was simply treading water. She hadn't gone out with a man since they'd split up. She hadn't had the slightest interest in starting up another relationship. She hadn't had the time to start up another relationship, for God's sake!

Yet he had. David, who hadn't had time to come home to her in the evening, who hadn't had time to get involved in anything that wasn't work-related, who hadn't – then – ever had time to come shopping with her for the children's birthday or Christmas presents – David had since found the time to meet somebody new and marry her. And in doing so he'd managed to rock the foundations of the life that Gemma had so carefully reconstructed.

She got up and brushed dry grass from her skirt. I hate her, she thought. And I hate him too.

↩

Orla Hennessy, until that afternoon Orla O'Neill, stood in the gardens of Kilkea Castle and gazed into the distance. The gardens were a spectacle of vibrant colour against the backdrop of the cloudless blue sky. The sun beat down on her shoulders, warming her through the thin fabric of her dress.

She closed her eyes. It had been the oddest day of her life, she thought. She didn't think that most people would regard their wedding day as odd, but for Orla it had been.

She couldn't help being acutely aware that David had done this before. That he'd looked at Gemma Garvey in exactly the same way as he was now looking at Orla O'Neill and that he'd said the same things to her and that, then, he'd meant them. The short ceremony had flashed past her in a blur. She was married before she even realised it and the thought scared her. She hadn't intended to get married until she was at least thirty but she loved David so much that it seemed exactly the right thing to do. The moment she'd first seen him there was an instant attraction and then, afterwards, when they'd finally gone out together she knew that he was the man she wanted to spend her life with. She knew that he loved her too. He'd told her often enough. She was very sure that they were doing the right thing. But she wished they'd done it abroad, where they wouldn't have had to worry about her family or his family and the obvious awkwardness that they felt about the relationship.

Orla walked down the gravel path and thought about their families. His parents hadn't been too bad, really. Perhaps because they were older and didn't much care what he did once he was happy. Although his mother had told her that she'd liked Gemma. That she still saw her because Gemma brought the children to visit and that she wouldn't stop seeing her just because David had married Orla. Nothing against Orla, of course, Mrs Hennessy had said and smiled at her so that Orla felt as though the woman probably meant it.

David's mother had, in fact, been much more relaxed about it than Rosanna O'Neill. Orla's mother hadn't approved of the marriage at all. Orla hadn't expected her to be pleased but she'd been completely taken aback by how against it her mother actually was. Rosanna O'Neill hadn't minced her words.

'Are you off your rocker?' she'd demanded. 'He's twice your age. And he's married with kids.'

'He's divorced,' said Orla calmly. 'And he's not twice my age. He's fifteen years and three months older than me.'

'Oh, don't be ridiculous.' Rosanna looked at her, eyes full of concern. 'You're a young girl. You're pretty. You've got brains. You can do a hell of a lot better for yourself than a cast-off man and his family.'

Orla bit back the words of fury that she wanted to hurl at her mother. She could understand how Rosanna felt. But she knew that David was the only man for her. And she was quite determined that she was going to marry him. As he was quite determined that he was going to marry her.

And now it had happened. They'd exchanged vows in the banal registry office ceremony and they'd come down to Kilkea Castle with a small number of family and friends to celebrate.

It was just that it didn't feel real, thought Orla, as she sat on one of the stone benches. It didn't feel as though she was married at all.

⌒

When Gemma got home she carefully unwrapped all her purchases and hung the clothes in the wardrobe. It wouldn't do for Keelin to see them yet. Her daughter would be furious if she knew that Gemma had blown their monthly budget on feel-good clothes. She wished that she felt good about them now. She ran her hand along the back of the orange jacket. It was lovely, though. It was a classic piece. She'd be able to wear it over and over again, even if orange was this season's colour. And she'd needed the shoes. Especially the low-heeled comfortable pair. She was on her feet so much that comfort was very important in shoes. All the same, she sighed, she really should have paid some of the accumulated bills instead of adding to them.

She went downstairs to the kitchen and poured herself a gin and tonic. It was still warm outside. The tiny back garden of the townhouse in Sandymount was a flower-filled sun trap. The scent of her favourite soft pink roses hung in the air and soothed her. She took her drink into the garden and sat on one of the wooden chairs. It was peaceful here. She almost liked it.

It could never be the same as the house in Dun Laoghaire though. That had been so wonderful, with its spacious rooms, its magnificent views and its expensive furnishings. I must have been mad, she thought suddenly, giving up everything I had for this little matchbox. Three tiny bedrooms. One living room. A combined kitchen and dining area. The whole thing would have fitted into the living room in the Dun Laoghaire house.

But I wasn't happy, she reminded herself. I wasn't happy with David.

She looked at her watch. The children would be home soon. She swallowed the gin and tonic in three gulps.

⌒

'Are you all right?'

Orla turned as she heard David's footsteps behind her. She smiled at him. 'Of course.'

'Why are you out here when everyone else is having a good time inside?'

'I wanted a few minutes on my own,' she told him.

'Don't tell me you're regretting it already?' He looked at her in mock horror.

'Not quite.' She smiled. 'I couldn't be happier.'

'What, then?' he asked.

'I thought I'd feel different,' she said. 'I know that's really silly of me. But I thought I'd feel different inside and I don't. I can't believe we've done it, David.'

'I can,' he said. 'When I see you here, wearing my ring, I can believe it.'

She laughed.

10

'It'll be all right, you know,' he told her.

'All right?'

'It'll be perfect. I know you worry sometimes, Orla.'

'I don't worry,' she said.

'You do. You're afraid that it won't work out.'

'Don't be silly.'

'But I love you more than anything.'

'More than you loved Gemma?' She couldn't help asking him.

He took her hands and held them tightly between his own. 'When I married Gemma I thought I loved her. But it was nothing like I feel for you, Orla. Nothing. And even though I never really wanted to split up with her, I'm so grateful that I did. Because otherwise I'd never have met you.'

'You'd have met me.' She grinned at him. 'But we would have had an illicit affair.'

'I much prefer being married to you than having an illicit affair with you.'

'I love you.' She touched him on the cheek.

'I love you too.' He kissed her on the lips.

⌐

The sun slid behind the trees at the back of the house. Dapples of shade fell across the patio. Gemma got up and poured herself another drink. She'd promised herself that she wouldn't get depressed today. But it was hard not to feel that way. Even though she should be feeling sorry for Orla O'Neill instead of resenting her.

She'd thought about driving down to Kilkea Castle. Of sneaking into the hotel and looking for David and Orla. Just to confirm for herself that they really had got married. Because, right now, it didn't seem real to her. She just couldn't believe that he'd done it. It seemed so much more final than the divorce had ever done.

⌐

Orla followed David inside and sat on the empty chair beside Abby Johnson.

'You look lovely,' said her friend. 'Really great.'

'Thanks.' Orla patted the back of her hair. 'I feel like I'm held together by spray and pins.'

'One wrong move and the whole thing comes apart.' Abby giggled.

11

'It looks nice like that, Orla. And I love the outfit.' Orla's dress was cream silk which came to just below her knee.

'Thanks.'

'Would you have preferred the whole church thing?' asked Abby.

Orla shook her head. 'You know me, Abby. I was never really into it very much. This suits me much better.' She grinned. 'Even if my darling mother doesn't think much of it.'

They both glanced in the direction of Rosanna who was sitting ramrod straight in her chair, an untasted glass of white wine in front of her.

'She'll get used to it,' said Abby. 'Statistically, I'm sure there are lots of younger girls marrying older, divorced men these days.'

'You think so?' Orla laughed. 'She truly thinks that David is a second-hand husband. I couldn't seem to get through to her at all. I didn't expect her to understand straightaway, but I thought she'd understand enough. She doesn't. And she freaks out every time she thinks of the kids.'

'Do you?' asked Abby.

'Sometimes.' Orla bit her lip. 'Let's face it, I'm only eleven years older than Keelin! Technically, I guess I'm her stepmother. But practically, I feel more like her older sister.'

'How does she feel about it?'

Orla shrugged. 'Hard to tell. I suppose she resents me. I know I would if I was her. But I didn't break up her parents' marriage. It wasn't anything to do with me. She shouldn't care about me too much one way or the other.'

'It's a bit of a task, taking them on.'

'I'm not!' Orla was emphatic. 'David sees them every week – but I don't have to see them with him each time. I haven't seen that much of them, to be honest. I suppose I'll see them more often now but I'm not going to get involved.'

'It all seems terribly grown up,' mused Abby. 'And so does David.'

'What do you mean?'

'Let's face it, Orla, he is grown up! He's older than us. He's not perpetually broke. He's different.'

'I'm not perpetually broke,' said Orla. 'But I know what you mean.'

'Probably the fact that he has kids makes a difference too,' said Abby.

Orla shrugged. 'Maybe.'

'Why didn't they come today?' asked Abby.

'Who?'

12

'The kids.'

'We talked for ages about it. David asked them. But they said no. I think it was Gemma's influence really but David didn't want them to feel pressurised. He's really good like that, Abby. And it might have been a bit emotional for them.'

'Perhaps.' Abby filled her glass with wine. 'Anyway, I hope you and David have a great life together, Orla. I truly do.'

'Thanks.'

'As long as you stay my best friend and don't turn into some old married woman.'

'How likely is that?' asked Orla and the two of them laughed.

Chapter 2

Frances Garvey parked her green Vokswagen Polo outside her daughter's house and took the keys out of the ignition

'Home at last,' she told Keelin and Ronan. 'Don't forget anything.'

'Are you coming in, Gran?' asked Ronan.

Frances glanced at her watch. It was still bright although it was almost nine o'clock. 'I suppose so.' She pulled her bag from beneath the driver's seat. 'But I won't stay for long.'

She knew that Gemma wouldn't want her to stay for long. Certainly not today. She followed Keelin and Ronan up the path and winced as her grandson put his finger on the doorbell and kept it there.

Gemma opened the door. Ronan rushed past her and into the living room. Gemma heard the click of the TV being switched on.

'Hi,' said Keelin who immediately went upstairs to her bedroom.

'Hello, Gemma.' Frances followed Gemma into the kitchen where she took some mugs from the cupboard while Gemma filled the kettle.

'How was the day?' asked Gemma.

'OK.' Frances picked up a tea towel and wiped the cups. Gemma fought the urge to grab the cloth from her. 'Brittas was absolutely crowded as you can imagine but it was beautiful. Keelin lay on the beach all day – I made sure she was covered in sun screen – but Ronan met a couple of kids and they went off to play football. We couldn't see him all the time but we could certainly hear him. Your father and I were on our own mostly. Keelin didn't say anything, she just lay there with her eyes closed. Very adolescent! We stopped off for burgers and chips on the way home so they're not hungry.'

'Keelin wouldn't have eaten burgers.' Gemma dropped a couple of tea bags into the bright yellow teapot. 'She's going through a vegetarian phase.'

'Don't I know it!' Frances grimaced. 'She had a vegetarian burger. She kept talking about eating the carrion flesh of dead animals and I wanted to throw up.'

Gemma smiled faintly. 'I know. She does the same at home.'

'When did she start this lark?' demanded Frances. She flicked the tea towel over the table then sat down.

'A few months ago,' said Gemma. 'She watched some bloody film about intensive farming.'

'It's not good for her,' said Frances sharply. 'And I'm not being conservative and stupid. She's thirteen years old. She's a growing girl – I'd swear she's shot up another couple of inches since last month. She needs vitamins and proteins.'

'Oh, I pack her full of supplements.' Gemma sighed. 'I was throwing vitamins down her throat and then I read some article saying that you can overdose on them. You can never bloody get it right. And yes, she has grown. With a bit of luck she'll grow out of the veggie phase until she's a bit older.'

She poured boiling water into the teapot. From the living room came the sound of AK47 gunfire punctuated by whoops of triumph as Ronan played his newest computer game.

'And how about you?' asked Frances eventually. 'How was your day?'

'Fine,' said Gemma. 'I went shopping.'

'I might have guessed,' said Frances tartly. 'That's always your solution, isn't it?'

'What do you mean?' Gemma turned to face her mother.

'Oh, come on, Gemma! Remember when you passed your exams? A shopping spree. And when you got the interview? A shopping spree. And when you got the job? A shopping spree. I pretty much guessed you'd be in town today.'

'It helps,' said Gemma defiantly.

'Once you have enough money to pay for it,' said Frances.

Gemma gritted her teeth. Her mother knew perfectly well that money was tight. And tighter, she thought, now that she'd gone right up to her card limit. Stupid, stupid, stupid! Frances would never have done that, she thought savagely. Frances would have walked around and looked at everything and realised that she could spend a couple of quid on a scarf and that would be that. She probably wouldn't even have bought the scarf. She would have been sensible. Frances was a very sensible woman. Strange then, Gemma mused as she brought the teapot to the kitchen table, that she'd had two very unsensible daughters.

'Have you been talking to Liz?' she asked, changing the subject.

'Not today.' Frances stirred her tea and took a ginger nut biscuit from the tin on the table.

'I was wondering how Suzy's arm is,' said Gemma.

'Bloody silly child!' Frances snorted.

'Liz or Suzy?' asked Gemma.

Frances looked darkly at her. 'Your sister,' she said. 'What on earth Liz was doing letting Suzy out on those roller blades I'll never know.'

'They're perfectly safe,' said Gemma. 'Usually.'

'Suzy is only four years old,' Frances snapped. 'Liz should have known better.'

'Plenty of four-year-olds have fun on roller blades,' protested Gemma. 'Admittedly she should have been wearing all that crash pad stuff, but it was a clean break in the end, wasn't it? So padding might not have made any difference.'

'I told Liz that she should cop on to herself,' said Frances.

'She was never great at copping on,' Gemma told her.

'Neither of you were,' said Frances. 'I often wonder where I went wrong.'

Gemma pursed her lips. She didn't want to hear the where I went wrong lecture. She'd heard it often enough when she was a girl. When she'd told Frances that she didn't want to study for the rest of her life, that she wanted to be a hair stylist. Frances had been appalled at that. The result was the 'wasting a good brain' lecture. When she'd gone on holiday with Niamh and three other girlfriends and her mother had seen the photos of them topless on the beach and not wearing very much else the rest of the time; that had brought on the 'you've got to respect yourself' lecture. And, of course, she'd delivered the big lecture, the definitive lecture when Gemma had announced that she was going to divorce David. Gemma might as well have told her that she was going to murder David for all the support Frances had given her. Not that Gemma had actually expected her mother's support but it would have been nice all the same.

She sighed. Nothing that either of her daughters had ever done had been good enough for Frances. At least, though, Gemma said to herself, I actually managed to get married. That kept her happy for a while.

Her sister Liz, younger by a couple of years, was still single. She hadn't been in a serious relationship when she'd arrived home and told them that she was pregnant. Gemma shuddered as she remembered her mother's reaction to that. She hadn't needed to hang around for Liz's lecture.

'Thanks for taking them today,' she said, breaking the silence. 'I know it's not easy for you to put up with them.'

'I wouldn't have if I'd known you were going to shop,' said Frances. 'I thought you'd have been thinking about your life, Gemma.'

'Thinking what about it?' asked Gemma. 'That it's shit?'

'Gemma!'

'Oh, lighten up!' Gemma snapped. 'That's what you think, isn't it? That I was a rotten daughter because I didn't go to college. That I was a rotten wife because I let my husband get away. That I'm a rotten mother because I have a vegetarian daughter and a hooligan son.'

'I don't think that,' said Frances.

'Don't you?'

Frances sighed deeply. 'I think you could have done things better,' she said. 'I mean, you must think you could have done things better yourself.'

'Of course,' said Gemma. 'But I did my best at the time.' She swallowed hard. She didn't want to cry in front of her mother. Frances would think that she'd won if Gemma cried.

'I suppose it was better than Liz,' admitted Frances.

'It wasn't Liz's fault.'

Frances raised an eyebrow. 'Even you can't think that.'

'Not entirely her fault,' Gemma amended.

'She should have told the father,' said Frances, 'and made him face up to his responsibilities.'

Gemma said nothing.

'At least Michael got it right.' Frances smiled slightly at the thought of her son.

'Sure,' said Gemma. 'He married the social climber and moved to London.'

'Debbie is a lovely girl,' said Frances fondly. 'And she adores Michael—'

'And they have two utterly wonderful children.' Gemma finished her mother's sentence for her. She'd heard this a million times before.

'They are nice children,' said Frances. 'So mannerly.'

'And mine aren't?'

Frances looked at her in annoyance. 'I didn't say that.'

'But you probably think it.' Gemma stood up and put her mug in the sink.

'It's different for them,' said Frances. 'Debbie is at home all day. She can look after them.'

'You're not saying the right thing,' said Gemma as evenly as she could. 'I can look after my children too.'

17

'Of course you can,' said Frances. 'It's just that Debbie has more time for Thomas and Polly.'

'Of course she has. I had more time when I was married to David. But I don't now.' Gemma gritted her teeth. 'And I'm doing my best.'

'I know you are,' said Frances. 'I know how much you do for them. It's just—'

'Drop it,' said Gemma wearily. 'I know you don't mean to make me feel like the worst mother in the world.'

'I don't,' said Frances.

'Then let's leave things as they are,' said Gemma. 'And thanks again for taking them today.'

'Whenever you need a break you know I'll take them,' Frances told her.

But you'd prefer them to be Thomas and Polly, thought Gemma savagely. You put up with my children. You love his children. The perfect children from the perfect family created by my perfect older brother.

⌐

Orla stood in the huge bathroom and disassembled her hair. By the time she'd removed the pins and clips, it fell around her face in sticky clumps. Anything less romantic than gelled and moussed hair she couldn't imagine.

She stared at her reflection in the mirror. Her mascara had smudged, her long-lasting lipstick had given up the ghost and her eyes were red from tiredness. She turned on the shower over the bath.

'What are you doing?' David called from the bedroom.

'I have to wash all this gunk out of my hair,' she yelled back. 'I can't stand it another second!' She stepped under the spray and let the water cascade over her face. Instantly she felt better.

David pushed the bathroom door open. 'Why?'

She pushed her wet hair out of her eyes. 'Why what?'

'Why can't you stand it?'

'It's making me itch,' she told him. 'I feel like there's half a can of spray in it.'

'Let me help.' David unbuttoned his shirt.

'You're joining me?' asked Orla.

'Oh, I think so.' He took off his trousers. 'You look like you need someone to help.'

'You might be right.'

18

'I know I'm right.' He stood in the shower beside her and caught hold of her hair. 'It feels all right to me.'

'It's not,' said Orla. 'It needs lots of shampoo.'

'OK.' David poured shampoo onto her head and began to massage it into her hair.

'That's nice,' murmured Orla.

'How about the rest of you?' he asked.

'The rest of me?'

'You probably need a good scrubbing.' He grinned at her. 'Come here, woman.' He tipped some shower soap onto his hands and began to slide them over her lean, taut body.

'Very nice,' she said languorously.

'Enjoying it?' he asked.

'Absolutely.'

'Glad to be here?'

'Where else could I be?'

'Happy to be Mrs O'Neill?'

'I pity anyone who isn't,' she said.

He put his arms round her and held her slippery body close to him. 'You know I love you,' he said.

'Mm?'

'More than anything else in the world,' he told her.

'Promise?'

'Of course.'

She wrapped her legs round him and he stumbled.

'Are you OK?' she asked anxiously.

'The bath is slippy,' he said. 'It's not designed for this!'

'That's what makes it exciting.' She grinned at him.

'Everything you do is exciting,' said David as she slithered against him again. 'Everything.'

⌒

Keelin stretched out on her bed. Her shoulders were sore. She'd burned them today even though she'd worn plenty of sun cream. But she hadn't managed to cover the very tips of her shoulder blades and they ached now.

It had been an awful day. It was all very well for her mother to come up with this great plan of going out with Gran and Granddad, but Keelin hadn't wanted to. She'd wanted to go to David and Orla's wedding. David had asked her if she wanted to go but she hadn't been sure then. And he'd noticed her uncertainty and told her not to worry, it didn't matter and maybe it was better if she didn't come. But she'd wanted to. It would have made it seem more real to her. It had been weird lying on the beach and thinking about it all the time. She couldn't quite believe that her father had married somebody else. That this woman, Orla, was now part of their family.

Well, not exactly, she supposed. And Gemma would have a fit if she thought Keelin was thinking of Orla as part of the family. But how else was she to think of the woman who'd married her father? Some kind of distant friend?

She sighed. It hadn't been comfortable, finding out about Orla. Her father had told her one Sunday as they had brunch in Bewleys.

'You'll like her,' he'd promised. 'She's a great person. I want you to meet her.'

'Not today.' Keelin had looked at him in horror from beneath her fringe. She wasn't ready to meet her father's girlfriend. She pulled at the sleeves of her green jumper.

'Next time,' said David. 'When we go bowling.'

He often took her bowling. It was the one thing that both of them were good at and both of them enjoyed. She didn't want this Orla person to be involved in their bowling. She didn't want her to be involved in their lives.

Keelin had looked at Orla with her mass of curly red hair and her twinkling eyes and her ultra-fashionable clothes and couldn't believe that she wanted to marry her father. David was positively ancient compared to the girl standing beside him who looked young and vibrant and fun.

Keelin couldn't help comparing her to Gemma who walked around with a perpetual frown and who wouldn't dream of wearing a skirt that revealed more than a centimetre above her knee. It wasn't as though Gemma couldn't be stylish – Keelin knew that a lot of Gemma's clothes were very stylish – but they had an indelible mark of maturity about them which the sky-blue miniskirt that Orla was wearing that day certainly didn't.

Keelin didn't want to compare Orla and Gemma. There was nothing about them that she should compare.

'I'm really hopeless at this!' Orla had just sent a second consecutive ball into the gully. So far, she'd hit one pin. 'You'll have to show me how you do it, Keelin.'

'I don't know how I do it.' Keelin didn't look up at her but lifted her 9lb ball and stood in front of Lane 2. She approached the lane and released the ball, swerving it from right to left so that it hit the pins perfectly for a strike.

'You really will have to show me,' said Orla again.

Keelin shrugged and sat down. She allowed her long black hair to hide her face and she pretended to be concentrating on the scores while she ignored the black looks emanating from her father who was clearly afraid to say anything out loud. She could sense how annoyed he was with her but she wasn't going to make it easy for him. He hadn't made it easier for her, had he? He'd left them to fend for themselves. So what if he'd given them money? He didn't give them enough, Gemma was always saying that. Anyway, it wasn't about money. It had never been about money.

Now he was going out with someone who could have been her older sister. Her prettier older sister. Her sexier older sister. Keelin shivered. There was something uncomfortable about it. Unreal about it.

Orla wouldn't have wanted her at the wedding. David had said that she was perfectly happy to have Keelin along but Keelin knew that, in Orla's place, she wouldn't have wanted her new husband's kids there to remind her that he'd been married already. That this wasn't the first time. That she was marrying a middle-aged man. Did she worry that her new husband was forty years old? Did it bother her? Did she ask David questions about what life had been like when he was still married to Gemma? When he'd lived with them in the five-bedroomed house in Dun Laoghaire and she'd had a huge bedroom with plenty of room for all her stuff instead of the little box that she had now.

'Can I come in?' Gemma tapped at the door and Keelin sat up.

'Hi,' said Keelin.

'Hi.' Gemma sat on the edge of the bed. She looked at her daughter thoughtfully. Keelin looked tired, Gemma decided. Her dark-blue eyes were solemn and her hair fell in disarray around her sunburned shoulders. 'Did you have a good day?' Gemma asked.

'It was OK,' said Keelin.

'Your shoulders look a bit red.'

Keelin shrugged. It hurt. 'I missed a few bits.'

'Do you want me to put some aftersun on them for you?'

'I did already.'

'Did you use the aloe vera gel?' asked Gemma. 'That's pretty soothing.'

Keelin shook her head.

'I'll get it,' said Gemma. She returned with a bottle of the green gel and gently rubbed some onto Keelin's shoulders.

21

'Thanks,' said Keelin.

'How were Gran and Granddad?' asked Gemma as she screwed the top back on the bottle.

'The same as always,' said Keelin. 'Gran told Granddad what to do and he did it.'

Gemma laughed and Keelin smiled tentatively at her.

'Poor old Granddad,' said Gemma. 'He didn't know what he was letting himself in for when he married your gran.'

There was a sudden silence.

'What did you do?' asked Keelin.

'Oh, bits and pieces,' said Gemma. 'I bought a few things.'

'I thought we didn't have any money.'

Gemma made a face. 'We don't.'

'So how could you buy a few things?'

'We don't have lots of money,' Gemma amended, 'but we're not destitute, Keelin.'

'We didn't have enough money for me to buy a leather jacket,' said Keelin.

'No,' said Gemma although she could feel herself blush. She hadn't liked the black leather jacket with the chrome zips that Keelin wanted. She'd told her daughter that they had better things to do with their money than waste it on an overpriced jacket. But it had cost less than the bag she'd bought in BT's.

'I'm going to get a job for the rest of the summer.'

'What sort of job?'

'I don't know,' said Keelin. 'But I want some money of my own.'

'Fine,' said Gemma. 'It's a good idea.'

They were silent again.

'Did you hear how the wedding went?' asked Keelin eventually.

'No,' said Gemma. 'I wouldn't, would I?'

Keelin shrugged. 'I just wondered.'

'I'm sure it went well,' said Gemma carefully.

'I suppose so.'

'You could have gone,' Gemma told her. 'I wouldn't have minded.'

'Yes, you would,' said Keelin.

Gemma smiled slightly. 'Well, I suppose I would. But I wouldn't have stopped you.'

Keelin bit her lip. 'I don't think Dad really wanted me there.'

'He asked you, didn't he?'

'But it was to be polite,' said Keelin. 'Not because he cared.'

'Oh, Keelin, of course he cared. He still loves you, you know.'

22

Keelin had to fight the sudden urge she had to cry. 'He doesn't show it much.'

Gemma sighed. 'That was the problem, Keelin. He didn't show it very much to me either.' She hugged her daughter, carefully avoiding her sunburned shoulders. 'Are you staying up here or do you want to come downstairs for a while?'

'I'll stay here,' said Keelin. 'I have some things to do.'

'OK.' Gemma smiled at her and left the bedroom.

Keelin lay back on the bed and closed her eyes again. It had been such a weird day. And it was weird hearing Gemma saying that David had never shown her how much he loved her. That was ridiculous. He'd bought her loads of things. Anything she ever wanted.

Keelin rubbed her eyes. She'd always secretly harboured the hope that one day David would come back. That Gemma would realise how much he loved her. That they could live together as a family again. Even after the divorce she'd clung to the hope that her parents might realise that they loved each other.

But there was no point in hoping that any more. He wasn't ever coming home again. Orla had changed everything.

The bitch.

Chapter 3

Orla stood by the rail and sipped her glass of champagne. David had insisted on champagne even though she didn't really like it very much. Too bubbly, she'd told him, but he'd laughed and said that absolutely everybody liked champagne.

She glanced down at the silver bucket near her feet. The bottle of Piper-Heidsieck was almost empty. They'd ordered it after dinner and David had drunk most of it. It was quiet on the top deck of the boat. Quiet and dark and peaceful. The night breeze was balmy as it gently caressed her bare shoulders. On the horizon she could make out faint points of light which, she supposed, were either the coast of Florida or one of the islands of the Bahamas. By morning they would have docked at Nassau. She'd always dreamed of a honeymoon in the Bahamas and it felt strange to realise that her dream had actually come true. The words of a Chinese saying sprung into her mind. 'Be careful of what you wish for. You might get it.'

She shivered suddenly and laughed at her moment of fear. She'd got what she wanted and she was the happiest woman in the world. She put down the half-empty glass and leaned over the rail.

'Not thinking of throwing yourself in already.' David slid his arms round her waist.

She turned to him. 'Would you dive in and rescue me?'

'No.' He grinned at her. 'That'd ruin my suit. I'd throw you a lifebelt.'

'Thanks.' She laughed and cuddled up to him.

'You're beautiful,' said David.

'Thank you.'

'No. I mean it.' He gazed into her hazel eyes. 'I've never known anyone like you before. I was watching you. From the doorway. And I couldn't believe that this wonderful, gorgeous creature was actually mine.'

'Why?'

'I don't know.' He shook his head. 'I look at you and I think that one day I'll wake up.'

'Don't be so silly.' She kissed him gently on the lips.

They stood side by side and gazed into the water for a while. Then they sat down on the sun loungers that still lined the upper deck. David closed his eyes. But he didn't go to sleep. He recalled the moment when he'd first seen Orla. He'd known, even then, that she was going to be important to him. But then he'd thought it would be a work thing. Because that was the way he was used to thinking. People he met during the day were either rivals or clients. From the second that Orla O'Neill had walked into the room, he'd marked her down as a rival. He'd been giving the lecture on sales techniques. He gave it every time Gravitas Life and Pensions brought in a batch of new salespeople. He was introduced as the top salesman for the past five years, easily beating the man in second place each year. He was there to tell them how to close a sale and how much money they could make if they did.

He'd started the talk by saying that the top ten salesmen all loved their jobs. And Orla O'Neill had interrupted him almost immediately.

'Are there any women in the top ten?'

He stared at her. She was wearing a charcoal-grey trouser suit. A white silk top. Gold earrings. Gold chain. And her long red hair was tied back behind her head.

'Pardon?' he said.

'Women?' said Orla. 'Are there any women in the top ten?'

'Not last year,' he replied. 'Last year, in fact, the top fifteen salespeople were all men.'

'Why?' asked Orla.

He raised his eyebrows in silent query.

'Why? Is this technique more suited to men? Do women feel uncomfortable with it?'

'They shouldn't,' said David. 'And if they do then it really is their problem, don't you think? After all, this is the technique that has allowed me to have an expenses paid fortnight for me and my family to Cape Town. And an expenses paid holiday to Aspen. It allows me to be in a golf club and drive a two-litre car and buy decent suits.'

'Hugo Boss,' she said.

'Pardon?'

'Your suit. Hugo Boss. It is nice.' Her lips twitched in a half-smile.

'Thank you,' he said. 'Now, if we can continue?'

He spoke for about an hour. He showed them the flash cards they used, the ones that said 'Would you like to have extra income on your retirement?' so that the customer had to answer 'Yes'. He'd led them through the series of questions that they asked and the way they should ask them. He brought them right up to the point where they should be closing the sale.

'And that's it.' He smiled at them. 'Peace of mind for your customer. Business for Gravitas. And money in the bank for you.'

The session co-ordinator walked in at that moment. 'Coffee and biscuits next door,' she told them. 'And David will be joining you so if you have any questions I'm sure he'll be pleased to answer them.'

He thought Orla would ask him a question. He'd put her down as the pushy type. The one who wanted to score points off you all the time. He loved them as customers. He could always get them eating out of his hand.

But she didn't. She stood in the corner of the room sipping her coffee and leafing through one of the company's brochures.

'Will you last the pace?' He stood beside her.

'What?'

'Can you do it?' he asked. 'Close a sale?'

'I don't know.' She grinned at him. 'It's a challenge, though.'

'Lots of people don't like it. Because you have to make them say yes. Lots of people are no good at making people say yes.'

'Why are there so few women?' she asked.

'Because they don't like selling pensions,' David told her. 'Or because they sell the less valuable products. They look at the family's outgoings and they think that they should keep them as low as possible. So they sell something cheaper.'

'Better for the customer?' asked Orla.

'You get what you pay for,' David answered.

She laughed. 'Next year,' she told him, 'I'll be number one sales-person.'

'No, you won't.' David laughed too. 'But I hope you have a damned good attempt at it.'

She wasn't the number one the following year. David was. She was number four. Henry Gilpin, the man she'd beaten into fifth, was astonished.

'Congratulations,' he said. 'Nobody thought you could do it.'

'Thanks.' She smiled and held her award close to her – a plaque and tickets for a weekend in New York.

'Didn't quite make it,' said David. 'But you sure put in a brilliant year.'

'I did my best,' she said. 'Beaten by a better man.'

'By three better men,' he reminded her.

'Oh, I'm not so sure about that.' She smiled and David wanted to take her to bed. He was astonished at how strong the desire in him was.

'What are you thinking about?' Her voice brought him back to the present. He opened his eyes.

'You,' he said. 'When we first met.'

'Ah.' She made a face at him. 'You were rude to me.'

'No, I wasn't!'

'You looked at me as if to say "Sit down, little girl, and don't be bothering me."'

'I'd never say that to you.' David regarded her in mock fear. 'And you're not little. You're an Amazon.'

She laughed. 'You know exactly what I mean. You tried to patronise me.'

'Not intentionally.'

'Absolutely intentionally,' she said.

'Maybe a little,' he admitted.

She stood up and stretched her hands above her head. Her body, draped in the fine indigo-blue silk of the dress she was wearing, was long and lean.

'Don't do that,' said David.

'Do what?'

'Stretch like that. You're driving me into a frenzy.'

She grinned at him. 'Good.'

'I haven't the energy to be in a frenzy,' he told her. 'Not yet.'

'Come on,' she said. 'Let's go to the disco and dance.'

'I've even less energy for that,' he protested.

'Trust me,' she told him. 'You'll enjoy it.'

⌐

Niamh and Gemma sat together in front of the TV. Keelin was babysitting for the couple next door. Ronan was in bed.

'Why should you feel jealous?' Niamh's legs were curled up beneath her and she took a chocolate from the box of Just Brazils that was open on the coffee table in front of them.

'Because they're on a cruise together. Because she's young and she's pretty. Because she's so different to me.'

'She's older than you were when you first met David,' said Niamh.

Gemma grimaced. 'But she looks much, much younger.'

27

'And what's stopping you going on a cruise with some desirable young man?' demanded Niamh.

'Oh, come on.' Gemma ran her fingers through her hair. 'Don't be bloody ridiculous. I wouldn't know a desirable young man if he was standing in front of me. And I can't afford it.'

'Borrow the money,' said Niamh. 'You deserve a break.'

'And what about the children?' asked Gemma. 'If I suddenly took off. What exactly would they be doing in my absence?'

'You could always let David look after them.'

'David!' Gemma looked horrified. 'I couldn't.'

'Why not?' asked Niamh. 'Now that he's married to Orla, he could take time off from work.'

'You mean they could go and stay with both of them?'

'Sure.'

'No,' said Gemma firmly.

'Why not?'

'Because I don't want them to stay with her.'

'Don't be silly, Gem.'

'I'm not,' said Gemma. 'I don't want her getting to know my kids.'

'She's bound to get to know them.' Niamh took another chocolate. 'Let's face it. Gemma, she'll hardly be out of the apartment whenever they're there.'

Gemma swallowed. 'No.'

'So she will get to know them.'

'OK,' said Gemma. 'But I don't want her to be friendly with them. And I don't want them to be friendly with her. And I definitely don't want them staying with him while she's there.'

'I think you're being a bit unreasonable,' said Niamh calmly.

'No I bloody am not!'

Niamh said nothing.

Gemma sighed and rubbed the base of her neck. 'I don't know why I feel like this,' she told Niamh. 'It's not as though I care about him any more, truly it isn't. And yet I just can't accept that someone like Orla O'Neill would marry him. And I absolutely can't accept that my children should get to know her.'

'Who did you think would marry him?' asked Niamh curiously.

'I guess I never thought about him getting married at all,' replied Gemma. 'I don't know what I expected. I suppose I thought things would carry on the way they were. We've been pretty civil about it ever since we split.'

'You decided it was over,' said Niamh. 'Not him.'

'He made me decide,' said Gemma shortly. 'It was me or his job and he chose his job.'

'What's happening about money now?' Niamh reached out and refilled their glasses with Californian Chardonnay. 'I don't like asking about it, Gemma, but surely he's providing for you.'

'He's still providing for the kids,' said Gemma. 'Until they leave school. And if they go to college he'll stump up the fees for that too.'

'But what about you?'

Gemma shook her head. 'He cut back on what he gave me once I went back to work for you,' she explained. 'He doesn't see why I should get paid by him at all though I keep telling him that raising two kids is bloody hard work and bloody expensive too!' She blushed as she remembered the carnage she'd inflicted on her credit card. She was going to have to economise again. All this time on her own and she still hadn't got the hang of economising.

'I'm sure it is!' Niamh agreed. 'Though I wonder how the new Mrs Hennessy will feel when she realises how much he has to pay towards the kids.'

'I don't give a shit how she feels,' said Gemma shortly. 'It's our money and we're entitled to it. Besides – she earns a fortune too, the bloody red-headed bitch!'

'Maybe they won't be happy in the long term.' Niamh steered the topic away from money although she wondered if she hadn't jumped from the frying pan into the fire.

'Oh, come on, Niamh!' Gemma put her glass on the table. 'Why wouldn't they be? David's over the moon and what does she have to care about that would give her grey hairs or worry lines or anything like that?'

'Who knows?' Niamh shrugged.

'Skinny cow.'

'But maybe she'll spread a bit as she gets older.'

Gemma looked at her. 'Why?'

'Well, if they have kids she'll hardly—' She broke off as she saw Gemma's expression. 'What?' she asked. 'What did I say?'

'He doesn't want any more children,' said Gemma. 'He told me that. When Ronan was five I asked him what he thought and he said that he didn't want any more.'

'But she might want them.'

Gemma shrugged. 'I don't think so. She seems to be as caught up in her career as he does, though God knows why. It's a rotten job. To be honest, I don't know when they have time to even see each other!'

'All the same.' Niamh looked doubtful. 'She's young, Gemma. She can't have made up her mind already.'

'Apparently she has.'

'Bet she changes it.'

Gemma picked up her glass and took a gulp of wine. 'I don't want her to.'

'Why not?' asked Niamh. 'That way at least he gets to see her in her unglamorous role as baby feeder and nappy changer.'

'I'd prefer if she didn't,' said Gemma. 'I don't like the idea of them having kids.'

'Why?'

Gemma shrugged. Suddenly her anger had disappeared and her voice trembled. 'I – well, the way things are, I'm the mother to his kids. It's unique to me. If she has them, then maybe he'll love her kids more than Keelin and Ronan.'

'Oh, Gemma, no.' Niamh leaned over and put her arm round her friend. 'He wouldn't think like that. You know he wouldn't. He adores Keelin and Ronan.'

Gemma blinked to keep back the tears. 'Now he does,' she muttered. 'But if Orla has children of her own, that might change. You can see that, can't you?'

'He wouldn't love them more,' said Niamh firmly. 'He'd love them, but not more.'

Gemma pulled a tissue from the pocket of her jeans and blew her nose. 'He wasn't interested in them,' she said. 'Not really.'

Niamh said nothing.

'He'd play with them, of course. But it didn't come naturally to him. When he talked to them it was as though he was talking to adults. He didn't make allowances for the fact that they were kids.'

'And does he now?' asked Niamh.

'I don't know.' Gemma sighed. 'When he picks them up I say goodbye and that's it. I don't see them together. That was part of the deal.'

'I'm sorry, Gem,' said Niamh. 'I'm sorry it didn't work out the way you thought it would.'

'So am I,' said Gemma ruefully. 'If we'd still been married maybe it would have been me on that cruise!'

'Did he pay for it?' asked Niamh curiously. 'Or was it one of the prizes this year?'

30

Gemma grinned shakily. 'I don't know. Maybe between them they brought in enough to be given the cruise!'

'You got some great holidays, though,' Niamh reminded her.

'Aspen,' remembered Gemma, 'and Cape Town. I loved Cape Town!' She sighed. 'I miss that, Niamh. I bloody miss the money. I hate having to budget all the time. I'm useless at it anyway. I see things and I want them so I buy them. Besides,' she grimaced, 'I can't always tell the kids that we can't afford things. They're entitled to whatever he can provide for them. It's me who should be walking around in sackcloth!'

Niamh laughed. 'It could be worse,' she told Gemma. 'You could still be married to him.'

'Or worse than that again,' said Gemma with forced gaiety. 'I could still want to be!'

Chapter 4

It was hot in Nassau. Orla sat beneath the shade of a palm tree and waited for David to come back. She stretched out her legs in front of her and checked for signs of sunburn. Nothing so far, thanks to the copious amounts of heavy-duty cream she was using. Unlike David, with his dark hair and his sallow skin, Orla burned easily. Even though she loved the warmth of the sun she always sought out the shelter of the shade.

She leaned back against the tree and closed her eyes. They had been almost back at the ship when David had cleared his throat and looked at her in a shamefaced way.

'What?' she asked.

'I have to go back to the shops,' he told her.

'Why?'

'I need to pick up some things for the kids.'

She looked at him in astonishment. 'Why didn't you do that earlier?' she asked. 'When we were walking the length of Bay Street? Or while we were at the straw market? There were plenty of things there that I'm sure they would have liked.'

'I know.' David looked apologetic. 'It was just that I didn't like buying them in front of you.'

'Oh, David!' She put her arms round him and kissed him gently on the lips. 'How bloody stupid!'

He smiled. 'I know. I just felt that – well it's our honeymoon, isn't it? It seemed a bit crass to say I wanted to buy gifts for the kids.'

'David, I expect you to buy gifts for the kids,' she told him. 'And I'll happily buy them with you. But not now,' she added darkly. 'I haven't got the strength to walk along that road again. I'll wait for you here, in the shade.'

'Thanks.' He ruffled her hair. 'I know I was being silly but I couldn't help it.'

'I rather like that you were being silly,' said Orla. 'It means there's hope for the rest of us.'

She opened her eyes again. It was typical of David that he didn't want to remind her that he had two children. Typical but stupid. His children were part of him. She had no intention of pretending that they didn't exist, much as a large part of her wished they didn't.

She still hadn't got her head around the fact that she was the stepmother to a thirteen-year-old girl and an eleven-year-old boy. She didn't feel like anyone's stepmother. The idea that she had some kind of authority, however tenuous, over a girl who could just as easily be her sister was ludicrous.

Orla had no problem giving orders to people who worked with her. They knew their place in the hierarchy and so did she. But she balked at the idea of ever telling Keelin Hennessy what to do. She didn't think that there was any love lost between Keelin and herself and she could understand that. Orla was certain that she would have found it difficult to come to terms with her father ever marrying again, so she could accept Keelin's point of view. If, indeed, that was Keelin's point of view. So far, her conversations with Keelin had been practically monosyllabic.

She shuddered as she remembered the day that she'd first met Keelin at the bowling alley. It had been David's idea to meet there. Help break the ice, he'd said, and Orla had reluctantly agreed.

Keelin had looked at her from dark-blue eyes beneath a long black fringe and had said hello in the bored tone that teenagers can use when talking to an adult. Then she'd proceeded to get on with the bowling and said nothing else. She'd looked pretty disgusted when Orla planted the bowling ball firmly in the gully on her first attempt and when she only succeeded in nicking one pin with her second. Keelin had taken her turn and immediately hit a strike. Even when Orla had laughed and joked about her own ineptitude, Keelin had simply smiled in a distracted sort of way and said, 'Never mind.' She'd made Orla feel completely inadequate. And later, as they sat down to pasta and salad, the younger girl had hardly spoken at all.

The other times they'd met had hardly been any more successful. David had been worried but they both agreed it would just take time. It wasn't a problem.

Like heck it wasn't, she thought, as she watched a dragonfly skim through the air. That girl doesn't like me. And, much as I love David, I'm not mad keen on his daughter either, even if she does have a lot to come to terms with.

A young Bahamian girl stopped in front of Orla. 'Want braids?' she asked.

Orla opened her eyes and shook her head.

'I can do them real pretty.'

'No, thanks,' said Orla.

'Real pretty. Whole head. Half head. Just one or two braids. You choose.'

'I don't want my hair braided!' Orla closed her eyes again and ignored the girl. They'd warned them on the ship about the hair braiders. Orla wasn't going to waste her money on some colourful plastic beads that would be impossible to sleep on and would fall out in a couple of days.

She wondered how Keelin really felt about her father's marriage. Did it truly bother her? Or did the fact that he'd already been out of the house for so long make it any easier? Was she simply wary of Orla because she didn't know her very well? Or did she see her as a danger to her concept of what her family should be?

Orla had half expected the children to be at the wedding. She'd told David that she'd be glad to have them there and, to be honest, she wouldn't have minded Ronan too much. He was a straightforward type of kid and he thought his dad could do no wrong. But when David told her they wouldn't be there, she'd felt relieved. The idea of Keelin watching her and reporting everything back to Gemma was too chilling. And Orla was fairly certain that Gemma debriefed Keelin every time she returned from a visit to David.

She sighed. She didn't want to think about David's first wife. Not today. Not while everything was so perfect. She yawned. The warmth of the sun was making her sleepy.

'Just a couple of braids.' The girl sat down beside her. Her own hair was a clatter of green and gold beads. 'You will like them. Yes, you will.'

'I don't want braids,' Orla told her. 'Braids will mean that I get my head sunburned!'

The girl laughed loudly, showing perfect white teeth. Orla laughed too.

'Little braids. Each side of your face. No sunburn,' the girl promised.

'Oh, all right.' Orla sighed in resignation. Another time and another place she would have walked off. But she was too hot and the girl had her trapped. She thought that the girl had potential to be a pensions saleswoman when she was older.

'What's your name?' asked Orla.

'Coco.' The girl began to separate Orla's burnished curls. 'You got curly hair, lady.'

'I know,' said Orla. 'So do you.'

Coco laughed again. 'Pick colours.'

'Pardon?'

'Beads. Which colours?'

'Whatever you like,' said Orla.

'Purple,' said Coco without looking at them. 'They'll go good in your hair.'

She deftly twisted the strands into a thin braid. She folded some tin foil round the end of the braid and slid the beads over it. Then she twisted the foil so that the beads wouldn't fall off.

'Turn around,' she commanded Orla.

Orla shifted so that Coco could do the other side of her head. She waved as she saw David walking towards them.

'What on earth are you doing?' he asked.

'What does it look like?' she asked. 'Getting my hair done.'

David looked at his watch. 'We have to be on the ship in twenty minutes,' he told her. 'You don't have time.'

'I'm only getting a few each side.' Orla grinned at him. 'Coco has promised they'll look real pretty.'

'They do.' Coco slid three beads onto the second braid and twisted the tin foil. 'See?'

Orla peered at herself in the tiny mirror. She looked like a red-headed version of the young Boy George with her braids and the hat that David had bought her earlier at the colourful straw market.

'How much is that costing you?' asked David.

'A few dollars,' said Orla.

'The beads cost less than a dollar,' he protested.

'She's paying me for my time,' said Coco seriously. 'And my expertise.'

Orla and David both laughed and Orla handed Coco the money.

'Come on,' said David, 'let's get back to the boat before you change your mind and get the whole lot done.'

They walked up the gangplank and held their hands under the ultraviolet lamp that revealed the stamp that had been put on them before they disembarked.

'Makes me feel like a spy,' muttered Orla as she followed David to their cabin. She flopped down on the bed. 'What did you buy?'

'Pardon?'

'For the kids. What did you buy?'

'Oh, nothing much.' David opened the wardrobe door and put the plastic bags inside.

'Don't be a spoilsport,' said Orla as she sat up again. 'Show me.'

'Just knick-knacks,' he muttered. 'Honestly, Orla.'

She reached into the wardrobe and pulled out a pink plastic bag.

'T-shirts,' he said. 'And shells. Things like that.'

She unfolded a T-shirt which said 'Jamaica Mon'. 'We're not actually in Jamaica,' she pointed out.

'Ronan won't care,' said David.

'And what did you get Keelin?' Orla deftly unwrapped a flat package and looked at it in surprise. 'A photograph frame?' The frame was about four by four and was made of silver.

'That's not for Keelin,' said David. He cleared his throat. 'It's for Gemma.'

'Gemma.' Orla stared at him. 'You've bought a present for Gemma?'

'I thought she might like something,' said David. 'She likes photographs. So I thought a frame . . .' his voice tapered off as Orla continued to stare at him.

'You bought Gemma a present?' Her tone was one of disbelief.

'Why not?' he asked. 'I thought it would be a nice gesture.'

Orla dropped the frame onto the bed. 'Why not,' she repeated. She pushed her fingers through her hair and the beads clattered.

'It's nothing special,' said David. 'But it seemed like I was bringing back lots of stuff for the kids and nothing for her. Besides, she's been pretty good about everything lately and . . .' He shrugged helplessly.

'You're divorced,' said Orla. 'There was no other way she could be.'

'But she could,' David told her. 'She could have kicked up a fuss about the kids. Anything like that.'

Orla sighed. 'Marrying me doesn't mean she can deny you access to the kids,' she said. 'Gemma's only ever done what she's supposed to do.'

'But it's the way she's done it,' said David. 'She's made things easier for me, Orla. And I appreciate that.'

Orla bit her bottom lip and then smiled at him. 'You're a nicer person than I'll ever be, David Hennessy,' she said.

'Not at all.' He put his arms round her. 'You can practise being nice to me now. I'm sure you have your little ways.'

'I'm sure I do,' said Orla as she kicked off her sandals. 'Just let me show them to you.'

Keelin was awake.

She'd been awake since the blackbird on the roof had started chirping at about half-four that morning. Every so often she'd drifted back to sleep again but it was only half-sleep and it was a sleep from which she'd suddenly jolt into wakefulness.

She looked at her radio alarm clock at around eight. The sun was streaming in the window. It was going to be a hot, hot day. Part of her wanted to get up but she had no intention of getting out of bed early in the summer holidays. So she lay there, looking at the crack in the ceiling, while she thought of her father and Orla O'Neill on honeymoon on a cruise ship.

She'd tried not to think about them but it was impossible to keep them out of her mind. They'd been the last thing she thought about before she'd fallen asleep and the first thing that had burst into her mind as soon as she woke up. Her father and Orla. She felt sick when she thought about them together. Had he seduced her? Or had she seduced him? Either way, it was disgusting.

Tears trickled down her cheeks. It was all very well for Mum to say that they were better off without Dad, but Keelin wasn't so sure. Keelin had liked knowing that Dad was there in the mornings when she woke up, even if he wasn't always there when she went to bed. She liked the way he looked sternly at her whenever she asked for something and then would laugh and say, 'Of course.' She missed him. Other people seemed to think that because he was living somewhere else she should just forget about him. But they didn't know anything about it – how could they? He was still her father and she missed him.

Gemma pushed open the door. 'Are you awake?' she asked softly.

'I am now.' Keelin sat up in the bed.

'I'm off to work,' said Gemma. 'Ronan is spending the day with Neville and Jack. Make sure that's where he goes, won't you?'

'Don't I always?' asked Keelin.

'Of course you do,' said Gemma. 'But I have to say it all the same. That's the way it works with mothers. We nag.'

A ghost of a smile flitted across Keelin's face. 'Too true.'

'Gran will come around to fix your tea,' Gemma told her.

'I can do it,' said Keelin. 'Nobody has to come and look after us. I'm old enough, for God's sake.'

'I know you are,' said Gemma. 'But I don't like leaving you on your own all day, Keelin. It's not fair.'

Keelin shrugged. 'I don't care. And Gran doesn't want to be here anyway.'

'That's not true,' said Gemma forcefully.

'Yes it is,' retorted Keelin. 'Gran moans at me all the time.'

'She means well,' said Gemma.

'Huh!' Keelin wasn't convinced. 'Anyway, I'm going to Shauna's today.'

'That's fine,' said Gemma. 'Just be back here by six.'

Keelin made a face. 'I might want to stay out later.'

'You can go out again afterwards if you like. But let the Fitzpatricks have their evening meal in peace. Show some consideration.'

'I do,' said Keelin. 'I'm considerate about everyone. It's just that nobody appreciates it.'

'I do.' Gemma sat on the bed beside her. 'You know I do, Keelin. I think you're the best daughter anyone could ever have.'

Keelin felt the sting of tears behind her eyes. She stared unblinkingly at her mother.

'I'll be home by eight,' Gemma promised. 'My last appointment is for seven.'

'Why don't you work the short days instead of the long ones?' asked Keelin. 'Why do you have to go in on late-night opening?'

'Because that's when they need me,' said Gemma. 'And that's when I get the best tips. So that I can keep you in the style to which you've become accustomed!'

'I thought Dad did that,' said Keelin.

Gemma looked at her but Keelin's gaze was fixed on the swirling pattern of her duvet.

'Mostly,' said Gemma finally. She got up and walked to the door. 'I'll see you later.'

'Mum?' Keelin called her back.

'Yes?'

'Will they have babies?'

Gemma felt as though there was a lump the size of a brick in her throat. 'I don't know.'

'She won't look so pretty then,' said Keelin. 'With a huge fat bump in front of her.'

'No,' said Gemma.

'But I'm not sure if I want them to.'

'Maybe they won't.'

'Maybe.' But Keelin didn't sound convinced.

Chapter 5

The rain was hammering against the ground when David and Orla arrived back at Dublin airport.

'I don't believe it,' said Orla as they sat in the bus that took them to the long-term car park. 'According to the news the weather here was great while we were away.'

'Typical.' David's mood was as black as the clouds above. The flight had been delayed for three hours at Miami so that they'd missed their connection from London and had to hang around for another three hours in Gatwick's overcrowded airport terminal. David hated crowds.

'Never mind.' Orla cuddled up to him. 'We'll be home soon.'

'I don't know whether that's a good thing or not,' said David. 'The apartment is probably freezing.'

'You're exaggerating,' she told him. 'It's summertime, David. It won't be that cold.'

'Hah!' He pointed to goose pimples on his forearm. 'And what do you think is causing those? A heat wave?'

She grinned. 'You're acclimatising again,' she said. 'Just because it was ninety in Florida.'

'I wish I was in bloody Florida now,' he grumbled as the bus moved off with a shudder.

Orla leaned her head on his shoulder. She was exhausted but with David in this kind of mood she didn't want to fall asleep. She wanted to cheer him up.

The bus pulled up near their parking bay and they got out.

'Shit!' David picked up both suitcases and sprinted towards the car. 'I'm getting soaked.'

'So am I,' panted Orla, 'and this dress is so light it's practically transparent with the water!'

'Really?' David half turned to look at her and stepped into a puddle. 'Oh, shit, shit, shit!'

Orla stifled a giggle and side-stepped the puddle.

David took out his keys and pressed the remote locking. Orla climbed gratefully inside, trying to hold her dress away from the seats.

'Right,' said David, having stowed the suitcases in the boot. 'Let's get going.' He turned the key in the ignition. Nothing happened. Orla glanced at him. His jaw was set. He turned the key again.

'Is it damp?' she asked.

'How the fuck would I know?' David turned the key and stamped on the accelerator.

'The Fiat used to give up the ghost whenever it rained,' she told him. 'I needed to use damp start on it all the time.'

'This car shouldn't need damp start,' said David. 'It's a BMW, for God's sake.'

'Well, even the best of them sometimes give trouble. Maybe it's been raining like this for hours.'

'I couldn't care less what it's been doing.' David released the bonnet. 'It should bloody well start.' He got out and peered into the engine while Orla squirmed in the seat, trying to dry out.

'There's nothing wrong with it.' David slammed down the bonnet. 'Let's try again.' He turned the key. This time the engine fluttered for a moment before dying.

'Could the battery be flat?' asked Orla.

'For crying out loud, Orla, teach your grandmother to suck eggs.' David looked at her in disgust. 'I know all of the things it could be.'

'I'm just trying to be helpful,' she told him.

'Yes, well, don't.' He turned the key again. As the engine fired he banged his foot down on the accelerator. Suddenly the car shuddered into life. He revved it for a couple of minutes. 'See.' He turned to Orla and smiled in satisfaction. 'I knew what needed to be done.'

'What needs to be done now is for me to get dry,' she told him through chattering teeth. 'I'm absolutely drenched, David. And I'm getting c-cold.'

'Give it a minute or two to warm up and I'll turn on the fan,' said David. 'It won't take you long to dry out.'

'I'll catch pneumonia,' she muttered.

'If I'd known you didn't mind getting wet I would've insisted you enter the Miss Wet T-shirt competition.'

She looked down at her body. The dress clung to every inch of her. She was so cold that her nipples were practically through the thin fabric of the dress.

'They're like little door knobs,' said David.

40

'David!'

'Well, they are,' he said. 'Or coat hooks. You could hang a duffel coat on them.'

'No you couldn't!' But she began to laugh and so did he.

'Come here,' said David.

'Oh, no,' she said. 'I'm too cold and I'm too wet and I'm sure we only have another couple of minutes to get out of this place!'

'Loads of time,' said David. 'They charge by the day not the hour. Come here.'

She leaned towards him and he put his arms round her. He kissed her gently on the lips. Then he undid the buttons of her wet dress and cupped her cold breasts in his hands. 'This'll warm you up,' he murmured.

She shivered. It should be exciting, she thought, but she was too cold. David seemed to have forgotten how cold he was. And how wet.

'Have you ever made love in a car park before?' he asked.

'No,' said Orla. 'And, David, I really can't now. I'm too wet and miserable. Besides, people will see us.'

'Who cares if they see us?'

'I do,' said Orla. 'Please, David.'

'Oh, all right.' He released her breasts and sat upright in the driver's seat.

'I'm sorry,' she said. 'Really, I—'

'It doesn't matter,' said David.

'But I don't want you to think—'

'It doesn't matter.' He slid the gear into drive. 'You're cold and tired and not in the mood. And, to be honest, neither am I.'

'I—'

'Forget it,' he said.

He reversed out of the parking space and drove towards the exit. Orla looked at him doubtfully. But he was fiddling with the heater again.

⌒

'Thanks, Ciara.' Gemma acknowledged the tip her client had left beside the mirror. 'Enjoy yourself tonight.'

'I'll do my best,' said Ciara, 'but I hope this rain stops. Don't want it to pour down over my new cut!' She slipped on her coat and took her umbrella out of the stand. 'See you next month.'

'Cheers.' Gemma smiled then rubbed the base of her spine. She'd been on her feet since eight that morning and it was almost five now.

She had another client due at a quarter past. In the meantime she intended to sit down in the tiny back room and have a cup of coffee.

Niamh was mixing a colour when Gemma walked in.

'Hazelnut Glimmer?' asked Gemma as she looked at the paste.

Niamh nodded. 'They all love it.'

Gemma pushed her own hair out of her eyes. 'I should get it done myself.'

'I'll do it for you later if you like,' offered Niamh.

'Thanks, but I have to get home. Keelin is on her own today and I don't want to be late. Otherwise she'll have murdered Ronan.'

'OK.' Niamh stirred the colour a little more. 'Maybe next week.'

'Sure,' said Gemma. 'And you could give me a trim too. I know I look a wreck at the moment.'

'You look tired,' said Niamh.

'I am a little,' admitted Gemma. 'I'll try for an early night tonight.'

Niamh nodded and took the plastic bowl of colour back into the salon. Gemma switched on the kettle, which was always full of water, and spooned some coffee into a bright blue mug.

Today had been their busiest Friday in ages. Her back and her legs were absolutely killing her. She sat down on the three-legged stool and waited for the kettle to boil. She could hear Niamh talking to her client as she applied the colour to her hair. 'Yes, it's busy,' Niamh was saying, 'which is great for us, Jackie, although I know sometimes the clients wish there were more of us!'

Niamh was right, thought Gemma, they could do with more people in the salon. They had a great client base which was something that Niamh had worked hard to build up over the years. She'd worked hard on the salon too, so that people felt relaxed and soothed when they came in.

It was now extremely profitable. It was ten years since Niamh had bought the dowdy local hairdressers in Marino and transformed it into the stunning modern place it now was. She had received offers from national chains who wanted to buy her out but she always refused. Sometimes Gemma found it difficult to be happy for Niamh who was doing what Gemma had most wanted to do with her life. The only thing that she'd done differently to Gemma's dream was in naming it Curlers instead of The Cutting Edge. Every time Gemma pushed open the plate-glass door with the name inscribed in gold leaf, she imagined what it would have been like if she, not Niamh, had been the one to buy the salon.

But instead she'd married David and got pregnant with Keelin and suddenly she became a mother who was staying at home with her child and nothing else mattered.

She didn't regret it, she told herself as she poured boiling water into the cup, she didn't regret one single second of the time she'd spent with Keelin. Or with Ronan. They meant everything to her. She loved them with an intensity that sometimes frightened her – since her divorce from David they were more important to her than ever. All the same, it was hard to come in here and know that, no matter how good she was, it was still Niamh's salon and it was still Niamh that made the decisions. When they'd worked together in town – before she'd ever met David Hennessy – Niamh had joked about Gemma's ambition.

'A place of your own! Far too much trouble!' she'd laughed. 'I'd never be able for it.' And she'd grinned at Gemma, looked at her watch and asked Gemma to do her hair because she had a hot, hot date with some bloke she'd met in Tamango's the previous night.

But Niamh was a different person now. She was a businesswoman. She called herself a female bachelor and told Gemma that she wasn't interested in getting married even though she had a number of regular dates. Her life was perfect the way it was. Why complicate things by dragging a man into it on a permanent basis? Niamh had been Gemma's support when her marriage with David had gone so wrong and had immediately offered her a job in the hair salon.

At first Gemma had been reluctant but soon the salon had become her life-saver. It had helped her to get things into perspective again. Helped her to realise that she'd been right to tell David that it was over. Helped her to realise that she needed to do things for herself. So she'd accepted Niamh's offer and it had been the best thing she'd ever done.

She drained her coffee and rinsed the cup. As she walked out into the salon again, her next client pushed open the door. A flurry of rain was blown into the warmth of the salon. Annemarie Connolly struggled to close the door behind her.

'Let me.' Gemma took her sodden umbrella while Annemarie closed the door.

'July, God help us,' moaned Annemarie. 'We were lulled into a sense of false security by the weather last month. It might as well be November now.'

'Isn't it awful?' agreed Gemma as she took Annemarie's coat. 'I keep having to rummage through my wardrobe to find something more suitable than the cotton tops and shorts I was getting used to wearing.'

'I'm going to emigrate.' Annemarie slid her arms through the protective gown that Gemma held out for her. 'I can't hack this much longer.'

Gemma led her to a basin. 'Have you gone on holidays yet?' she asked.

'No.' Annemarie closed her eyes and sighed with pleasure as the warm water ran through her hair. 'We're going in September. September! It's months away.'

'Won't be long coming,' said Gemma.

'Probably not. But right now I wish it was here.'

So do I, thought Gemma, but not for the same reasons as you. I wish it was September because I feel so bloody guilty about working when the kids are at home. I hate having to ask Mum to keep an eye on them – it's no wonder she thinks me and Liz are useless. Especially when she looks after Suzy too. And I really hate when they spend the day at their friends' houses. She gritted her teeth as she thought of the other mothers either resenting her for dumping her kids on them, or pitying her for being a single mother forced to work.

'Have you been on any holidays yourself?' asked Annemarie.

'Oh, not me.' Gemma turned off the water and wrapped a towel round Annemarie's head.

'You look peaky,' said Annemarie. 'You could do with a holiday.'

'It's a while since I managed one,' Gemma told her. She'd been on one holiday since she'd separated from David. She'd gone to the south of Spain with Liz and it was the first time they'd ever gone on holiday together. It would probably be the last, Gemma thought. They'd both felt guilty about having left the children behind and they didn't enjoy doing the same things. Gemma just wanted to sit in the sun while Liz had gone windsurfing and paragliding and managed to get herself involved in any activity that was going. Including a brief flirtation with a bloke from England, Gemma remembered sourly and with a twinge of envy. No one had bothered to chat Gemma up.

'Where are you going in September?' she asked Annemarie as she began to snip at her hair.

'Jamaica.' Annemarie was unable to keep the excitement out of her voice. 'I've never been there before but James, my boyfriend, has gone a few times. He says it's wonderful. Very romantic!' She giggled.

Everyone was going to the bloody Caribbean this year, thought Gemma morosely. For their bloody romantic holidays. Two of her clients that day had either gone or were coming back from sun-soaked fortnights in Jamaica or Barbados.

'Whereabouts in Jamaica?' She steadied Annemarie's head and checked to see that the cut was even.

'Montego Bay,' said Annemarie dreamily. 'Doesn't it sound fabulous?'

'Fabulous,' murmured Gemma.

They were due home today, she remembered. David and Orla. Back from sunny Paradise. Her forty-year-old ex-husband and his new, improved wife.

'Not too short,' said Annemarie anxiously as Gemma snipped again. 'I'd like to keep the length in it.'

They always wanted to keep the length in it, thought Gemma irritably. Why the hell did they want it cut if they always wanted to keep the length in it?

⌐

Orla was still cold and wet as she walked into the apartment. She shivered as she peeled off the thin cotton dress and pulled her fleecy sweatshirt from the wardrobe. David changed into jeans and a sweatshirt too.

'I'm sorry,' he said.

'Pardon?'

'For snapping at you.'

She looked at him. 'It's OK.'

'No,' said David. 'It's not OK. I was pissed off at things and I took it out on you.'

'You didn't mean to.'

'Just because I didn't mean to doesn't make it any better.' He pulled her towards him. 'Are you warm enough now?'

'Getting there,' she said.

He kissed her on the lips.

'I know I should rely on just body warmth,' she told him, 'but would you mind if we had a cup of tea or something first?'

'Romance!' But he laughed as he let her go.

'Old married couple!' She grinned at him.

'I love you,' he said.

'I love you too.'

She went into the kitchen to make the coffee. He followed her. He slid his arms under her sweatshirt and pulled her towards him.

They had the coffee later.

Chapter 6

O rla's mobile phone began to ring just as she was opening the apartment door. So did the phone in the apartment.

'Bugger,' she muttered as she scrabbled in her bag with one hand for the mobile and made a grab for the apartment phone at the same time. 'Hi, it's Orla, hold on a moment please.' She'd answered the apartment phone first. 'Hello?' she said into the mobile.

'Hello, is that Orla O'Neill?'

'Yes.'

'Orla, this is Sara Benton. You called to see me and my husband about a savings and pension plan.'

'Oh, yes, Sara. Hi. Can you just hold on there for a moment?' Orla put the mobile to one side and concentrated on the apartment phone again. 'Hi, sorry to keep you.'

'It's me,' said David. 'What's going on?'

'Oh, nothing,' she told him. 'I've got a prospective client on the mobile. You both rang at the same time. Will you ring back in a couple of minutes?'

'I just called to say I won't be home until later tonight,' David said. 'I'm meeting a client myself. In Delgany. The meeting isn't until seven.'

Orla glanced at her watch. It was six now.

'Bloody hell, David,' she said. 'Look, I'm busy. I'll call you back.' She replaced the receiver and picked up the mobile again. 'Hi, Sara, sorry to keep you. Have you had time to consider the proposal I sent you?' she asked brightly.

'Yes,' replied Sara. 'And I have some questions. Well, my husband has some questions. We need to clarify a few things.'

Orla sighed. She'd been through everything with Sara Benton already. In her experience, it was usually the woman who made the final decision and she couldn't think of anything else she could say that would make any difference to Sara.

'Of course,' she said. 'Would you like to talk it through now?'

'Actually, I'd prefer if you could call out to us,' said Sara. 'Maurice would like to meet you.'

'When would be convenient?' asked Orla. Calling to their house was a positive sign.

'What about tonight?' said Sara.

'Well . . .' Orla dithered.

'Around half eight,' suggested Sara. 'It'll give Maurice time to put his feet up for a while after dinner. Put him in a better mood.'

Orla's heart sunk into her boots. The Bentons lived in Balbriggan, about twenty miles to the north of the city. Going through the proposals with them would take up to an hour. And it would take her another hour to get home. She groaned under her breath. Commission was all very well, she thought, but there were limits!

'Sure,' she said. 'Half eight it is.'

She took off her light linen jacket and threw it onto the sofa. There seemed to be a conspiracy to prevent her having just one decent evening alone with her husband. She sat down and dialled his number.

'Hi,' she said. 'What was all that about a meeting in Delgany?'

'Sorry, Orla,' said David. 'I couldn't get out of it.'

'We were supposed to be going to the pictures tonight,' she reminded him.

'I know. I'll make it up to you. And I'll stop off and get a video and some Chinese food on the way home.' He knew that she loved Chinese food.

'It doesn't matter,' she said. 'I've arranged a meeting myself.'

'Have you indeed? Who?'

'A couple called the Bentons,' she told him. 'I've been talking to them for ages and I didn't think I was getting anywhere. But she was the person that called at the same time as you. She called into the office a few months ago and Tony Campbell asked me to deal with her. I was beginning to think that he was just setting me up for a fall but now she wants me to call out and meet them and talk things over. Only problem is that they live in Balbriggan, so I rather think you'll be home before me in which case you'll have to eat the Chinese alone.'

'Bentons?' David's voice crackled. 'In Balbriggan. Is she a smallish woman? Fortysomething? Ash-blonde hair – dyed? Wears country casuals?'

'Y-es,' said Orla slowly. 'That sounds like her.'

'Celine? Sandra? Susanna?'

47

'Sara,' said Orla.

'And he's a weedy sort of bloke. Weak chin. Straggly beard?'

'I don't know,' she said. 'I never met him.'

'I think I know them,' said David, 'and if you go out there you'll be wasting your bloody time! I tried to get them last year. Spent ages talking to them. I got dodgy vibes after my second visit and thought I'd be better off forgetting about them. But I got stubborn. Wanted the deal. And I'd had a poor month. They were looking at a high-paying policy. I called to see them three times, Orla, and in the end they didn't do anything.'

Orla grimaced. This wasn't what she wanted to hear. 'Maybe they're ready this time,' she said.

'I know that sort,' David said firmly. 'They won't do business with you. They love having someone call to the house and go through things. Makes them feel important. But they won't do anything.'

'I'll use my feminine charms,' said Orla. 'This time they might.'

'Not a chance,' said David. 'If I couldn't do it, you can't.'

'Rubbish!' she cried indignantly.

'Look,' he said, 'I will bet you the commission you'd get on that sale that they don't deal with you.'

Orla laughed. 'David, that's ridiculous.'

'If you insist on going out there at all,' he added. 'But if you just stay home, put your feet up and wait for me to come home with the food and the video, I'll give you half my next commission.'

She laughed again. 'Tonight's commission?' she asked. 'For an entire company pension?'

'What do you take me for?' asked David. 'The next one to go through is for that guy I saw last night. But it's not a bad one, Orla, you'll get a new suit out of it.'

'Thanks but no thanks.'

'You don't have to prove anything, you know.' His voice faded as he drove under a bridge.

'Prove anything?'

'To me,' said David. 'You're a good saleswoman, Orla. You've done spectacularly well. But you don't have to take me on, you know.'

'I'm not,' she said indignantly. 'I want to do well. I want to sell lots of policies.'

'I know. I want you to do well too. But there's no need to kill yourself rushing around town when I'm doing enough business for both of us. I honestly think you're wasting your time with the Bentons. I turned all of my magnetic charm on that woman and I might as well have been talking to a rock! I'll bring home enough food for you anyway. Just in case.'

'I bet you I land the deal,' said Orla. 'And you'll be eating your words as well as the sweet and sour!'

'See you later,' said David. 'Take my advice, though, stay in and put your feet up. You'll have a better evening that way.'

'Maybe,' said Orla. 'See you.'

She hung up. Now she definitely wanted to land the Bentons. It wasn't really about proving anything to David, but who the hell did he think he was telling her that he was doing enough for both of them? OK, her last couple of weeks hadn't been great but she was as good a salesperson as him any day.

Anyway, just because the Bentons hadn't dealt with David didn't mean they wouldn't deal with her. Maybe the reason David hadn't got on with Sara Benton was that she didn't like salesmen. Maybe she preferred dealing with a woman. Orla hoped so. It was a matter of pride to get the business and show him that she wasn't like his stay-at-home demanding wife. 'Ex-wife,' she said out loud. Gemma Garvey was his bloody ex-wife!

She got up, made herself a cup of coffee and walked out onto the balcony. Despite everything, she'd have preferred not to trek to Balbriggan tonight but with David out anyway, what else would she be doing? Surely it was better that both of them were out at the same time?

David had been busy every night since they'd come home from their honeymoon and she was getting tired of being in the apartment on her own. He'd told her that he had to make up for the time they were away. Her reply was that a honeymoon wasn't something you had to 'make up' on and he'd had the grace to look embarrassed.

She hadn't realised just how much effort he put into his work. He was meticulous in his preparation and he thought nothing of driving from one side of the city and back again as many times as necessary during the day so that he could meet clients at their convenience. She just wished he wasn't out so much in the evenings. She still wasn't comfortable being in the apartment on her own. It didn't feel like home to her yet although she was slowly getting used to it.

The apartment was on the top floor of a four-storey block. It was big, with two bedrooms, bathroom, galley kitchen and a large living room with doors which opened onto the balcony to give wonderful views across Dublin Bay. Unlike Gemma, David had chosen to stay in Dun Laoghaire after their separation. It was a very stylish apartment.

49

David had hired an interior designer, given her a free hand, and the result was very modern and very fashionable. Which was exactly to Orla's taste anyway although her friend Abby thought that she should redo some of it. 'Put your stamp on it,' she'd said as Orla brought her round to show it off. 'Make it yours.'

But Orla didn't want to change anything except, perhaps, to get rid of the bronze statue of a naked African woman in the corner of the room which gave her the creeps every time she saw it. She liked the Amtico floors, the pale pine furniture and the pastel-coloured walls. And yet she knew that Abby was right. Somehow she hadn't managed to make it hers yet. She still felt as though she was visiting and that she should get up and leave every night.

She sipped her coffee and gazed across the bay. There were hundreds of small sailing boats out on the water, their multi-coloured sails making vivid splashes of colour against the blue of the sea and the sky. David had sailed when he was younger. He'd owned a boat – only a tiny Laser – but he'd won a number of competitions and had been good at racing. He'd learned in Australia, he told her, when he'd spent a few months there. Gemma had hated boats and sailing and hadn't much liked David spending all his free time out on the water. She'd complained endlessly about him sailing on Saturday mornings. Nagged him, David told her, until it was easier to stop going rather than to listen to her moaning. I can understand that, thought Orla wryly as she finished her coffee, it's not like he has a lot of free time anyway! If he took up sailing again I'd probably nag too. She shivered at the thought of agreeing with his former wife on anything. Gemma sounded like the kind of woman Orla despised, the kind who lived her life through her husband and had no life of her own.

She left for Balbriggan at a quarter past seven which, she hoped, would give her plenty of time to get to the seaside town. She practised her sales talk on the way, though she couldn't think of anything new to add to what she'd already told Sara Benton. She hoped that David was wrong and that they were ready to buy a savings plan this time. It would really piss her off if they were wasting her time and she was missing her video and Chinese for nothing.

She turned off the motorway and pulled up in front of the Bentons' neat little dormer bungalow at exactly eight thirty. She gathered her equipment and locked the car.

'Come in,' said Sara Benton. 'I'm glad you're on time.'

'Nice to see you again.' Orla followed her into the chintzy living room. She was glad that David hadn't decorated his apartment like this. The room was a clutter of ornaments and bric-a-brac and was dominated by a huge settee covered in a busy floral design.

Maurice Benton was sitting in an armchair. He nodded at Orla.

'Now,' said Sara as she settled down on the settee. 'I want to talk to you about the regular savings plan.'

Orla went through just about every product that Gravitas Life and Pensions sold. She explained them in minute detail, answering all of Maurice Benton's pedantic questions. She told them why some of the products weren't suitable for them and tried to emphasise the ones that were. And when she was finished, they thanked her for her time and told her they'd be in touch. They told her in such a way that Orla knew that they wouldn't.

David had been right after all, she thought as she flung the computer onto the back seat of her car. A whole night wasted on those bloody people. Why hadn't she listened to him? He had a feel for this kind of thing. He had more experience than she did. He was better than her after all.

She turned onto the motorway and pressed down hard on the accelerator. The sooner she was home the better. Then she gasped as the steering wheel pulled viciously to one side and she had to struggle to get the car back on line. Her heart was pounding and her mouth was dry. But she knew what was wrong. She'd got a puncture.

Nobody stopped to help her. In some ways she was glad because it was getting dark and she felt nervous about anyone she didn't know offering to help. But it would have been nice, she thought, as she struggled to lift the spare tyre out of the boot, to have someone else doing the hard work.

It took her half an hour to change the tyre. When she'd finished, she realised that she had tyre marks on her suit. The perfect end to a perfect day, she thought sourly as she headed home again.

It was after eleven by the time she got back to the apartment. When she opened the door she saw David lying on the sofa, his eyes closed. The air reeked of sweet and sour sauce. An empty plate was on the table behind him. She kissed him gently on the lips.

'Hi there,' he murmured. 'How did it go?'

'Need you ask?' She put her laptop and paperwork onto the table.

'Waste of time?' He opened his eyes.

'Utter,' she said. 'I should have listened to you.'

'I know,' he said. 'But one of the reasons I love you is that you don't!'

'Thanks.' She sat on the floor beside him.

'Never mind.' He ruffled her hair. 'You'll catch up on this month.'

'I don't care about this month,' she said. 'But I care about driving fifty miles for nothing. And getting a bloody puncture!'

'Oh, Orla!' He sat up. 'You didn't.'

'I did.' Suddenly she felt her eyes brim with tears. She blinked rapidly to stop them from falling but she was too late. A tear slid down her cheek, around her chin and plopped onto the floor.

'Orla!' David stared at her. 'What's the matter?'

'I'm tired.' She sniffed. 'I'm fed up. I should have been home with you and instead I was jacking up the car on the side of the motorway miles from home!' She bit her lip. 'I'm sorry. It's nothing to cry about.'

'Poor baby.' David put his arms round her and held her close. 'It's OK. I'm here. I'll look after you.'

She leaned against his chest. It was nice to have someone to look after her. But she wished she didn't need to be looked after. She'd wanted to return home in triumph, having landed the Bentons, instead of slinking in with no sale and dust all over her clothes. Maybe it is about proving myself after all, she thought wryly.

'Would you like some tea?' asked David.

She nodded.

'Hungry?'

She nodded again.

'There isn't any Chinese left,' he said apologetically. 'I'm afraid I ate everything. But I'll make you some toast if you like.'

'Toast would be fine,' she said, even though the smell of sweet and sour was driving her crazy with hunger. But toast was better than nothing.

'Did you close the deal?' she asked him.

'Yes,' he said.

'Congratulations,' she said.

'You'll get the next one,' he told her. 'You know you will.'

'Maybe.'

She thought he sounded pleased with himself but she didn't want to think that. David wouldn't have wanted her to fail just to prove a point. Would he?

Chapter 7

Niamh switched off the hair dryer and surveyed Gemma's hair.
'Hazelnut Glimmer suits you,' she said. 'It brings out the colour in your cheeks.'

'Don't be utterly ridiculous,' said Gemma. 'I'm not one of your clients!' She leaned her head to one side. 'But I like it, Niamh. Thanks.'

'You're welcome,' said Niamh. 'And you're wrong, you know. It does do something for the colour in your cheeks. Makes you look healthier.'

'Anything that does that is worth it.' Gemma sighed. 'I feel so sluggish lately. Everything is such an effort.'

'I'm thinking of joining a gym,' said Niamh. 'I've put on a few pounds over the last couple of months and I just have to do something about it.'

'You haven't put on any weight.' Gemma looked at her in the mirror.

'Yes, I have.' Niamh sighed. 'So it's the treadmill for me, I think. Why don't you join with me? It'd be fun.'

'I don't think so,' Gemma said as she turned her head again so that she could judge how well the colour looked.

'Why not?' asked Niamh.

'I was never one for hopping around on those damn machines,' Gemma replied. 'I don't mind going for walks, or even playing a little tennis now and again. But gyms are so boring! Even when David took out family membership in Riverview or Friarsland or whatever it was, I only went a few times. And that was to sit in the Jacuzzi.'

'That was because they were populated by women who were already skinny,' Niamh told her. 'How could you enjoy doing an aerobics class with a set of stick insects?'

Gemma smiled. 'How right you are. And all of them decked out in designer gear. Actually, I bought some, you know. A bright pink leotard. It was revolting. I looked like a piece of quivering candy floss.'

'Gemma, you're not fat,' said Niamh.

'Oh, I am.' Gemma pinched more than an inch around her waist. 'Look. It's no wonder David traded me in.'

'David didn't trade you in. You gave him the push.'

'Ah, but if I'd stayed a size ten . . .'

'Don't be ridiculous, Gemma.' Niamh applied some wax to Gemma's fringe.

'I'm not,' said Gemma. 'I was skinny when he met me. I know he used to say I was too skinny but he never really meant it. Let's face it, you only have to look at Orla O'Neill to know that he goes for leanness.'

'You dumped him, Gemma. And before he ever met Orla O'Neill. I think you've forgotten that.'

'I haven't forgotten.' Gemma sighed. 'How could I forget? Mum never shuts up about it.'

'She really didn't like you divorcing him, did she?'

'She doesn't believe in divorce.' Gemma tilted her head so that Niamh could apply some more wax. 'She's of the "you made your bed now lie in it school".'

'They forget that nobody actually wants a divorce,' said Niamh. 'They think it's a big cop-out whereas it's probably the most stressful thing you can do.'

'As if you'd know.' Gemma grinned at her. 'You've happily managed to avoid the trip up the aisle in the first place.'

'Doesn't interest me in the slightest.' Niamh stepped back to admire her handiwork. 'What d'you think Gem? Good enough to go clubbing on a Saturday night?'

'As if I would!'

'Maybe not clubbing,' Niamh acknowledged. 'But you should get out and about a bit more, Gemma. When you got divorced first, you were always out.'

'That was reaction,' said Gemma. 'And I ended up with a massive guilt complex about the kids.'

'Your problem is that you're perpetually guilty.' Niamh pulled up one of the comfortable leather chairs and sat down beside her friend. 'Stop feeling as though you should blame yourself simply because you married the wrong man.'

'I don't.'

'You do! You're always wondering if you did the right thing by getting rid of him. Well, you did. So forget David, forget Orla, find someone for yourself.'

Gemma laughed. 'For heaven's sake, Niamh, who'd be bothered with me? Thirty-five. Running to plump. A bit of a mess. And two kids.'

'Lovely blue eyes. Great bone structure. Not anorexic. And, when you put your mind down to it, bloody good fun to be with.'

'And the two kids?'

'Great kids,' said Niamh loyally.

'I like you.' Gemma leaned over and hugged her friend. 'You say the nicest things.'

'Have some fun, Gemma.' Niamh stacked some yellow perming rollers in the tray in front of her. 'Don't let him mess up the rest of your life.'

Gemma sighed. 'Sometimes I feel as though I've messed it up already. Married with two kids by twenty-five. Divorced with two kids by thirty-five. What's left to mess up any more?'

'You're still young, Gemma. Stop feeling as though, you're past it. I'm telling you get a man and have some fun. It doesn't have to be serious, you know.'

'A man wouldn't be any fun for me right now,' said Gemma. 'Although it doesn't seem fair that he's having fun.'

'David?'

'Don't you think he's having fun?' Gemma glowered. 'With those twenty-four-year-old legs wrapping themselves around him every night?'

Niamh laughed. 'What a thought!'

'Of course, maybe he's not able for it every night.' Gemma's face brightened. 'Maybe she's absolutely voracious and she has him completely exhausted.'

'So he can't get it up any more and she keeps telling him that she understands, it could happen to anyone!'

'And he's so totally humiliated that it makes him even worse!' Gemma grinned at Niamh.

'There,' said Niamh. 'You see. Not so bad after all.'

'It's more likely that they have bloody fantastic sex every night and twice a night at weekends,' said Gemma, her tone suddenly bitter. 'And that she's made a new man out of him. And that he absolutely loves it.'

'No,' said Niamh firmly. 'It's definitely that she has him worn out and worried about his performance. I guarantee it.'

⌒

Keelin Hennessy sat down in the carriage of the DART and put her feet up on the seat in front of her. Her friend, Shauna, sat beside her.

'Where'll we go?' asked Shauna. 'Henry Street or Grafton Street?'

'I can't afford anything in Grafton Street,' said Keelin. 'Let's go to the ILAC Centre. They have better bargains there.' She sighed. 'I get paid buttons.'

'But at least you have your own money now,' said Shauna. 'You don't have to keep begging your mum for more. And I'm sure working in the convenience store is a lot better than nothing at all!'

'Maybe,' acknowledged Keelin. Actually, she didn't mind working in the store even though she'd had to lie about her age to get it. But she looked older than thirteen nearly fourteen. In the last few weeks particularly she'd lost her childish looks.

'What are you going to buy?' asked Shauna.

Keelin shrugged. 'No idea. Something different though. Something nice.'

'You always have nice clothes,' said Shauna.

'Oh, come on!' Keelin turned to look at her. 'I haven't had anything new in ages. People must look at me and say, "there's Keelin Hennessy, what a surprise, she's wearing her grey sweatshirt and black jeans!"'

Shauna grinned as Keelin pulled the sleeves of the sweatshirt down until only the tips of her fingers were showing.

'It's a nice sweatshirt,' she said seriously.

'It's practically worn out,' grumbled Keelin, 'and the only reason I can still wear it is because I made Mum buy it in extra large size.'

'It fits you perfectly now,' said Shauna.

'But it's last year's sweatshirt!'

'I like it,' said Shauna. 'You're just a fashion victim, Keelin Hennessy.'

Keelin laughed and suddenly her face looked brighter and younger. 'I wish,' she said. 'But I do want to get something new. And I'd be waiting a long time for Mum to buy me anything.'

'Money tight at home?' asked Shauna sympathetically.

Keelin's face clouded over again. 'She keeps saying so. But she still blew an absolute fortune on clothes the day Dad got married.'

'Therapy,' suggested Shauna.

'Selfishness,' snapped Keelin. 'She goes on and on at me about how we have to look out for each other and be careful about money and not want too much because everything is different now. And then what does she do? Buys jackets and skirts and tops and shoes. And she went to Grafton Street to buy them. No economising for her.'

'Do you think it's anything to do with the fact that your dad got married again?' Shauna asked the question carefully. Although she'd been friends with Keelin ever since primary school, the break-up of her parents' marriage was not something that they ever discussed in any detail. Keelin wasn't the kind of girl who told you everything. And Shauna wasn't the kind of girl who asked. She pushed her curly hair out of her eyes and looked inquiringly at Keelin.

'Probably,' replied Keelin. 'At first I thought she didn't care. She kept saying she didn't care. But I suppose she does. And you know my mum, Shauna, there's nothing that'll stop her buying something to make her feel better about things.'

'What about you?' asked Shauna as the train pulled in to Connolly Station. 'Do you mind?'

'A bit.' Keelin stood up. 'Sometimes. Sort of.' She pressed the button on the door and stepped out onto the platform. 'Come on,' she said to Shauna. 'Like mother like daughter. Let's go shopping!'

~

Orla went up to the bar and ordered two gin and tonics. She carried them back to the table where Abby was sitting.

'I got us some dry roasted peanuts as well,' she said. 'I didn't have lunch today and I'm starving.'

'We can go and eat if you want,' said Abby.

Orla shook her head. 'David will be home at seven,' she told her, 'and we're getting a takeaway. We were supposed to do it earlier this week but it all went wrong.'

'Don't tell me there's trouble in Camelot already.' Abbey poured the bottle of tonic into her gin.

'Don't be silly.'

'Well, what went wrong this week?'

'Oh, he had to go and meet a client. I had to go and meet a client. Bit of a mess. And things have been busy since we got back. Talk about coming back to earth with a bump!'

'Did you have a good time on your honeymoon?' asked Abby. 'Was the cruise fun?' She looked at Orla appraisingly. 'You look fantastic.'

'It was bliss,' said Orla. 'And I put on half a stone! So probably just as well I haven't had time to eat since I came home. You wouldn't believe the amount of food that's on a ship. It's obscene!'

'And the Bahamas?'

'Gorgeous,' said Orla. 'The water was so clear, the weather was fantastic . . .' She sighed as she remembered lying on the white sandy beach beside David. She'd spent most of her time in the shade of a

57

huge beach umbrella, but he'd lain out in the sun. By the end of the holiday his body was a deep mahogany brown which Orla thought was very sexy.

'Hello!' Abby waved a beer mat in front of Orla's face. 'Are you still on planet Earth?'

Orla blushed. 'Sorry, just remembering.'

'Obviously nice memories,' said Abby. 'But you'll have loads of exotic holidays now that you've hitched up with Mr Mature, Committed, Financially Stable Hennessy.'

'Sod off.' But Orla grinned. 'He's not necessarily any of those things.'

'I thought he was all of them.'

'Well . . .' Orla considered. 'I suppose he's committed – we're married! Mature? He's more mature than some of the blokes I've gone out with, I have to admit that! Financially stable – I hope so, although he keeps muttering about giving more money to the kids.'

'Why?' asked Abby. 'I thought you told me all that sort of thing was decided.'

'It is,' said Orla. 'He just feels that he should do as much for the children as he can.'

'Don't let him overdo it.' Abby looked shrewdly at Orla. 'Don't let him spend guilt money on them. You've got to think about yourself.'

'I don't need him to spend money on me,' said Orla. 'I'm an independent woman, after all.'

'But what if you have kids yourself?' asked Abby. 'You won't want him throwing his money at Keelin and Ronan if you have kids of your own, will you?'

'That won't be for ages,' said Orla confidently. 'If ever.'

'Don't you want kids?' asked Abby.

Orla shrugged. 'Maybe. But not yet.'

'And how have his taken to the whole remarriage business?'

'I don't know,' said Orla. 'He hasn't seen them yet. They're coming to lunch on Sunday.'

'Wow!' Abby waved at a lounge boy and ordered another couple of drinks. 'Will you be there?'

'Yes.' Orla nodded. 'David was supposed to have met the kids last week – without me. But they were sick. At least, so Gemma said! Both of us were highly suspicious but David didn't want to make a fuss. I think she just didn't want him to see them, Abby, but there's nothing she can do about that. He has his rights. Besides, he thought the lunch thing would be a good idea instead. And he thinks I should meet them

58

and break the ice. Get things off on the right foot so that everyone knows where they stand.'

'It must be difficult,' said Abby.

'For who?' Orla stuck her little finger in her glass and swirled the ice cubes around.

'For everyone,' Abby replied. 'He probably finds it difficult because he loves you and he doesn't want you to feel intimidated by his children – or by his ex-wife. They're probably afraid that you're some kind of wicked stepmother-type creature who'll force them to eat things they don't like and do things they don't want to do. And I'm sure you find it difficult to love him and his children.'

'I don't need to love them,' Orla said simply, 'just put up with them. And feed them on Sunday, which is the difficult part!'

'What'll you cook?' asked Abby.

'Pasta,' said Orla. 'Keelin is a veggie and Ronan likes pasta. And it's the only thing I can cook!'

'Are you worried about it?'

'Worried? About the cooking? A little, I suppose.'

'Not about the cooking, you idiot! I know you can't cook. About the kids, about meeting them again.'

Orla shrugged. 'How bad can it be?'

'They're his kids, Orla. You're their wicked stepmother.'

'Don't be utterly ridiculous,' said Orla. 'And don't forget I've met them already. It's not as if they don't know me.'

'But up till now they've only known you as a friend of their father's. This is different, Orla.'

'Not that different,' Orla said.

'Very different,' said Abby firmly.

Orla shrugged again and took the slice of lemon from her glass. She sucked at it and winced at the tartness of it. She wouldn't admit to Abby how nervous she actually was about Sunday. She hated the idea of them appraising her as she knew they would. She dreaded the thought of Keelin walking around the apartment as she looked at her things in the place that had once been her father's sole preserve. She was less worried about Ronan because Ronan seemed to be such a balanced, happy-go-lucky sort of child. Although, who knows? she asked herself. He might be one of those kids who was placid on the surface and a complete handful underneath. She didn't even want to think about sullen, truculent Keelin.

'You OK?' asked Abby. 'Only you've gone into a trance again.'

59

'Thinking about the shopping,' said Orla. 'I've loads to do before Sunday.' She grimaced.

'Forget what I said earlier.' Abby smiled at her. 'They're only kids, they don't bite.'

'I hope you're right!' Orla drained her glass and waved at the lounge boy to bring another.

Gemma was already at home when Keelin arrived back from her shopping expedition. She heard her daughter tramp upstairs and slam her bedroom door shut behind her. Gemma wondered whether that meant that Keelin was in a bad mood or whether she just wanted to be on her own. Gemma remembered times when she was a child and she'd gone to her room in a sulk, half wishing that Frances would poke her head round the door and ask her if she was OK. But Frances never had, no matter how hard Gemma had willed her to. Yet whenever Gemma looked round Keelin's door, her daughter made it perfectly clear that she preferred to be alone. All the same – Gemma sighed. She had a horrible feeling that no matter what she did with Keelin it was wrong.

She walked into the living room where Ronan was sticking Manchester United player cards onto a team sheet.

'She's very noisy,' he said.

'Who?'

'Keelin.' Ronan smoothed the last sticker and looked at the sheet in satisfaction. 'She makes an awful lot of noise.'

Mother and son smiled at each other as Keelin turned on her hi-fi and the house was suddenly filled with rap music.

If I tell her to turn it down I'll feel like my own mother, thought Gemma. And if I don't, we run the risk of being deafened. She rubbed her forehead. When do you stop being a person and turn into a nagging mother? she wondered. Or was being a nagging mother just a state of mind?

'I told you she made noise,' said Ronan.

'You're dead right.'

It was another ten minutes before the rap was turned off and Keelin came downstairs.

'How was the shopping?' asked Gemma.

'OK,' said Keelin. 'But I don't earn enough to buy anything really nice.'

'What did you get?' asked Gemma.

'Some tops,' said Keelin laconically.

'Are you going to show me?'

Keelin shook her head. 'You'll see them when I wear them.'

'Are you going to wear one when we go to see Dad?' asked Ronan.

'Maybe,' said Keelin.

'Were they expensive?' asked Gemma.

'Not by your standards,' said Keelin coolly.

'Young people can get away with wearing less expensive clothes,' Gemma told her. 'Your figures are better.'

There was a tense silence then Keelin shrugged and looked closely at Gemma. 'Have you coloured your hair?'

'Yes,' replied Gemma.

'Why don't you just let it go grey?' asked Keelin.

'Why should I?' asked Gemma. 'Besides, it's not that grey!'

'Natural is better,' said Keelin.

'Wait until you get a grey hair. You'll soon change your tune,' Gemma retorted. 'Besides, I work in a hairdresser's. The customers expect me to have decent hair!'

'There's nothing wrong with grey,' Keelin said. 'Shauna's mother has grey hair.'

'Shauna's mother is ten years older than me.'

'I like Shauna's mother,' said Keelin. 'You know where you stand with her.' She turned her back on Gemma and picked up a magazine.

Gemma contained her anger with difficulty. 'Would you like something to eat?' she asked eventually.

'Sausage and chips,' said Ronan. 'It's my favourite.'

'Keelin?' She spoke to her daughter's back. 'What would you like?'

'Nothing.' Keelin flicked through the magazine. 'I'll make my own later.'

'You need something to eat,' said Gemma.

'I know. I said later.'

'All right.' Gemma had had enough. She didn't want to fight.

'No black bits on the sausage!' called Ronan as she walked into the kitchen. 'And lots of chips. And tomato sauce!'

Chapter 8

David left Orla chopping peppers for a mixed salad while he went to pick up Keelin and Ronan. She barely looked up from the task as he kissed her on the cheek and told her he'd be back soon. From the look on her face, David wondered if anytime would be too soon for her. He couldn't understand why she was so uptight. It was only lunch and they were only kids.

He drove along the coast road to Gemma's house. The sun sparkled on the water of the bay as groups of people walked briskly along by the strand. Just like he and Gemma had done once, he remembered. Every Sunday during the summer they would walk along the stretch from Sandymount to Merrion and back again. The kids were smaller then, of course, which was why they would all hold hands together, Gemma and David either side of the children. He'd loved those walks. They'd made him feel grown-up at last. He'd been proud of his two strong, healthy children and his pretty, carefree wife. It hadn't been that bad a marriage, he thought as he turned onto Gemma's road. They'd just become different people who'd wanted different things.

He pulled up outside the redbrick townhouse near Sandymount village. She'd paid a lot of money for it, David knew, but it was in a good location so it was also a good investment. All the same, he thought, it might have been better if she'd spent less on the house and kept more money for day-to-day expenses. She was a complete innocent when it came to money – he'd always had to look after that end of things. Even simple things like shopping in the supermarket turned into a major expedition for Gemma. Unless the trolley was full to overflowing she didn't feel as though she'd done a good job. He knew that she struggled these days to keep things on an even keel. Sometimes she'd phone him, panic-stricken, to tell him that she'd messed up and was there any chance he could lend her a couple of hundred until the end of the month. He usually did – although not before lecturing her on her bad spending habits and her inability to budget properly. Eventually she would play him back. But still, he mused, she was not the best person in the world to be living on her own!

He grimaced. Not that he cared, of course, but he sympathised with her. Some people were good with finances, others weren't. She was one of the former and he still felt as though he should keep an eye on her. He'd thought that after the divorce he would feel differently but, if anything, he felt even more strongly that she needed someone to check up on her and not just because he wanted to make sure that the kids were being properly provided for. People expected him to hate her but he didn't. She would always be a part of his life and he would always be part of hers, no matter how much either of them wished differently.

Gemma answered the door. She looked better than he'd seen her in a while, he thought. Her hair was brushed back from her face and seemed to glint in the morning sun. She was wearing a loose navy dress with tiny appliqué flowers on the bodice. Navy suited Gemma. It brought out the blue in her eyes.

'Hi,' said David.

'Hello.' She smiled tightly at him. 'They'll be ready in a second. Do you want to come in?'

'Sure.' He stepped into the hallway and followed Gemma into the kitchen. The worktop was laden with vegetables – tomatoes, aubergines and peppers. It was almost a mirror image of the worktop in his apartment. He blinked. 'Market gardening?' he asked.

'Making vegetable lasagne,' Gemma told him. 'I'm doing a couple so that I can freeze some in separate portions for the kids.'

'Good idea,' said David.

'We're all eating at different times now,' explained Gemma. 'Keelin's working in the shop, Ronan is doing his summer camp project at school and I'm out at work.'

'Busy lives.'

'Yes,' said Gemma.

David cleared his throat. 'I have something for you.'

'Oh?'

'Just a token, Gemma. You know. Something to say thanks.'

'Thanks?' She looked at him in surprise.

'For being so understanding.'

Gemma turned away from him and filled the sink with cold water.

'You've been great about Orla, especially with the kids and everything. You've never hassled me or abused me or tried to turn them against me and you could have done.'

63

'Why?' she asked. 'Why would I do that?'

He shrugged. 'Jealousy, maybe? You're on your own. I have a new woman in my life. That sort of thing.'

'Oh.'

'I'll always care about you, Gemma. You know that.'

'A bit late now.' Gemma dropped the peppers into the water. 'You didn't care enough a few years ago. That might have been a help. And, of course, you—'

'I'm sorry,' he interrupted her. 'I really and truly am sorry, Gemma.'

'I know,' said Gemma.

'Anyway,' said David brightly. 'Here's your present.'

She dried her hands and took the package from him. She turned it over but didn't open it.

'It's something you'll like,' he assured her. Gemma loved photographs. The walls of the house were covered with portraits of the kids at various ages, or enlarged photos of places that they'd visited together.

'Thank you.'

'Daddy!' Ronan burst into the kitchen and wrapped his arms round David's waist. 'It's ages since you've been here.'

'Because he was on his honeymoon.' Keelin followed her brother into the room. 'In the sun. With Orla.' Her dark eyes darkened even more.

'And very nice it was too,' said David firmly. 'OK, if you're ready, let's go.'

'Have a good time,' said Gemma. 'They've to be back by six, David.'

'I know,' he said. 'I'm aware of the rules.'

'Sorry.'

They were always apologising to each other, thought Gemma. Since the divorce they apologised more than they ever had when they were married.

David put his arms round the children's shoulders. 'We'll be back in plenty of time. Don't worry.'

'See you later.' Keelin turned to look at her mother. 'Have a good day.'

Ronan sat in the front of the car beside David. Keelin didn't care even though, as the eldest, she felt entitled to sit beside their father. But she didn't really want to sit beside him today. He looked great, she thought, as she glanced at him surreptitiously in the driver's mirror. His face was tanned and healthy. He didn't look like someone who was a creaking forty years old. Maybe he didn't look absolutely ancient beside Orla. But sixteen years! More than the amount of time she'd even lived! It was disgusting to think about it. People must laugh when they saw them together.

Orla heard David sliding the key into the latch. She checked the table again to make sure everything was OK. She'd put together an enormous bowl of salad with just about everything she could think of in it – raddichio, baby tomatoes, cheese, scallions, peppers, onion and little ears of corn. The pasta and the sauce were both bubbling on the hob. The garlic bread was warming in the oven. An aroma of tomato and garlic wafted through the apartment. Orla felt pleased with herself. Nobody would guess how nervous she felt.

'We're here!' called David.

'Great!'

She hadn't seen Keelin in weeks. She was sure that the girl had grown another couple of inches. She was almost as tall as David, and thin as a reed. When she filled out a little she'd be incredibly pretty, thought Orla. Lucky for Keelin that she appeared to take after David rather than blobby Gemma.

'Hi,' she said. 'It's nice to see you again.'

'Hello,' said Ronan. 'Dad was telling us about your cruise. It sounded great fun. I want to go on one.'

'Maybe the next time,' said Orla. 'How are you, Keelin?'

'Fine.' Keelin pulled at the sleeves of her top.

'You've grown, I think,' said Orla.

'Probably,' said Keelin shortly. 'I'm at a growing age.'

'Would you like something to drink?' asked David. 'Ro, what about you? We have lemonade or juice.'

'Do you have YoYo?' asked Ronan.

David and Orla exchanged worried glances.

'It's a yoghurt drink,' Keelin explained.

'It's my favourite,' said Ronan.

'We don't have it, I'm afraid,' Orla told him. 'We have Fanta. Or juice.'

'What sort of juice?'

'Orange or apple.'

'No blackcurrant?'

'I don't think so,' said Orla.

'You like apple juice,' said David. 'I know you do.'

'I used to,' Ronan told him. 'But I've gone off it. Orange juice will do.'

'And you, Keelin?' asked Orla.

'Water.'

'Fizzy or still?'

'Still.'

'OK.' Orla went to get the drinks.

David sniffed the air appreciatively. 'Something smells good, doesn't it?' he asked the children.

'Garlic bread,' said Ronan. 'It stinks.'

Keelin ignored David and walked out onto the balcony. She leaned over the rail and looked down into the flowerbeds below.

'Don't fall.' David stood behind her.

'I won't.' She turned and looked at him. 'What d'you take me for?'

'Sorry,' said David. 'It's automatic.'

They stood side by side in silence while Ronan sat on the sofa and drank his orange juice. Orla had left Keelin's water on the table.

'Your mother tells me you're working in the convenience store,' said David. 'Aren't you a bit young?'

Keelin shrugged. 'I'll be fourteen in a few weeks.'

'Do you like it?'

She looked at him pityingly. 'It's a job. I get money. I'm not supposed to like it.'

'I suppose not,' said David.

Keelin fiddled with her earrings.

'Nice earrings,' said David.

'I bought them with my first wages,' she told him. 'And I bought this top as well.'

It was clingy lycra in pillar-box red. David thought the style hideous but the colour suited Keelin's sallow complexion.

'And what does your mother think about the job?'

'She must be pleased,' said Keelin. 'Means she doesn't have to worry about providing for me.'

'She's supposed to provide for you,' said David. 'I pay her to provide for you.'

Keelin shrugged.

'Do you mean that there isn't enough money?' asked David. 'What's she spending it on, for God's sake?'

Keelin shrugged again.

66

'Lunch is ready.' Orla appeared at the balcony doors. 'I hope you're all hungry.'

David and Keelin walked into the living room. The round table was laden with Orla's salad bowl, the garlic bread and brightly coloured pasta dishes which she'd bought the day before.

'This looks great.' David rubbed his hands together and sat down.

'Where do you want me to sit?' asked Keelin.

'Wherever you like,' said David.

She looked inquiringly at Orla.

'Wherever you like,' said Orla.

Keelin sat down opposite her father. Orla brought a huge Le Creuset pot full of penne to the table and spooned the pasta into the bowls. A few pieces were stuck to the bottom but she ignored them. She brought the empty pot back to the kitchen and put it in the sink. Then she returned with another pot of sauce.

She hadn't made the sauce herself. She'd read how to make it in her only cookery book but when she'd gone to the supermarket they were doing a two-for-the-price-of-one offer on jars of pasta sauces and she decided that it would be a lot more stress-free to simply buy the sauce and heat it up. After all, she'd decided, they're only kids. It's no big deal.

She ladled the sauce over the penne. 'I hope you're hungry,' she said. 'There's plenty more sauce. And more salad if you want it.'

'Did you make this sauce?' Keelin poked at the pasta.

'I'd love to say that I did but I have to confess that I didn't,' admitted Orla.

David laughed. 'Orla hasn't quite got all of the domestic science skills yet.'

'She hasn't quite got the hang of vegetarian food yet either.' Keelin pushed her bowl away. 'This is bolognese sauce. There's meat in it.'

They stared at her in silence.

'She's right,' said Ronan cheerfully. 'But that's OK, Orla, I'll eat hers.'

'Are you certain?' asked David.

Keelin looked at him pityingly. 'Of course I'm certain.'

He exchanged glances with Orla who looked stricken.

'I'm sure the jar said tomato and basil sauce,' said Orla. 'I checked, Keelin. I know I did.'

'It doesn't matter,' said Keelin. 'I can eat the garlic bread. And the salad.'

'It does matter,' Orla told her. 'I looked at the label.'

'Well, you can't have,' said Keelin baldly. 'Look at those pieces. What do you think they are, Orla? Chocolate?'

'Keelin!' David glared at her.

She shrugged. 'It's meat. And I don't eat meat.'

Orla got up from the table and went into the kitchen. She looked at the two jars. The nearest one clearly stated tomato and basil. The second jar contained bolognese sauce. She gritted her teeth. The two jars had been banded together as part of the special offer. She'd assumed that they were both the same. How could she have been so stupid?

'I'm sorry,' she said as she walked back into the living room. 'You're right, Keelin. I bought one jar of tomato and basil and one jar of bolognese. I didn't look properly.' Her cheeks were burning with the embarrassment of being made to look a complete idiot in front of a thirteen-year-old child. She didn't dare glance at David.

'Doesn't matter,' said Keelin shortly. 'I wasn't very hungry anyway.'

'Is there any of the tomato and basil sauce left?' asked David.

Orla shook her head.

'I told you, it doesn't matter.' Keelin tore off a piece of garlic bread. 'I can eat this instead.'

'Maybe I could make you some more pasta,' offered Orla.

'No thanks.'

'There's some soup in the cupboard,' Orla suggested. 'You could have that.'

'No thanks.'

'But—'

'Leave her,' said David. 'She can eat the bread and the salad. She won't starve.'

'I can have some lasagne at home if I'm still hungry,' said Keelin. 'Mum makes a really nice one. She does the sauce herself.'

Orla sat down again and pushed her food around her plate. She wasn't hungry either. She'd been too nervous about getting everything right to be hungry. And now she'd managed to get everything wrong.

'You're making short work of your food anyway.' David smiled at Ronan. 'You must like it.'

'It's OK,' said Ronan. 'Mum says when you're hungry you'll eat anything.'

Keelin choked back a giggle. Orla bit her lip. David glowered at Ronan who was unconcernedly pushing pasta into his mouth.

68

They ate in silence. Keelin was finished first and she stood up.

'Where are you going?' asked David.

'To the loo,' she said.

'You should ask permission before you leave the table.'

'Why?' she asked rudely. 'You didn't ask permission before you left us.'

Ronan stopped eating and looked at his sister and his father with interest. David's eyes were almost black. His face was grim. Keelin tossed her hair over her shoulders and walked away.

'I'll kill her,' said David. 'I really will.'

'David.' Orla touched his arm. 'It doesn't matter.'

'It certainly does,' he said.

'Not now.' Orla couldn't believe that she was the one who was trying to calm David. Not when she felt such a wreck herself.

'Why not now?' asked Ronan.

'Eat your lunch,' said David. 'I don't want any lip out of you!'

'I'm finished.' Ronan put his fork on the table. Orla winced as it left blobs of tomato sauce on the polished wood.

'There's dessert,' said Orla. 'Ice cream.'

'What sort?' asked Ronan.

'Vanilla,' she said. 'It's very nice.'

He screwed up his face. 'At the moment I'm only eating banana ice cream. But it's not because of any special reason like Keelin. It's just because I like it.'

'Would you like vanilla ice cream with chopped up banana?' asked Orla desperately. 'I could do that if you like.'

'No thanks,' Ronan said politely. 'It's not the same.'

Keelin could hear the hum of their conversation. She wondered if they were talking about her. She didn't care if they were. David was probably muttering things about 'sulky adolescents' or 'difficult teenagers'. As if he knew anything about it! He wasn't around for her being a teenager. He didn't love her enough. He loved that red-headed cow with the long legs and the short skirts. How could he? Didn't he see how utterly ridiculous the whole thing was?

She sat on the edge of the bath and looked around. Most of the stuff in the bathroom was different to the stuff they had at home. Gemma liked Palmolive shower soap. Orla used Body Shop. Gemma used Clairol shampoo. Orla used John Frieda. It was beside David's bottle of Head and Shoulders.

Keelin picked up a bottle of Christian Dior body cream. This was one product that both Orla and Gemma used. Keelin unscrewed the cap and massaged some into her arms. It smelled nice. She hadn't got as far as doing that at home because Gemma had come into the bathroom just as she was opening the bottle. Her mother had snatched it from her hands and yelled at her that it was far too expensive for heavy-handed kids to use. Keelin rubbed some more of Orla's cream onto her arms before screwing the cap back on.

She switched on the light over the bathroom mirror and studied her face. Bits of her were definitely like David. Her hair especially. But that was the worst part because her hair was thick and long and difficult to keep tidy. Gemma trimmed it for her every couple of weeks and was forever suggesting that she cut it a little shorter. But Keelin didn't want Gemma to cut her hair. She didn't even like her trimming it.

She opened the bathroom cabinet. David's nasal spray was there. He suffered from hayfever. Keelin could remember his sneezing fits when he'd lived with them, which made Gemma collapse with laughter as he staggered around the kitchen with tears streaming down his face. It hadn't been malicious laughter, though. It had been fond amusement. And she'd always rushed to get his spray or his eye drops for him. Keelin was tempted to empty the spray down the sink and fill it with water. Or, she thought wickedly, fill it with his aftershave. But she thought the better of it. There was a packet of Tampax in the cabinet too. She swallowed the lump in her throat. It disgusted her to see Orla's hygiene products beside her father's nasal spray.

She closed the bathroom cabinet, washed her hands and left the bathroom.

'We're having coffee.' Orla's voice was strained. 'Do you want some?'

'OK,' said Keelin.

'Sure you don't have any ethical objections to coffee?' asked David sarcastically. 'Or moral reasons why you can't drink it?'

Keelin sat down on one of the armchairs. 'I'd prefer if the growers weren't exploited,' she said. 'We buy a special blend at home where the profits go direct to the growers. Of course it's a little more expensive but Mum says it's a small price to pay.'

'You're trying my patience, young lady.' David's voice was grim. 'You really are.'

'Why?'

'You know perfectly well why. Orla has gone to a lot of trouble today and you're acting like a child.'

'I didn't ask her to go to any trouble,' Keelin said indignantly.

'Now, look—'

'Here,' said Orla hastily as she thrust a cup at Keelin.

'Thank you.'

Orla sat on the sofa. She knew it was difficult for Keelin. And for Ronan. She hadn't expected today to be easy. But, she realised, she'd imagined herself glossing over any minor incidents. Being mature and friendly with them. So that, by the end of the visit, they would have respected her. And liked her. Maybe she'd even harboured a vague hope that they'd think she was better fun than Gemma. Had she? She wasn't sure. She didn't trust how she felt. Other than the feeling that she was a complete failure.

Sod them, she thought, as she drained her cup. They were David's kids but she didn't have to like them. And they didn't have to like her. An element of civility might be nice but she wasn't going to lose any sleep over it. It wasn't as though they were living with her, as though she had to step into Gemma's shoes. She could forget about them if she liked.

At half past five, after what seemed an interminable afternoon at the apartment, David drove the children home.

'I was very disappointed in you,' he told Keelin.

'Why?'

'You know why.'

'That's a great phrase parents use,' said Keelin, 'when you don't have a clue what they're talking about.'

'Keelin, you were rude to Orla.'

'No I wasn't,' objected Keelin. 'She shouldn't have given me a bolognese sauce. I mean, it's not as if she didn't know. Stupid cow,' she muttered under her breath.

'What did you say?'

'Nothing.'

'I don't expect everything to be perfect,' said David. 'I'm not asking you to accept Orla as someone you want to be with all the time. But she is my wife and I expect you to treat her with common courtesy. Is that clear?'

Keelin shrugged.

David glanced in the rear-view mirror. 'Is that clear?' he asked again.

'Perfectly.' She stared out of the window.

When Gemma opened the door, the first thing David could smell was the aroma of Italian cooking. It was a richer smell than had been in the apartment, he realised. He could identify the sun-dried tomatoes and the hint of basil and oregano.

71

'Did you have a good time?' asked Gemma as Keelin and Ronan both disappeared upstairs.

'Depends on what you mean by good.' David followed her into the kitchen.

'Were they trouble?'

'Orla bought bolognese sauce by mistake,' said David.

'You're joking!' Gemma smothered a laugh and tried to clamp down on the feeling of elation that the flame-haired bimbo bitch had been stupid enough to buy a meat sauce for her vegetarian daughter.

'Keelin made it quite clear that she wasn't going to eat any of it.'

'Obviously not,' said Gemma. 'When you don't eat meat, you don't eat any meat.'

'Well, it's bloody silly,' snapped David. 'Why do you let her get away with it?'

'She's entitled to her view.'

'She's a proper little madam,' David said. 'And she needs a good talking to.'

'David.' Gemma looked steely. 'She's a young girl. There are a lot of things going on in her life now. And her father has just married someone nearer to her age than his. Give her a break.'

The anger disappeared from David's face. 'I'm sorry,' he said. 'I didn't think of it like that.'

'I know.'

'I want to do what's right for them,' he said. 'I want us all to get along.'

'You want the impossible then,' said Gemma wryly. 'But then, you always did.'

Chapter 9

Gemma didn't want to open the envelope. She knew that it was the credit card bill and she didn't want to see it. She deeply regretted her impulse buying on the day of David's wedding. If she looked at the statement and saw everything itemised she'd see all over again how bloody stupid she'd been.

She bit her lip. Why couldn't she manage things better? Why couldn't she resist the temptation of a pretty skirt or a pair of earrings and just walk by? She seemed to lurch from one payday to the next with no clear idea of what she'd spent the money on. At the time every purchase seemed completely necessary. It was only afterwards she would realise that she already had a cotton dress or tan shoes or natural pink lipstick.

She stuffed the envelope behind the wine rack. It was something to worry about tonight, not now. She glanced at her watch and grabbed her bag. Her sense of time was almost as bad as her sense of money, she told herself as she left the house. She hated being late for work but she always seemed to arrive with mere seconds to spare.

As always, when she pushed open the glass door of Curlers she felt the stab of regret that it wasn't hers and that Niamh had succeeded where Gemma hadn't even tried. But it had been a stupid dream, she told herself as she hung her jacket on the coat stand. She would never have been able to cope with the financial side of things. With the best of intentions she'd probably have driven her business into the ground in under a year.

It was a frantic morning. Niamh propped the door of the salon open so that fresh air could circulate because the weather had turned again and it was sweltering. Gemma had a full appointments book which meant that she had very little time to think about the fact that David had just got a new company car and that Orla had brought in a new pensions account which, for the first time, had made her the top salesperson for the month.

David had told her this when he'd dropped the children back the Sunday following the disastrous lunch. This time, he'd taken them out on his own. Gemma had noticed the car immediately.

'Nice, isn't it?' he'd said.

'What did you do with the old one? Did you give it to Orla?' she asked.

'Not at all!' David grinned. 'She has her own. She'll be passing me out soon – she brought in a brilliant account last week.' And he'd told her about how well Orla was doing.

As if, Gemma thought as she snipped angrily at Stella Martin's golden locks, as if she cared about Orla. Men were so blind. She pursed her lips. David simply didn't see that she hated hearing about how fucking marvellous Orla was. He thought that, just because their marriage was already over, she would be pleased and happy for him to have married a paragon. Well, she wasn't. She was jealous that he'd found someone and she was envious of their bloody perfect life together and the fact that they didn't seem to have a care in the world, while she was struggling along on what should have been enough money but wasn't and it was all her own fault.

'Are you OK, Gemma?' Stella Martin was getting worried. This cut was shorter than she wanted.

'Sure,' said Gemma.

'It's just that I'd like to leave a bit of length in it,' explained Stella. 'I think you might be taking it a little short.'

'Oh.' Gemma looked at her handiwork. Maybe Stella was right. 'Don't worry,' she told her. 'It'll be fabulous when I've finished.'

⤳

Orla sat in front of her computer terminal and called up her client list. There were some really good accounts there, she thought with pleasure. Some that would have more business to do and some that had contributed magnificently to the fact that she was top salesperson in July. She'd beaten David and, although he wasn't top salesperson every month, he'd never been beaten by a woman before. She was very, very pleased about that.

She clicked the mouse and looked at her prospective client list. It wasn't as long as she'd have liked and if she wanted to stay at the top of the tree she'd need to bring a few of them in as clients. She wished there were more companies on the list – it had been the successful sale of a company pension that had pushed her into the top spot this month. She scratched her nose and wondered which of the four that were there were most likely to deal with her.

Blanca was a kitchens and floorings company. Heron Security Services sold sophisticated alarm systems. Tiger Computing and Aggressive Defence were both software companies. Which, she asked herself, was the best prospect? Who would she call first on Monday morning? It was pointless calling on a Friday. Nobody was interested in talking about pensions on a Friday. She highlighted the name of Blanca Kitchens & Floors who were advertising like crazy on TV at the moment, extolling the virtues of their new line in natural wood products. If they were expanding so much, then maybe they'd think about a pension scheme for their employees if they didn't have one already. And she, Orla Hennessy, would be the person to sell it to them!

'Hello.'

She turned round, startled. She hadn't heard David walking up behind her.

'Hi.' She smiled at him. 'How are you?'

'Bored,' said David. 'I haven't got the strength to deal with anyone today. The sun is shining, the sky is blue and I don't feel like talking to people about what provision they've made for serious illness or sudden death!'

Orla laughed. 'It's a pretty morbid business when you come down to it.'

'Exactly,' said David.

'But profitable.'

'Death and taxes.' David grinned. 'The only two certainties in life.'

'And that I love you,' said Orla. 'That's a certainty too.' She leaned back in her chair and touched him gently on the cheek. David felt an explosion of desire.

'Want to go home?' he asked. 'It's nearly four o'clock.'

'I was going to go through my prospects again,' said Orla.

'Leave them.'

'How else will I stay top salesperson?' she teased.

'Don't try,' said David. 'I'll beat you overall, you know that, don't you?'

'I know nothing of the sort,' responded Orla. She shut down the open application on the computer. 'But maybe going home has its advantages.'

'You know it has,' said David. 'I'll see you back in the apartment. Twenty minutes?'

'Twenty minutes,' agreed Orla.

It was crazy that they both came into the office separately, she thought. But inevitable since they actually spent very little time in the office itself since mostly they were out on the road meeting clients. They both needed their cars. But it was silly now when they wanted to go home together.

She slipped on her jacket and picked up her bag. Her phone rang.

'Shit,' she said. She thought about ignoring it for a moment, then decided that she'd better answer it. You never know, she thought, as she put her bag on her desk, it could be someone who wants to buy a policy.

'Orla Hennessy,' she said.

'Hello, Orla, this is Sara Benton.'

Orla groaned. Why had she bothered? She didn't want to waste any more of her time on stupid Sara Benton and her stupid husband.

'Hello, Mrs Benton,' she said.

'I wanted to ask you another couple of questions about your serious illness policy.'

I am *not* in the mood for this, thought Orla. There are times when you can take all sorts of shit from people, but not at four o'clock on a beautiful sunny Friday when you know that your husband is waiting for you at home.

'Mrs Benton, I went through that policy with you in great detail when I was at your house,' she said politely. 'I really don't think that there's anything I can tell you that I haven't told you already.'

'You were very helpful,' Sara conceded.

'And I've spent a lot of time talking to you,' said Orla. 'I know, too, that you met with another one of our salespeople last year. It seems to me, Mrs Benton, that you are unable to make up your mind on any of our policies. And that being the case, I really don't think it would be a good idea for you to buy one. You'd never be happy. You'd always think that you could have got something else.'

'I just wanted to be careful,' said Sara. 'You hear such awful stories about misselling that I just wanted to be careful.'

'I understand that.' Orla tapped her hand impatiently against the computer. 'But you have to understand that it's not worth my while to make lots of calls to people who are not ready to buy anything.'

'I'm sorry,' said Sara. 'I didn't mean to waste your time.'

'It's not a waste if you end up with a product that suits your needs,' said Orla. 'But it is if you don't think any product is going to suit your needs. And that's the way I feel about your business, Mrs Benton.

76

Nothing I try to sell you will really suit your needs. Because you don't know what those needs actually are.'

'I want something for serious illness.' Sara's voice quivered. 'My brother-in-law was brought into hospital this morning. He's thirty-five years old. He had a massive heart attack. He's critically ill.'

'I'm sorry,' said Orla gently. 'It must be a hard time for you.'

'It could have been me,' said Sara. 'Or Maurice.'

'You don't have a history.' Orla closed her eyes as she remembered the answers to the lifestyle questionnaire they'd filled in. 'In fact, as far as I remember, you're both very healthy.'

'I know,' said Sara. 'We are. But what if something happens? What then?'

'That's why we brought out the policy,' said Orla.

'I want to buy it,' said Sara. 'And I want to buy it today. And I want to do the regular savings plan too.'

'Are you sure?' asked Orla.

'Certain,' said Sara.

'Well, OK, Mrs Benton.' Orla kept her tone neutral. 'I'll call and see you later this evening.'

'As soon as you can,' said Sara. 'I don't want to mess around any longer.'

'Not before eight.' Orla was thinking about the traffic. By the time she got home to the apartment, made love to David, had a shower and got out again the traffic would be dreadful. Better to wait until later.

'Can't you get here before then?'

'Don't panic, Mrs Benton,' she said. 'I'll be with you later. You have my word.'

She replaced the receiver and jigged around with delight. It wasn't that the Benton's were such a good account, but it was the fact that she hadn't entirely wasted her time in dealing with them after all that cheered her up so much. Then she felt guilty for being so pleased. It wasn't exactly sensitive to be hopping around the office with pleasure when the poor woman's brother-in-law was critically ill. That was the problem with selling insurance, she thought bleakly. You revelled in other people's fears. She sighed, then looked at her watch. Twenty past four! David would be wondering what on earth had happened to her. She gathered her belongings again and sprinted for the lift.

⌐

David was tidying the apartment. The bowls from breakfast were still sitting in the sink when he arrived home, the bed was unmade and there was a general air of untidiness around the place. It had never been this untidy when he'd lived on his own, he thought, irritably. Why did Orla need to leave a pile of magazines on the floor beside the sofa? What was wrong with putting them in the magazine rack? Or, he muttered, as he realised that the magazine rack was crammed with back issues of *Cosmo*, *Marie Claire* and *House and Garden*, why didn't she throw some of them out?

Making the bed was easy, it was just a matter of straightening the sheets and tidying the duvet. But the dressing table was a jumble of perfumes and jewellery, of hair clips and combs. Why did she need so much of everything? Gemma had been a much neater person. Gemma kept all her jewellery in a lacquered trinket box that David had bought for her. She'd worn the same perfume – L'Air du Temps – all the time that David had known her. She kept one bottle of it on the dressing table. Gemma had cut her long, curly hair soon after they'd married and so she never bothered with the scrunchies and ribbons and clips that Orla used.

David bit his lip. They were different people. Gemma had never loved him the way Orla did and he hadn't loved Gemma the way he loved Orla. He felt suddenly guilty at the thought. He had loved Gemma, he'd loved her enough to marry her and have two children with her. He'd even tried to save their marriage by telling her that he'd change. He'd loved her, but differently. It was odd that he should now be comparing her, almost favourably, to Orla. He shook his head and looked at his watch. What on earth was keeping her? He was home ten minutes already and there was no sign of her. He was gripped with a sudden fear that something might have happened to her. That she'd crashed the car, perhaps. She wasn't a great driver and traffic was always dreadful on Fridays. She could easily have driven into the back of another car while she was talking on her phone or something. She had a hands-free phone but when she used it in the car she kept looking down at it, as though she could see the person speaking to her. It terrified him. He hoped she hadn't crashed the car.

He arranged her perfume bottles in a neat row on the dressing table, the tall, tapered Issey Miyake at the left, graduating in size down to the small, stubby blue Monsoon bottle. Thinking about car crashes was utterly ridiculous. His imagination was getting the better of him.

It was another ten minutes before she arrived home. He felt a huge sense of relief as he heard the key in the door, although it was tinged with anger with her for having worried him.

'Where the hell were you?' he demanded.

'Sorry I'm late.' She beamed at him. 'The phone went just as I was leaving. The Benton woman. She wanted me to call out there and then to sign her up!'

'She's jerking you around,' said David.

'No. Apparently her brother-in-law keeled over with a heart attack and she's now panicking about serious illness cover! She was practically crying down the phone.'

'Make sure she really wants it and she can't try and claim undue pressure,' said David.

'Not for serious illness anyway.' Orla dropped her bag on the floor. 'She can always stop paying. No problem. I said I'd call out to her later this evening.'

'Tonight!' He looked at her, aghast. 'I thought we'd go out for something to eat tonight.'

'Oh.' Orla bit her lip. 'Tomorrow night, maybe. I really want to get this woman tied up, David. She's cost me so much time and effort already.'

'Leave it until the morning,' said David. 'You're home now and I don't want you to go out again.'

'I don't either.' She leaned her head on his shoulder. 'But I have to. You know how it is.'

He sighed. He knew exactly how it was. He'd had this conversation with Gemma a hundred times before. Although, in that case, it had been Gemma trying to persuade him to stay in. It felt odd to be on the other side of the equation.

'Come on!' Orla kissed him on the lips. 'We didn't come home early to talk about serious illness policies!'

'No.'

She dragged him into the bedroom and stopped in surprise. 'You've tidied things up.'

'It was a disaster area,' he told her. 'So was the rest of the place!'

'I would have done it tomorrow,' she said. 'I always tidy up on Saturdays. You know that.'

'Sure, but I was here and—' he shrugged. 'It just seemed like a good idea.'

'Handy around the house.' She smiled at him.

'A new man,' said David.

'Huh.' Orla began to unbutton his shirt. 'It's the old man I'm interested in here.'

He put his hands over hers. 'You don't think I'm old, do you?'

She looked at him. 'It was a figure of speech,' she said. 'And you're only forty, David. It's not like you're ready to retire yet.'

'Certainly not.'

She finished undoing the buttons. 'Besides which,' she added, 'you have a great body.' She kissed him on his chest. 'And I love you.' She unbuckled the belt of his trousers and gently slid the zip downwards. 'I suppose you do love me?'

He gasped as her lips closed around him. 'You know I do,' he told her. 'You know that you're the best thing that ever happened to me.'

She was incredible, he thought afterwards. She'd never been so good, so wonderful, so bloody marvellous. He lay beside her, his arm draped across her naked stomach, until she finally slid from his hold and off the bed.

'I need to shower,' she told him. 'I can't face the Bentons until I shower.'

'Don't.' David opened his eyes. 'I want you to go like you are.'

She laughed. 'Naked? I don't think so!' She kissed him on his chest. 'I'll be back. We'll have an encore later.'

Chapter 10

D avid stepped out of the doorway and groaned. It was raining – soft, drizzling drops that soaked you before you even realised you were wet. David looked up at the sky. It had been blue and clear when he'd entered Trinity Hall as a guest speaker to give a lecture on sales and marketing, now it was grey and gloomy. He'd never known such a changeable summer. He glanced up and down Pearse Street then walked briskly towards O'Neill's bar. He was starving. Lecturing always made him hungry.

The bar hadn't yet filled up with lunchtime customers from the nearby offices. David chose a seat, ordered soup and a sandwich and took out his Filofax.

Orla always laughed at him about his Filofax. She said it was boringly eighties, it said more about him than his birthday, or the pale blue shirts and neat ties that he wore, or his sneaking fondness for BMW cars. A Filofax had him marked down as an eighties man in Orla's eyes. She used a palm pilot. David hated computer notebooks.

He had two meetings in the afternoon. One in Dalkey and one in Stillorgan. Not great planning, he thought. Even though they were on the same side of the city, traffic would be dreadful between the two destinations. But they were both potentially high-earning accounts and he wanted to land at least one of them to get his averages back up. He'd been horrified when Orla had beaten him as salesperson of the month – even though her numbers had been inflated by the very lucrative company pension she'd brought in out of the blue. An old friend who knew Orla was working in the pensions industry had called her and had handed the business to her on a plate. It was that simple.

The trouble with me is that I've run out of old friends that I can tap for business, thought David as he snapped the Filofax closed. I need new contacts all the time. And it's not always easy to find them.

'David?'

He looked up. He recognised the voice.

'David? How are you doing? Haven't seen you in ages!'

David grinned. 'Kevin McCabe! Nice to see you.'

Kevin sat down beside him. 'I didn't think this was your local,' he said. 'I thought you were in Mount Street.'

'Oh, I was lecturing in Trinity,' said David.

'Still guesting?' Kevin laughed. 'I would have thought you'd be tired of that by now.'

'I don't mind doing it occasionally,' said David. 'Although it wastes an awful lot of time. Still, I've made some contacts at it. So all in a good cause.'

'Still grafting away for Gravitas?' asked Kevin.

David nodded.

'And you're married again,' said Kevin. His eyes narrowed. 'That was very sudden, wasn't it? What happened?'

'I met a gorgeous girl,' David told him. 'Her name's Orla and I think it was the best thing I've ever done.'

'It was a shame about you and Gemma, though,' said Kevin. 'I liked her, David. Though I know there were problems.'

David shrugged. 'Irreconcilable differences, as they say. We couldn't manage to work it out. Just as well, I guess, because I've got the better part of the bargain now! How's Eve?'

'Very well, thanks. She asks after you a lot.'

'She was very good to me after Gemma and I split,' said David. 'You both were. I'm sorry that we've been out of touch the last few months. Remember when you asked me over to dinner and Eve produced that female friend of hers – funny name – dark-haired girl, lots of teeth?'

'Valentina,' said Kevin.

'That's the one. Did Eve ever offload her on anyone?'

'I doubt it,' said Kevin. 'God, she was a horror. Why Eve thought you'd be interested I'll never know.'

'Probably thought I was desperate.' David laughed. 'Maybe I was! Gemma had given me the elbow. I was living in a rented place on my own. She felt sorry for me, I suppose.'

Kevin flagged a passing lounge boy and ordered a ham sandwich and a couple of pints. 'You'll have a pint, David?'

'Why not.' David nodded. 'Anyway, I'm glad to say that I managed to do better than Eve's offering.'

'So what's the new Mrs Hennessy like?' asked Kevin. 'Word on the street is that she's a right little honey.'

'Is it?' David basked in the thought that people considered Orla to be a honey.

'Oh, absolutely. I met Sean Williams. He'd seen you a few days before the wedding. Told me she had a chest like Melinda Messenger and a mouth like Marilyn Monroe.'

David laughed. 'Not quite. Though she's generously endowed.'

'You were always a bit of a tits man, weren't you? Gemma wasn't exactly small in that department either!'

'It isn't essential,' said David, 'but, yes, I like them curvy on top.'

'And is it true she's only twenty?' asked Kevin.

'Where do people get these stories from?' David shook his head. 'She's twenty-four.'

'Twenty, twenty-four. What difference does it make?' Kevin looked enviously at David. 'I can't see myself ever ending up with a twenty-four-year-old!'

'Not while you're married to Eve anyway,' said David.

'I can dream though.' Kevin sighed.

'How long have you and Eve been married?' asked David.

'Twelve years. Thanks.' Kevin nodded at the lounge boy who'd placed the sandwich and pints in front of them.

'Time flies,' said David.

'Frighteningly,' agreed Kevin. 'A CV landed on my desk today from someone who was born the year I left college! It made me feel ancient.'

'Oh, I know the feeling,' said David. 'We were watching *Apollo 13* on TV the other night and I told Orla that I remembered it happening. She looked at me as though I'd walked out of her history book.'

'And when she gets a bit older, are you going to trade her in?'

David grinned. 'You never know. If she doesn't keep up to scratch!'

'Tell me, how are the kids?' asked Kevin. 'Do you get to see them?'

'Oh, yes.' David nodded. 'Once a week. To be fair to Gemma she's been really good about it. No tantrums or anything like that, but then she was always determined that the kids wouldn't take sides.'

'And how do they get on with wife number two?'

'So-so,' David admitted. 'But I think things are improving all the time.'

'And does she get on with them?'

'She tries too hard to be nice to them, to tell you the truth. I keep telling her not to worry, but I know she wants everything to be perfect. She's not naturally good with kids. She's the youngest in the family so she didn't have anyone to practise on. Still, I reckon things are going pretty well.'

83

'So everything's worked out perfectly?'

'Not perfectly,' said David. 'Let's face it, Kevin, divorce isn't something you really want to happen. I know that all the news articles say it's difficult but you always get the impression that people cope. It took me a while to start coping again. I didn't like living on my own and I missed the kids. In a funny way, I missed Gemma too.'

'Wasn't there any chance of you two getting back together?' asked Kevin.

David shook his head. 'She was adamant. I would have tried, Kevin, I told her as much. But she said I wouldn't be able to change and she was perfectly miserable with me at home.' He shrugged. 'In the end, it was easier to let it all happen. And I'm glad it did because Orla's a great girl.'

'I'll have to see her for myself to pass judgement!' Kevin laughed.

'Well, why don't you?' asked David. 'Why don't you and Eve come over for dinner some night? We used to do dinner together a lot.'

'That was the girls,' said Kevin. 'You know how women are. Organising to see each other. Wanting to compete at the cooking!'

'Seriously,' said David. 'I'd like you to come over. I often meant to ring you and get together for a pint. It'd be fun.'

'All right,' agreed Kevin. He took out his diary. 'When?'

David opened his Filofax again. 'Next Saturday?' he suggested.

'Sounds good to me,' said Kevin, 'but I'll have to check with her indoors first.'

'Great.' David slid a business card out of the Filofax. 'My home and mobile number are on the card. I'll write the address on it for you. Dun Laoghaire. The apartments near the seafront. If Eve is OK about it, how does eight o'clock sound?'

'Great. It should be a bit of a laugh,' said Kevin. 'We can do some catching up. And I'm dying to see Mrs Hennessy Mark Two.'

'You can keep your filthy hands off her, McCabe.' David punched him gently on the arm. 'She's all mine!'

⤺

'You've what?' Orla hit the mute button on the TV remote control and stared at David in horror.

'Asked him and his wife to dinner,' repeated David. 'What's wrong with that? I thought you'd like to meet some of my friends. You're always complaining that we don't meet enough people.'

'No, I'm not,' said Orla. 'I said – just once – that it's difficult to

84

make a whole new set of friends that don't have baggage about you being married before. And that we don't meet enough people to fill that gap. It's completely different.'

'Well, Kevin and Eve are a nice couple,' said David complacently. 'You'll like them.'

'I never even heard you mention them before,' said Orla. 'Who are they?'

'Kevin and I used to work together in Irish Life when we started out. He moved into banking. I moved to Gravitas. His wife worked in Irish Life too and she's terribly nice. We used to have some great evenings together.'

'We used to?' repeated Orla. 'You mean you and Gemma used to?'

'Sure,' replied David. 'Look, it's no big deal, Orla. It's just a couple of people coming to diner.' He leaned over and kissed her on the neck.

'But they were friends of you and Gemma. They'll see me as some kind of intruder.'

'That's bullshit, Orla, and you know it. Of course they were our friends. That doesn't mean they won't like you.'

She bit her lip. She didn't want to sound petulant in front of him and yet she wanted to stamp her foot and tell him that it was utterly ridiculous of him to invite friends from his previous marriage to dinner now.

'Did Eve and Gemma know each other well?' she asked.

'Only through Kevin and me,' replied David, 'although I think Gemma did Eve's hair a couple of times. I can't remember.'

'And you want me to cook dinner for them,' she said. 'I can't cook dinner for people, David, you know I can hardly cook dinner for us.'

'Do what you did when the kids were over,' suggested David. 'Pasta. That was OK.'

'David, I can't cook pasta and heat up a jar of sauce. And, if you remember, I didn't even do that properly.' Orla pushed her fingers anxiously through her red curls. 'I couldn't do that, I really couldn't. They'll be expecting something else.'

He shrugged. 'Like what?'

'I don't know!' she snapped. 'But whatever it is I can't do it.'

'Don't be silly,' said David. 'There's nothing to it. Christ, Orla, if Gemma – who hasn't half your brains or ability – could rustle up a dinner without any trouble I can't see what your problem is.'

'David, cooking and entertaining is a skill. Not one that I have. I've never cooked for people before and I don't even know how to go about it.'

'It's only food,' said David. 'You put it in the oven and you turn on the timer. I'll look after the wine. It's not difficult, Orla, really it's not.'

She rubbed her temples. 'David, the only catering I've ever done for people is sausage and pizza parties with lots of beer and wine so that they don't know what they're eating. I honestly can't do this.'

David sighed. 'You're being stupid,' he told her. 'It's not something I normally associate with you. I married you because you weren't stupid.'

'You also married me because I wasn't Gemma,' snapped Orla, 'but you're expecting me to entertain friends that she used to entertain.'

'Kevin is *my* friend,' said David. 'We go back years. He's married to Eve. I can take her or leave her. But he's a good mate. OK, I don't see him so much now, but I like him. And I want him to come over. I'm not asking you to kill yourself, Orla. Just cook something simple.'

She bit her bottom lip. He didn't understand. He really and truly didn't. He was looking at her now, a puzzled expression on his face.

'Have you any suggestions?' she asked finally.

He looked thoughtful. 'There was a duck dish that Gemma used to do,' he remembered. 'Though I'm not sure exactly what. It was very nice though. Lots of flavour. And she did a sauce with it.'

'Orange sauce?' guessed Orla.

'No.' He shook his head. 'A red sauce. Berries, I think. Cranberries maybe. Or perhaps that's only with the turkey at Christmas.'

Orla sighed. She hoped he wasn't going to expect her to cook some massive turkey at Christmas. She got up from the sofa and pulled her cookery book from the shelf. 'I suppose I could practise something from this,' she mused.

'You don't have much time to practise,' said David. 'Unless you're staying in every night this week.'

'No,' said Orla. 'I've got a meeting tomorrow. I was supposed to meet Abby on Wednesday. Maybe I'll cancel that and cook instead. We've got a team meeting Thursday. I can do the shopping on Friday.'

'It's not a military operation,' said David. 'And I was joking about practising. I'm sure whatever you do will be fine.'

'David, I don't cook. It's that simple. I need to try out something.'

'All women can cook,' David told her. 'It's just a matter of confidence.'

'Don't give me that bullshit.' She flicked through the cookery book. 'Look at this picture! That woman has her hand inside the chicken. You think I'm going to do that? You have another think coming!'

'Chicken is pretty simple,' said David. 'You can't go wrong with chicken.'

'I could,' said Orla darkly.

'Then do the pasta thing,' said David. 'They won't know if it's jars of sauce.'

'They will,' Orla told him. 'Even I can tell when something is heated up.'

David sighed. He hadn't realised that she'd get into such a flap about this. He'd thought it was a good idea. He'd imagined she'd be pleased at the idea of meeting more of his friends. At the time of their wedding, when they'd kept the guest list strictly to only their closest family and friends, she'd said that it was a pity they couldn't invite more. But they'd decided to keep it low-key because theirs was the first divorce and remarriage in either family and they thought low-key was better. Not that it had made much difference in the end, he thought now. In fact it might have been better to have a raucous celebration instead of the quiet, sophisticated affair that they'd had.

'Whatever you want to do is OK by me,' he said eventually. 'And even if it tastes revolting, I'll eat it anyway.'

She smiled wanly. 'You'd better. Otherwise I'll force it down your throat. And I won't care if it chokes you.'

⌒

This is ridiculous, thought Orla the following day as she stood in Hughes & Hughes bookshop and flicked through the cookery books on display. There were hundreds of them – *Learn to Cook, Cooking Made Easy, Cooking for Family and Friends.* Cooking with chicken, with lamb, with meat. Italian cooking. French cooking. Cooking in one pot. Cooking in the microwave. Cooking in the oven. It seemed to Orla that there were at least a thousand ways to cook a breast of chicken and she didn't even know one of them.

She sighed. It was all very well for David to suddenly decide he wanted to engage in a bit of suburban-style entertaining, but he hadn't married her for her prowess over the hob. He'd married her precisely because she was nothing like his ex-wife and now he was trying to turn her into some domesticated clone, even if he didn't see it himself. And yet she didn't want to let him down. She didn't want to let herself down either. Her mother was a decent cook. Surely it must be in her genes somewhere. It couldn't possibly be that bloody hard, could it?

Duck with grape sauce. She looked at the picture in the *Step-by-Step Cooking Course* book and wondered if that was the dish Gemma had made for them before. The duck was roasted to a dark honey colour and decorated with whole grapes. It seemed to be sitting on something made of pastry. Orla skimmed through the recipe. The duck was, in fact, perched on a deep-fried croute. She wasn't exactly sure what a deep-fried croute was. The recipe didn't tell you how to make one. Not duck, she decided. Something simpler than duck. Anyway, she didn't much like duck herself.

She turned over the page and nearly threw up. The next recipe was for pheasant and the little birds were decorated with real feathers. It looked disgusting. No wonder Keelin Hennessy was a vegetarian!

She flicked through the book again. The desserts looked nice, she mused. The Nesselrode pudding, a high tower of eggs and cream mixed with fruit and surrounded by chestnuts looked absolutely fantastic. But the recipe was terribly complicated. And Orla wasn't at all sure how you managed to turn the whole thing into a kind of tapered spire. She might be better off with the blackcurrant and raspberry water ice. All you had to do was puree the fruit, freeze it and throw a few raspberries on top afterwards. She couldn't go too far wrong with that.

⌐

'I wish I could help,' said Abby that evening as they sat in Bewley's and sipped hot, milky coffee. 'But it was never my thing either. Remember our parties?'

Orla nodded. 'Takeaway pizza and cocktail sausages. Everyone said they were great parties!'

'They were,' said Abby. She nibbled on her sugar-coated doughnut. 'Remember the one where Claire Hobson and Patrick Maguire locked themselves in the bathroom?'

Orla laughed. 'Must have been the quickest moment of passion in the history of the universe with everyone banging on the door and yelling at them to hurry up, people needed to use the facilities!'

Abby smiled. 'I miss having you share with me,' she said. 'Janet is a nice girl, but it's not the same.'

'Actually, I rather miss it myself sometimes,' admitted Orla.

Abby stared at her. 'Miss it? Why? Aren't you happy?'

'Of course I'm happy!' Orla was forceful. 'Of course I am, Abby. It's just that being married is different.'

'How?'

'You have to think of someone else all the time,' she said. 'You can't just do something off the top of your head. I was late home one day last week and David went crazy. He thought something awful had happened to me. All I'd done was go for a drink with one of my team members. Nothing terrible at all. And I thought David was meeting a client himself. But his client cancelled, he went home and he freaked out when I wasn't there.'

'Actually I think it would be nice having someone worry about you,' said Abby. 'I could disappear off the face of the earth and no one would ever know.'

'I'd know,' said Orla.

Abby sighed. 'I suppose you might notice eventually. It's not that I'm ready to settle down or anything myself, but I envy people who've found the right person.'

'And I know I've found the right person,' said Orla. 'It's just that our lives together seem terribly grown-up. We don't seem to do silly things any more.'

'Orla, you never did silly things. You were always one of the oldest young people I ever knew.'

'No I wasn't,' amended Orla.

'Oh, comes on,' said Aldoy. 'You were one of the only people I know who spent their time in college actually studying!'

Orla laughed. 'Not all the time.'

'Most of it,' said Abby. She grinned at her friend suddenly. 'Except for the Jonathan Pascoe episode.'

Orla blushed as she remembered her six-month passionate relationship with the muscular engineer she'd gone out with at college. From the moment she'd set eyes on Jonathan she'd wanted to go to bed with him. She'd never felt like that before. He'd told her, later, that he'd felt exactly the same way. It had been her first serious relationship and she'd broken up with him precisely because it had become serious.

'Getting back to the original topic,' said Orla as she dragged her mind back to the present, 'I've got to be serious about this entertaining lark. I still haven't a clue what to cook for them.'

'Have you talked to your mother?' asked Abby.

Orla shook her head.

'Oh, Orla, don't tell me she's still giving you grief about David?' Abby looked surprised.

'No,' said Orla. 'We haven't talked long enough for her to give me grief about anything!'

'That's a shame,' said Abby. 'I thought you were close to her.'

Orla nodded. She missed her mother. She missed the easy relationship that they'd once had. She'd always considered Rosanna to be a fairly relaxed sort of person and, even in her more turbulent teenage years, she'd never had a major row with her. She couldn't believe that they'd had one over the man she loved.

'Have you called her?' asked Abby.

'No.' Orla dropped another sugar lump into her half-finished cup of coffee. 'She was so mad at me about David, Abby. And she said some awful things about him. Really hurtful things. I can't call her.'

'That's silly,' said Abby. 'I bet she's over it by now.'

'She's an obstinate bitch when she wants to be,' said Orla. 'She can call me, I'm not calling her.'

'But she might be able to offer some advice on the cooking front,' said Abby. 'She can cook, Orla. I've eaten her food.'

'She must wonder about me then.' Orla giggled. 'I obviously got Dad's genes in the cooking scenario!'

'Call her.' Abby drained her coffee. 'I bet she's dying to hear from you. And she'll give you a recipe for something simple that'll look fantastic so David will think you're utterly perfect.'

'He thinks that anyway,' said Orla. She finished her coffee too. 'Come on, I'd better get home before he does. Otherwise he'll be climbing the walls again.'

Chapter 11

G emma stood in front of the TV and pressed the remote control. Nothing happened. She shook the remote and pressed it again. Still nothing.

'I told you,' said Ronan. 'It's broken.'

'Maybe the remote needs a new battery,' said Gemma. 'Let me try without it.' She kneeled down and pressed the button on the TV itself. There was a sudden surge of light and picture onto the screen which faded almost immediately.

'It's definitely broken,' said Ronan.

'It doesn't look great,' admitted Gemma.

She sat back on her heels and looked at the TV. She couldn't think of what might be wrong with it. And she was pretty sure that whatever it was, it would cost almost as much to fix it as it would to buy a new set. She sighed deeply. This was not a good month. She'd embarked on a major economy drive but the washing machine had suddenly started dumping water all over the place and she'd had to get someone out to fix it. Rather embarrassingly, the trouble had been caused by the wire from one of her underwired bras getting caught in the machine – the mechanic had roared with laughter as he held it up in front of her. The house insurance had also fallen due and she'd arranged monthly instalments with the insurance company but the telephone bill, which she'd forgotten about, was astronomical. She knew that this was because Keelin spent so much time on the phone to Shauna Fitzpatrick but she didn't want to nag her about it. Keelin had also saved up almost enough money to buy the leather jacket she so desperately wanted and Gemma, in a perpetual state of guilt about her daughter, had given her the extra money she'd needed to buy it. Which was kind of worth it, Gemma thought as she looked at the blank screen, because Keelin was almost speaking to her again. If adolescent girls ever really did speak to their mothers.

She switched off the TV and switched it on again. There was a loud bang and a puff of smoke. Gemma and Ronan both dived for cover.

'It's not on fire,' said Ronan shakily as he peered over the back of the armchair.

'But it's definitely broken,' conceded Gemma.

'Can we get a new one?' asked Ronan. 'Wide-screen, Mum. With Teletext. And can we get Sky Sports?'

'I don't know,' said Gemma.

'We need a new one,' said Ronan. 'And Sky Sports would be brilliant! I'd be able to watch the Premiership.'

'I know,' said Gemma.

'Everyone else in school has Sky Sports,' said Ronan. 'Why don't we?'

'Because it—' Gemma stopped. It wasn't fair to keep on saying that they couldn't have things because they cost money. If she was better at managing it in the first place, if she didn't spend it as some kind of comforter, they probably could have afforded a dozen new TV sets all with Teletext or digital or whatever it was that Ronan wanted.

'Can we have a really big TV?' asked Ronan. 'Maybe PowerCity will do a portable one free with a big one. Then I can have one separate for my games!'

'It's probably those bloody games that have broken this one,' said Gemma sharply. 'I'm sure they can't have done it any good.'

'Everyone plays games on the TV,' said Ronan. 'It's not my fault.'

'No. I know.' Gemma rubbed the bridge of her nose. Televisions weren't that expensive any more, she thought. She could pick one up cheaply enough. Not, perhaps, a wide-screen but Ronan wouldn't know the difference anyway. Maybe.

'Can we go now?' asked Ronan. 'Otherwise I'll miss *Ace Ventura*. It's on at eight o'clock.'

Gemma thought about her options. She couldn't buy anything on the credit card. Her overdraft was up to its limit and so she couldn't put it on her laser card either. And she had the grand total of seventy-eight pounds in her purse, with the week's grocery shopping still to do. David's maintenance was due, though, and it should hit her account sometime in the next week.

'I'll have to think about it,' she told Ronan. 'And we can't get it tonight.'

'But . . .' He looked aghast. 'But *Ace Ventura* is on tonight.'

'I know,' said Gemma. 'I'm sorry.'

'I can't even play Zelda,' cried Ronan. 'I've nothing to do!'

'Read a book,' said Gemma.

'I don't want to.'

'Go outside and play,' she told him. 'It's a nice evening.'

'It's cold.'

'Look, Ronan, I can't buy a new TV tonight. That's it. Sorry.'

Ronan got up and stomped out of the room. Gemma closed her eyes.

She was still sitting in front of the TV with her eyes closed when Keelin walked in.

'What's the matter with you?' asked Keelin.

'Nothing,' said Gemma.

'Why are you sitting there like that?' Keelin's tone was anxious.

'No reason,' said Gemma.

'Why isn't the telly on?' asked Keelin.

'Because it's broken,' Gemma told her.

'What's the matter with it?'

'It went bang and emitted a cloud of smoke,' said Gemma.

Keelin giggled. 'Really?'

Gemma opened her eyes and looked at her daughter. 'Really.'

'So it's completely knackered?'

'I guess so.'

'Do you want to go and get a new one tonight?' asked Keelin.

'Why do you and Ronan both think we can wander up to the shops and buy a new TV just like that?' asked Gemma.

'Well, this one is broken. We need a new one. PowerCity is open until nine,' said Keelin. 'It's only eight now. We have an hour.'

'But we don't have the money,' Gemma said.

'Why?' Keelin stared at her. 'Dad gives you lots of money for us. He told me. And you get paid by Niamh. How come you never have any money?'

'It's not as simple as that,' said Gemma wearily.

'It is,' said Keelin. 'You had money to buy this house. It's not like you have to pay loads every month. We've done accountancy and economics in school, you know.'

'Perhaps you'd like to manage the money then,' said Gemma acidly.

'I'd probably do a better job than you!'

They glared at each other. Then Keelin walked out of the living room and thumped her way up the stairs.

I am utterly useless, thought Gemma. Hopeless. And she's right. She probably would make a better fist of things than me.

Orla stood outside the house. It seemed silly to be nervous but she was. She didn't know what to expect. Since her marriage to David, she could number her conversations with Rosanna on the fingers of one hand. And those conversations had been terse. Her relationship with her mother had never been terse before. And it upset her to think that things had changed.

She took a deep breath and pressed the buzzer.

'Hello, stranger!' Her brother, Tony, two years older than her, answered the door.

'Hi.' She stepped inside. 'How are things?'

'Fine,' said Tony. 'And you? How's life with the almost pensioner?'

'He's not almost a pensioner,' she said sharply. 'You're as bad as Mum.'

'No, I'm not!' Tony grinned at her. 'I fight your cause, you know.'

Orla sighed. 'Is she still pissed off at me?'

'She's getting over it,' said Tony. 'But you know our mum. Obstinate.' He smiled. 'Just like you.'

'I'm not obstinate,' objected Orla. 'I just know what I want.'

'Exactly,' murmured Tony as he opened the living-room door.

'Well, this is an honour.' Rosanna O'Neill looked up as Orla walked into the room. 'We haven't seen you since you came back from the Caribbean.'

'I called over as soon as I got home,' objected Orla. 'I brought you presents, didn't I?'

'And we haven't seen you since.'

'You didn't make me feel awfully welcome,' said Orla. 'I thought I'd spare you the effort of having to try again.'

The two women stared at each other. Tony left the room.

'Why don't you like him?' asked Orla.

'I've told you a hundred times,' said Rosanna. 'He's too old. He has kids. He has an ex-wife. He has baggage, Orla.'

'But he's my husband now,' said Orla. 'So no matter what you think you've got to accept that.'

The older woman sighed. 'I know.'

'And I love him,' said Orla. 'He's kind. He's generous. He's fantastic to me and he's fantastic to his kids.'

'And what about kids of your own?' asked Rosanna. 'How exactly does he feel about that?'

Orla shrugged. 'Supportive,' she said, 'if I want to have any. Which I'm not certain about just yet. I'm only twenty-four.'

'I know exactly how old you are,' retorted Rosanna. 'But the point is, Orla, let's say you want kids when you're thirty. Let's imagine you wait that long. He'll be fifty-six! It's not a great age for a man to start a family. You have to agree about that.'

Orla shrugged again. 'Lots of men have children when they're older. In a lot of cases they're better fathers second time around. They have more time for them.'

Rosanna smiled faintly. 'It doesn't matter what I say, does it?'

'Not now,' said Orla. 'I've married him and that's that.'

'OK.' The anger left Rosanna's voice as she reached out and took Orla by the hand. 'No fighting over it. Not now. So why are you here and not with him?'

Orla smiled and squeezed her mother's hand. 'Because he wants me to cook something,' she told Rosanna. 'And I haven't the faintest idea what to do!'

⌒

David was reading the paper when the phone rang. He folded it and picked up the receiver, expecting it to be Orla. He'd encouraged her to call round to see her mother this evening. He knew that she was unhappy about the strain between herself and Rosanna and he hoped that the two of them would manage to resolve things. Orla often told him that, until she'd met him, she'd got on very well with her mother. He'd been surprised at how unhappy Orla was that the relationship between them was so strained – Gemma's relationship with Frances had always been strained and Gemma never voluntarily dropped round to Frances. But Orla had seemed happy, if nervous, about calling round to her mother's house again. David sighed as he tried to understand the complexities of the mother-daughter thing. His relationship with his parents was simple. They'd brought him up to be independent and he was. His mother kissed him whenever they met and his father slapped him on the back and asked after work. It had never gone much deeper than that, although he knew that neither his mother nor his father had been very happy about the break-up of his marriage to Gemma. They'd liked Gemma and she'd got on well with them too. She'd sometimes told him

95

that she got on better with his mother than she ever had with Frances.

David wondered if Orla was calling to say that she'd be late, that Rosanna was giving her a cooking lesson. He was feeling terribly guilty about having landed Orla in the deep end as far as entertaining was concerned but he hadn't really thought it would have been so big an issue for her. It was the kind of thing that Gemma had taken completely in her stride.

'Hi,' he said easily.

'David?'

'Gemma?' He sat upright. 'Is anything the matter?'

Gemma tightened her grip on the receiver. 'No, nothing at all. Nothing's the matter, David.'

'So why are you ringing me?' he asked. 'You only ever ring if something's the matter.'

'No, I don't,' she said. 'I ring to organise things.'

'Or to change our arrangements.'

'Not unless I have to – David, this is stupid,' she said. 'This sounds like one of our old conversations!'

'I know,' he said, 'I'm sorry. What did you call for?'

'I wanted to ask you something.'

'Ask away.'

'I was wondering if you could lend me some money.'

'Money?' he repeated. 'What for?'

'A new TV,' she said.

'TV?'

'Yes.'

'What's wrong with the one you have?'

'It blew up,' said Gemma.

'Blew up?'

She was getting really tired of him repeating everything she said. 'Yes,' she told him.

'Anyone injured?'

'It wasn't as dramatic as all that,' she told him. 'It just emitted a puff of smoke and died.'

He laughed.

'It sounds funny, I know,' said Gemma. 'But, of course, for Ronan it's a complete disaster. He's missing all his favourite TV programmes.'

'Do him good not to sit glued in front of it all the time,' said David.

'I know. But you can't tell him that,' said Gemma. 'And, of course, there's the games thing. He can't play games either.'

'Playing those games is just as bad,' said David.

'You always used to enjoy them,' said Gemma. 'As I recall, it was you who wanted the Playstation in the first place.'

'Why can't you just buy a new TV yourself?' asked David. 'It's not as though you're destitute, Gemma. You can't keep running to me every time you have a short-term financial problem, you know. I've been generous enough as it is.'

'I know you have.' She moistened her lips. 'And I really appreciate how good you've been.' She made a face at the phone. 'But I'm a bit short of ready cash at the moment.'

'Use your credit card,' he said blithely.

'I can't,' she told him.

'Why?'

'Because I just can't. I'm up to my limit.'

'What the hell have you been spending the money on?' asked David.

'It's none of your business,' she snapped. 'I'm up to my limit. That's all you need to know.'

'Well, what about an overdraft?' he suggested.

'David, if I could get an increase in my overdraft then I wouldn't need to call you, would I?'

'You mean you're up to your overdraft limit too?' His voice was incredulous.

He's doing it again, thought Gemma miserably. He's making me feel like a child. He's going to start lecturing me any minute and I just can't bear it!

'Really and truly, Gemma,' said David, 'you'll have to get a grip on how you manage your money. In the past I've always been ready to help you out. But I'm married now, I have other responsibilities. I can't be your lender of last resort all the time. If you come running to me every time you have a little financial problem you'll never manage to sort it out for yourself. Will you?'

Fuck off, you pompous bastard, she thought. And how can you call the flame-haired bimbo bitch a responsibility? Doesn't she have a job of her own?

'So you won't give me anything then,' she said.

'It's not a question of can't or won't,' said David. 'It's what's good for you, Gemma.'

'It's good for me to be without the TV, is it?' she asked.

'Surely it won't take you long to get the money together,' he said. 'After all, you can pick up a telly for under a couple of hundred these days.'

'Ronan wants a wide-screen,' she said.

David laughed. 'Who does that kid think he is?'

'He doesn't understand,' she told him. 'He thinks because everyone else has one, he should have one too.'

'Well, he'll have to learn, won't he? He can't have what everyone else has.'

'He knows that already,' said Gemma. 'He doesn't have a father at home, does he?'

David was silent for a moment. Gemma could sense his fury. She could picture the tightening of his jaw, the narrowing of his eyes and the all-over tension that filled his body when he was angry.

'That's unforgivable,' he said finally. 'You were the one, Gemma! You were the one that decided the marriage was over. You were the one who said that it was better for the children to have no father than me as a father. You decided that you were keeping them. You brought solicitors into our private lives and you tried to screw me for every penny you could! So don't, *don't* give me any shit about Ronan not having a father at home!!'

She bit her lip. She hadn't meant to antagonise him. 'I just mean—'

'Oh, I know what you meant!' David raged. 'You want to picture yourself as some poor abandoned ex-wife who struggles to keep home and family together under difficult circumstances.'

'I—'

'Well, your circumstances aren't that bloody difficult, Gemma, you make things difficult for yourself! And you can't decide now that it was a mistake to get divorced.'

'It certainly wasn't mistake,' she retorted, 'it was the best thing I ever did.'

'Likewise!' said David and slammed down the receiver.

Gemma stood in the hallway and leaned her head against the wall. Great work, she told herself glumly. That wasn't exactly how you wanted the converation to go.

Chapter 12

It was easier to get people to buy insurance policies, thought Orla, as she laid out the ingredients for her cooking fest on the marble-topped counter. You knew where you were with people, you knew what you wanted and what they wanted and you could figure it out. But this! Mounds of meat and vegetables and spices waiting for her to create something that would make people exclaim with delight or at least not turn away in disgust. She shook her head. Even with the help of Rosanna's favourite cookery book, this was going to be a nightmare. Rosanna had insisted on Orla taking the cookery book home – she thought the pictures would help.

Orla had quite enjoyed sitting with her mother, chatting about the dinner party. In Rosanna's house, steeped in memories of her mother's effortless hostessing, Orla felt perfectly capable of rustling up something sensational herself. But she was afraid of doing a roast. People were picky about how they liked their meat cooked. And so was she. If it ended up being rare, she wouldn't be able to touch it. Rosanna had suggested goulash. After all, she said, it was basically just a stew and even though it took time to prepare you didn't have to do anything once it was in the oven. That would then give Orla the opportunity to entertain her guests.

'They're not my guests,' she told her mother. 'They're David's.'

Rosanna had raised an eyebrow at that but said nothing.

'How long does it take?' David looked up from the weekend supplements.

'A couple of hours,' Orla replied. She scraped at a carrot.

'Isn't a bit warm to have something in the oven for a couple of hours?' asked David.

'It means I can concentrate on your friends not the cooking.' Orla sucked her finger which she'd nicked with the sharp knife.

'Our friends,' David corrected her.

99

'Your friends at the moment,' said Orla. 'They might be our friends one day, but right now their yours.'

'Touchy, touchy.'

'I'm not,' said Orla. 'It's true. I haven't even met these people.'

'You'll like them,' David assured her. 'Kevin is a really decent bloke.'

'And Eve?' asked Orla. 'What does Eve do?'

David shrugged. 'She job shares in some telephone company. Two and a half days a week.'

'Nice,' said Orla.

'Ideal, I'd call it.' David yawned. 'I'd love to work half a week.'

'You'd get bored.' Orla dropped the carrot into a bowl of cold water.

'No, I wouldn't,' said David.

'I would,' Orla told him. 'I know it sounds great but what the hell would you do for the other two and a half days?'

'Relax,' David told her.

'You're not the relaxing sort,' said Orla. 'You never were.'

David laughed. He walked into the kitchen and put his arms round her. 'Want to bet?'

She held the knife in front of him. 'I'm armed.'

'I'll just have to disarm you then.' He slid his hand under her T-shirt.

'David!'

'Come on,' he said. 'You look incredibly sexy with a knife in one hand and a carrot in the other.'

'I can't possibly.'

'But you do.'

'David, I'm trying to cook!'

'You have time,' he said. 'I said eight o'clock. It's only five now.'

'But I have to do loads of things,' cried Orla. 'And this takes two or three hours. I won't get it into the oven before half five!'

'And we won't be eating it until later.'

'I still have to get the starter ready.'

'You've got smoked salmon,' said David. 'I saw it. All you have to do is stick it on a plate! Not much to do there.'

'But then I have to get ready myself!'

'Orla, for God's sake! Take time out. You've been on the go all day. Rushing off to the supermarket. Playing around with all that fruit. Buying candles. Relax. It's not some kind of competition, you know.'

100

'I just want to make it perfect,' she told him.

'And it will be perfect.' He kissed her gently on the nape of her neck as he undid the button of her jeans. 'I promise you, Orla, it'll be absolutely perfect.'

She was as tight as a drum. David kissed her and caressed her. He held her closely to him and murmured that he loved her. But she kept thinking about how long it might take to peel half a dozen carrots and whether it was really enough just to wipe the mushrooms with a damp cloth. What if she left some spots of earth clinging to them? Would people notice? She couldn't believe that she was thinking about things like this while David was kissing her. Usually she abandoned herself to him completely, but right now she simply couldn't.

She gasped as David pushed himself into her. He grunted slightly and she squirmed so that it was more comfortable. He groaned with pleasure.

She looked at him. His eyes were closed, his face was set in a mask of concentration. She wondered why he looked like that, why he didn't seem more relaxed. She'd never looked at him while they were making love before. Her eyes had always been squeezed tightly shut because that way she could feel him more intensely. She wrapped her legs round his back and winced. She really wasn't in the mood and her body was telling her that she wasn't in the mood. If she squirmed a bit more, she thought, he might hurry up and then she could get back to the cooking.

'Oh, Orla.' He bit his lip. She noted, with interest, that the vein in his forehead stood out. She wriggled underneath him again.

'Oh, God.'

Smoked salmon was the wrong starter. She'd chosen it precisely because all she had to do was put it on a plate but it didn't go with goulash. They'd be horrified. She tightened her grip on David as she imagined their faces when she replaced the salmon with goulash. They'd wonder what on earth she was thinking of.

'Oh, Orla!'

She hoped that the blackcurrant and cherry ice concoction that she'd made earlier had frozen like it was supposed to. She shuddered as she imagined turning it out of the newly-bought mould only to see it dissolve into a puddle of dark red liquid in front of everyone.

'Oh, yes!' David shuddered too and exhaled slowly. He dropped onto Orla's body and lay there, his head between her breasts.

If I'd had boob implants, she thought, they wouldn't fall to the sides like they do now. They'd be like a cushion either side of him. The thought made her want to giggle.

'David, I have to get up.'

'That was wonderful.' He lifted his head to look at her.

'Yes,' she said.

'You sure?'

'Absolutely,' she told him.

He kissed her gently on each nipple. 'I love you.'

'And I love you too, but I really need to peel a few carrots.'

'Romance is not dead,' he said and rolled to one side.

⌇

She hadn't realised it would take so long to peel and slice and chop things. It was nearly six o'clock by the time she poured oil into the huge copper saucepan and slid it onto the hob.

'I thought you were doing it in the oven,' said David who had come into the kitchen and was now poking at the chopped onions.

'I am,' Orla told him. 'But you brown the onions and meat on the hob first. I'm just letting the oil heat up for a couple of seconds.'

She left the kitchen and surveyed the dining table which she'd already set. It looked good, she thought. I can do this. I can do entertainment things in a grown-up kind of way. It doesn't have to be takeaway pizza and burnt cocktail sausages.

She yawned.

'Tired?' David followed her.

'A little,' she said.

'Post coital,' he told her. 'I'm exhausted.'

'Post nothing,' said Orla. 'It's from chopping those onions. My eyes are ruined.'

'Gemma had a trick about—' he stopped as he saw the expression on Orla's face. 'It never worked,' he said.

She smiled slightly. 'What was it?'

'I can't remember,' he said. 'Honestly.'

'You think it's fine,' said Orla, 'and then suddenly your eyes start to water and they just won't stop.' She sniffed suddenly. 'Do you smell something?' she asked.

'Something odd.' David stood up. 'I thought you were just heating oil.'

'I was.' She followed him back to the kitchen. A wave of blue-grey smoke met them. There was a strong but undefinable smell.

'Jesus Christ!' David rushed over to the hob and switched it off. 'What on earth were you doing!!'

'What? What?'

He looked at her. 'We're lucky the whole place hasn't gone up in smoke.'

'What did I do?' Her voice was almost a squeak.

'You switched on the wrong plate,' said David. 'And you left this on the one that you actually turned on.' He held a piece of melted plastic in front of him. It was the bowl in which she'd left her carefully chopped carrots. Some were embedded into the plastic, some were scorched. She stared at him in horror.

'Didn't you look?' he demanded. 'Didn't it occur to you that you were switching on the wrong plate?'

'Of course not,' she snapped. 'If I'd known I was switching on the wrong one I wouldn't have done it, would I?' She coughed. The acrid smell of the plastic caught in her throat.

David switched on the extractor fan and the smoke began to filter out of the kitchen. 'This smell is awful,' he said.

'It'll be gone before Kevin and Eve arrive,' said Orla.

'It better be.' David wiped his own eyes which were beginning to water. He threw the melted plastic bowl and its decorative carrots into the bin.

Orla followed him back into the living room. A film of smoke clouded the air. David opened the balcony doors.

'I'm sorry,' she said as he stepped outside. 'It was an accident.'

'I know,' he said. 'I'm not blaming you.'

'It feels as though you are.'

'Of course I'm not.' He put his arm round her. 'You've never done this before. You're probably nervous. It's easy to make a mistake.'

'Don't patronise me!' She shook his hand away.

'I'm not bloody patronising you!'

They glared at each other. Orla was horrified to realise that she was going to cry. She bit the inside of her lip.

'I'm sorry,' said David. 'Maybe I did sound patronising. I didn't mean to be.'

She pulled at her earlobe. 'It's OK,' she said.

'Friends?'

'Sure,' she said.

'OK.' He smiled at her. 'Come on, you'd better peel some more carrots.'

'I don't have any more.'

She looked like a child, he thought, who'd done something wrong. He was overcome by love for her. He wrapped his arms round her and held her to him. He hadn't realised that this would be such a trial for her. He was so used to seeing her in control of things, talking to customers, giving orders, knowing what she was doing, that this new, uncertain Orla was a revelation to him. He liked the feeling that he was protecting her.

'It doesn't matter,' he murmured as he stroked her hair. 'They won't notice.'

'I'll notice,' she said.

'I'll ply them with drink,' he assured her, 'and I promise you they won't notice.'

⌒

Kevin and Eve arrived at exactly eight o'clock. Eve carried a huge bouquet of flowers while Kevin handed David a bottle of St Emilion.

'Great. Thanks.' David patted his friend on the back.

'I know you like it,' said Kevin. 'It used to be one of your favourites.'

'It's perfect,' said David.

Orla took the flowers into the kitchen. She had nowhere to put them. David's interior designer had specified vases but had filled them with dried flowers. Orla took a bucket out from beneath the sink, filled it with water and shoved Eve's bouquet into it.

'Drinks,' said David. 'Gin and tonic, Kevin? And the same for you, Eve?'

They nodded and David took some glasses out of the drinks cabinet.

'So.' Eve smiled at Orla. 'It's nice to meet you at last.'

'And you.' Orla smiled back. 'I've heard a lot about you.'

'Not as much as I've heard about you, I'm sure,' Eve said.

Orla kept the smile on her face as she studied Eve. Eve had light blue eyes, ash-blonde shoulder-length hair and long nails which were perfectly manicured and painted pale pink. She wore large gold earrings, a gold chain round her neck and two gold bracelets. Orla wasn't sure whether she liked the older woman or not. It was hard to judge exactly how old she was, she thought. Somewhere between thirty and forty she guessed, and nearer forty, surely, given the crow's feet around her eyes. You're being bitchy, Orla told herself as she contemplated her own line-free skin. But it's nice to think bitchy thoughts.

104

'So, David.' Eve sat back in the ultra-modern armchair and tapped her nail against her glass. 'Tell us all about how you and Orla met. It's great to see you back in the saddle, so to speak, after so long.'

David laughed. 'That's a charming way of putting it, Eve.'

'I didn't mean it to sound quite so crude.' She smiled at him. 'But I suppose you get the drift.'

'We met in work,' said David. 'I was giving her a lecture.'

'What kind of lecture?' Eve turned to Orla.

'How to be a star salesperson,' Orla replied. 'Although, as I recall, he kept saying salesman.'

'I told you at the start that I didn't have time for all this salesperson rubbish,' said David. 'I have no problem with saleswomen or salesmen, but salesperson sounds utterly ridiculous.'

'I agree,' said Kevin.

'Me too,' said Orla calmly, 'when you're talking about one or the other. But when you have a room full of people of both sexes, I think you should defer to that. And David didn't.'

'Still didn't stop you lunging at him!' Kevin laughed.

'Kevin!' Eve leaned over the arm of the chair and gave him a gentle dig. 'For all we know it was David who lunged at Orla.'

'There was no lunging by either of us,' said David. 'We only spoke to each other that day. It was later before we really got together.'

'And what did you see in him?' Eve turned to Orla.

'I liked him,' said Orla simply.

'The grey hair, false teeth and short sight didn't put you off?' asked Kevin.

'He doesn't have false teeth!' cried Orla and then blushed as they grinned at her. 'I'll just check on things in the kitchen,' she said hastily and got up.

'She's adorable,' said Eve as Orla left the room. 'And very beautiful, David.'

'Isn't she?' He smiled smugly.

'I wish I did know what she sees in you,' said Kevin glumly. 'I don't think that any of the girls I know that have legs up to their armpits and a perfect figure would even go for a drink with me. Let alone marry me.'

'That's because you're very securely married to me,' said Eve firmly. 'And I don't want you getting any ideas about young, nubile women in your office, thanks very much!'

They laughed and David got up to refill their glasses.

105

Orla could hear them laughing. They were probably laughing at her, she thought, as she opened the oven door and slid the pot out. She hoped that it was cooking properly. It had been nearly half past six before she'd finally put it into the oven. She sniffed. It smelled OK and there was no hint of the aroma of melted plastic around the place. She returned it to the oven and peeped into the fridge. Her smoked salmon was fine. It didn't matter that it was being followed by goulash.

'We were just saying,' Eve turned to her as she walked into the room again, 'that David's designer did a wonderful job on the apartment.'

'Yes,' agreed Orla. 'It's lovely.'

'Of course David was used to lovely things,' she continued. 'Remember those paintings you had. They were beautiful, David.'

'They were,' he said.

'Did Gemma get them?' asked Kevin.

David shook his head. 'We sold them.'

'What a shame.' Eve pouted. 'If I'd known I would have bought the one of Dublin Bay. Is Gemma still living in Sandymount, David?'

Orla moved uneasily in her seat.

'Yes,' he replied. 'The children love it there.'

'And do you see them often?' asked Eve.

'Every week,' David told her.

'And what about you, Orla?' Eve turned her huge blue eyes to Orla. 'Do you get on with them?'

Orla shrugged. 'It's hard to say. I take it easy with them.'

'Poor things,' said Eve. 'I mean, David, I know absolutely that you and Gemma had to break up, of course you did, she was far too self-centred, but it was hard on the children, wasn't it?'

'Of course,' said David, 'but Gemma wasn't self-centred, Eve. You know she wasn't.'

'She always wanted things her way, though, didn't she?' asked Eve.

'I suppose so,' said David, 'but it was my fault too. I wasn't there enough for her, or for the kids. And I know she drove me crazy – she still does every time I see her – but she's a good mother to them and she does her best.'

Orla bit her fingernail. It snapped off between her teeth.

'Anyway, it's great to see that you've started all over again with someone like Orla.' Eve's voice was warm.

Why was it, Orla thought, that she felt sure the woman didn't mean a word of it?

'As I told you, you're a lucky devil!' Kevin grinned at Orla. 'You're probably miles too good for him, the creaky old bastard.'

106

Orla smiled tentatively.

'How old are you?' asked Eve. 'Don't answer if you don't want to!'

'Twenty-four,' said Orla.

'Oh!' Eve made a face at her. 'How I wish I was twenty-four again. Mind you,' she laughed, 'I don't know if I'd get married at twenty-four again.'

'You were twenty-five when we got married,' said Kevin. 'Nearly twenty-six, in fact.'

Eve made a face at him. 'I was still miles too young.'

'How long are you married?' asked Orla.

'Twelve years.' Kevin sighed. 'I can hardly believe it myself sometimes.'

So that made Eve thirty-seven or thirty-eight, thought Orla. She supposed that the woman was well-preserved for someone who was thirty-seven or thirty-eight. She wondered would she feel old when she was that age. Nearly forty, she told herself. Gemma's age – almost. David's age – absolutely.

She suddenly felt very young and very out of place. Twenty-four isn't that young, she told herself viciously. And forty isn't old. She was allowing them to make her feel like this.

'I'll check things in the kitchen again,' she said.

'Would you like some help?' asked Eve.

Orla shook her head. 'I can manage.'

'Really, though, David, do you keep in touch with Gemma?' asked Eve when Orla had left the room. She drained her gin and tonic and put the glass on the coffee table in front of her.

'When I see the kids I usually see her.' David reached for the bottle of gin and refilled Eve's glass. 'So I can't help but keep in touch with her.'

'And how does she feel about this?'

'This?' He dropped a couple of ice cubes into her drink.

'Your marriage, for heaven's sake!' Eve laughed. 'What does she think about you hurtling into matrimony with someone half your age?'

'She's not half my age,' said David. 'And she's a very mature person. Very together.'

'I know,' said Eve. 'But look at her, David! I know she's very attractive and everything but you'd think she was about seventeen.'

'I wouldn't,' said David. 'Anything but!'

'David, that figure under that little black dress! It's coltish, to say the least.'

'You're just jealous,' said Kevin. 'You couldn't fit into it any more.'

'I've had three kids,' said Eve. 'I have my excuses!'

Orla couldn't hear what they were saying but she was convinced they were talking about her again. Or, even worse, talking about Gemma. She reached into the oven and lifted the lid off the pot. She banged her hand against the side of the oven, cried out as it burned her, then dropped the lid which fell onto the tiled floor with a crash that echoed around the tiny room.

'Orla! Are you all right?' David rushed to the doorway of the kitchen, Kevin and Eve behind him. Orla held her hand against her chest as the waves of pain washed over her. Tears glistened in her eyes.

'Let me.' Eve pushed past the two men and put her arm round Orla. 'What happened?'

'Burned it.' Orla blinked furiously to keep the tears at bay. 'I'll be OK in a second.'

'Let's see.' Eve looked at Orla's hand. A dark red weal ran across it. Eve winced. 'Looks painful.'

'It is.'

'Do you have a first-aid box?' she asked David. 'I'm sure you must have some antihistamine cream or something like that.'

'I don't know,' said David. 'I'll check in the bathroom.'

'It'll be OK,' said Eve.

'I'm fine now,' said Orla. 'I got a fright more than anything. My hand just seemed to stick to the oven.' She blew gently on it. 'Honestly, it's OK.'

'Here.' David brandished some cream. 'It says burns and stings.'

'Excellent.' Eve squeezed some out and rubbed it gently onto Orla's hand. 'You'll be fine.'

'I know.' Orla was recovering her composure although her hand was hurting badly. But she was annoyed at herself for being so bloody stupid and for making a fuss. 'Why don't you go back outside? I can manage now.'

'You sure?' asked Eve.

'Certain.' She nodded, although it made her feel light-headed.

'OK,' said Eve. She put the cream on the draining board, beside the bucket of flowers. 'Glad to see you've got a container big enough for them!' She laughed, but Orla wanted to die.

Chapter 13

Gemma lay in bed, wide awake although her eyes were closed. She'd always been the kind of person who was alert at night but, in the last few years, sleep seemed to elude her no matter how tired she was. In the first few weeks after David had left, she'd taken sleeping tablets. They'd worked by sending her into a deep, almost comatose sleep, from which she'd struggled to wake up. And when she finally opened her eyes she'd have a slight, nagging headache pinned behind her forehead. So she'd thrown the tablets down the loo and tried Niamh's suggested cure of camomile tea. The tea didn't work as well as the tablets – didn't work at all in fact – and she didn't much like the taste of it either, but it was soothing to drink and she pretended it was helping.

She sat up. Some tea would be a good idea now, she thought. It was three o'clock in the morning and she hadn't been able to still the thoughts that chased around her head for even a fraction of a second. Making tea would distract her, no matter how temporarily.

She slid out of bed and pulled her dressing gown around her. The sound of snoring came from Ronan's room. She pushed open the door and smiled as she saw him lying, arms outstretched, sideways across the bed. It didn't matter that she tucked him in every night by morning he was usually spread-eagled. She pushed open the door of Keelin's room too. Her daughter was lying on her side, her arms clutched around her own body.

She looks tense even though she's asleep, thought Gemma sadly. It's my fault she's like that. Mine and David's. We were too young to get married and too young to have children.

The stairs creaked as she made her way down to the kitchen and she held her breath in case she woke them. But they slept on as she filled the kettle then dropped a tea bag into her china cup. She always used her china cup for camomile tea.

Why do I get it wrong so much? she wondered as she stared out into the back garden. Why is it that everything I try to do somehow goes awry? Why couldn't I have put money aside after I bought the house and the car and the furniture instead of buying toys and clothes and all sorts of ridiculous things for the children? How come I look every day of my thirty-five years and yet feel as though I haven't really changed from the kind of person I was ten years ago? Why do I sometimes wish David was still here, even though I cried every night of the last six months we were together?

She leaned her head against the kitchen door and blinked away the tears that had begun to fall. And what was the bloody point in crying? she demanded. Where was that going to get her?

The kettle boiled and she poured water over the tea bag. She wrinkled her nose at the slightly oily smell of the tea.

David was a pig, she told herself, as she swirled the tea bag around. He could have given her the money for the TV. It was something for the kids, after all. Not just for her. And she hardly ever asked him for money any more. She hadn't kicked up a fuss when he told her that he was entitled to cut back on what he gave her because she'd started working. She'd been perfectly reasonable and understanding about it. She could have stopped working and made him carry on paying her. But she wasn't that sort of person.

She was a stupid sort of person, she muttered. A stupid, silly old bat. On her own.

She shivered. She hadn't thought about being on her own very much. She hadn't had time to think about it. But tonight, for the first time since the divorce, she realised that she was an adult woman who wanted an adult companion. Who missed having someone to share her thoughts and her fears. And who missed a man in bed beside her.

She sipped her tea. Sex wasn't something that she even thought about these days. Sex with David had turned into an exercise in avoiding each other and then, occasionally, coupling as though by mistake. She'd cried every time they'd made love in the last year they were together. She hadn't missed it since. Despite reading all the magazines in the hair salon, which invariably carried articles about how to improve your sex life and how important regular sex was, she hadn't felt the slightest interest in it. She couldn't imagine anyone putting his arms round her and kissing her on the mouth. She couldn't picture him opening the buttons of her blouse, or sliding the zip on her skirt, or pulling her close to him. Sex was just a sensation, she told herself as she wrapped her hands round the china cup. And not always a very pleasant sensation. Completely overrated, no matter how great it had been at the start. It didn't stay that way. It became mechanical. It would be like that with anyone.

She swallowed the remainder of the tea and went back upstairs to bed.

'Dad's here!' Ronan thundered down the stairs and opened the front door.

'Hi, big man,' said David. He put his arm on Ronan's shoulder.

'Did you hear?' asked Ronan. 'Our telly is broken.'

'Yes, I heard.' David followed his son into the kitchen. 'Who broke it?'

'Mum,' said Ronan.

'Typical.' David grinned at him.

'What's typical?' asked Gemma as she walked into the kitchen with a basket of laundry.

'Ronan says you broke the TV,' David told her.

'Oh, does he?' She smiled at her son. 'More likely it was you, Ronan. If it wasn't the games, it was the way you kept channel-hopping.'

'It wasn't my fault,' protested Ronan. 'Really it wasn't.'

'I know. It was nobody's fault.' Gemma opened the washing machine and began to load it with clothes.

'New skirt?' asked David.

'Pardon?' She straightened up.

'New skirt?'

She glanced down at the denim skirt she'd bought the day he married Orla. How the hell did he keep track of what she wore?

'Not very,' she lied.

'It's nice,' said David. 'Suits you.'

'Thanks.' She glanced at him to see if he was laughing at her but his face was expressionless. He looked tired, thought Gemma. He had bags under his eyes. 'Late night?' she asked.

'What?'

'Did you have a late night last night?' She blushed as she suddenly realised that her ex-husband could have spent the night making passionate love to his new wife.

'We had – some people over for dinner,' said David. He'd almost told her who they were but stopped himself just in time. He wasn't sure that she'd appreciate hearing that Kevin and Eve had been their guests.

'Oh.'

111

'Poor Orla nearly killed herself,' he added.

'How?' Gemma threw the washing tablets into the machine and switched it on.

'First of all from worry,' David said. 'She's not in your league when it comes to cooking, I'm afraid. And then she burned her hand on the inside of the oven.'

'Ouch.' Gemma winced.

'It probably looked worse than it was,' said David, 'but it looked awful.'

'Burns are painful,' Gemma said. 'Remember when we were out one night and someone knocked over a flaming sambucca? Caught the side of my arm? That really hurt.'

'I remember.' David looked at her. 'It was my birthday. We went to Mezza Luna. It was fun.'

'Yes.' She half-smiled. They'd still loved each other then.

'Are you ready to go?' Keelin opened the kitchen door. 'I'm waiting.'

'Sure,' said David. 'We're going bowling today.'

'I know.' Keelin looked aggravated. 'You said so last week. That's why I'm wearing my jeans.'

'Have fun,' said Gemma. 'Don't be late.'

'They're never late.' David's voice had lost the warmth of earlier and just sounded annoyed. 'You know they're never late.'

Gemma made a face at his retreating back and hauled the vacuum cleaner out of the cupboard. She always did the housework on Sundays.

⤙

Later that afternoon she called over to her parents' house. She seldom visited them because she never felt like giving Frances the opportunity of commenting on how well Michael and Debbie were doing and making her feel utterly useless.

She rang the doorbell. She didn't have a key to the house.

'Hello, Gemma!' Her father beamed at her. 'What drags you over to see us?'

'Hi, Dad.' She kissed him on the cheek. 'Just wanted to drop by.'

'I don't think so.' He smiled. 'Come on, I'm sitting in the garden. Your mother and Liz have gone to the park with Suzy.'

She followed him through the house and into the south-facing back garden. Her father loved the garden and spent a lot of time in it. 'To stay out of your mother's way,' he'd once told her and she believed him.

She sat down on one of the wooden chairs and he sat opposite her.

'You look pale,' he said. 'Is everything OK?'

'The telly blew up,' she said.

'What?'

'The telly blew up.' She started to giggle. 'It went bang, there was a puff of smoke and it died.'

'Gemma!' Her father looked worried. 'Was anyone hurt?'

She shook her head. 'I'm making it sound more dramatic than it was. But Ronan and I hid behind the sofa all the same.'

Gerry Garvey smiled. 'Is it under warranty?' he asked.

'No,' said Gemma. 'I checked this morning.'

'Oh well, you can pick up a TV cheaply enough these days,' said Gerry. 'It's not like when I was young and it was all tubes and valves and it cost almost as much as the house.'

'Not cheaply enough,' said Gemma.

Gerry looked at her speculatively. 'Money problems?'

'Oh, Dad.' Gemma sighed. 'I try, I really and truly do. But I'm hopeless at it. Absolutely hopeless.'

'Is that why you're here today?' he asked. 'Want to touch the old man for a loan?'

Gemma smiled at him. 'Probably,' she admitted. 'I wouldn't have said anything if Mum had been here – you know how she is about money, Dad, she can't understand how people don't survive on a tenner a week!'

'I know,' said Gerry. 'But you've got to remember that she was brought up in a different era, Gemma. When money was really tight. And being poor didn't mean no telly, it meant no anything.'

'I know.' Gemma nodded. 'I understand all that, Dad. It's just that she makes me feel so useless sometimes.'

'She doesn't mean to,' said her father. 'She loves you, you know.'

Gemma was silent. She supposed her mother did love her in the way that all mothers love their children. She simply didn't think her mother liked her very much.

'She worries about you,' said Gerry.

'Maybe,' said Gemma noncommittaly.

Gerry looked at her and sighed. 'So how much do you want?'

'I – don't know exactly,' said Gemma. 'A few hundred.' She bit her lip. 'Oh, Dad, I'm sorry. I shouldn't really have come. I don't need the money, I can manage really.'

'What else will I spend it on?' asked her father. He stood up. 'Come on, let's go to the shops now. Pick out one you like.'

'I don't—'

'If yours has blown up you'll want one tonight, won't you? And I'd like to see what you're getting.'

She smiled. 'Thanks, Dad.'

'Don't thank me, I didn't say you could have the most expensive one in the shop.'

She plugged it in and switched it on. It was lovely, she thought. She'd chosen the cheapest model that was there and then her father had suggested this one which was a hundred times more stylish, and much more expensive, and he wouldn't take no for an answer. Ronan will be pleased, she thought. It was a wide-screen.

She heard David's car pull up outside the house. Six o'clock. Exactly on time. That was one of the things that had driven her crazy about David. If he said he'd be somewhere at a certain time, he was. Practically to the second. But she was never on time and usually remembered a last-minute thing that just had to be attended to while David stood tapping his foot and waited for her.

She opened the hall door. Keelin stalked past her and upstairs to her bedroom. Gemma looked at her retreating back.

'Ro, go into the kitchen,' she said. She didn't want her son running out and telling David about the TV.

'Can I call down to Neville first?' he asked. 'Dad gave me a new video. I can watch it there.'

'OK,' she said, much to Ronan's amazement. He'd been expecting her to tell him that he should leave the Crawfords in peace. He scampered down the road before she could change her mind.

David got out of the car and walked up the path. Gemma closed the living-room door so that he couldn't see inside.

'Have a good day?' she asked.

'It was OK,' said David.

'Did you do anything interesting?'

'What interesting things can you do?' he asked. 'We went bowling, as we do so often. Then I took them for a walk along the pier.'

'Did Orla come too?' Gemma's tone was neutral.

David shook his head. 'Her hand was too sore to come bowling,' he said. 'She stayed at home.'

114

'Did they have something to eat?'

'Of course.' He looked affronted. 'I always give them something to eat.'

'Sorry.'

They were silent for a moment. Gemma waited for him to go but he stood awkwardly beside the door.

'Is something the matter?' she asked finally.

'No,' he said.

'Did you want to come in for some reason?'

'No,' he said again.

'Well, don't you think you'd better get home? I'm sure Orla will be waiting for you.'

'Is that an attempt at sarcasm?' asked David.

'No,' said Gemma. 'A statement of fact, I thought.'

'I wanted to give you this.' He pulled an envelope from the pocket of his jeans.

'Oh?' She looked at him quizzically.

'The TV,' he explained. 'I felt bad about it. Ronan told me again and I knew that I was a bit short with you. Take it.' He held out the envelope.

'There's a TV in this?' Gemma smiled.

'Financing,' said David shortly. 'But don't ask for anything else, Gemma.' He turned and walked back to the car.

Gemma stared at the cheque for three hundred pounds. She'd have to give it back, she knew she would.

But maybe not today.

Chapter 14

Orla reached behind her head and tugged at the zip of her short, purple linen dress.

'Let me.'

She turned and smiled at David as he walked into the bedroom.

He slid the zip gently upwards. 'You look stunning,' he said.

'Thanks.'

'I'll be sitting here worried sick about you,' he told her, 'and what might happen to you.'

'Happen to me?' She tightened the butterflies at the back of her tiny gold earrings. 'What do you think is going to happen to me?'

He looked at her long legs, her breasts barely contained by the low-cut neckline of the dress and her generous, full lips and shrugged.

'Don't you trust me?' she asked.

'Of course I do.'

'Well, then?' She looked at him in annoyance.

'You're so touchy,' he said. 'All I meant was that I can't help but imagine blokes looking at you and wanting you.'

'David!'

'When I see you – every time I see you – I want you.'

'That's OK, then.' She sprayed some Allure behind her ears. 'You have me.'

'But generally speaking, men are pigs. You know that. We look, we want, we take.'

'That's a horrible generalisation.' But she was smiling at him.

'So, I worry.'

'Well, you know that there's no need to worry tonight,' she told him. 'It's an engagement party. I really don't think that any of the girls will be looking at me in the way you fear.'

He laughed. 'I know. I'm sorry. I'm an idiot and I can't help it.'

She kissed him gently on the lips. He returned the kiss more passionately.

'Not tonight,' she told him breaking the embrace. 'I don't have time.'

He caught hold of her hands and she winced.

'I'm sorry.' He looked at her right hand and at the still visible scar from where she'd burnt it on the side of the oven. 'Does it still hurt?'

'Occasionally,' she said.

'I felt so sorry for you,' he told her. 'I could see that you were in agony and you had to sit there talking to them all night.'

She shrugged. 'It doesn't matter.'

'Kevin really liked you,' he said.

'Eve didn't.'

He stared at her. 'Of course she did.'

'Don't be a fool.' Orla picked up her handbag. 'She patronised me all night. I could see it in her eyes, David. She thought I was naïve and silly—'

'She liked you,' David interrupted her. 'And, as I told you the next day, everything was great. The food was lovely. The table looked fantastic. They had a good time.'

'I was on display,' said Orla. 'They were curious about me.'

'Of course they were,' he said. 'You can't blame them for that.'

'I was an interloper,' she told him. 'They were friends with you and friends with Gemma. They didn't really want to know me.'

'Of course they did!' He caught her by her unburnt hand. 'You're being paranoid, Orla.'

'Maybe.' She slid her hand out of his grasp. 'I have to go, David. I said I'd meet Abby at eight.'

'OK,' he said. 'Take care.'

'I will,' she told him.

⌐

She caught the DART to Lansdowne Road and then walked to Slattery's pub where Valerie Brown, a long-time friend of both Orla and Abby, was holding her engagement party. Slattery's was more of a stag party venue, Orla thought as she looked at her watch, but she was looking forward to a night out with the girls. She hadn't been out with anyone other than Abby since she'd married David. It was now almost a quarter past eight. She'd hurried out of the apartment and she was almost certain that she'd be one of the first there. She'd had to get out because she'd sensed that David had wanted to make love to her and she hadn't wanted him to.

The evening breeze blew a wisp of hair across her face and she tucked it behind her ears. Why did he always make a lunge at her whenever she was busy? she wondered. She'd noticed it a couple of weeks after they'd moved into the apartment. Anytime she said that she had to go and meet a client; any time that she busied herself with her paperwork; anytime she got involved in anything that excluded David, he would walk up behind her and put his arms round her until his hands were cupping her breasts and he would kiss her gently on the cheek and tell her that he loved her.

She knew he loved her. He told her often enough. It was something that most of her girlfriends complained about in their boyfriends – 'He never says he loves me. I'm supposed to just know!' But David told her. Over and over again so that she was secure and content in the knowledge of his love.

She sighed. There must be something really wrong with me, she thought as she ran across the road, if I get upset because my husband says he loves me.

She pushed open the door of the pub and walked inside. The smell of beer and smoke hit her and her eyes began to water. The pub was already crowded, with a crush of people lining the bar and people standing in every available space. The hum of conversation was more of a roar, she thought, as she scanned the area for any sign of her friends.

'Orla!' Abby waved at her from the other end of the room. 'We're back here!'

She pushed her way through the crowds.

'It's packed,' she said to Abby. 'I didn't think it would be this full.'

Abby made a face. 'Saturday night, what do you expect?'

'Somewhere to sit down,' said Orla.

Abby laughed. 'No chance.'

'Is Valerie here yet?' asked Orla. 'I'm surprised you are, I thought I'd be the first.'

'She's over there.' Abby nodded to where a tall, black-haired girl was chatting. 'Everyone's here, we all obviously have the need to get drunk! Can you believe that Valerie's engaged?'

'Of course I can,' said Orla. 'I was engaged myself once!'

'I can't believe you're married now either,' said Abby. 'I think you're all mad.' But she smiled to show she was joking. 'Do you want a drink? I was just about to order.'

'Vodka and tonic would be great,' said Orla.

Abby called the order to a barman. 'What's David doing tonight?' she asked while she waited for the drinks.

'Sitting in,' said Orla. 'He wasn't too amused about it.'

'Why?'

'I don't think he likes being in when I'm out,' explained Orla.

'But you're never out,' objected Abby. 'How many times have I asked you to come for a drink and you can't?'

'That's because I'm meeting prospective clients,' Orla told her. 'That's completely different.'

'Does he go out much without you?' asked Abby.

'Not with his mates,' replied Orla. 'He meets clients in the evenings too, though.'

The barman put their drinks on the counter.

'Cheers.' Abby raised her glass of Bacardi.

'Cheers.'

'So when do you two get to meet?' asked Abby.

'What?'

'If you're out meeting clients and he's out meeting clients, when do you get to see each other?'

'When we're not meeting clients!' Orla laughed.

'But how many nights a week are you both out?' persisted Abby.

'Two or three,' replied Orla. 'Not that late, though. We're both home by nine.'

'At least there's weekends,' said Abby.

Orla made a face. 'Not always,' she told her friend. 'Sometimes Saturdays are good days to see people.'

'What a foul job,' said Abby. 'Why on earth did you give up the job with the building society for that?'

'Because the building society paid peanuts,' Orla told her, 'and they were never going to be taken over by a bigger institution.'

'But what you do now is nearly all commission based,' objected Abby.

'That's why we have to work so hard,' conceded Orla. 'But when we sell, we get good bonuses. I earn a lot more than I ever did at the building society.'

Abby sighed. 'At the expense of your personal life.'

'Not at all!' cried Orla. 'Everyone works odd hours these days, Abby. It's not nine to five any more. Even the building society wasn't nine to five.'

'I can see why he doesn't want you to go out without him, though.'

'It's nothing to do with that.' Orla laughed. 'It's because he's afraid I'll be attacked and ravished by someone.'

'No, really?'

'So he says.' Orla grinned.

'We're at an engagement party,' said Abby, 'no chance of you being ravished here.'

'That's exactly what I told him.' Orla giggled and drained her glass. 'Come on, Abby. Do you want another drink?'

⤺

David closed his laptop and slid it into its carrying case. He'd updated his files and, looking at the business he'd brought in this week, it was much better than last. He was relieved about that because, for the first time in years, he'd felt anxious about turning his prospects into actual clients. But he'd had a great hit rate in the last couple of days and he suddenly felt as though he was back on track.

It had been a shock when Orla had beaten him. He hadn't believed it at first. He'd been beaten in a week or a month before, but always by one or two of the best known salesmen. Never by a woman. And that the woman was his wife made it all the more difficult to bear.

He wondered why he should feel like that. Surely, he thought, he should be happy that Orla was doing so well. He shouldn't resent her bringing in the amount of business that she did. After all, the money came into the house no matter who earned it. But he didn't like it. He didn't like feeling that she'd done better than he had and the more he told himself that he was being particularly silly about feeling that way, the worse he actually felt.

He looked at his watch. Nearly eleven. He wondered how she was enjoying her friend's engagement party and what time she'd be home. He didn't like being on his own in the apartment. This, he knew, was even sillier than resenting her bringing in more business than he did. He'd lived on his own in this apartment since the break-up of his marriage and he'd never felt the need of somebody there with him in all that time. But, now that he was married to Orla, he couldn't help feeling that she should be there whenever he was. He knew that it was irrational but he couldn't help himself. Gemma had never gone out when he was home. Although, he thought wryly, maybe it would have been better if she had.

He sighed. He hated to think of Orla with a gang of her girlfriends, having a good time without him, getting drunk and maybe having to

120

fend off the unwelcome advances of other men. He knew that Orla was well able to fend off any unwelcome advances but he didn't like to think of them being made. And a part of his mind worried that the advances of men who were closer to her own age wouldn't, after all, be that unwelcome.

He got up and took a beer from the fridge. This was stupid thinking, he told himself. Orla had had plenty of opportunities to meet men nearer her own age before she'd met him. And, he thought angrily, as he pulled the ring on the can, he wasn't that bloody old. He was only forty! Maybe twenty or thirty years ago people gave up on themselves when they were forty, but not now. He was in good shape, the grey in his hair was only a sprinkling and Orla said that the gold-rimmed glasses that he wore when he was reading were distinguished, not ageing.

So, he thought, he was forty and looked distinguished. He sighed. He'd really rather be twenty and looking like a sex symbol.

Why had she married him? he wondered. What was it that she'd seen in him? He knew what he'd seen in her – intelligence, independence, humour and a body that mesmerised him. They enjoyed the same things – they liked work, they liked travel, they liked eating out. But she could have got all that with somebody younger. She hadn't needed to marry him.

He pressed the remote control on the TV. He was being stupid and introspective and there wasn't any point. She'd married him because she loved him and she'd told him a hundred times that she loved him. Surely that was enough for anyone?

⌒

'. . . and he said, "Only when I'm having sex!"' Abby spluttered with laughter as she revealed the punchline to her joke. Orla joined in the laughter, her shoulders shaking with mirth.

'Anyway, all I can say is that Owen is very well-endowed,' Valerie Brown told them. 'And we are utterly immense in bed together!!'

'Lucky thing,' said Abby. 'It's so long since I've had sex that anyone would seem immense to me.'

'Who was your last?' demanded Valerie.

'Jack Moran,' said Abby, 'and I regret to say that he wasn't exactly God's gift. Either in the size department or the brains department. Made me quite nostalgic for Brian Phillips, actually.'

'I liked Brian.' Orla picked at the packet of peanuts in front of her. 'He was kind of cute.'

121

'He was gorgeous and he knew he was,' Abby told her. 'Every time we went out he used to check his appearance in shop windows. It was exhausting. And when we were in bed, I swear to God he was visualising how we looked together! I couldn't take it any more.'

'What's he doing now?' asked Valerie.

Abby shrugged. 'I've no idea, and I care less.'

'You'll have to find someone new,' Valerie said. 'Look at us all – I'm engaged, Sarah's engaged, Deirdre's living with her boyfriend and Orla's gone and done it already!'

'And how is married life, Orla?' Sarah Merchant peered through red eyes at her. 'Is it everything you ever dreamed of?'

'I never dreamed of anything,' said Orla. 'I didn't think I'd get married at all!'

'Why not?' asked Valerie.

'I don't know.' Orla yawned. 'I thought I'd be in my thirties at least. Just goes to show, doesn't it?'

'How do you get on with his ex-wife?' asked Sarah. 'I have to say I wouldn't be too keen on someone with an ex-wife.'

'Oh, she's all right,' Orla replied. 'I don't see her much. Not at all, in fact.'

'And the kids?' asked Valerie. 'I think it's really weird that he has kids, Orla.'

She made a face. 'So do I. But they're OK.' She stretched her hands over her head. 'Excuse me, call of nature.' She picked up her bag.

'It's not perfect,' Abby told the others as they watched her walk towards the Ladies. 'There's an edge to it somewhere but I can't find out exactly where.'

'It's all very well hitching up with someone who's been married before,' observed Sarah, 'but you take on an awful lot more, don't you?'

Abby nodded. 'And I don't think she even knows about the half of it yet.'

Orla peered at herself in the mirror. Her eyes were red and irritated. She took her contact lens case out of her bag and unscrewed the lids. Then she popped out her lenses and put them in the case. She was blind as a bat without them, but she'd got to the stage where she couldn't see much with them either. She blinked a couple of times to hydrate her eyes. Then she took out her lipstick and reapplied it. She wished she was one of those people who could keep lipstick on their lips all night, but no matter what sort of lipstick she bought and how much she blotted it and applied it again as they told her in magazines, it never stayed on.

122

She made a kissing motion at herself in the mirror. Back to the fray, she thought. Back to them wondering about me and David and why we got married and didn't just shack up with each other.

She sighed. Maybe it would have been a good idea. But David had been so sure, so certain and he'd made her feel sure and certain too. And she still did feel sure and certain, it was just that living with David was different to what she'd expected. The thing was, she told herself as she pushed open the door and walked back into the bar, she really wasn't too sure what exactly she had expected.

She peered short-sightedly through the throng of people. She was utterly hopeless without her lenses.

'Hey, Orla! Over here!' Abby waved at her. 'You shouldn't take those lenses out!'

'Sorry,' she said as she reached her friend, 'but the smoke is killing my eyes.'

'Mine too,' agreed Abby. 'Still, all in a good cause. Guess who's just come in?'

'Who?'

'Martin Keegan. Remember him?'

How could she have forgotten? Martin and Abby had been an item for a year at college at the same time as Orla had been going out with Jonathan Pascoe, Martin's friend. Abby and Martin split up soon after Orla had dumped Jonathan.

'I haven't seen him in years,' said Orla. 'What's he been up to?'

'I don't know,' said Abby, 'but I'm going to find out. Hey, Marty!!' She pushed her way towards him, dragging Orla with her. 'Guess who!'

'Abby Johnson.' Marty beamed at her. 'How's it going?'

'Not bad.' She kissed him on the cheek. 'And you?'

'Great,' he said. 'Absolutely great. Hi, Orla.'

'Hi, Marty. How're you doing?'

'Not so bad,' he said. 'You're looking stunning, as always, Orla.'

'What about me?' Abby pouted. 'No chance of you saying I look stunning, is there, and breaking the habit of a lifetime?'

Martin grinned. 'You were always looking for flattery.'

'That's because you never gave me any!'

They laughed together. If Jonathan had been there, thought Orla, it could almost have been five years ago. Martin didn't look in the slightest bit different. She told him so.

'You should have seen me a few weeks ago,' he said. 'I've just come back from the Falklands. I was researching a book.'

123

'About the war?' asked Abby. 'I didn't think you were into that sort of thing, Marty. I thought you were more a fiction writer.'

'It's about a sheep,' he told her.

'You're joking!'

'No, deadly serious. I've got a publisher and everything.'

'Congratulations,' said Abby. 'I always knew you could do it. I just never realised that when you finally broke into print it would be to tell the story of a Falklands sheep. There aren't enough in the west of Ireland for you, I take it?'

He put his arm round her and hugged her. 'That's what I like about you, you bring me down with a bump. I've been wandering around for the past six months thinking that I'm about to write the work the world has been waiting for, and you tell me that there are plenty of sheep around.'

'Well, there are,' said Abby. 'Honestly, Martin, you were always far too pretentious for your own good!' But her eyes twinkled at him.

'How's Jonathan?' asked Orla. 'What's he doing these days?'

Martin looked from Abby to Orla and shrugged. 'He's been in the UK,' he told her. 'Got a job near London. Having a whale of a time but he's been offered a job back here. Don't know if he'll take it though.'

'Oh,' said Orla.

'He never got over you,' Martin told her.

'Stop spoofing,' she said.

'Well, OK, he got over you. But he was devastated for months after you split up.'

'He was so devastated that every time I saw him he had an even more gorgeous girl on his arm,' said Orla.

'That was nothing.' Martin smiled at her. 'That was just to make you jealous.'

'Why did we split up?' Abby turned to Martin. 'Remind me again?'

'I don't know,' he said. 'I can't think of any good reason right now.'

'Neither can I.' She smiled at him.

Orla walked away from them. They were wrapped up in each other, maybe only for tonight, but she was definitely one too many for them. She looked at her watch. It was getting late and she didn't want to have to queue for hours for a taxi. She looked around until she saw Valerie.

'Val!' She waved at her friend. 'Val, I'm heading off now.'

'Already?' asked Valerie.

124

'Yes.' Orla nodded.

'Aren't you going to come clubbing afterwards?'

'Oh, not for me!' Orla laughed. 'I was never much for clubbing.'

'I always thought you enjoyed it,' said Valerie.

'You grow out of it pretty quickly,' said Orla. 'Anyway, Val, best of luck.'

'Thanks,' said Valerie.

Abby and Martin were leaning against a pillar. Their faces were only centimetres apart.

'Hi, Abby, sorry to break things up but I'm heading home now.'

'Already!' Abby straightened up.

'It's getting late and I don't want to hang around for a taxi,' explained Orla.

'Sure, but—'

'Anyway, poor old David is at home on his own and I'm sure he's warmed a spot in the bed for me by now,' she said.

'Oh, well, if you—'

'So I'll give you a call.'

'OK, Orla. Look after yourself.'

'It was nice meeting you again, Martin,' she said.

'You too, Orla.'

She turned away from them and walked out of the pub. She'd expected to stay longer but seeing Martin had brought back a rush of memories that she didn't want to have. She'd behaved really badly to Jonathan Pascoe. When he'd tried to persuade her not to break off the relationship she'd said some things to him that she wished she'd never said. Hurtful things, simply to make him go away. She hadn't meant to, of course, but she'd been young and immature.

As if you're so bloody mature now, she thought, as she flagged a passing taxi to take her home.

Chapter 15

Orla's desk was beside the window. She liked the fact that she could look out onto Mount Street and see the traffic pass by, the people walking along the streets, the lorries delivering barrels of beer to the nearby O'Dwyer's pub. She liked noise and activity even when, as now, she was trying to concentrate.

The phone rang and startled her. She looked up from the computer print-out of policy renewals and reached for the receiver.

'Orla O'N— Hennessy,' she said.

'Hello, Orla.'

She didn't recognise the voice at the other end. 'Who's that?' she asked.

'Can you talk?' asked the man.

'Who is it?' she repeated.

'My name is Bob Murphy. I'm with Serene Life and Pensions,' he said.

'Oh?'

'I was wondering if you'd have time to meet for a chat.'

'What sort of chat?' asked Orla.

'We have a proposal to put to you,' said Bob.

'A job proposal?' asked Orla.

'Possibly.'

She sat back in her chair and looked out of the window. Serene Life and Pensions was a big company. It was owned by one of the international life companies and Orla knew that it had a very large market share. What sort of job might they offer? she wondered.

'When had you got in mind?' she asked.

'This evening?' suggested Bob.

'What time?'

'Half six, seven.'

'Half six,' she said. 'Where?'

'How about the Davenport Hotel?' asked Bob. 'It's convenient for both of us.'

'All right,' said Orla. 'Will you recognise me?'

'A clue would be good,' said Bob.

'I'm wearing a silver-grey trouser suit,' she told him.

'That's enough,' said Bob, 'I'll recognise you.'

'Fine,' said Orla. 'See you then.'

She replaced the receiver and grinned. Head-hunted, she thought. Maybe.

She turned back to her list and sighed. After a tremendous month last month, this one was turning into a bit of a nightmare. She'd had numerous appointments cancelled at the last minute and a client who she'd been convinced was ready to sign on the dotted line had suddenly informed her that he'd taken out a different policy with another company. It had been a Serene policy.

She glanced through this week's prospects. The MD at Blanca Kitchens & Floors had put her off again. Orla was totally pissed off with Blanca Kitchen & Floors. The apartment was now littered with brochures about expensive new kitchens, all of which made their current one seem drab and old-fashioned by comparison. And instead of reading a book in the evening, as she normally did to relax, Orla found herself flicking through the brochures over and over again. She would have preferred to finish her book – *The Company She Keeps* – about a girl who takes over a business from under the nose of her rivals which was an enthralling read, but she felt that she should know as much as she could about fitted kitchens and natural wood floors so that Damon Higgins would realise what a competent person she was.

Her phone rang again.

'Orla Hennessy,' she said.

'Hi,' said David.

'Hello.' Her voice softened. 'Where are you?' He'd gone to Waterford that morning to give a talk to some of the sales managers in the region.

'Almost home,' he said. 'I'm going to sit in tonight and put my feet up. I wondered if you'd like me to cook dinner for you.'

'That'd be lovely!' she exclaimed.

He laughed. 'Good. What time will I have it ready? Will you be home by six?'

She was about to say yes when she remembered her meeting with Bob Murphy. 'No,' she said slowly, 'I've a meeting at half six.'

127

'Oh, Orla.' He groaned. 'I thought you said you had a light schedule this week.'

'I have,' she said. 'Mostly. This only came up a few minutes ago.'

'Worthwhile prospect?' he asked.

'Maybe.' She didn't want to tell him what the meeting was about. Not yet. Not until she'd heard more.

'Seven?' he suggested.

'Better make it nearer half,' she said. 'The meeting is at six thirty and it'll probably take half an hour.'

'OK,' said David. 'Half seven. But don't be late.'

'I won't,' she said. 'And I can't wait to get my dinner served up when I get home.'

She arrived at the Davenport at exactly half six and went into the lounge area. There was no man on his own looking as though he was waiting for someone. She ordered a Ballygowan and sat in one of the comfortable armchairs.

It was nearly a quarter to seven when he arrived.

'Orla,' he said as he stood in front of her. 'Bob Murphy. I'm terribly sorry I'm late.'

She stood up. She was taller than he was, she realised. He was only about five feet two. It was very disconcerting.

'I got caught up in another meeting,' said Bob. 'I didn't realise how long it would go on.'

'It happens,' said Orla.

'Would you like a drink?' he asked.

She shook her head. 'I'm fine.'

'OK.' He beckoned a lounge boy. 'Are you sure?'

'Ballygowan,' she said.

'A Ballygowan and a pint of Guinness,' he ordered. 'Thanks.'

Orla observed him as he settled back in his seat. Besides being short, he was practically bald. But he was immaculately dressed in a smart navy suit, white shirt and navy tie with tiny red stripes. His shoes were polished so that they shone almost as much as his head under the bright lights.

'OK, Orla,' he said. 'Let's get down to business. You've got a good reputation in the industry and Serene is always interested in people with good reputations. I believe you were top salesperson in Gravitas recently.'

128

'How the hell do you know that?' she asked.

'I have my sources.'

'I see.' She took the Ballygowan from the lounge boy.

'We could do with another strong salesperson at Serene,' Bob told her. 'We have some really good teams as it is. But we're always looking to improve them. With you, I think we would.'

She shrugged. 'Perhaps. But I like Gravitas.'

'As I expected you to say, of course.' Bob smiled. It was the sort of smile Orla used to her customers. Sincere and caring, used even when she didn't feel sincere and didn't care very much. 'But let me talk to you about Serene and see if we can't change your mind.'

He was a good salesman, thought Orla. He went through Serene's figures and painted a picture of a strong and growing company. He made her wonder how on earth Gravitas managed to get any business while Serene personnel were around. 'Of course,' he told her as he closed his folder of brochures, 'you'd be a team leader.'

Team leaders co-ordinated each sales team. They were rewarded by a percentage of each salesperson's commission. Henry Gilpin, the man Orla had beaten into fifth place last year, was still her team leader.

'I'll have to think about it,' she said.

'I know,' said Bob.

'And the salary?'

Salaries at Gravitas were pretty basic. All of the sales team made their real money on commissions. But Serene's salary was very generous. It was all Orla could do to stop herself shouting 'I'll take it' straightaway.

'We don't like hard sell,' said Bob. 'That's why we pay you a reasonable amount up front. We find it works better – the salespeople sell the right product, the customer is happier and we get much more repeat business as a result. Mind you,' he added, 'if you don't perform, you're out. But I'm sure you'd perform, Orla.'

'I'll think about it,' said Orla.

'Let me know as soon as you can.' Bob stood up. 'By next week, if you can.'

She nodded. 'I'll call.'

She watched him walk out of the hotel, then she finished her Ballygowan and went home.

The aroma of chicken tikka met her as she opened the door of the apartment. David didn't cook very often, but when he did it was always with the aid of a jar of Chicken Tonight. Orla sometimes wondered how he would have existed if it hadn't been for jars of Chicken Tonight. He was good at boil-in-the-bag rice too.

'Hi,' he said as she walked into the kitchen and dumped her laptop on the counter. 'Can you move that, dinner's ready.'

'Let me change out of my suit first,' she said, moving the laptop out of his way. 'I'll only be a couple of minutes.'

'OK,' David stirred the pot, 'but don't take too long, the rice is cooked and it's awful if it goes cold.'

'I won't.' Orla went into the bedroom, hung up her suit and pulled on a sweatshirt and jogging pants. She took the scrunchie from her hair and ran her fingers through it. Then she sprayed herself with Monsoon and went into the living room.

David had set the table. He really was good, she thought, as she sat down. He cared so much about her.

'How was your meeting?' he asked as he slid a plate of chicken tikka and rice in front of her.

'Fine.' She picked up her fork and swirled the food around the plate.

'Any business?'

'Perhaps.' She almost told him about Bob Murphy but something stopped her. She didn't know why.

'I landed a good one today,' said David. 'Family plan for a family of six.'

'I didn't think there were families of six these days.' Why didn't she just come out and say, 'I was offered a job by Serene'? What was holding her back? She wanted to tell him, she knew she did.

'Father, mother, two sons, two daughters,' said David. 'All happy and healthy.'

'Let's hope they stay that way.' Every passing second made it harder to tell him. If she said something now he'd want to know why she hadn't told him straightaway.

'No histories of any ill health,' David continued. 'Nice bunch of people. Live in Sandyford.'

'Great,' said Orla.

'I should have a good week.'

'Mine isn't great.'

'Never mind,' he said consolingly, 'it happens to the best of us.'

She washed up after their meal while David watched Sky News on TV.

She didn't tell him about Bob's offer that night. She needed to think about it herself for a while, sort out how she felt first. She didn't want David summing up the pros and cons for her and expecting her to agree with him. She didn't want to listen to his advice just yet.

130

Using the money that David had given her, Gemma bought a small TV for Ronan so that he could play his computer games in his room and not interfere with the TV downstairs. She was capitulating, she knew. Ronan had always wanted his own TV and she'd held out against it on the basis that she preferred him playing downstairs, with the family, than on his own.

But downstairs with what family? she asked herself as she wrote a cheque to PowerCity. Keelin spent her whole life either in her bedroom or out with Shauna Fitzpatrick. If there was any sitting around at home it was Gemma who sat around and waited for someone to join her.

She couldn't blame the children, of course. What kid wanted to sit around with their parents? She certainly hadn't. She remembered nights of lying on her bed listening to the then pirate radio stations while her parents watched TV downstairs. Michael had been in his room too, although he was studying. Liz had been out with friends – Liz always had loads of friends. None of them had wanted to sit around as a family with Frances and Gerry.

But that was normal, wasn't it? No teenage children wanted to be anywhere near their parents, did they? So why had she ever expected it would be different with her children? She hadn't even been able to keep her husband so it was hardly surprising that the children wanted to be somewhere else too!

While they were married she'd constantly complained to David that he was away too much, that he was home too late, that he didn't care about them enough. At the time, she'd thought it was true. But perhaps her constant nagging had made him stay away more, come home later, care about them less. It was her fault, in the end, that things had gone wrong. She was just hopeless at people and relationships. She never seemed to know what sort of person people wanted her to be.

Ronan was delighted with the TV. He bundled together his console and his games and he set it up without any help from her in his room. The familiar sound of gunfire ricocheted around the house. I'm probably raising some kind of psycho, Gemma thought despairingly as she peeled potatoes.

'I'm going out.' Keelin told her.

'Where?' Gemma dropped a potato into a basin of water.

'To Shauna's.'

'It's Sunday,' said Gemma. 'They'll be having dinner.'

131

'No they won't,' said Keelin scornfully. 'They don't have dinner until five o'clock on Sundays.'

'Where are you and Shauna going?' asked Gemma.

Keelin shrugged. 'Dunno. We'll just hang around. It's so nice to be able to hang around on a Sunday instead of being hauled around with Dad.'

Gemma turned to look at her. 'Don't you want to go out with your father on Sundays?'

'Not every Sunday,' said Keelin. 'I mean, it's like having your whole life mapped out, isn't it? Every single Sunday with him. It's my day off too, you know.'

'I thought you wanted to see your dad every week.'

'I do,' said Keelin. 'But it's a routine, isn't it?' She pushed her long black hair out of her eyes. 'I want to do something exciting with my life. I hate everything being so predictable. School and Dad, weekdays and Sundays.'

'You're not at school now,' Gemma pointed out.

'It's only a couple of weeks until we go back,' said Keelin. 'And it'll be the same old grind over and over again.'

'You won't be at school forever.'

'No.' Keelin sighed. 'I'll probably get some crummy job and despair because I'll never have enough money.'

'Don't be so silly.' Gemma dried her hands and hugged Keelin. 'You'll get a great job with loads of travel, a glamorous life and then you'll meet some gorgeous hunk who'll make you very, very happy.'

'Did you think that's what would happen to you?' asked Keelin.

Gemma frowned. 'I liked my job – I still do. I did travel quite a bit with your dad. And I have two great kids.'

'But no gorgeous hunk to make you very, very happy,' said Keelin. 'And you never have enough money.'

'Well,' said Gemma, 'I guess you can't have everything.'

'Why?' asked Keelin.

'I don't know.' Gemma frowned. 'It just seems to me that when one part of your life is working out OK, a different part is causing you all sorts of problems. But think of all the people who do have everything and go for it!'

Keelin smiled at her. It was a tentative smile but, thought Gemma, it was the first smile she'd seen on her daughter's face in ages.

'Did you have many boyfriends before Dad?' asked Keelin.

Gemma thought about it for a moment. There'd been a few, particularly in her last year at school – she sincerely hoped that

Keelin would never get up to what she'd got up to in her last year at school!

'Not as many as I should have,' she said finally.

'They're a waste of time,' said Keelin flatly.

'No, they're not.'

'They are.' Keelin's tone was firm. 'They're juvenile and silly.'

'Do you have anyone special?' asked Gemma, half afraid of what Keelin's answer might be.

Keelin shook her head.

'Anyone likely?'

Keelin shook her head again and Gemma sighed with relief.

'Why can't we go on holidays?' asked Keelin suddenly.

'Holidays?'

'Yes,' said Keelin. 'Everyone's been away this summer. Shauna went to Florida. Why can't we go somewhere nice?'

'Well—'

'I know really,' Keelin interrupted her. 'We can't afford it.'

Gemma bit her lip.

'If Dad had stayed we would have gone on holidays,' Keelin said. 'We always went on holidays when he was here, only I was too young to appreciate it.'

Gemma almost smiled at how worldly-wise her daughter sounded.

'Why did you ask him to leave?' asked Keelin. 'I mean, it wasn't that awful when he was here. It wasn't as though he was thumping you around the place. It wasn't as though you were screaming at each other all the time. Why didn't you want to stay with him?'

I was screaming inside, Gemma wanted to say. It doesn't have to be about being hit or shouting at each other or anything like that. It really doesn't.

'You could have stayed with him,' Keelin continued. 'You chose to marry him, didn't you? Would it have been so terrible to stay together?'

Gemma was silent. Keelin's lower lip trembled.

'I'm sorry,' said Gemma. 'I'm sorry we made a mess of it. I really am.'

'Will he make a mess of it with Orla too?' asked Keelin, recovering her composure.

'I doubt it,' replied Gemma. 'After all, he's hardly going to marry someone else if he doesn't love them.' It was hard to say that, she realised. When she got to the word 'love', she had to force herself to say it.

133

'It's just . . .' Keelin sighed. 'When he was living somewhere else it was awful but he was still Dad. Now that he's married to her it's different.'

'I know.' Gemma put her arms round Keelin again. 'I know.'

∽

David and Orla sat beside each other on the bench in Rosanna and Roger O'Neill's back garden. David hadn't taken the kids out today because Orla's parents had invited them to Sunday lunch. Her two married brothers and their wives had been invited too.

'It's a good sign you've been asked,' Orla had told him fiercely. 'You can't refuse to come!'

He'd known that but he hated ringing Gemma and telling her that he wouldn't be seeing the children this Sunday. And he hated the fact that she hadn't even asked why. He'd asked to talk to them but Gemma told him that they were both out. Out where, he wondered, but he hadn't felt able to ask.

He sighed. Lunch had been OK, he thought. Not too awkward although there had been the occasional uncomfortable silence. But mostly those silences had been interrupted by one or other of Orla's four brothers. There was a camaraderie among Orla's family that he really liked. They seemed to actively enjoy each other's company, something that had never been the case in either his own family or Gemma's.

He looked around the garden. It was very like Gerry Garvey's garden, thought David. A neat lawn, tidy flowerbeds filled with roses and pansies. A neat, flagstone patio with a variety of flower-filled tubs. Almost identical, David said to himself, except that Roger's garden was full of children running around the place. Nobody ran in Gerry's garden. He'd liked Gerry, though. Gerry was an easygoing, relaxed kind of man. He spent time in the garden to get away from Frances who had never been easygoing or relaxed in her life.

Maybe that's why Orla and Gemma were such different kinds of people even though their backgrounds seemed to be so similar. Maybe your parents had a much greater influence on you than you ever thought. And what kind of influence was he having on his children? he wondered. He shivered suddenly.

'Are you OK?' asked Orla.

'Of course,' he told her as he pulled her towards him. 'I'm fine.'

134

Chapter 16

It suddenly seemed very important to Gemma to take the children on holiday. It wasn't fair that Keelin and Ronan should be the only ones not to go away. Keelin had worked hard all summer and she deserved a break. And so did Ronan, anything to get him away from his bloody computer games. Gemma was concerned about how much time he spent in front of the screen shooting people, although when he wasn't playing them he seemed perfectly well-adjusted. But she worried all the same.

I need to sort the money side of things out, Gemma thought as she snipped at Eileen Devanney's newly highlighted hair. And I will. I'll get it all under control soon. But I need David to pay for a holiday for the kids. I can make a good case for it. They deserve a holiday, they really do. And so do I – but I'll pay for my part myself. I won't have him saying that I'm trying to scrounge off him.

There was no point in phoning him until the evening. He was almost impossible to get during working hours – another thing that had been a problem in their marriage. If she ever needed him, she could only leave messages on his mobile phone. And he never answered her messages. Because, she remembered bitterly, he never thought they were important enough.

She put down her scissors and picked up her hair dryer. Eileen was going to a dinner tonight, she'd asked Gemma to be extra careful. As if it mattered, Gemma thought, as she began to dry Eileen's hair. She was always careful. She took pride in her work.

'It's lovely, thanks,' said Eileen when she'd finished.

'Have a great time tonight,' Gemma told her.

Eileen made a face. 'It's a company thing for Philip,' she said. 'I can't imagine it'll be much fun listening to them nattering on about combustion engines or whatever, but at least I'll look good.'

'You'll be stunning,' said Gemma. 'And I'm sure it'll be great fun.'

That was a lie, she told herself. She'd never had fun at David's company nights out. But maybe that had been her own fault. Maybe she hadn't tried to have fun.

'Can you work Saturday morning?' Niamh walked over to her, a worried frown on her face. 'Cilla is off on Saturday, she's going to a wedding. Janice was going to cover for her but she sprained her wrist yesterday and she's not sure if she'll be able.'

'Sure,' said Gemma. 'Keelin is working all day and Lorraine Crawford is taking Neville and Ronan out for the day. I was going to give the house the once-over but I'll work.'

'Thanks,' said Niamh. 'I appreciate it.'

'No problem,' said Gemma. 'Every day I appreciate that you gave me a job here.'

'For goodness sake!' Niamh looked at her. 'Why? You're good, Gemma. I needed someone. You make it sound as though I tolerate you. You're a better stylist than me, you know you are.'

'I'm not.'

'You bloody well are. I don't know why you're so lacking in self-confidence. Remember when we worked together before? Your book was always full. Every day. Cop on to yourself, Gemma, and stop selling yourself short!'

Gemma stared at Niamh in astonishment. In all the years they'd been friends, Niamh had never before spoken to her so forcefully.

'I don't sell myself short,' she said.

'You do,' Niamh told her. 'All the time.'

'No, I don't. I know I'm a good stylist.'

'It's not just the hairdressing,' said Niamh. 'It's everything, Gemma. You think that you're useless at money. Useless with the kids. You're always complaining about your weight or your looks or something. You're terrified of your mother. There hasn't been a time in the last few years when I've heard you talk positively about yourself.'

'You're exaggerating,' said Gemma mildly.

'Maybe.' Niamh sighed. 'I just want you to feel good about yourself. Think about it, Gemma. You got divorced. You're raising two kids on your own and doing a great job. You work with me and you do a great job here. You just don't appreciate how good you are.'

Gemma smiled at her. 'Sounds like you've been reading one of those empowerment books you're so keen on. Feel the fear and do it anyway!'

Niamh looked guilty. 'Actually—'

'No, don't tell me.' Gemma laughed. 'And you're right, I suppose. It's just that I don't feel like I'm doing a particularly good job. Keelin

136

walks around the place in a state of perpetual rage. Ronan spends more time in front of the TV than in front of real people. I still haven't got to grips with my finances in any meaningful way and – and this is obviously the big one – I put on another four pounds over the weekend!'

'Oh, Gemma!' Niamh grinned at her. 'Of all of those things, which is the worst?'

'The four pounds, of course,' said Gemma. 'Why on earth would you think it was anything else?'

~

She decided to phone David that evening. She would talk to him, discuss the finances, tell him about spending the TV money on a portable for Ronan (she still felt guilty about that) and ask him if, for this one time only, he'd consider lending her some money so that she could take the kids away for a week. It couldn't be longer than that anyway – the summer holidays were nearly over and Gemma had no intention of keeping them out of school.

It was nine o'clock when she called. Keelin and Shauna were upstairs in Keelin's bedroom. Ronan and Neville were playing football on the road outside the house.

'Hello.'

Gemma gripped the receiver more tightly. She hadn't expected Orla to answer although she knew that it was a possibility. But it was one which she always refused to consider. She thought about hanging up but decided that would be particularly stupid. Orla was only a girl, for heaven's sake!

'Hi, Orla. It's Gemma.' She kept her voice light.

'Hello, Gemma.' Orla's tone was neutral.

'Is David there?' she asked.

'Not at the moment,' said Orla.

'Oh.' Gemma glanced at her watch again.

'Can I take a message?' asked Orla.

'Could you get him to call me please?'

'Urgently?'

'No,' said Gemma, 'it's not urgent but I really would like to talk to him.'

So would I, thought Orla. 'I'll give him the message,' she said. 'I'm not sure what time he'll be home.'

'Out with clients?' asked Gemma.

'Yes,' lied Orla.

'You should be out with a few yourself.' Gemma was surprised at herself for making this feeble joke.

'I've seen too many today already,' said Orla.

'I understand,' said Gemma. 'He can call me tonight if he's home at a reasonable hour.'

'I'll tell him,' said Orla. 'Goodbye, Gemma.'

'Goodbye,' said Gemma, but Orla had already replaced the receiver.

~

Orla sat and stared at the TV screen. David had gone out for a walk. He'd gone after they'd had a row about the Serene job.

'They've offered you what?' he asked when she finally told him about it.

'A better salary, a bigger car and the position of team leader,' she told him.

'Why you?' he asked.

'Why not?' She stared at him. 'Don't you think I'm good enough? Weren't you a team leader at my age?'

'Actually, no,' said David. 'If you recall, I'd spent some time travelling before I started in the pensions industry.'

'Well, I think it's a great opportunity,' said Orla. 'Serene are growing their sales force in Ireland. There will be other chances for me to do well. I might even move out of sales and into management. Who knows? But there isn't a hope in hell of that happening at Gravitas. Let's face it, David, it's a good company but it's much, much smaller than Serene and the opportunities are much less.'

'So you think we work in a second-rate outfit, do you?'

'No!' She stared at him. 'But I'm thinking about my future, David. Let's face it, you and your gang have everything pretty well sewn up at Gravitas. I know you want to stay in sales but maybe not forever. Anytime there's a management position you're a candidate. So's Eamonn and Henry and Angus. I'm so far down that particular pecking order as not to matter very much. And besides, Gravitas favours its male workers. You know that.'

'We don't discriminate!'

'Not especially,' conceded Orla. 'But you don't help a lot either.'

David stared at her. Her hazel eyes were angry, her cheeks flushed. She looked particularly sexy when she was angry, he thought, amazed to find that he wanted to have sex with her when he was mad at her

138

because Bob Murphy had offered her a job five days ago and she'd waited until this evening to tell him about it. He was hurt that she hadn't confided in him before now and resentful that she seemed so eager to take it. David wanted her to stay working in Gravitas.

'So that you can keep an eye on me?' she'd demanded and he'd said no, that was rubbish, while having to admit to himself that she was partly right.

'I think there are good opportunities for you at Gravitas,' he said. 'I know that Liam McDaid thinks very highly of you. He's said so to me often enough. And if the managing director thinks highly of you, then there's every reason to think you'll do well in the company.'

'Of course,' said Orla. 'But you're talking about doing well at some nebulous time in the future. Serene are talking about me doing well now. They're prepared to put their money where their mouth is and pay me for my expertise and my abilities. You're talking about some vague possibilities. Don't you think I should be taking the opportunities that are available to me?'

'Why rush into something?' asked David.

'Rush?' She stared at him. 'I've been working at Gravitas for nearly two years, David. It's not rushing.'

'But we want to develop your career,' David told her. 'If you take on too much too soon you could burn yourself out.'

'What a load of bullshit!' She stood up. 'You just want to keep me under your thumb, don't you? You want to be the person in charge, the one bringing in the most money. You want to know that no matter how good I am I'll never be better than you because you've been at Gravitas longer than me and you'll always have the ear of the MD. You just don't want me to succeed, do you?'

'That's crap.' David was angry at her. 'I can't believe you're spouting all that nonsense, Orla. I thought you were a more sensible person than that!'

'Sorry to disappoint you then.' She was keeping her voice level with the greatest of difficulty. She couldn't believe that she was having a row with David. They didn't row. They disagreed sometimes but that was completely different. This was a row, a real argument, and it was about her life and her future.

'Yes,' said David. 'You do disappoint me.' He picked up his jacket. 'I thought your future was caught up with mine. I'm going for a walk. I'll see you later.'

That had been two hours ago. Orla couldn't imagine where he'd been walking for two hours. Had he done this when he argued with

Gemma? she wondered. They'd had lots of rows, David had told her about some of them. Blazing, screaming rows which always ended up with Gemma in tears and David struggling to keep calm. But maybe Gemma had a reason to be in floods of tears, thought Orla anxiously, if David had been as unreasonable with her then as he was being with Orla now. She bit her lip. What on earth did Gemma want? Why had she called them at home? Gemma never called David at home. Orla knew that they spoke to each other, obviously they had to talk about the children and David saw her every Sunday when he called to pick them up, but she was never around whenever David spoke to his ex-wife. She assumed that he usually called her from work or from his mobile. She thought it was actually very sensitive of him not to call Gemma from the apartment, and it was equally considerate of Gemma not to call him at the apartment. So, if Gemma was phoning tonight, maybe there was something really urgent she needed to talk to him about. Maybe one of the children was sick. She bit her lip. Perhaps she should phone Gemma back, take a message.

Don't be so bloody silly, she told herself. If it had been anything really important Gemma would have alerted her. She would have sounded more anxious too. As far as Orla could tell, Gemma had sounded particularly relaxed.

What had Gemma and David's marriage really been like, she asked herself. He never said more than that they'd been too young when they got married, that they'd married in a rush of passion which hadn't lasted and that then they'd stuck it out because of the children. But Gemma had suddenly decided that the children weren't a good enough reason for them to stay together and she'd asked David for a divorce. Orla had liked the way he told her about it – he hadn't made it seem as though he was fed up with Gemma and had walked out or anything like that, he'd admitted that he probably would have stayed in the marriage but that Gemma had been the one to finish it.

'How did you feel?' she'd asked when he told her about it.

'Devastated, at first,' he'd replied. 'Then relieved.'

He'd always been upfront with her about his relationship with Gemma. That was why she never felt jealous of the other woman or anxious about his relationship with her now. Gemma wasn't a threat. She was his past. Orla didn't believe in living in the past.

It was nearly ten o'clock by the time David came in, bringing with him a rush of cool air, smoke and beer. She wondered how far he'd walked before he decided to stop off in the pub. His eyes were bright.

'You're back,' she said.

'Yes.'

'Good walk?'

'Yes.'

'Nice evening for it.'

'Not bad,' he said.

He took off his jacket and hung it over the chair. He went into the kitchen where she heard him fill the kettle. She flicked through a copy of *Image* magazine.

He returned a couple of minutes later, a cup of coffee in his hand.

'I know you don't drink coffee this late,' he told her. 'Otherwise I'd have made you some.'

'It's OK, thanks.'

He sat in his armchair and picked up the remote from the table. 'Anything on TV?'

She shook her head. 'I don't think so.'

He zapped through the channels and stopped at Sky News. Their financial correspondent was giving a rundown of the day in the markets. Orla knew that David liked to keep in touch with what was going on in the markets on a day-to-day basis so that he could talk more knowledgeably about the products that he sold. He was thorough like that.

'Meet anyone while you were out?' she asked.

'No,' he said.

She turned over another page of the magazine. I'm not going to be nice to him, she decided. He's in the wrong here. He's making me feel bad because I want to better myself. I don't see why I should pander to him.

'I'm going to bed,' she said finally.

'OK,' he said.

'Will you be long?'

'It's only a quarter past ten. I'll watch the news.'

'Fine,' she said.

She went into the bathroom and carefully removed her make-up. She took her time over it, hoping that by the time she'd finished David would be sitting in the bedroom waiting for her. She wanted him to be the one who was waiting for her.

She had a spot on the side of her nose. She peered at it in the mirror, wondering how on earth she'd managed to get a spot. She squeezed it but only succeeded in making the area around it go bright red.

He wasn't in the bedroom. She could still hear the low hum of the

TV in the living room. Fuck you, she thought as she slid under the duvet. I don't care!

⁓

David woke up with a jump. The TV was still on and, according to the little clock at the bottom of the screen, it was nearly half one. He rubbed his eyes and looked around. He had a slight headache, caused, he supposed, from the four pints of Heineken he'd drunk earlier. He never drank four pints of lager in the middle of the week. And certainly not in an hour and a half which he'd done tonight. But he'd been so annoyed with Orla. Hurt, more than anything, he'd decided as he walked along the pier at Dun Laoghaire.

He was hurt that she hadn't told him straightaway about the offer from Serene and he was hurt, too, that she seemed so keen to take it. He knew that it was silly to feel like this, that she had every right to take any opportunity that came her way. And yet, by saying that she'd like to work for another company, he felt as though she was trying to move away from him. He told himself, as he watched the water lap against the side of the pier, that he was being incredibly childish over the entire affair. That if Orla had behaved like this he would have made some joke about her youth and inexperience and lack of maturity. But he couldn't help himself. While she worked at Gravitas she was under his wing. If she moved to another job she'd be standing on her own two feet.

She's twenty-four years old, he reminded himself. It's not actually all that young. The only reason I think it is, is because at twenty-four I'd just got my first real job. She's been working for a few years. But I spent five years hitch-hiking around Europe, the States and Australia. I didn't care about promotion and doing well when I was twenty-four. I was just shell-shocked at having got a job at all. And at meeting Gemma and falling head over heels in love with her.

He rubbed the back of his neck as he recalled meeting Gemma and falling head over heels in love with her. He remembered the way she'd run her fingers through his too-long hair and how she'd turned him from a layabout into a businessman in fifteen expert minutes. He remembered the feeling of her breast against his shoulder as she'd leaned forward for a moment. He remembered her bright smile and her shining eyes and her blonde hair piled into a loose knot on the top of her head. She'd been cheerful and bubbly and there'd been an instant spark between them.

142

When, after a week of training, he'd been told to go and trawl any acquaintance he knew for business, the first person he'd thought of had been the pretty young hairdresser with the tomato-red sandals and the hip-hugging jeans. He wasn't sure whether he'd picked her because he thought he had the faintest chance of getting business from her or simply because he'd wanted to see her again.

In the end, he'd succeeded on both counts. Gemma, Niamh and two of the other stylists in the salon had taken out policies with him. And he'd asked Gemma for a date. They'd gone to the movies together. She'd spent most of the time huddled in his arms – *Terminator* had scared her witless. He'd chosen it for that very reason. She'd been so exciting, he remembered. The scent of her perfume, the touch of her hand, the softness of her lips – they'd all turned him on in a way that no one ever had before. And he'd wanted to keep her for himself, not share her with anyone. Besides which, he'd been in love with her. So he'd asked her to marry him. And he'd been ecstatic when she'd said yes.

Chapter 17

'Gemma! It's for you.' Hazel, one of the juniors, waved the phone at Gemma who was almost finished blow-drying a new client's hair. Gemma nodded at the junior and took her time about completing the blow-dry. It was probably David on the phone, she thought, and he could wait. She was annoyed that he hadn't returned her call the previous night and had wondered whether or not Orla had even bothered to pass on the message. Maybe Orla didn't think that phone calls from David's ex-wife were important enough to tell him about. She strolled over to the phone and picked up the receiver.

'Hello,' she said coolly.

'Hi, Gem, do you leave everyone hanging on this long?'

'Liz!' Gemma was surprised. The only time Liz phoned her at the salon was to make an appointment and the last time she'd phoned, Gemma had been too busy to fit her in. At which Liz had rung off in a huff and said that she'd get her hair done somewhere else. 'Is anything the matter?'

'Why should anything be the matter?' asked Liz. 'Other than the fact that you seem to think I can wait all day for you to pick up the phone.'

'I'm sorry,' said Gemma. 'I was finishing with a client. I didn't think it could be you – you're not due a cut. And you only ever phone me if you need a cut or if something is the matter.'

'No, I don't.' Liz sounded aggrieved. 'I'm just busy, that's all.'

'So, if it's not a cut and nothing's the matter, why are you ringing?'

'I was going to phone you last night, but whenever I phone from home Mum's ears flap like crazy and it's impossible to have a conversation.'

Gemma giggled. 'You sound like you're sixteen again.'

'She makes me feel like I'm about fourteen,' said Liz. 'Look, Gem, I was wondering if you'd like to meet me for lunch.'

'Lunch!' Lunch with her sister was almost unheard of.

'Be a sport,' said Liz.

'There must be something wrong,' Gemma said. 'We never meet for lunch.'

'We never meet,' said Liz, 'unless it's for me to get my hair done and, if you ask me, that's more wrong than anything else. We're sisters, for God's sake. I shouldn't be meeting you just to get my hair cut! We've got out of the habit of meeting for a chat. We used to, when we were younger.'

'Liz, you haven't been drinking or anything, have you?'

'I'll pretend you didn't say that,' said Liz. 'It's eleven o'clock in the morning, Gemma. Even in my worst excesses I never drank at eleven o'clock in the morning!'

'I know. I'm sorry.'

'And I'd be booted out of my oh-so-important job in the corporation if I was drinking at eleven o'clock in the morning.'

'I said I was sorry.'

'Yeah, well, OK. Anyway, do you want to meet for lunch?'

'Lunch is impossible today,' said Gemma. 'At least at the drop of a hat it is. I've got an appointment at twelve and I always stay here until two to cover any unexpected drop-ins. Can't we meet this evening?'

'We could,' said Liz, 'but it means asking Mum to look after Suzy and I hate asking her to look after Suzy. You know how she is. It's such a chore as far as she's concerned. I hate feeling under a compliment.'

'Oh, Liz, I'm sure she doesn't think of it as a chore.' Gemma crossed her fingers. She was sure Frances probably did.

'Want to bet?' asked Liz darkly.

'I can't do lunch, I really can't,' said Gemma. 'Call over this evening. Bring Suzy with you. I'll get Keelin to keep an eye on her.'

'Sure?'

'Yes, absolutely.'

'OK,' said Liz. 'I'll be over around seven. Is that OK?'

'Yes,' said Gemma. 'Liz, you're sure there's nothing wrong?'

'Honestly,' said Liz. 'I just want to ask my big sister for advice.'

Advice! Gemma stared at the phone. Liz had never once asked her for advice! And, if she had, Gemma would never have known what advice to give her. Gemma found her own life difficult enough to deal with, she certainly couldn't think of any useful advice to give to a sister whom she'd always considered smarter than her anyway.

She replaced the receiver and wondered what on earth Liz could want.

And why hadn't David phoned? He was probably stringing her along, knowing that she wanted to ask him something, guessing it had to do with money. And he was on his regular power trip refusing to talk to her until he was ready, making her wait, making her anxious. He'd always made her anxious. Well, she thought as she mixed some colour for Sharon Kelly's hair, she wouldn't let him get to her. And if he hadn't phoned by later on this evening, she'd phone him again.

Keelin looked at her in disgust when she told her that Liz and Suzy were coming over and she wanted her to look after Suzy.

'I'm meeting Shauna,' wailed Keelin, 'I don't want to look after anyone.'

'You hardly ever see your cousin,' said Gemma. 'It'll do you good to look after her for a couple of hours.'

'No it won't,' said Keelin. 'What good will it do me?'

'Oh, come on, Keelin,' she wheedled. 'Why don't you ask Shauna to come over and you can keep Suzy amused while Liz and I chat.'

'Why do you and Liz want to chat?' asked Keelin suspiciously. 'You never chat.'

'Not lately,' said Gemma. 'We've both been too busy.'

'Are you going out?' asked Keelin.

'I don't know,' replied Gemma, 'we didn't decide. Would you prefer if we stayed in or went out?'

'Will Ronan be here too?'

'I suppose so. If we go out we won't go far.'

'You can go out. But I'm not looking after him as well,' said Keelin. 'He's weird.'

'No he's not.'

'He's a boy,' said Keelin. 'That's enough.'

Gemma laughed and Keelin reluctantly joined in.

'I'll ring Shauna,' said Keelin. 'But I'd rather not have to baby-sit.'

'I'd rather be a millionaire,' said Gemma. 'It's not likely to happen, though.'

146

Liz arrived exactly on time carrying a bottle of wine and a box of chocolates.

Gemma looked at her in amazement. 'I'm trying to lose weight,' she said. 'I'll never manage to do that on Faustino and Ferrero Rocher.'

'You look fine,' said Liz impatiently.

Not as fine as her sister, though, Gemma thought. Liz had always been the prettier, with her smooth skin and her high cheekbones and her sparkling blue eyes. Her auburn hair (cut just a little too severely this time by whoever she'd nipped in to, thought Gemma) gleamed with health and vitality. She was wearing a white cotton shirt and stonewashed jeans pulled tight at the waist – a waist that looked a lot slimmer than the last time she'd seen her. In fact, Gemma thought, except for the somewhat inexpert haircut, Liz looked bloody fantastic!

'I broke my arm.' Suzy, who always waited for a couple of minutes before speaking, tugged at Gemma's skirt.

'I heard about it. You poor thing.'

'I fell,' said Suzy.

'Did it hurt?'

Suzy's bottom lip wobbled and she nodded.

'But she was very brave,' said Liz briskly, 'and she didn't cry one little bit, Gemma. Wasn't that great?'

'Absolutely,' asserted Gemma. She smiled at her niece. 'You're a great girl, Suzy. And if you look carefully, I think you'll find some jelly beans in the jar on the kitchen counter. Walk,' she called after the little girl who'd sprinted along the hallway, 'don't run!'

Keelin came down the stairs. Her black hair fell in a curtain across her face. She was wearing a black T-shirt, black jeans and black CAT boots.

'Shauna will be here later,' she told Gemma. 'Ronan is down with Neville. I told him to be back by half eight. You can go out if you like.'

'Actually, we were thinking of staying in,' said Gemma. 'Liz brought a bottle of wine.'

Keelin looked at her mother from behind her hair. 'But you said you were going out. Shauna's coming over.'

Gemma glanced at Liz who shrugged. 'We can walk to the pub,' said Liz. 'Leave the kids alone. If Keelin is babysitting we might as well get out and about.'

'We won't be late,' Gemma told her. 'I promise. And I'll bring the mobile so you can call me if there's a problem.'

'There won't be a problem,' said Keelin.

'I'm sure there won't.' Liz smiled at her. 'Thanks a million, Keelin.'

Keelin smiled back. Gemma had to stop herself from commenting on the fact that her daughter actually looked pretty when she smiled and that the smile was the first genuine one she'd seen Keelin give in weeks.

Gemma and Liz walked along the sunny side of the road. The sea breeze chilled the air, but in the sun it was still warm.

'What's with the black?' asked Liz.

'Keelin?' Gemma glanced at her.

'Who else?'

'It's a phase, I presume.' Gemma sighed. 'She's been impossible all summer, Liz. And since David got married she's been even worse. I can't seem to connect with her at all. She's living in some world of her own and I don't know the way in.'

'She's thirteen,' said Liz. 'I wanted to be in a world of my own when I was thirteen.'

'She's almost fourteen,' Gemma told her. 'I thought they didn't go through the teenage angst stuff until they were older.'

Liz wrinkled up her nose. 'I'm not sure. I have a feeling that nobody understood me when I was thirteen!'

Gemma laughed. 'Nobody ever understood you, Liz. It was part of your charm.'

They crossed the road, walked past the people standing outside the pub in the warmth of the evening sun, and went inside.

'What would you like?' asked Gemma.

'Bottle of Miller,' said Liz. 'And don't look at me like that! I know I'm driving. I'll be moderate.'

'I wasn't looking at you like anything,' protested Gemma. 'Grab a seat, I'll bring them over.' She paid for the drinks and a couple of bags of Scampi Fries. 'I know I shouldn't,' she told Liz as she tore one open, 'but I can't resist.'

'I'm sure the Ferrero Rocher would've been better for you.' Liz grinned at her.

'So.' Gemma sat back on the seat and regarded her sister thoughtfully. 'What is it exactly that you need my advice about?'

Liz poured her beer into the stubby half-pint glass and took a mouthful. 'Mum will ask me if I've been drinking,' she said. 'She sniffs my breath every evening when I go out.'

'I remember,' said Gemma.

'You only had to put up with it when you were in your teens,' said

Liz. 'I'm thirty-three years old. I'm a grown woman. Not, I'll admit, always the world's most sensible woman, but I'm old enough not to have my mother sniffing at my breath.'

'She'll never change.' Gemma took a sip of her own beer.

'I know,' said Liz. 'Controlling old bitch!'

'Liz!' Gemma looked at her in horror. 'You can't say that about Mum.'

'Why?' asked Liz. She tucked a stray hair behind her ears. 'Why can't I call her controlling? Or manipulating? Or patronising? Take your pick.'

Gemma bit her lip. She agreed that Frances had all of those qualities but she was also their mother and it seemed disloyal to say those words out loud.

'It's just the way she is,' said Gemma.

'She should never have had kids.' Liz popped one of the cereal snacks into her mouth. 'At least, not daughters. Daughters that might have become nuns, maybe. But not normal daughters.'

Gemma giggled. 'Maybe if we'd spent more time reading *Good Housekeeping* and less time on *True Romance* it might have been different.'

'She's just so old-fashioned.' Liz sighed. 'She couldn't cope with us being out late and having multiple boyfriends.'

'Repressed,' said Gemma.

'Do you think so?'

'Could be.' Gemma shrugged. 'I dunno. She wants perfection all the time. She likes things that I hate. Remember how crazy she went if we left things in the wrong place?'

Liz nodded. 'Although it was only us she complained about. Never Michael.'

'I know.' Gemma sighed. 'It must have been her upbringing. You're right, Liz, she'd have done better with just sons. Michael is the apple of her eye. It's us that have been the problem.'

'But maybe not always.' Liz sighed. 'You know, she was so proud of you, Gemma, when you got married. I was quite jealous.'

'Not really?' Gemma drained her glass.

Liz nodded. 'Absolutely. And, even though your divorce was so traumatic for her, she goes on and on at me about how at least you had the decency to get married before you had kids.'

'Why don't you move out?' asked Gemma.

Liz signalled for another drink. 'I couldn't afford to,' she said. 'Let's face it, I don't earn a fortune and renting a place would mean having to get someone to look after Suzy.' She grimaced. 'I feel very guilty that I've said horrible things about Mum when she looks after Suzy for me. It's just that she makes me feel as though I should be grateful all the time as though it's such a big favour that she allows me to live there.'

'Having to be grateful to someone is the worst thing in the world,' agreed Gemma. She took her fresh drink from a lounge girl who looked barely older than Keelin. She wondered whether or not Keelin had this type of conversation with Shauna – complaining that Gemma didn't love them enough, that she was always out at work, that she wouldn't spend enough money on them, that she was always nagging at them to tidy their rooms and hang up their clothes. Maybe I'm looking at Mum the wrong way, thought Gemma. Maybe I'm exactly like her. She bit her lip. She hoped not. She wanted to believe that her children loved her and didn't see her as simply a figure of authority. Authority, she snorted to herself, she had no authority over her kids!

'Actually, it wasn't to talk about Mum that I dragged you out.' Liz broke in on her thoughts. 'It was to ask you about something completely different.'

'Fire ahead,' said Gemma, 'although I've never been much for giving you advice.'

'I know,' said Liz. 'Maybe if you had I might have listened.'

'Probably not.' Gemma smiled.

'OK.' Liz sat back in her chair. 'I've met someone.'

'A man?' asked Gemma.

'Well, of course a man.' Liz grinned.

'You're joking!'

'Why should I be joking?' Liz looked offended.

'I'm sorry,' said Gemma quickly, 'I didn't mean it like that. It's just that I didn't realise you were trying to meet someone.'

'I wasn't,' said Liz. 'It was one of those really stupid things. I'd taken Suzy to Herbert Park, we were running around having fun, I tripped and this bloke helped me up.'

'Liz!'

Liz grinned. 'He's a nice guy, Gem, he really is. His name's Ross Harrington, he works in a bank – which is good news – and he's thirty-six years old.'

'You lucky thing.' Gemma was conscious of a sudden spurt of jealousy that Liz had found a 36-year-old, nice man.

'We clicked straightaway,' said Liz. 'He asked if he could give me a hand, I said another ankle would be better because I thought I'd twisted mine, and he helped me to one of the benches.'

'Are you sure you're not making this up?' demanded Gemma. 'Does he look like George Clooney as well?'

'Better,' said Liz.

'I won't believe that.'

'He's not bad at all,' Liz told her. 'Dark hair, a little bit of grey, not much. He's tall. He's a tiny bit overweight, but just enough so that I feel OK about an extra pound or two myself.'

'Liz, you can't weigh more than seven stone,' said Gemma.

'Eight two,' said Liz.

'Bitch.'

Liz smiled. 'I've lost a few pounds, to tell you the truth.'

'That's the bloody best thing about falling for someone.' Gemma sighed. 'Weight just slides off.'

'I didn't say I'd fallen for him,' said Liz.

Gemma eyed her thoughtfully. 'It sounds like it.'

'He's really nice,' Liz told her again. 'He was great with Suzy, too. And his own kids.' She looked definatly at Gemma.

'His own kids?'

'He has two,' said Liz. 'A boy named Shane and a girl name Anita.'

'And the mother of his children?'

'They're separated,' Liz told her. 'They're getting a divorce.'

'How old are the kids?'

'Shane is eight and Anita is six.'

'Does he have custody of them?'

'Are you mad?' asked Liz. 'No, his wife has custody of them.'

'What's her name?'

'Jackie. She left him, Gemma. She walked out when she was pregnant with Anita.'

'Why?'

'That's what I want to know,' said Liz. 'Why does a woman decide to walk out on her husband? Why did you decide to divorce David? What was the trigger, Gemma?'

Gemma sat back in her seat and stared into space.

'Well?' asked Liz, after a minute's silence. 'What is it, Gem? I never asked you before. I didn't want to influence you. Get involved. Maybe that was wrong but—'

'I didn't want anyone to be involved,' said Gemma. 'You know, I'd thought about it for ages and ages before I realised what way it would end up.'

'And why?' asked Liz.

151

'Because I knew that David wasn't the guy I thought I'd married. I married someone who'd backpacked around Europe. Who'd gone surfing in Australia. Who hadn't had a proper job at all until the day I met him! I married someone for the fun of it, Liz, and when all the fun went out of it I realised that I'd made a mistake.'

'But you were married to him for a long time.'

'It didn't take long to realise it was a mistake. It took a lot longer to realise it wasn't one I could live with.'

'OK.' Liz lit a cigarette and Gemma made a face at her. 'I only smoke when I'm under pressure,' Liz told her. 'And I feel a bit pressurised right now. So, Gem, you decided you didn't love him any more and you wanted a divorce. Did you ever feel that you shouldn't have gone through with it? And do you ever regret divorcing him?'

Gemma wriggled uncomfortably on the seat. These were questions she didn't really want to answer. Because she sometimes wasn't sure of the answers herself.

'There were times I thought I should say to him that I'd changed my mind, that I didn't want the divorce,' she admitted. 'But that was copping out, Liz. It wouldn't have changed anything and I would have ended up being even more miserable. The thing is, David and I changed and we didn't love each other enough to accommodate those changes.' She rolled the empty Scampi Fries bag between her fingers. 'I still care about him, but I don't love him. It's funny, but love can disappear in a split second. One minute it's there. And suddenly it's gone.'

Liz exhaled slowly. 'Do you think it's a good idea – me and Ross?'

'How the hell would I know?' asked Gemma. 'I'm the first wife, Liz. Not the new, improved trendy model!'

'I'm not a new, improved trendy model,' said Liz. 'I'm the same age as Jackie. I have a kid of my own! It's not quite the same as David and Orla. Presuming you're assigning the role of new, improved and trendy to her?'

Gemma smiled ruefully. 'Of course she's new and improved and trendy. That's why he married her.'

'I thought you were dealing with it OK,' said Liz.

'Which – the divorce or his re-marriage?'

'Both.'

'Actually, getting the divorce wasn't the worst part. You think it will be but it isn't. And there was a great sense of freedom afterwards. I didn't have to plan my life around someone who wasn't at all dependable any more. But seeing him married again – that's more difficult. Especially to someone with legs like Orla O'Neill.'

'I don't know why Jackie left Ross,' said Liz. 'I haven't asked him yet and I have a horrible feeling he'll say something like "because she didn't understand me".'

'Aren't you jumping the gun a bit?' asked Gemma. 'After all, you've only just met the guy.'

'I know,' said Liz. 'But I have a feeling that he's the one, Gemma. I can't stop thinking about him. I want to be with him all the time. Every moment I'm not with him seems such a waste.'

'Wow.' Gemma grinned. 'You've absolutely fallen for him, haven't you?'

Liz nodded. 'But you're right. Maybe I should wait and discover what his fatal flaw is before getting in too deep.'

'The problem is,' Gemma drained her glass, 'that most of us don't find the fatal flaw until it's far too late!'

Liz stared into the distance for a moment. Then she brought her gaze back to Gemma. 'I know you're right,' she said. 'But I never thought I'd feel like this about anyone, Gemma. And it's wonderful and scary all at the same time.'

Gemma nodded. She remembered what it was like too. She just wondered if she'd ever feel that way again.

Chapter 18

O rla was exhausted. She hadn't slept at all the previous night and her eyes hurt. She'd spent the last two hours at her computer screen in the office trying to reconstruct a file which she'd accidentally deleted. It was nearly nine o'clock in the evening and she'd abandoned her attempts to locate the file on her hard disk, deciding instead to let one of the IT department have a go. Something, she thought, which she should have done from the start instead of wasting so much time. But she'd wanted to stay in the office and messing around with the computer was a good excuse.

In the week since she'd told David about the Serene offer, life in the apartment had been impossible. She'd tried to be bright and cheerful whenever he was around. She'd asked him to help her with stupid things, like opening the lid on a jar of sauce, or checking out the VideoPlus system on the video recorder. He'd taken the jar of sauce from her, opened it and handed it back without a word. He'd shrugged about the video recorder and said that he hadn't got a clue about it. He was forty, he told her, he wasn't a man of the technology era. Surely she, of all people, knew that. She'd tried in other ways to coax him out of his black mood. She'd asked him his opinion on a dress she'd bought which she never normally bothered to do and he'd glanced at it, told her that grey wasn't his favourite colour but that she'd bought the dress now so what difference did it make?

Finally (and with growing despair) she'd suggested an early night together the previous night. He'd simply told her that he didn't have time. He had a lot of admin work to do. Better, he said, if she went to bed early herself if she was that tired.

She reached for a non-technology friendly pencil and snapped it in two. Really, she thought, men were such bloody children! She was the one who was supposed to be the immature one, but she reckoned that David was behaving like a four-year-old. And yet she couldn't entirely blame him for being annoyed. He cared so much about her, about every part of her life, that she could understand his feeling of hurt at being excluded from her thoughts on the new job. But she'd never be able to explain to him that she hadn't told him precisely so that he couldn't influence her.

She heaved a sigh and called up her completed business file. The spreadsheet in front of her showed an absolutely abysmal performance. Apart from the Bentons, she'd only signed up two new clients and they were minimal accounts and minimal commission. Serene Life and Pensions would shudder if they realised that they'd offered a loser a job.

She couldn't take it. She couldn't walk in and pretend that she was in any way competent as a saleswoman on the basis of these numbers. They'd laugh her out of the office. But she wanted the job. Now that the opportunity had been given to her, she wanted to grab it with both hands and see how good she could be. It was the first time anyone had ever approached her about working for them and it made her feel satisfied about herself. But she wasn't satisfied with the figures in front of her which showed her worst time ever.

She closed her eyes and leaned back in her seat. She was the only person left in the office. It was the first time she'd ever been here on her own and it was a little creepy. It was never normally quiet here, there was a constant buzz of chatter and ringing phones during the day. The silence at night was unnerving.

But she didn't want to go home yet. David wouldn't be there – he'd gone to dinner with the managing director and one of the people from their London office. Although she'd known about the dinner, she felt that it was just another way for David to ignore her and show her how annoyed he was with her. After his comments the previous night, she'd gone to bed early but she hadn't been able to sleep. At one o'clock she'd got out of the bed and padded into the living room and seen him, sleeping soundly in front of the TV. She'd thought about turning it off and waking him up but she'd decided against it. His moods were so volatile at the moment she didn't want to make things worse. Later, she'd heard him turn off the TV himself and slide into the bed beside her. She'd waited for him to put his arms round her but he hadn't, he'd rolled away from her onto his side.

She'd cried at lunchtime. She'd been sitting in the Merrion Square park and she'd suddenly felt utterly miserable. Tears had come from nowhere to spill down her face while she tried to hide behind her hands so that nobody would notice. It was stupid, she knew. They'd just had a silly row which hadn't even been a row. It had been nothing

– nothing at all. Which was why it was so hard to rationalise. Why had David been so horrible to her? Why did she feel so terribly upset over nothing at all? Why was she so frightened?

Hormones, her brothers would say. They always did when she got upset. 'Orla's oestrogen levels are too low!' they'd laugh. Or too high. Whatever.

She'd suddenly been gripped with the dreadful fear that maybe it was hormonal. Only the wrong kind of hormonal. Maybe she was pregnant! She began counting backwards in her head but couldn't work it out. And then, when she'd come back to the office and checked, she realised that it would be very, very unlikely. Which had disappointed her rather than cheered her. And made her feel like crying again.

She closed down the spreadsheet and switched off the computer. She hadn't wanted to go back to the apartment and sit in on her own. But she didn't have any appointments for the evening. Another black mark, she thought bleakly. I should have someone I could call, someone who needs my financial advice.

She looked at her watch again. She'd have to call Bob Murphy but she dreaded calling him. She didn't know what to tell him. That she couldn't take the job because her husband didn't like it? How would that make her look? Pathetic, she told herself, it would make her look absolutely pathetic. But if she took the job, would it mean that David would spend even more time being horrible to her? She chewed the inside of her lip. It was time to get things into perspective. David was being stupid about this whole affair, not her.

She picked up the phone and dialled Bob's number.

'Hi, Bob,' she said when he answered.

'Orla. I was beginning to think that you weren't going to call me.'

'Of course I'd call,' she said.

'So? What news do you have?'

She hesitated, then sat up straight in the chair. 'I'm going to take your offer, Bob,' she said.

'That's great.' He sounded genuinely pleased, thought Orla. He really did.

'I'm glad you're pleased,' she said.

'Of course I am. We are,' he told her. 'We're always looking for new people who have drive and ambition. Do you want to meet me tomorrow and thrash out all the details?'

'That'd be great,' she said.

'Six o'clock suit you?'

'Fine,' said Orla.

'Same place?'

'Suits me.'

'OK,' said Bob, 'I'll see you then. I'll have a contract for you. And we're really delighted to have you on board.'

⌒

It was ten o'clock when she got home. She pulled the curtains and switched on the standard lamp in the corner. As always, it lit up the bronzed African woman sculpture and threw a long shadow across the room. I really hate that bloody thing, thought Orla. It's ugly. It doesn't look nice. In fact, it scares the shit out of me.

She pulled it away from the wall. It wasn't as heavy as it looked. She pushed it across the living room and into the narrow hallway. There was a tiny storage room at the end of the hall and she opened the door and shoved the sculpture inside.

'Stay there,' she commanded as she slammed the door shut.

She heated up a Tesco ready meal for one in the microwave and sat in front of the TV. It was almost like being back with Abby, she thought, as she flicked through the channels. Except that David's apartment was much bigger and much nicer.

The telephone rang and startled her. She dropped a piece of chicken and bacon tagliatelle on the light-blue sofa.

'Shit,' she muttered as she picked up the receiver. 'Hello?'

'Hello, Orla.'

Bloody hell, she groaned to herself as she recognised Gemma's voice. I didn't tell David that she'd called. Now she'll be pissed off at me and think I didn't want to tell him. Or she'll be pissed off at him because she'll think he's ignoring her. Which, of course, he should be.

'Orla?'

'Hi, Gemma,' said Orla. 'I'm sorry, you caught me at a bad moment.'

What sort of bad moment? wondered Gemma. Had they been making love when she called? Was David now lying on the bed, his arms spread out to one side as he liked while his wife sat astride him? She swallowed at the thought. 'Will I phone back?' she asked.

'Yes, if you want to talk to David,' Orla told her. 'He's out tonight.'

'He didn't ring me,' said Gemma.

'Yes, well, I'm sorry, that was my fault.' Orla tried to sound cheerful. 'I know it was awful of me but I forgot to tell him you called.'

157

'Oh,' said Gemma.

'It was just that I was in bed when he got home and I forgot about it this morning,' explained Orla.

'He was out late last night too?'

Bitch, thought Orla, trying to score points off me, is she? 'He had meetings,' she told Gemma. 'And he's out to dinner with the MD and the UK MD too tonight.'

'God, I hated those dinners.' Gemma sighed. 'He was always trying to make me come to them and they were so awful! I couldn't bear it. I'm sorry you have to put up with it now.'

'It's different,' said Orla. 'I work in the company so I don't get invited.'

'Don't you?'

'No,' said Orla tersely.

'You're better off,' said Gemma. 'Obviously it'll be too late tonight but will you please ask David to phone me in the morning?'

'Sure,' said Orla.'

'Thanks.'

'You're welcome.'

Orla put down the receiver and turned to the tagliatelle on the sofa. The cream sauce was drying into a horrible stain. David would go mad, she thought, as she scrubbed at it ineffectually with a tissue. He liked everything to be just so.

⤺

Gemma went back into the living room. She wondered if Orla had been telling the truth. Was David really out to dinner with Liam McDaid and Oliver Smith? Or had he been right there beside her, shaking his head, telling Orla that he didn't want to talk to Gemma. She sighed.

It was certainly true that he used to dine with Liam and Oliver any time the Englishman visited Ireland. He'd been to dinner with them the night Ronan was born. Gemma had gone into labour desperately trying to contact David – he hadn't had a mobile phone in those days and he'd given her the name of the wrong restaurant. He'd always claimed it was a mistake but Gemma had never been quite sure. Deep down she thought that he'd deliberately given her the wrong number so that her labour wouldn't ruin his important dinner. In the end she'd phoned Frances who had been the last person in the world she'd wanted to call. At least, not in the particular circumstances. Frances had already agreed to look after Keelin when Gemma went into hospital but Gemma hated having to explain that her father would have to drive her because David was nowhere to be found.

The birth itself had been easy and the labour short (unlike Keelin's which had ended with a Caesarean section) and by the time they tracked down David and he arrived at Mount Carmel Hospital, Ronan Kevin Hennessy was already two hours old.

Gemma sat down and picked up the TV guide but she didn't read it. She was remembering later, when Ronan was a little older, and she'd thought that another child might be a good idea. She loved them so much when they were helpless babies. She loved both her children all the time, of course, but there was something special about them when they were too small to answer back, so tiny that she was almost afraid to pick them up. David had loved them as babies too. David got up in the middle of the night when they cried and he changed their dirty nappies and he wiped up after them when they were sick.

But David hadn't wanted another child. The worst thing was that he'd been perfectly right when she broached the subject and he told her, dismissively, that she wanted a baby for all the wrong reasons. Two was enough, he'd said, no matter what the circumstances.

Sometimes she still wanted a baby. She couldn't quite believe that she'd never have one again, that her childbearing years were, to all intents and purposes, over. When David had left them first she'd thought about babies all the time. She'd closed her eyes and remembered their smell of milk and talc and she'd remembered how special they'd made her feel. She'd gone for long walks along the seafront and she'd imagined what it would be like to have a child by another man. But she hadn't wanted another man; the one she'd asked to leave had been more than enough. And yet she'd felt the need to have a child so strongly that it was all she could do not to reach into a pram and take one. She'd thought about it one day as she sat on one of the wooden benches overlooking the bay. A girl, not much older than Keelin was now, had sat down beside her. She was looking after a baby in a pram and a little boy who Gemma guessed was about four years old. He'd suddenly run away from the girl, racing along the grass so that she'd jumped up from the seat, looked anxiously at Gemma and said, 'Keep an eye on her, I'll be back in a second,' and sprinted after him. For a moment both of them were out of view and Gemma had fought the almost irresistible urge to let the brake off the pram and push it quickly in the opposite direction. She'd thought about it, visualised it, imagined arriving home with the baby. She'd even thought that

159

she could explain it away although she couldn't now remember the story she'd concocted.

Then the girl had come back into her line of sight, dragging the little boy behind her and yelling at him that she'd give him what for if he ever ran off like that again. She'd muttered 'Thanks' to Gemma and pushed the pram away. Gemma had cried then, and she hadn't even known why.

ᔖ

Orla looked at the TV guide. Sky One was showing a rerun of *Buffy the Vampire Slayer*. Orla liked *Buffy the Vampire Slayer*. She'd often thought about taking self-defence classes and learning to kick people just like Buffy did. David thought it was the most incredibly stupid piece of television he'd ever seen. He said it wasn't realistic. Orla told him that it wasn't meant to be realistic. David had laughed. So had she.

She curled her legs beneath her and rummaged under the cushions for the remote control. If she was spending the night in she was going to watch Buffy, followed by *Ally McBeal* (another series that David refused to watch on the grounds of its being unrealistic – 'And that woman is too stupid to be a lawyer,' he'd added) and then back-to-back episodes of *Friends*. David didn't like *Friends* either. David watched sports programmes. Orla never minded him watching sport – with four brothers she knew that soccer on Saturday nights was almost sacrosanct. She never even complained when he watched terminally boring events like sailing on Eurosport. She never criticised him.

She pressed the button on the remote.

David still hadn't arrived home by twelve-thirty. Orla stacked her crockery in the dishwasher and wrote a note for him.

Gemma rang, was all it said.

Chapter 19

It was raining at Faro airport. Gemma couldn't believe that she was in Portugal at the end of August and that it was actually raining. Not only that, but it was chilly. It was six o'clock in the evening, the sun was hidden behind a thick layer of grey clouds and she had goose pimples on her arms.

Keelin and Ronan sat in the coach beside her. Keelin's Walkman was firmly anchored to her head while Ronan was playing with a Gameboy. Keelin had looked at the sky as they got off the plane, crossed her arms in front of her and muttered that if she was going to be cold she might as well be cold at home.

Ronan had looked at Gemma, his eyes big and worried and asked why it wasn't hot, like Gemma had told him.

'It will be,' she said hopefully. 'This will probably blow over really quickly.'

But the tour rep told them that it was forecast to last for at least another day. 'I'm really sorry,' she said and giggled infuriatingly. 'It's been lovely all week but it turned bad yesterday. We're getting the edge of a weather system in the Atlantic.'

Great, thought Gemma. I'm the only person in the whole world to come on a sun holiday and get caught in the middle of a weather system.

David had been unexpectedly generous about the holiday. Gemma explained to him that she really and truly felt that the children needed the break, that Keelin desperately wanted to go on holidays like everyone else in school and that, with her birthday coming up in a couple of days, it would be a fantastic present. She'd expected David to tell her that he wouldn't let her out of the country with the children. He'd told her that before, just after they'd split up and she'd had the most dreadful row with him because she'd arranged the trip with Liz to Majorca. But when he'd rung her the day after she'd spoken to Orla, Gemma thought he sounded distracted.

'I know I'm getting away too,' she'd said quickly, 'and I understand that you won't pay for me, David. But it would be really good if you could do it for the kids. I'm sorry. I know it's pressure.' She made a face at the phone and continued. 'I don't mean to pressurise you, really I don't—'

'OK,' he'd interrupted the gabble. 'Where do you want to go?'

'I saw a late break for Portugal,' she said breathlessly. 'Only a couple of hundred a head. The Algarve.'

'OK,' he said again. 'Give me the details and I'll book it on my credit card.'

'Are you sure?' she asked, then kicked herself for putting a doubt into his mind.

'You're right,' he told her. 'The kids should get the same things as they would if we were still together. And if we were still together I'm sure we'd be taking them abroad on holidays. So it's fair, Gemma. And I don't mind paying for you because I know that it's not exactly a bed of roses looking after them.'

She'd stared at the receiver in utter amazement. He'd never spoken like that about her or the children before. She wondered if he was feeling OK but she didn't want to ask.

'It's Budget Travel,' she said. 'Oh, David, thank you. I know they'll be utterly thrilled.'

They were. Keelin's face had lit up and she looked almost like the old Keelin, the one that had liked and respected Gemma. Ronan had grinned and said, 'Cool', and Gemma had basked in a feeling of satisfaction that she'd managed to do the right thing at last.

'It's your dad's treat,' she told them, although she really wanted to keep the glory for herself. 'He's paying for us all.'

'He must love us.' Keelin glanced at Gemma. 'To send us on holiday he must love us.'

'Of course he does!' Gemma hugged her. 'Well, he loves you and Ro – I guess that'll have to do.'

Keelin's good mood had lasted until they bumped their way through the heavy cloud and she'd been sick in a paper bag. Gemma knew that it was embarrassment that upset her more than anything and she'd said nothing. She realised from the set of Keelin's jaw that she should leave her daughter alone.

Was I this difficult? she wondered. Of course, Frances and Gerry had never brought her or Michael or Liz abroad on holidays. They booked a week in a cottage in Donegal every year – and no matter what week it was, all Gemma could remember was a constant misty rain which meant

162

that they were soaked every day. Sometimes they went away for bank holiday weekends – she remembered an August weekend in Wexford when it had, unexpectedly, been blazing hot and they'd all managed to get burnt. Holidays with her parents had never been very successful. She just hoped that she wasn't carrying on the tradition.

The coach shuddered to a halt outside the whitewashed apartment building. Gemma and the children followed the rep inside, got the key to their apartment and took the lift to the fifth floor.

'Where's my room?' asked Keelin as she dumped her backpack on the floor.

'Keelin, you know that we have to share,' said Gemma. 'It's a one-bedroomed apartment. You and I will share the bedroom and Ronan can have the sofa bed out here.'

'Great!' Ronan jumped onto the sofa and bounced experimentally on it.

'Stop it!' Gemma ordered. 'You don't want to break it, do you?' Foolish question, she thought. Of course he wants to break it. He breaks everything!

'I'm hungry,' said Ronan. 'I'm too light to break it. I'm fading away.'

Gemma hid a grin. 'We'll get something soon.'

'Very soon, I hope,' said Ronan seriously, 'otherwise I might just collapse!'

'It's cold.' Keelin hugged her arms round herself. 'Why are we the only people in the whole world to come to a hot place and find out that it's cold?'

'You heard the rep.' Gemma walked over to the patio doors and opened them. 'It's a weather system. It'll clear up tomorrow.'

'Actually she said it'll last another day,' said Keelin. 'It might not clear up tomorrow. And I'll have to spend another day in this sweatshirt because I don't have another one.'

'Nobody will notice,' said Gemma.

'I will,' muttered Keelin.

Gemma stood on the balcony and looked out. If she craned her neck she could just about make out the sea through a gap between the apartment blocks opposite her. The water was sludge-green and white-flecked. Rather like Dublin Bay in autumn, she thought.

'Come on.' She turned back to them. 'Let's unpack our stuff and get something to eat so that poor Ronan doesn't fade away.'

'OK.' Keelin smiled crookedly at her.

It took them half an hour to unpack. Gemma also made up Ronan's sofa bed so that it would be ready when they got back. When she'd finished she pulled on the navy-blue Ralph Lauren sweatshirt Niamh had brought back for her the last time she'd gone to a convention in the States. When Gemma and David had been married, Gemma had been the one to buy Ralph Lauren in the States.

'I like that sweatshirt,' said Keelin. 'It suits you.'

'Thanks.' Gemma looked at her in surprise.

'Are you two ready yet?' demanded Ronan. 'I'm utterly, utterly starving.'

'Let's go,' said Gemma. 'I'd hate to think that my only son would starve.'

Despite the chill in the air, there were a lot of people strolling along the streets of Albufeira. The trees in the cobbled square swayed in the breeze while the birds chattered busily. Brightly lit stalls were already set up selling trinkets to the tourists. Keelin studied the displays of rings and bracelets, coloured stones and scarves. They were the same as the ones at home, she realised. She wondered if she could learn to do it and travel the world selling trinkets.

'Come on, Keelin.' Ronan tugged at her sleeve. 'I'm really hungry.'

They went into a pizzeria on the first floor of a three-storey white-washed building. The waiter showed them to a table near the window so that they could look out onto the thronged street below them where people were walking around in T-shirts and shorts despite the chill of the evening.

'What would you like to eat?' asked Gemma as she studied the menu in front of her.

'Can we have anything?' asked Ronan.

'Anything at all,' she said.

He beamed at her and bent his head to read the menu. Keelin sat back in her chair to read hers. Gemma felt her heart swell with pride and joy in them – her troublesome daughter who was going to be stunningly beautiful one day, and her happy-go-lucky son who was so easy to manage. I'm lucky, she thought suddenly. I really am. I have two great kids and I'm coping. OK, so things haven't turned out exactly as I'd always wanted, but what does? And, even though I'm divorced, my ex-husband does his best for us. Things could be a damn sight worse than they are for me.

The waiter returned, notebook in hand, and looked at her questioningly.

'You first,' she said to Keelin.

'Can I have garlic bread?' asked Keelin, ignoring the pained expression on Ronan's face. 'And vegetable risotto.'

164

'Certainly.' The waiter looked at Gemma expectantly.

'Your turn, Ronan,' she said.

'I want the pizza del Mundo,' said Ronan.

'Would you like a starter, sir?' asked the waiter.

Ronan looked at Gemma. 'You can share a salad with me,' she told him.

'OK,' he said.

'Can I have the mixed salad, please?' she ordered. 'And I'll have the risotto too.'

'Will I bring some bread rolls?' asked the waiter.

'Yes, please,' said Ronan.

'And a bottle of Vinho Verde,' said Gemma as she closed the menu.

They sat in silence for a few moments. In the bar opposite, someone had started to play the guitar and sing Elvis Presley songs. Gemma hummed along and then told herself that Elvis was her parents' generation and that, just because she knew the words, she didn't have to sing the songs.

The waiter brought Keelin's garlic bread and the rolls and butter. He uncorked the bottle of Vinho Verde and poured some for Gemma to taste.

'Lovely,' she said.

He filled her glass and looked at her questioningly.

'Would you like some?' Gemma asked Keelin.

'Some wine?'

'You'll be fourteen tomorrow,' Gemma told her. 'If we lived in France you'd probably have drunk gallons of the stuff by now.'

'Yes please,' said Keelin who smiled with pleasure as her glass was filled.

'Can I have some?' asked Ronan. 'Most probably if we lived in France I'd have drunk gallons of it too.'

'Most probably.' Gemma grinned at him. 'You can have half a glass. But drink it slowly, Ronan, it's not lemonade.'

He sipped it suspiciously. 'It's a bit – dry,' he said.

'Goodness!' Gemma stared at him. 'A connoisseur.'

'What?' asked Ronan as he tried it again.

'Wine expert,' said Keelin. She sipped her wine self-consciously. 'It's nice.'

'Good,' said Gemma. 'I'm glad you like it.'

'It's kind of fizzy,' said Keelin.

'Only a little,' Gemma told her.

'Is champagne fizzier than this?' asked Keelin.

'Much,' Gemma assured her. 'When you were born your dad brought a bottle of champagne into the hospital and we drank it over your cot.'

'Was I in it at the time?' asked Keelin.

Gemma laughed. 'Yes. Sound asleep.'

'While my parents were getting drunk!'

'It was only a small bottle,' Gemma said. 'And we didn't get drunk.' Although, she reflected, as she sipped her wine, she'd felt light-headed after almost the first sip. David had helped her back into the bed and she muttered that she'd probably curdled her milk and that her poor baby would have an atrocious hangover. She remembered it clearly. The yellow paint on the walls of her private room. The enormous vases of flowers on the windowsill. The cards lined up between them. The cover on the bed was yellow too. If she closed her eyes she could remember being that Gemma, the married Gemma, the one who had loved and been loved.

'Are you OK?' Keelin's voice was anxious.

'Of course.' Gemma smiled at her. 'I was just remembering when you were born, that's all.'

'What was I like?' asked Keelin.

'You were beautiful,' said Gemma. 'The first day you were red and wizened and kind of angry-looking, but that wore off. By the time we left the hospital everyone was saying that you were the most beautiful baby there.'

'That's rubbish.' But Keelin flushed with pleasure.

'Yes, it's rubbish.' Ronan nodded wisely. 'You're not beautiful now.'

'Ronan!' Gemma nudged him. 'Your sister is beautiful.'

'No, I'm not,' said Keelin. 'My eyes are too small and my mouth is too big!'

'And you've got big feet,' said Ronan.

Gemma stifled a giggle as Keelin glared at him. 'I have not!!'

'Children, children,' she said. 'Please don't fight over whether or not one of you has big feet.'

Both of them smiled. 'We're not fighting,' said Ronan. 'We're debating.'

'Well, let's not debate body shapes,' said Gemma. 'I don't think that's a good idea.'

'I like your body shape,' said Ronan. 'It's kind of squishy.'

Gemma swallowed a piece of roll without chewing it and had to drink copious amounts of water to dislodge it.

'Are you all right?' asked Keelin after Gemma had regained her composure and wiped her eyes.

'I guess so,' said Gemma. She sighed. 'It's not every day that someone calls you squishy and means it as a compliment.'

'You're not squishy,' said Keelin. 'You're just – comfortable.'

'I don't really want to be comfortable,' Gemma told her. 'I want to be tall and thin and elegant.'

'Like Orla,' said Ronan.

It was just as well, thought Gemma, that she didn't have any food in her mouth this time.

'Do you think Orla is elegant?' she asked.

'She's very tall,' said Keelin carefully.

'And skinny,' said Ronan. 'You can see her ribs.'

'Really?'

Keelin shook her head. 'No, but she's awfully thin all the same.'

'But is she elegant?' asked Gemma again.

Keelin considered the question. 'Not exactly,' she said finally. 'But she's – she's kind of modern, you know?' She looked at her mother helplessly.

Gemma smiled at her. 'Well, she's a lot younger than me.'

'I like her,' said Ronan, 'but I wouldn't swap you for her!'

'That's the nicest thing you've ever said to me,' said Gemma. She took a mouthful of wine and this time had to swallow hard because of the lump in her throat.

༄

Gemma lay in the single bed and stared at the ceiling. She'd put some blankets on the bed but she was still cold. She'd always found it difficult to stay warm and when she was cold she couldn't sleep. She hoped the weather would be a little better tomorrow. If it was just hot enough to sit outside with a glass of wine and her book, she'd be perfectly happy. There was a kids club attached to the apartments so she hoped there'd be something for Ronan to do even if it wasn't that hot. She wasn't sure about Keelin.

She rolled onto her side and looked across the room. Keelin was facing her, her eyes closed, her arm hanging over the side of the bed. She looked untroubled in sleep tonight, thought Gemma. So unlike other nights when she'd looked in on her. Perhaps her daughter was changing. Perhaps her relationship with Keelin was changing too. Gemma exhaled slowly. If this holiday meant that they grew closer together, David would have done them the biggest favour of his life.

Chapter 20

Gemma woke with a start. She sat up in bed and looked around her in total confusion. It took her a few seconds to remember where she was and then to realise that she was alone in the room. She looked at her watch. Almost eleven! She never stayed in bed until almost eleven – in fact she hadn't expected to sleep at all in the lumpy single bed. She swung her legs over the side of the bed and grimaced as she felt the chill of the tiled floor beneath her feet. She looked around for her flip-flops and found them, upturned, at the end of the bed. She slipped them on and went into the living area. The sheets from the sofa bed where Ronan had slept were rolled into a pile at the sofa end but there was no sign of the children. Gemma's heart beat faster. Where had they got to?

She opened the patio door and looked out. The sky was still grey although the air was noticeably warmer. She leaned over the iron balcony and surveyed the garden area but there was nobody around. She turned back into the apartment and then she saw the scrap of paper they'd propped up against the coffee pot. 'Gone out,' it said in Keelin's neatly sloping handwriting. 'Have taken swim stuff in case weather gets better.'

'Shit.' Gemma pulled off her pyjama top as she hurried back into the bedroom. Gone where? she wondered as she scrambled into her jeans and T-shirt and pulled a brush through her hair. How in God's name hadn't she heard them? Either she'd been more tired than she'd realised or they'd tiptoed around the apartment in a most uncharacteristically quiet way!

She walked out of the apartment and closed the door carefully behind her.

There were a number of people wandering around the reception area but there was no sign of either Keelin or Ronan. Gemma told herself not to worry, that they were perfectly capable of looking after themselves, but she couldn't help feeling anxious all the same. She didn't know how long they'd been up and out. She just wanted to know where they were. She clamped down on visions of them crossing the busy and dangerous dual carriageway that ran by the front of the apartment to get to the McDonald's on the other side. She knew that she was being ridiculous. Keelin was – fourteen today! Gemma bit her lip as she remembered her daughter's birthday. Fourteen was old enough to wander around on her own, Gemma told herself. She'd felt perfectly adult at fourteen even if she'd struggled to convince her parents of the fact. But it seemed to Gemma now that the older she became, the less certain she was about anything! And the more she worried about the children.

She shook her head and told herself to stop worrying. Keelin was sensible. Even when she was being silly, she had a core of common sense. Gemma trusted her. She walked around the outside of the block and eventually came to the pool. A small group of people sat around on the sunbeds but they were talking quietly to each other, planning, Gemma presumed, what you could do on a potentially rainy day in Portugal.

And then she heard a high-pitched laugh that was unmistakably Keelin's. She felt a surge of relief and she hurried over to the nearby tennis courts.

Keelin and Ronan were playing tennis against a girl and a boy of about their own ages. Gemma opened the gate and let herself into the court area.

'Here you are,' she said.

Ronan swung for the ball and missed. 'You've put me off, Mum,' he complained.

'I'm sorry,' said Gemma. 'But I wanted to find out where you were.'

'We waited,' said Keelin. 'We thought you'd wake up but you were sound asleep. So we had the croissants you bought last night and came out.'

'You could have said where you were going.' Gemma kept her tone as mild as she could.

Keelin shrugged. 'We didn't know. But we weren't going to sit around.'

'I understand,' said Gemma. 'Who are your friends?'

'I'm Fiona,' said the slim, tanned girl beside Keelin.

'And I'm Ian,' said the boy.

'They're Irish,' Keelin told her. 'They're staying here too.'

'That's nice,' said Gemma. 'And how long have you been here?'

'A week,' Fiona told her.

'The weather was great last week, Fiona says,' Keelin pouted. 'Trust it to be lousy while we're here.'

'It'll get better,' said Gemma hopefully. 'Can you come here a minute, Keelin.'

Keelin sighed and dropped her tennis racquet. She walked over to Gemma.

'I wanted to wish you a happy birthday,' said her mother. She kissed Keelin on the cheek and Keelin shrugged away.

'Not in front of people!' she muttered.

'Well, happy birthday anyway,' said Gemma. 'I do have something for you, Keelin, but I left it in the apartment. I'm sorry, I came rushing out to check where you were.'

'Nothing was going to happen to us,' said Keelin. 'We weren't going far.'

'I know,' said Gemma. 'But I'm a mother. I panicked.' She smiled at Keelin who raised her eyes to heaven. 'So, what do you want to do today?' asked Gemma.

'Fiona's mum is going to take us playing crazy golf,' said Keelin. 'They were going anyway and she said if it was OK with you we could go too.'

Gemma stared at her. 'Where's Fiona's mother?'

Keelin shrugged. 'In the coffee dock,' she said. 'I told her it would be OK. It is, isn't it?'

Gemma scratched her head. She hadn't envisaged her two children disappearing with some strange adult on the first day of their holiday. 'I'll have to talk to her,' she said.

'She wants us to come,' said Keelin. 'She offered, Mum.'

'Maybe she was just being polite,' said Gemma.

'No,' said Keelin. 'She said it would be fun!'

'It's OK,' interjected Fiona. 'We want them to come. Honestly.'

'I'll talk to your mother,' said Gemma.

She followed the crazy paving through the rustling palm trees back towards the apartment, then veered to the left to the small terraced area where a few people were sipping coffees. She identified a taller, slightly heavier version of Fiona almost immediately.

'Fiona's mother?' asked Gemma.

The other woman looked up at her and smiled. 'Selina Ferguson,' she said. 'You must be Keelin and Ronan's mum.'

'Yes.' Gemma nodded and sat down on one of the plastic seats.

'Gemma Garvey. The children tell me you want to bring them playing crazy golf.'

'If you don't mind,' said Selina. 'Mine would enjoy it so much more with other people to play against! And they're not forecasting the weather to clear here until later this afternoon. So I thought it might be a bit of fun. It's a big course, not a piddling little thing. It takes a long time to get round it.'

Gemma smiled tentatively. Selina seemed OK, but she balked at the idea of letting her children go off for the day with someone she hardly knew.

'We come here every year,' said Selina. 'I know the road well. They'll be perfectly OK. There's a restaurant and a pool at the complex too, so we can spend some time there after the golf.'

'I don't like to think of them being in the way,' said Gemma.

'They won't be,' Selina told her. 'And you're perfectly welcome to come too, Gemma, only it'll be a bit of a squash in the car if you do. And I thought, perhaps, you might like some time on your own.'

Why would she think that? Gemma wondered. Had the children said something to make her think that she would want to be on her own?

'I don't mind if you'd prefer them to stay with you,' said Selina. 'But I know my two would like the company.'

'How old are yours?' asked Gemma.

'Fiona's thirteen. Ian is twelve. There's a bare nine months between them.' She smiled. 'A mistake, but it worked out in the end!'

Gemma looked around. 'Is your husband with you?' she asked.

Selina shook her head. 'I came on holiday with the children and my brother,' she said. 'Frank died last year.'

'Oh, God!' Gemma stared at her, aghast. 'I'm so sorry.'

'No need to be,' said Selina. 'At least, no need to feel bad about Frank. To be honest, I still feel kind of strange without him. That's why my brother came with me. I wasn't up to the holiday thing on my own.'

'I can understand that.' Gemma bit her lip. 'I truly am sorry, Selina.'

The other woman smiled wryly. 'Life is like that,' she said.

They sat in silence.

'When were you going to set out?' asked Gemma eventually.

'Fairly soon,' said Selina.

'And you're sure you don't mind taking them?'

'Positive,' Selina assured her.

Gemma still felt doubtful. But she knew that the children wouldn't forgive her if she said no. 'OK,' she said at last. 'But don't take any nonsense from them.'

'I won't,' Selina grinned. 'I promise.'

Gemma went back to the tennis courts and told Keelin and Ronan that it was OK to go playing crazy golf. She smiled at their enthusiasm and felt good that she'd agreed, then she returned to the apartment and had a shower. She felt better once she'd freshened up and less worried about letting them go off with the Fergusons. She'd just finished towelling her hair dry when Keelin and Ronan banged at the door.

'You've certainly made friends quickly,' said Gemma.

'They're nice,' Ronan told her.

'Good.' Gemma went into the bedroom and brought out a wrapped package for Keelin. 'Here you are.' She kissed her daughter on the head. 'Happy birthday.'

'Thanks.' Keelin undid the paper and took out the Armani sunglasses that Gemma had bought. 'They're great.'

Gemma laughed. 'Though you hardly need them today.'

'Bru says it'll get bright later,' Keelin told her.

'Bru?'

'Fiona's uncle. He was coaching us in tennis earlier.' Keelin popped the sunglasses on and grinned at her mother. 'He's very, very sexy!'

'Keelin!'

'But he is,' said Keelin. She took off the sunglasses. Her eyes sparkled. 'He's gorgeous.'

'If he's Selina's brother he's too old for you,' said Gemma.

'I don't know.' Keelin sighed. 'I find all the guys my age so incredibly childish.'

Gemma choked back the laughter.

'You've plenty of time to meet someone who's a mature teenager.'

'How old were you?' asked Keelin. 'When you first went out with someone?'

Gemma considered the question. 'Fifteen,' she lied. She'd actually been fourteen but she wasn't going to tell Keelin that. She didn't want Keelin to feel that she now had a licence to consider every guy she met as fair game.

'And how long did it last?'

'About an hour.' That much was the truth. She'd met him at the school gates where gangs of adolescent males hung around waiting for the girls. His name was Billy. She couldn't remember anything else about him. They'd walked along the main road, spent an hour sitting on the low wall beside the local corner shop and he'd put his arm round her and tried to kiss her. Gemma had been so surprised that she'd let him. She hadn't enjoyed the experience and she never even spoke to him again after that day.

'Why so short?' asked Keelin.

'We'd nothing in common,' said Gemma. 'Is this brother of Mrs Ferguson going to the golf with you?'

'No,' said Keelin. 'He said he's got things to do.'

Gemma was relieved. She wasn't too sure about the sound of Selina's sexy brother and her fourteen-year-old daughter with the sparkle in her eyes.

⌇

It was after twelve by the time they left. Gemma waved them off, clamping down on the feeling that she could be making a terrible mistake in letting them out of her sight. By now there were a couple of hazy blue patches amid the grey clouds and she began to think that she might actually manage to catch a few rays of sunshine before the evening. She really wanted to lie by the pool with the book she'd picked up off the shelf at the airport bookshop. *The Company She Keeps* had looked very promising.

But it wasn't yet warm enough to lie by the pool. Gemma went back to the apartment, put her swimsuit and her book into her bag, and decided to go for a walk until the skies cleared a little. She'd changed out of her ancient grey T-shirt into a crisp white one and exchanged her jeans for a pair of neat, red shorts. She brushed her hair again and looked at herself in the mirror.

Her blue eyes looked back solemnly at her. Her eyes had always been her best feature. David had once told her that looking into her eyes was like looking into a fathomless lake and she'd laughed at him and told him not to be so silly. But they were an interesting shade of blue, she thought, and enhanced by the faint traces of colour left over from the few sunny days that they'd had earlier in the summer. It was, she knew, terribly unfashionable to like a tan but Gemma always felt better with a hint of colour. She turned a light honey-brown that made her look and feel a million times better than she ever did during the depths of winter.

She leaned forward and examined her face more closely. There were tiny lines around the outside of her eyes, but they were very fine and hardly noticeable unless she frowned. I must be more serene, she told herself, trying to compose her features into a mask of calmness. She giggled, she couldn't help it. She turned sideways to look at the rest of her body. Legs – in fairly good shape. A little flabby at the thighs, perhaps, but that was neatly hidden by the red shorts. Stomach – the less said the better. She inhaled deeply and held in her stomach for as long as she could. If I could keep it like this, she thought, as her face reddened with the effort, it might be OK. She exhaled loudly with relief. She couldn't be expected to have a flat stomach after two kids. It was pointless feeling bad about it. She ended her survey by looking at her chest. The children had caused a further expansion in her already generous chest area. She'd never been sure whether she liked it or not but, in the right clothes, her boobs could look pretty sensational.

Maybe it's not as bad as I sometimes think, she concluded as she turned round slowly. But if I bothered to get off my bum (a little bigger than I'd really like) and go to the damned gym with Niamh, maybe I could look better.

All this obsession with how you look! She shook her head. Who damn well cared how she looked, after all? The only man in her life was Ronan and he liked her squishy!

She took the narrow winding road from the apartments that led to the beach. The waves were huge, crashing against the soft biscuit-coloured sand with a steady thud and leaving dark patches as they slid back into the sea. David would have loved that, she thought suddenly, as she remembered the photographs of him surfing in Australia. It had been the surfing photographs that had made up her mind about David. He'd looked so fantastic as he rode the waves, his body lean and taut, his dark hair held back in a curly ponytail. He'd looked fun and she'd wanted to marry someone who was fun. She'd ached for some fun, couldn't wait to leave the sterile house that Frances ruled with her rod of iron.

She walked along the beach, kicking at the sand. It wasn't fair to think of the house as sterile. Her father had laughed and joked a lot. And Frances had laughed with him – she couldn't ignore the fact that her mother had laughed. It was just that, with Frances, it was hard to believe that it was genuine.

Frances had hated them doing things that weren't useful. When Gemma came in from work and lay on the sofa, her legs hanging over the arms, Frances would click her teeth and ask Gemma if she'd

174

nothing better to do. When she brought home glossy magazines, Frances would ask if she hadn't something better to read. When she bought ultra-fashionable clothes, Frances would look at them with ill-concealed dislike and ask if Gemma couldn't have spent her money more wisely. Maybe it was her mother's strict Catholic upbringing that had made her live her life as though anything frivolous was a waste of time. It was no wonder, thought Gemma, as she sat down on a huge rock that stuck out of the sand, that she'd fallen for a man who looked like fun was his middle name.

And then David had gone into the insurance business. Gemma grimaced and took her book out of her bag. Any business less likely to bring fun to the lives of all concerned she simply couldn't imagine. David had changed almost immediately from a ponytailed windsurfer into a slicked-back salesman who thought that money was everything and that fun was something for other people. And the worst of it all was that she'd helped him to become that person by cutting his hair in the first place! She sighed deeply and opened her book.

The heroine in *The Company She Keeps* wasn't having much fun. Gemma turned the page and smiled to herself as she read about Kira O'Brien complaining to her best friend that nobody at the office took her seriously. Particularly the loathsome managing director. He thought that blonde hair and blue eyes equalled stupidity. And he thought that all women could be bullied. But he was wrong, she said. He'd completely misjudged her and one day he'd regret it.

What would it be like, Gemma wondered, to be a girl like Kira O'Brien? What would it be like to be so ambitious that you'd consider dying your natural blonde hair a dull mid-brown just so that you'd look the part? She wondered which sort of dye Kira would use and what sort of stylist would agree to turning a colour that everyone wanted into boring brown. She flicked over the page. Even though she was nothing like Kira, she was enthralled by the story.

Quite suddenly, a drop of rain fell onto the page. Gemma looked up at the sky in surprise. She hadn't noticed the bank of grey cloud roll in from the sea but she saw it now and it looked heavy with rain. She closed the book and put it into her bag. She didn't like the look of that cloud. It was too much, she thought despairingly, to have come to the Algarve only to get pissed on while she sat on the beach!

The raindrops grew heavier. Gemma glanced around her. The nearest shelter was a beach bar a hundred metres or so along the strand. She fastened the Velcro strips on her red Springer sandals and walked as quickly as she could in the direction of the bar. She cursed the softness of the sand as her feet sank into it, particularly as it was now getting wet and sticking to her. She ran the last few metres, breathing heavily. Her legs ached. She should really have joined that gym with Niamh!

By the time she stood on the wooden deck of the bar, she was soaking. Her hair hung around her face in rats' tails and water dripped from her face. She hoped Selina and the children had managed to shelter more successfully than she had.

A man sprinted up the steps to the bar. He was wearing faded denim jeans and a black T-shirt. His dark hair, in need of a decent cut, thought Gemma, was almost as wet as her own. He leaned over the bar and shouted something in Portuguese to the barman.

Gemma studied him surreptitiously. He was very attractive in a Mediterranean sort of way. She'd glimpsed brown eyes in a strong, tanned face as he'd raced up the steps. She wondered if he was a local fisherman. There were half a dozen boats drawn up on the beach and he had the sinewy arms and lean body of someone who did physical rather than mental work. He was barefoot, too, and Gemma had some idea that fishermen wouldn't bother with shoes. She grinned to herself. Maybe a hundred years ago, she thought, but now they probably wore technologically manufactured, enhanced-gripping power footwear. More likely, she told herself, he owned the bar and hated fish!

He turned round and caught her looking at him before she had a chance to look away.

'Hello,' he said. 'You get caught out too?'

She was so surprised at him speaking English – and with a hint of an Irish accent at that – that she was momentarily speechless.

He frowned. 'You're not English?'

'No,' she answered, when she had regained her wits. 'I'm Irish. Only I didn't realise – I thought you were a local!'

He laughed, throwing his head back and showing even, white teeth. She smiled cautiously.

'Would that I was,' he said.

'You speak Portuguese.'

'Badly,' he told her. 'I worked the Algarve for a summer while I was at college. I picked it up but not terribly well. I'm always saying the complete opposite of what I mean.'

She smiled again. 'I can't make head nor tail of it,' she said. 'It's all I can do to say *obrigada* and *bom dia*. And I know I don't pronounce it properly.'

'It's difficult,' he admitted. 'You kind of say everything through your teeth.'

'It hardly matters,' she said. 'They all speak such good English and German and French. It's embarrassing.'

'I keep telling them that English is much easier than Portuguese but they don't believe me.' He suddenly pulled off his T-shirt to reveal a well-built body, as tanned as his face. He wrung out the T-shirt and hung it over the back of a white plastic chair. 'I'm sorry,' he said, 'I just can't keep that on. It's too wet and too cold.'

'I know.' Gemma shivered although she wasn't sure whether it was because of her own wet clothes or because of the effect his body was having on her. I haven't seen a man like that in years, she thought, as she tried not to look at him. A gorgeous, attractive, sexy man who's exactly the sort of bloke I used to go for in a big way. She smiled to herself. She should have grown out of the casual surfer look by now. She knew how they turned out after all.

She leaned over the rail and looked up at the sky. 'I think it's easing off a little,' she said.

'I hope so.' He ran his fingers through his damp hair. 'I'm not good when it's cold.'

'Me neither,' said Gemma. 'I came here hoping for some warmth.'

'It's supposed to clear by late afternoon,' he said authoritatively. 'And I think it will.' He grinned at her. 'In the meantime, would you like a coffee? It'll warm you up and you look like you could do with some warming up.'

'Thanks,' said Gemma. 'That would be lovely.' She sat down, trying to ignore the fact that her shorts were still damp and uncomfortable.

'Here you are.' He set two cups of steaming coffee on the table then went back to the bar. 'And here's a little extra to help.' This time he put two glasses of brandy down.

'Thank you,' said Gemma. 'But—'

'Don't tell me you don't like brandy,' he said. 'It's a nourishing, warming drink.'

She laughed. 'I do like it, as a matter of fact,' she told him. 'But I don't drink it very often.'

'What do you drink?' he asked as he stirred his coffee. 'No, let me guess – white wine would be your thing, wouldn't it?'

'Wine?' Gemma shook her head. 'Well, sometimes. I'm more a beer drinker myself.'

'I had you pegged as a chilled white,' he said. 'Chardonnay. Or Frascati if you're feeling lazy.'

She laughed again. 'I'll come clean. At home I drink Chardonnay. But I also like beer. I'm not a fussy person.'

He grinned. 'You're a woman, aren't you? Women are always fussy.'

She blushed. An ageing mother of two children was what she was. She might be a woman but she didn't feel like the sort of woman he was talking about. Fussy women who drank white wine were tall and willowy, with blonde streaked hair. She knew them well – many of them frequented the hair salon! She wondered if he preferred willowy women who drank white wine to comfortable ones who swigged bottles of beer.

'You OK?' he asked.

She looked up from her coffee cup. 'Fine.'

'Sam,' he told her.

'Sorry?'

'My name. Sam McColgan.'

'Gemma Garvey,' she said.

'Nice to meet you, Gemma.' Sam lifted his brandy glass. 'Cheers.'

'Cheers.' She drank a mouthful of brandy. At once she felt it course through her body, radiating instant warmth. She coughed and Sam laughed.

'Firewater, isn't it?' he asked happily. 'It's the local brew. Absolute rotgut but fabulous when you're cold.'

'Interesting.' She sipped it more carefully this time.

'So are you on holiday, Gemma Garvey?' he asked.

She nodded.

'How long have you been here?'

'Only since yesterday,' she told him.

'So all you've seen are grey skies.' He smiled at her, his brown eyes full of sympathy. 'Never mind, I promise you things will be better by tomorrow. Rui says so.'

'Rui?'

'The barman,' he told her. 'This was one of my haunts in my misspent youth. Rui looks on me as the reckless son he doesn't have.' Sam grinned. 'Rui's son is a banker in Lisbon. Rui is very, very proud of him.'

'And you?' Gemma swirled the brandy in its glass. 'What do you do?'

'Oh, just admin,' said Sam dismissively. 'Nothing exciting, I'm afraid.'

'Where?' she asked.

178

'Dublin City University,' he told her. 'I'm on the organising side of things. I don't give lectures or anything like that.'

She looked at him curiously. 'Would you like to?'

'Me? Lecture?' He laughed.

'Why are you laughing?' she asked. 'What's so funny?'

'I wouldn't have the patience,' he told her. 'That's always been my problem.'

'What do you mean?' She took a sip of the brandy. It was doing a great job of warming her up.

'Nothing really.' He shrugged. 'My parents wanted me to study more when I was younger. They thought I had potential. I wasn't really into it, though. Did barely enough to get through Commerce. Dad was disgusted.'

'At least you qualified,' she said.

'Not quite good enough for my dad, though,' said Sam lightly. 'Good isn't enough. He wants great. And I think he had some vague notions that I could hack it in the world of academia.'

'Sounds awful,' said Gemma.

Sam smiled. 'Oh, I can't entirely blame him. Dad has a Mensa level IQ but, like lots of people his age, he left school with no qualifications and ended up working as a warehouse manager. He was very clever, but not smart. Less intelligent people than him moved through the ranks and Dad – well, he did OK in the end but I think he feels that he never gave it his best shot.'

'Which is why he thought you should become the academic torch bearer?'

Sam nodded. 'Terribly unfair, though. I think, in lots of ways, we all disappointed him. My sister gave up her high-flyer job when she got married. My brother, Malachy, turned down a job as Third Secretary in the Department of Foreign Affairs to work on a magazine.' He smiled. 'Dad's a bit snobbish about what we do, I guess.'

Gemma nodded in understanding.

'I don't know why I'm telling you this,' said Sam. 'I'm sure you've better things to do than listen to a complete stranger's life history!'

'Oh, I'm used to it.' Gemma grinned at him. 'I got a little of the same from my own mother after I left school. I became a hairdresser which she thought was "a lowering of my expectations"! I ask you! She thought "my daughter the bored-out-of-her-mind office worker" sounded better than "my daughter the hairdresser". Besides,' she said impishly, 'hairdressers are practically trained shrinks. You wouldn't believe the sort of stuff that people tell us when we have scissors in our hands.'

179

'Like what?' asked Sam.

'I can't betray client confidences,' she told him, her eyes dancing. 'I'd be disbarred!'

'I could do with getting mine cut.' Sam pulled at his hair. 'I never think about it.'

'It suits you like that,' said Gemma.

'Wet?'

She grinned. 'Long. Needs a bit of weight off it, though.'

'I bet that's what you say to all the boys.'

'Probably.' Suddenly she thought of him as a hunk again, and blushed.

'So what would you have done if you hadn't gone into hairdressing?' he asked.

She leaned back in her chair and clasped her hands behind her head. 'Nothing,' she said. 'It's all I ever wanted to do. Except I'd have liked my own salon but I have the business brain of a retarded newt.'

'I doubt that,' said Sam.

'It's true,' Gemma told him. 'But I have the next best thing. I work with a very close friend of mine and I enjoy it a lot.'

'Must be nice to really enjoy your job,' said Sam.

'Don't you?'

'Enjoy admin?' He looked at her scornfully. 'Who does! But I like working with the students and I get involved in other things.'

'Like what?' she asked. 'Mountaineering? Windsurfing? Athletics?'

'Why on earth would you think that?' he asked.

She blushed. 'It's just that you – you look like someone who works out a lot,' she said. 'When I saw you first I thought you—' she broke off in confusion.

'You thought I what?' he asked.

She bit her lip and looked at him from beneath her eyelashes. 'I thought you were a fisherman,' she admitted.

He laughed so much that his eyes watered. I'm glad I'm amusing him, she thought wryly.

'I tried fishing when I was here before,' he said. 'I was utterly useless at it. I felt guilty about the fish.'

This time it was Gemma who laughed.

'I do use the college facilities during term time,' he admitted. 'And I play a bit of tennis. But that's for fun. It's not working out.'

'Huh.' But she smiled.

'You know, the rain has stopped,' he said. 'And what's more, there's a patch of blue beginning to appear.'

180

'Really?' Gemma got up and leaned over the rail beside him. Her head brushed against his shoulder as she peered at the sky. 'That's a relief.' She moved away from him.

'You really feel badly about this rain, don't you?'

'Yes,' she said simply.

'I promise you it'll be better tomorrow.'

'If it's not, I'll blame it on you personally,' she told him.

'Anything planned?' he asked.

'Planned?'

'For tomorrow,' he said. 'When it's not raining.'

'I'm going to lie out in the sun,' she told him. 'I want to let the heat penetrate my bones and warm me up completely.' She smiled. 'That sounds very lazy. I'm sure you think I should be doing something more energetic.'

'Why?' he asked.

'To become commando fit – like you.'

He grinned at her. 'I'm not into GI Jane sort of women! I like mine with a little less muscle and a little more tenderness.'

She said nothing.

'Are you doing anything special this evening?' he asked.

'Oh, I'm sure I'm pretty busy,' she said hurriedly.

'That's a shame,' said Sam. 'It might have been nice to meet up for dinner later.'

She stared at him.

'If you don't want to, that's fine.' He swallowed the last of his brandy. 'But I'd like it if you did.'

Dinner! For the first time since David had left, a man had asked her to dinner. Actually, for the first time in years and years because, in the latter stages of their relationship, David hadn't taken her out to dinner at all. He hadn't taken her anywhere. She swallowed. She liked the idea. Especially the idea of dinner with someone who had brown eyes and a washboard stomach and who was easily the best-looking bloke she'd seen in ages and who . . . hang on, she told herself, get a grip. You can't go to dinner with anyone. You've got the kids to think about. She wondered how keen he'd be on dinner if he realised that she was the mother of two children, one of whom was now fourteen years old. She looked at him more closely. She couldn't go to dinner with him. Anyway, he was clearly younger than she was. She wasn't sure how much younger, but definitely younger.

'I'm sorry,' she said. 'I can't.'

181

'Ah.' He smiled wryly. 'Never mind.' He pushed his damp hair from his forehead and sat down again.

She wanted to change her mind. She wanted to say that she'd love to go to dinner with him. That there was nothing she'd rather do than sit in a restaurant and simply look at him. But she couldn't. Anyway, she told herself severely, she should have grown out of the holiday romance phase of her life a long time ago. Besides, despite the fact that he seemed so nice, it was more likely that he was like all the blokes she'd seen on *Ibiza Uncovered*! He probably kept a record of the number of women he picked up at beach bars on a chart hanging over his bed.

'I'd better get back,' she said. 'I've things to do.'

'Where are you staying?' he asked.

'Oh, an apartment block,' she said vaguely. 'The far end of the beach.'

He nodded.

'Thanks again for the coffee. And the brandy,' she said.

'Anytime,' he said.

'I hope not.' She laughed. 'I hope it won't be raining again.'

'I promise you it won't,' he said.

'I really have to go.' She picked up her bag.

'Maybe we'll meet again,' said Sam.

'Maybe.' She smiled brightly at him and hurried down the wooden steps. And pigs might fly, she thought as she trudged back along the beach.

Chapter 21

'We had a fabulous time!' enthused Keelin. 'It's brilliant – you go through a kind of jungle and everything!'

'And what did you do when it started to rain?' Gemma smiled at her daughter. She hadn't seen Keelin look as animated in ages.

'Luckily we hadn't started at that stage so Fiona's mum said we could have lunch. Then, after lunch, it got sunny.'

'And it was really hot,' Ronan said. 'Steam was coming off the ground.'

'Yes,' said Gemma. 'That happened here too.'

The sun had appeared about an hour after the torrential rain. Gemma had stood on the balcony of the apartment, turned her face to the blue sky and revelled in the warmth. But every time she closed her eyes she saw Sam's attractive, smiling face in front of her. She told herself how ridiculous it was, but she couldn't help it. She felt exactly the same way as she had when she'd first set eyes on David Hennessy. And much good that did you, she'd said out loud as she pulled up a patio chair and waited for the children's return.

'Anyway, Mrs Ferguson said that they're eating in the restaurant next door tonight,' said Keelin. 'She said we're to join them.'

'I thought we'd eat in tonight,' said Gemma.

'But Mum!' Keelin stared at her. 'It's my birthday. We have to go out for my birthday.'

'We could just go out ourselves,' suggested Gemma. 'The three of us.'

'We did that last night,' objected Keelin. Then she saw the expression on Gemma's face. 'I mean, it was fun, Mum, really it was, but . . .'

Gemma sighed. She'd looked forward to another evening with the children but she could understand how Keelin felt. And it was her birthday after all. She smiled. 'OK.'

'Great!' Keelin flung her arms round Gemma. 'Thanks. And it'll be fun for you too,' she told Gemma. 'You'll have Mrs Ferguson to talk to.'

'And her brother,' said Ronan.

'Oh, yes,' said Keelin quickly. 'Him too.'

Gemma looked at her daughter curiously but before she could say anything there was a knock at the apartment door.

Fiona Ferguson stood outside. 'Do you want to go for a swim?' she asked Keelin.

'It's OK, isn't it?' Keelin looked at Gemma.

'Sure,' said Gemma. 'Have fun.'

⌒

Maybe I'm getting it right at last, she thought as she gently brushed her hair. Maybe Keelin and I are moving onto the same wavelength. Maybe I'm not such a rotten mother. And, she thought as she remembered Sam McColgan, maybe I'm not a dried-out wizened old woman either. He must have liked her, even a little, to suggest dinner. She wasn't sure why he'd suggested it. It wasn't as though he'd seen her at her best – she'd been a sodden, shivering blob. A man like Sam – a good-looking man – wouldn't want to be seen with someone who was edging close to her sell-by date. She bit her lip as she thought of him in term time, surrounded by dewy-skinned students who probably were sparkling and witty and who didn't have stretch marks. Students who were even younger than Orla O'Neill with her damned clear skin and skinny body.

She hadn't thought about Orla in – well, a couple of days anyway. She couldn't help thinking about the leggy bitch, wondering how the marriage was going. It was frightening, thought Gemma, how often she wondered about David and Orla's marriage, how often she mused about the fact that they were so much more suited to each other than she and David ever were. Orla would understand when he came home late in the evenings. She'd be able to talk to him about 'with profits' policies and Peps and Pips and Pops or whatever the latest pension product was. She wouldn't be terminally bored with looking at target figures and she wouldn't be trying to tell him about the children's aches and pains and other moans.

I moaned all the time, Gemma told herself. It was my fault as much as his. She sighed and sprayed herself liberally with Clinique's Happy which she'd bought in the airport shop. The one thing that she'd changed forever after her divorce was her perfume. David had loved

184

the subtle floral fragrance of L'Air du Temps but after he'd left she'd never worn it again. Now she enjoyed experimenting with different scents. Happy had seemed appropriate for a week in the sun.

Ronan was sitting in the living room picking at a scab on his knee when Gemma was finally ready.

'Leave your knee alone,' she said automatically. 'Where's Keelin?'

'Still in the bathroom.' Ronan made a face. 'She's doing her face.'

'Doing her face!' Gemma looked at him in surprise. 'Keelin never does her face.'

'Well, she is now.' Ronan yawned.

The bathroom door opened and Keelin emerged. Gemma gasped as she looked at her daughter. Keelin had tied back her long, black hair and had fastened it with a bright orange scrunchie. She'd robbed some of Gemma's make-up and her skin was an even golden tan. She'd used the chocolate-brown eyeshadow on her eyes and a tiny amount of blusher on her cheeks. Her lips were painted coral pink. She wore her black denim jeans and a plain white T-shirt.

'You look – very nice,' said Gemma. She looked about seventeen, she thought frantically as she gazed at the tall, slim and elegant creature in front of her. Seventeen, and sophisticated. But she was only fourteen. And innocent.

'Thanks,' said Keelin. She smiled uncertainly at Gemma. 'Do you really think so?'

'Yes.' Gemma could still hardly believe the transformation. 'You make me feel ancient.'

'Why?'

'Because you look so much older like that.'

'Do I? Oh, excellent!' Keelin beamed and suddenly she was fourteen all over again.

'Would you like to borrow some of my perfume?' asked Gemma.

'Yes, please.' Keelin looked delighted and Gemma basked in her daughter's approval. She took the bottle out of her bag and gave it to her, trying not to wince as Keelin doused herself liberally with it.

'That'll keep the mosquitoes away,' said Gemma as she returned the bottle to her bag.

Keelin laughed and hugged her. Gemma suddenly remembered a moment when she'd hugged Frances. Her mother had bought her a Madonna single that she'd wanted. Gemma couldn't remember now which one it was but she'd been delighted when Frances had handed it to her. And she'd thrown her arms round her so that Frances had stepped back and told her that she'd crease her blouse. She hadn't thought about that incident in years. She hadn't even known that it was lodged in her memory.

She hugged Keelin back – fiercely, so that her daughter protested that Gemma was squeezing the life out of her. Gemma released her and kissed her on her made-up cheek. Keelin made a face at her.

The Fergusons were already in the restaurant by the time they arrived. Keelin waved frantically at Fiona and pushed her way through the tightly packed tables.

'Hi!' Selina stood up as they arrived. And so did her brother.

Gemma stared in shock at her brother while Keelin beamed at him. 'This is Bru,' she said. 'This is Fiona's uncle.'

'Hello.' Sam McColgan smiled at her. 'I didn't think I'd get to meet you again so soon.'

Gemma was unable to speak.

'Have you met before?' Keelin looked uncertainly between Sam and Gemma.

'We bumped into each other earlier,' said Gemma. 'Only I didn't realise—' She frowned and looked at him. 'Bru?'

'The kids always call me that,' he said. 'After the drink. You know – Irn-Bru? Even my sister calls me that from time to time. But my name is Sam.'

'I see.'

'Why don't you sit the other side of Sam,' Selina told Gemma. 'And Keelin, you sit opposite.'

'Oh, let me sit beside Bru!' Keelin squeezed into the empty seat and smiled happily.

Gemma bit her lip. She'd hoped that Keelin's tied back hair, make-up and the liberal use of Happy were not really for the benefit of Selina's sexy older brother although she'd been suspicious of Keelin's motives from the start. But how could she even have suspected that Selina's brother and Sam McColgan were the same person? Selina didn't even look very much like her younger brother. A brother who was much, much too old for Keelin. And too young for herself, though she found him so attractive. She looked at Sam and then at Keelin who was smiling up at him, an expression of adoration on her face. This isn't real, she thought. I can't really be in a situation where my daughter and I fancy the same man!

'Bru works in Dublin,' said Keelin. 'At university.'

'Really?' Gemma busied herself with her napkin. 'When did he tell you that?'

'This morning,' said Keelin. 'When you were snoring your head off in bed.'

Gemma felt her cheeks burn.

'He's good at tennis,' said Ronan. 'He can serve the ball really fast and it swerves.'

'He's brilliant at windsurfing too.' Fiona Ferguson broke in on the conversation. 'He tried to teach me but I keep falling off.'

'I'm afraid that everyone thinks Sam is wonderful,' said Selina dryly. 'It's a lot to live up to.'

'They only think I'm wonderful because I'm around when good things are happening,' said Sam. 'If they saw me every day they'd change their tune a bit.'

'We used to see you every day. I wish we still did,' Ian proclaimed. 'Then you could take me playing football.'

'Are you wonderful at that too?' asked Gemma tartly.

Sam grinned. 'Nope. But I'm bigger than him so I win. One day, it'll all be very different.'

The waiter came and took their orders. Gemma said the first things she saw on the menu, totally unable to concentrate.

'Did you dry out eventually?' Sam looked across the table at Gemma.

'Dry out?' asked Keelin.

'When I met Sam earlier it was raining,' explained Gemma. 'I got wet.'

'Your mum looked like a drowned rat,' said Sam cheerfully. 'Very unappealing.'

Keelin giggled. 'Nice to know you were at your best, Mum!'

The waiter arrived with their food. Gemma looked at the asparagus she'd ordered and knew that she wouldn't be able to eat any of it. She didn't even like asparagus!

She glanced up from her plate and realised that Sam was looking at her. She dropped her fork and it clattered to the ground. 'I'm sorry,' she said as she scrabbled under the table to find it.

'Clumsy,' said Keelin.

'I'll get you another.' Sam signalled to the waiter.

They seemed to be in the restaurant for hours. Gemma listened to the conversation going on around her but she couldn't say anything. She only barely managed to join in the toast to Keelin and almost choked when Sam called her the prettiest fourteen-year-old in the Algarve. Although, Sam said, when Fiona turned fourteen there might be a bit of competition. Keelin smiled at him in a new, sultry kind of way that

187

made Gemma want to drag her away from the table. Fiona smiled. The two boys fought over the last bread roll. Selina watched them tolerantly.

Later, they went back to the bar at the apartment block. Sam ordered drinks while Gemma and Selina sat at one of the tables and the children walked round the swimming pool, deep in conversation.

'Your brother seems too good to be true.' Gemma couldn't help blurting out the words. Part of her had wanted to sit in silence, not to show any interest, but the opportunity of finding out about Sam was one she couldn't pass up.

Selina grinned. 'About bloody time. He was a holy terror when we were kids. Always pulling my hair, putting spiders in my bed, scaring the life out of me.'

'The kids seem to love him,' said Gemma. 'Keelin thinks he's the best thing since sliced bread.'

'He's been great with them since Frank died,' said Selina. 'I was a complete mess for a while, Gemma. It was so sudden – one day he had a headache, the next he was in hospital. A month later . . .' She bit her lip.

'I'm sorry.' Gemma looked at her sympathetically. 'I didn't mean to upset you.'

'Oh, I need to talk about it now,' said Selina. 'I couldn't for ages. But now I kind of welcome the opportunity.' She heaved a sigh. 'When you lose someone, nobody quite knows how to behave with you. At the start they think you should be in tears all the time, only you're actually quite frozen and you can't cry. Later, when you want to, everyone thinks you should have got over it!' She smiled faintly. 'Don't worry, I'm not going to cry.'

'I don't mind if you do,' said Gemma.

'Thank you.'

The two women sat in companionable silence for a moment. Sam walked over and left the drinks on the table. 'I'll be back in a couple of minutes,' he said.

Selina picked up her glass and nodded to Gemma. 'Cheers.'

'Cheers.' Gemma clinked her glass against Selina's.

'Does Sam live with you?' she asked.

'Oh, goodness, no!' Selina looked at her in surprise. 'That's why the kids like to see him so much. No, he stayed with me for a couple of months after Frank died – and that was a real hassle for him because we live in Wicklow and it was a nightmare for him to travel up to Dublin every day, but he did it. At first I didn't think I'd want him to leave, but eventually I did. I wanted my own space back again. The kids were disappointed, though. Still, I keep telling them, he wouldn't be half as good to them if he was living there all the time.'

'As I said, too good to be true,' said Gemma.

Selina's eyes twinkled. 'You think so?'

'Paragon brother? Wonderful with kids? And, let's face it, Selina, pretty good-looking as I think Keelin has already decided.'

'They all hero-worship him,' said Selina. 'My two probably built him up for Keelin's benefit too. Kids are like that.'

'Somehow I don't think Keelin considers herself a child any more,' said Gemma dryly.

'She's going to be a hell of a good-looking woman.' Selina glanced across the pool to where Fiona and Keelin were standing together. Keelin was smiling, her face young and innocent, her long black hair flowing down her back.

'I know.' Gemma followed Selina's look. 'And I want her to be lovely, of course I do. But, right now, I think I'd prefer if she had braces on her teeth and bottle-top glasses.'

'Oh, Gemma!'

Gemma glanced at her. Selina's eyes, brown like her brother's, were full of amusement.

'He's much too old for my daughter,' said Gemma.

'Of course he is,' Selina agreed. 'But why are you worrying about them?'

'I'm afraid Keelin – well, what if she's attracted to him?'

'If she is it'd only be a crush,' said Selina. 'But I don't know what you're concerned about. She and Fiona spent their time on the crazy golf course eyeing up two German boys who were ahead of us. There wasn't a word passed between them about Bru. You're worrying about nothing, Gemma. Besides,' she smiled at Gemma, 'Bru wouldn't dream of encouraging her. He's had quite a bit of practice, you know, working in college. Because he looks OK, students are always falling for him. He lets them all down very gently. I promise.'

'I just don't want her hurt, you know.'

'Of course you don't,' said Selina. 'But I honestly think you're barking up the wrong tree, Gemma. Keelin's just practising being a teenager and Sam is the one she's practising on.'

'I hope so.' Gemma twirled the ends of her hair round her finger.

'Believe me,' said Selina. She leaned back in her chair and looked at Gemma appraisingly. 'Sam hasn't exactly been all that lucky in the female department.'

'Why on earth not?' asked Gemma.

'It's because of his looks,' Selina told her. 'Don't laugh, Gemma! I'm serious! Lots of women see him and think he's the man of their dreams and, of course, he isn't. Sam's a laid-back kind of guy. He likes interesting women, not pushy ones. But somehow he always seems to end up with the pushy ones.'

'I bet he doesn't say no, all the same.'

'Maybe not,' admitted Selina. 'But it's time he had a decent relationship again. The last one was a complete disaster.'

'Why?' asked Gemma.

'I'll let him tell you himself,' she said.

Gemma stared at her. 'I hardly think he'll have the opportunity to tell me.'

'No?' Selina looked at her appraisingly.

'Of course not!'

'He's really nice, my brother,' she said. 'He's a nice person, I mean. Not just easy on the eye.'

'Well, sure.' Gemma looked at her in confusion. 'Only you're getting the wrong end of the stick completely if you think – if you thought – that . . .'

Selina smiled as Gemma fumbled for the words.

'Anyway,' said Gemma as she regained her composure. 'I'm much too old for him.'

'Too old!' cried Selina. 'How old are you, for heaven's sake?'

'Thirty-five,' said Gemma.

'Gemma, Sam's thirty. It's five years. Nothing at all.' Selina's voice was scathing.

'I thought he was even younger,' said Gemma. 'But it makes no difference. You're getting it completely wrong, Selina. Really you are.'

⮑

Later in the evening a band set up and began to play. It was warm now, the clouds had long since disappeared, and the sky was studded with stars.

'Come on!' cried Sam, 'let's dance.'

The band was playing the Corrs, one of Keelin's favourites. Gemma watched while she twisted and turned in front of Sam. She looked very beautiful, thought Gemma. She'd never thought of Keelin as beautiful before. Until now, her daughter had just been difficult.

Gemma wondered whether Keelin would return to her beloved all black when she got home or whether she thought that this new look was more her style now. I knew, thought Gemma, that one day she'd turn into a young woman. I just didn't think that today would be that day.

She turned away from Sam and Keelin and danced with Ronan and Ian who were engaged in a kind of kick-boxing rather than dancing. I suppose he'll break someone's heart too, one day, thought Gemma. She found it hard to imagine some girl pining for the love of Ronan Hennessy, but it could happen!

After fifteen minutes' vigorous exercise she sat down and sipped her beer. Keelin and Fiona were each holding one of Sam's hands, twirling around him, laughing and smiling. Gemma swallowed a large mouthful of beer. She wished that the boys from the crazy golf course were around.

The band stopped for a break and everyone sat down again.

'I'm knackered,' complained Sam, 'those girls are just full of energy.'

'You're having a great time,' Fiona told him. 'Admit it, Bru!'

'I certainly am,' he said. 'Best holiday ever.' He smiled at Selina. 'How are you, sis?'

'Fine,' she said.

'And you?' He looked at Gemma who felt her heart flip over.

'Fine,' she said too.

'You sat down.'

'Yes, well, I'm not as young as I used to be,' she said. 'And all that jumping around was just too much.'

'Poor, ancient Mum!' Keelin giggled.

'We'll have to get her up when the music slows,' said Sam.

Gemma finished the last of her beer and shook her head. 'I don't think so,' she said. 'We'll probably head off to bed soon.'

'Not before you dance with me,' said Sam. 'At least once.'

'We'll see.'

'She doesn't want to dance,' said Keelin. 'She's a bit of a stick-in-the-mud, my mother.'

Is that how she sees me? wondered Gemma. A boring, predictable stick-in-the-mud?

'Come on.' Sam grabbed Gemma by the hand and dragged her to her feet as the band began to play 'I Will Always Love You'. 'Just one. Then I've got to dance with Keelin.'

'I was surprised when I saw you,' he told Gemma as he slid his arm

191

round her waist and drew her towards him. 'Though it was a pleasant surprise. And I got to have dinner with you after all!'

'Yes.' Gemma was conscious of his dry, warm hand on hers and the closeness of his body as they moved together.

'I would never have guessed that you had two kids,' he said.

'Well, now you know,' she told him. 'As Keelin told you, I'm ancient.'

'Hardly ancient.'

'Thirty-five,' she said sharply. 'Older than you, I believe!'

'Has my sister been ratting on me?' he asked. 'I don't remember telling you how old I was.'

'It came up in conversation,' said Gemma primly.

He laughed. 'Must have been a very interesting conversation if you got around to the topic of my age.' He held her more tightly and Gemma fought the urge to rest her head on his shoulder.

'We were talking about your childhood actually,' said Gemma.

'How do women do that?' asked Sam. 'You barely know each other and then suddenly you're telling each other stories about your childhood!'

'It's a girl thing.' She badly wanted to rest her head on his shoulder.

'Of course it might be your hairdresser psychological stuff, I suppose.'

'No,' said Gemma, 'it's a girl thing. Definitely.'

'Women fascinate me.' Sam held her more tightly. 'You're so bloody well in touch with everything!'

'My daughter is infatuated with you, you know.' Gemma's tone was suddenly brisk.

'Not really,' he told her. 'I get on well with kids, that's all.'

'Don't be so dismissive of her,' said Gemma sharply. 'She's not a kid either.'

'I'm not.' Sam looked down at her. 'Honestly. And I realise that she's growing up. I'm probably just the first adult male that's talked to her like an adult too.'

'She spent hours in the bathroom for your benefit,' said Gemma.

Sam smiled. 'I'm flattered. I like her, Gemma, she's chatty and bubbly and she's a nice girl.'

'This is the first time I've seen her chatty or bubbly since her father and I were divorced,' said Gemma.

'Oh.'

'She's at an awkward age,' Gemma added.

192

'Every age for a woman is an awkward age,' said Sam. 'Believe me, I know. I have a sister.'

'You might be right.' Gemma smiled faintly.

'I'm always right,' said Sam. 'And I promise you, Gemma, I absolutely promise you that I would do nothing to encourage your delightful daughter in any infatuation she might have for me.' He smiled at her. 'Not that I believe she's really infatuated anyway. She's just having fun.'

'Even so,' said Gemma. 'Please don't hurt her.'

'Oh, Gemma.' His eyes were soft. 'I wouldn't dream of hurting her. Or you.'

When the song ended she firmly disentangled herself from his hold and went back to the table where Keelin and Fiona were in deep discussion.

'So, Keelin.' Sam smiled at her. 'Will you do me the honour?'

Keelin had no qualms about resting her head on his chest. Gemma watched them, her mind in turmoil. She didn't want Keelin to be hurt but she was going to be. Sam was an adult. Keelin was a child. A child who had just discovered men, but a child all the same.

'You look worried.' Selina sat down beside Gemma.

'I'm truly afraid that she's fallen for your brother,' said Gemma anxiously. 'And she'll get terribly hurt.'

'Gemma, I promise you that she'll spot someone nearer her own age on the beach and she'll drop Sam like a hot potato.'

'I wish,' said Gemma.

'You worry about her a lot, don't you?'

'I just want to make sure I get it right with her, you know? She really hasn't had much adult male company. Whenever she meets her father it's in such an unrealistic setting that it makes a mockery of the whole male role model thing.'

'She's a lovely girl,' said Selina.

'I want everything to be easier for my kids.' Gemma rubbed her forehead. 'I don't want her to have a broken heart and spend months getting over the man who broke it.'

'And you?' asked Selina.

Gemma stared at her. 'I don't have anything to get over.'

'Don't you?'

'I've been divorced for a long time, Selina. I got over my husband ages ago.'

'But have you got over being divorced?' Selina poured some Vinho Verde into Gemma's glass. 'I think it must be really hard, Gemma.

193

When Frank died, I felt as though part of me had gone with him, corny though that sounds. But I could grieve for him and people let me grieve. Your marriage broke up and I'm sure it was pretty awful yet you still have to see your ex-husband and be civil to him. I can't imagine what that must be like.'

'Oh, you learn to live with it,' said Gemma lightly.

'And other men?' asked Selina.

Gemma shrugged. 'I don't have time.'

'Maybe you do now,' said Selina.

'I've had my fill of men.' Gemma shook her head. 'There's only so many times you can listen to the same shit before you realise that they're all the same at heart.'

'Oh, Gemma.'

She smiled. 'Maybe not all. But all the ones I pick. I promise you.'

'And Bru?'

'Selina, I know he's your brother and you're probably mad about him, but I've only just met him! And I'm not planning to run off with him or anything.' Gemma laughed.

'No?'

'Absolutely not,' said Gemma. 'And you've been drinking too much wine if you think anything else.'

Chapter 22

Orla sipped her glass of Bud and looked across the sea of people to where David leaned against the bar. He was talking to Avril Grady, the managing director's stunning raven-haired, blue-eyed personal assistant. Avril leaned towards David and put her hands on his shoulders. She whispered something into his ear and they both laughed. Orla's grip on her glass tightened.

'Hey, Orla!' Abby Johnson pushed past a group of men from the west Dublin sales team. 'Sorry I'm late, traffic was shit.'

'Hi, Abby. Can I get you a drink?'

'Gin and tonic,' said Abby. She looked around Scruffy Murphy's pub. 'Are all these people from Gravitas?'

'Yes.' Orla nodded. 'All come to wish me well even though I'm deserting the Gravitas ship.'

'All coming for free drink.' Abby grinned at her. 'Where's David?'

'Over there.' Orla waved in the general direction of her husband while she ordered Abby's drink.

'Good grief,' said Abby. 'Who's the girl?'

'Avril Grady. The office tart.'

'Orla!'

'Well, she is.' Orla grimaced. 'The girl's a menace. Every time we have a company do, she gets herself wrapped around someone.'

'Does she know David is married?' asked Abby. 'I mean, she's trying to play tonsil tennis with him.'

'I'm sure he's well able to look after himself.' Orla handed Abby her drink and turned to look at David and Avril again. David was leaning towards her now while her hand rested gently on his arm.

'Are you worried about them?' Abby followed Orla's gaze.

'No.' Orla shrugged. 'She does it all the time.'

'But not with David surely?'

'With anyone who stands in the one place long enough,' said Orla. 'Honestly, Abby, it's nothing.' She said the words lightly, as though she meant them. But she wished she believed them. She wished that she felt as secure in her love for David and his love for her as she had a few short weeks ago. Now she wasn't so certain. David had shrugged when she told him that she was taking the Serene offer. He'd wished her well, as though she was a complete stranger, and he'd asked her when she was handing in her notice because they'd want to get someone in straightaway. Business was booming at the moment, he'd said. They'd be extremely busy without her.

'You don't mind?' she'd asked.

'What?'

'That I'm taking the job?'

'You're a grown woman, Orla. You can do what you like. You don't need my approval or my permission.'

She'd wanted to shout at him then, and ask him why he was behaving so childishly, but she hadn't. She'd said nothing at all and he'd looked at his watch, told her he had a meeting with some clients and gone out. It had been nearly eleven by the time he'd come home again.

They were like two strangers in the house now, she realised as she looked at him and Avril. It was as though they'd never walked hand in hand along the beaches of the Bahamas, or made love in the back seat of his BMW, or shared popcorn and nachos at the cinema together. But why had it happened? Why weren't they able to talk about it?

'Will you miss us, Orla?' Nigel King, one of her team, came up to her.

'Not one little bit.' She grinned at him to show that she was joking. 'Nigel, this is Abby Johnson, a friend of mine.'

'Hi, Abby. You in sales too?'

'No, thank goodness,' said Abby. 'I even can't persuade my boss to give me a rise so I don't think I'd do very well as a saleswoman.'

'Do you need a personal pension?' asked Nigel.

'Nigel!' Orla dug him in the ribs with her elbow. 'Abby's my friend, not a prospect!'

'Suppose she's signed you up with Serene already,' said Nigel. 'Oh well, if you ever need anything . . .' He grinned at Abby and continued to walk across the room.

'Honestly,' said Orla. 'He's so pushy.' She glanced towards the spot where David and Avril had been. There was no sign of them. She felt her heart lurch and she scanned the throng of people anxiously.

'Are you all right?' Abby looked at her curiously.

'All right? Of course. Why?'

'Because you look worried,' said Abby, 'and generally people don't look worried when they're moving from their old job to a much better paid new one!'

'I'm not worried,' said Orla. 'I'm looking forward to it. Although it's a pain not being able to start straightaway. I have to do a week's training in Cork first.'

'That'll be fun,' said Abby.

'It's awful,' Orla told her. 'You have to sit around doing these role-playing games. You know, you're the client and I'm the sales rep and I have to make you buy a policy. I hate it.'

'It's a week away,' said Abby. 'I'd give anything for a week away.'

'Why didn't you go on holidays this year?' asked Orla.

Abby shrugged. 'No money. Don't forget, I was on my own in the apartment until Janet moved in and the rent was astronomical for one. I might get away in October.'

'You should.' Orla looked around the pub again. She still couldn't see David or Avril anywhere.

'I might get one of those late breaks,' said Abby brightly. 'You know, pay on Thursday go on Friday sort of thing. The difficulty will be getting someone to go with me.'

'What about Janet?' asked Orla.

'Oh, I need a break from Janet,' said Abby.

'Why?' Orla stopped looking around the pub and turned to her friend.

'She's irritating after a while,' said Abby.

'Don't you want to share with her any more?'

'Being truthful, probably not,' said Abby. 'But I don't know who else I can share with.' She smiled. 'You're so lucky you don't have to worry about that any more!'

'Yes, I am.' Orla's smile didn't get anywhere near her eyes.

'We must go out some evening,' said Abby. 'We haven't been out in ages.'

'Sure.'

'Orla, are you certain everything's OK?' asked Abby.

'Yes. Why?'

'Because I'm talking to you and you're answering me but I feel as though I might as well be talking to that damned potted plant over there!'

'Why?' asked Orla again.

'Because the lights are on but nobody's home!' cried Abby. 'I could say something like "I'm going to take all my clothes off" and you'd still nod and agree with me. You're not listening, Orla.'

197

'I am,' protested Orla half-heartedly. 'I've probably just had too much to drink, that's all.'

'Really?' Abby looked at her suspiciously.

'Really,' said Orla as earnestly as she could. 'We've been here since half five, Abby. It's almost nine now. So it's hardly surprising I'm a bit disconnected.'

'Oh, well, if it's only drink . . .'

'It's only drink,' lied Orla as she scanned the pub yet again.

⁓

She saw Avril first. The PA was feeding coins into the cigarette machine. Orla looked around for David but couldn't see him. She sighed with relief that at least he wasn't with Avril. Then she saw him coming out of the Gents and she cut across the pub to intercept him.

'Hi,' she said.

'Hello. Having fun?'

'Not much,' she told him.

'Why?' he asked. 'I'd have thought you'd be having a fantastic time. You've cut your links with Gravitas. You're going to a job with better basic, better bonus structure and a new car – and I don't know many girls that have had two new cars in a year!'

'You're right,' she said. 'All of that sounds great. All of that is why I took the job in the first place.'

'So, what's the problem?'

'You're the problem,' she told him. 'Why are you still treating me as though I'm some kind of traitor? It's my going-away drinks tonight and you've hardly spoken to me at all.'

'Orla, darling, I can speak to you any night of the week,' said David.

'But you don't.'

'What's that supposed to mean?'

'You don't speak to me. You've hardly said two words to me since I told you about the offer.'

'Don't be stupid,' he said.

'It's true. You're ignoring me.'

'How can I ignore you?' asked. 'We live in the same house.'

'Easily.' She was close to tears.

'Look, I wasn't very happy when you took the job, I'll admit that. But it was your choice, Orla, and I'm not standing in the way of your choices. That's it. End of story.'

198

She bit her lip. 'It doesn't feel like that's it. It feels like you still resent me.'

'Don't be utterly ridiculous,' he said. 'Why on earth should I resent you?'

'No reason,' she said shakily.

'So. There. You're being silly.'

'But, David—'

'Let's talk about this some other time,' he said. 'I really don't think it's appropriate for us to have a heart-to-heart in the middle of the pub, do you?' He kissed her lightly on her head and turned away. He walked straight over to the cigarette machine and Avril Grady.

There was a sledgehammer going off in Orla's head. She opened her eyes and closed them again. Even the dull light of the sun through the curtains was too much for her. She groaned as she rolled onto her side and waves of pain bounced around her skull. She opened one eye and peered at the clock.

It was a quarter past eleven. It was ages since she'd stayed in bed until a quarter past eleven on a Saturday morning. David was always out of bed early and this habit, which had shocked her at first, had eventually rubbed off on her. Since they'd married, she was usually up by half nine. It was impossible to sleep anyway with David clattering around the apartment, making breakfast, turning on the radio, rustling the newspapers.

But she couldn't hear him this morning. She pressed her hand to her forehead. By now he'd have finished breakfast and tidied up the kitchen. He'd have run through any appointments he'd set up for the day because he quite often had appointments on Saturdays. He'd have read the *Irish Times* and the *Observer*. And he'd no doubt have had dark thoughts about her who couldn't haul ass out of bed before now.

She eased her way out of the bed and pulled her white towelling robe round her. She slid her feet into her slippers, not looking down because she was afraid that her head would fall off if she did. Then she padded slowly across the room, pushed open the door and walked into the lounge.

David had left a note propped up on the table. Orla felt her heart pounding in her chest and her headache pounding in her head. She was afraid to pick up the note, afraid of what David had written.

She edged towards the table. You are being so silly, she told herself. Silly and childish and immature.

She picked up the note and focused on his writing with difficulty. 'Some appointments. Back by three.' There, she told herself. That's not so bad. He's coming home.

She flopped into the armchair and closed her eyes again. Why should she feel so relieved? Why had she allowed herself the faintest shred of doubt? How could she have possibly thought that he might not come home?

Because of Avril Grady, she told herself as she massaged her temples with the tips of her fingers. Because, after she'd spoken to him last night, he'd spent the rest of the night stuck to Avril Grady while Orla had drunk progressively more and more until she'd tripped over a handbag that someone had left on the floor and cracked her chin on the edge of a table. She remembered it more clearly now. She remembered a crowd of people gathering around her and someone – Abby? – asking where David was and eventually she remembered him helping her up and asking her was she hurt. But his tone had been brisk and practical. He hadn't asked her in the way he'd asked her when she'd burned her arm on the oven door. Or the way he'd asked her when she'd been bitten by a mosquito while they were in the Bahamas and her leg had swollen up horribly. Then he'd sounded tender and concerned. Last night he'd been annoyed with her.

She felt sick. They'd been married less than three months and already he was tired of her. How could it be? Surely she couldn't blame it all on her wanting another job? It was impossible to believe that it was simply because of the job. Was this what had happened with blobby Gemma? Had he just got tired of her? He'd always said that it was Gemma who asked for the divorce but maybe she'd felt forced to ask because she couldn't stand his indifference any more.

She got up and took some paracetamol. The pounding in her head began to subside. She had a shower and stood so that the spray hit her shoulders and eased the tension.

If it was all about the job then she would sit down with David and talk it through. Obviously he felt threatened in some way by her move and that was the problem. But they could talk about it – they'd promised each other before they were married that they wouldn't be afraid to talk things through. And she'd also talk through with him his totally unacceptable behaviour last night with Avril Grady. She'd been on her way to break up the duo when she'd tripped. That was why she hadn't seen the handbag, she'd been concentrating too much on David and Avril.

He couldn't really fancy Avril, though, could he? David wasn't so shallow as to be taken in by those full red lips and those artless blue eyes. Avril was as thick as two planks – everyone knew that the only reason Liam McDaid had appointed her was that she looked so spectacular. He didn't really need a PA at all. Until recently, he'd shared the administrative and secretarial help with his deputy.

The phone rang and she wrapped a towel round her. She picked up the receiver, hoping that it was David but wondering what on earth she'd say to him. He probably hadn't been overly impressed by her almost knocking herself out in the pub.

'Hi, Orla, it's me.'

'Oh, hi, Abby.' She tried to sound enthusiastic.

'How are you feeling?' asked her friend. 'I was worried about you.'

'Worried about me?'

'You gave yourself an almighty wallop last night. We all thought you must have broken your jaw at least.'

'No.' Orla touched her face gently. The area around her chin was slightly swollen but otherwise she was fine.

'Must have been the drink,' said Abby. 'You know how it is when you've had a few – you feel no pain!'

'I felt it this morning,' said Orla. 'It was as though an army of road workers was digging inside my head.'

'That was probably the fall as much as anything else,' Abby told her.

'Do you think so? I thought it was just because I was pissed out of my tree.'

'You'd had a few all right,' admitted Abby. 'It's ages since I've seen you get blitzed like that. Quite like old times.'

'Yes, well, my head feels rather too much like old times,' Orla said. 'I've taken some paracetamol and I feel a bit better.'

'Didn't David bring you orange juice and tablets in bed?' Abby teased.

'David is out with clients at the moment,' said Orla.

There was a brief silence before Abby said, 'Busy man, your husband.'

'Too busy,' said Orla, 'but I can't stop him.'

'He usen't to be like this,' Abby said. 'When you lived here he was on the phone to you every minute or else camping on our doorstep.'

201

'Things are a bit different now,' Orla told her. 'But he's still . . .'
Still what? she asked herself. Still mad about me? Still in love with me?
She closed her eyes.

'Orla? Are you OK?' Abby sounded anxious.

'I'm fine,' said Orla. 'It's just my head, Abby. I think I'll lie down for a while. David's due back soon and I'll wait for him to put cool towels on my forehead.'

Abby laughed. 'OK. Take care, Orla. I'll give you a ring next week.'

'Sure,' said Orla. 'I'll talk to you then.'

She replaced the receiver and then went to dampen a towel herself.

Chapter 23

Gemma lay face down on the sunbed and felt around underneath it for her sun cream. She couldn't be bothered to raise her head and look, she was so comfortable the way she was. But she could feel the scorching heat on the tops of her shoulders and she wanted to protect them from burning.

'This what you're looking for?'

She opened her eyes. Sam McColgan's brown eyes were inches from her own. She sat up hurriedly, sliding the straps of her swimsuit back over her arms.

'You didn't have to sit up,' he told her. 'I'd have rubbed it in for you.'

'Would you?' she asked.

'Of course.' He grinned at her. 'It would have been a pleasure.'

'Sorry to deny you,' she said. 'I can manage.'

'Don't be daft.' His voice was teasing. 'Nobody can put cream on their own shoulders.'

'How did you know I wanted it for my shoulders?'

'Easy.' He touched the top of her arm gently and she nearly shot off the sunbed. 'Little bit red just here.'

'Well, thanks.' She took the bottle from him.

'So would you like me to do this for you?' he asked.

'No. Really. It's fine.' She looked around the pool area. 'Where's everyone gone?'

'Selina's having a cup of tea in the café. Keelin and Fiona are at the tennis courts having a lesson. Ian and Ronan are playing football. There's just you and me here.'

Gemma fought the urge to reach out and run her fingers through his dark hair. She'd wanted to do it the first time she'd seen him, at the beach bar. She always wanted to do that when she was attracted to a man. She would imagine what it was like to touch their hair and to twist it around her fingers. She'd fallen for David Hennessy the moment he'd leaned his head back into the basin and she'd touched his long, black locks.

I fancy him, she thought. He makes me feel dizzy. It's a physical thing. I've stayed away from him as much as possible but it makes no difference. I really, really want to touch him.

'What time is it?' she asked.

He looked up at the azure blue sky. 'Four o'clock.'

'You can't tell by looking at the sky,' she protested.

'I'm telling you, it's four.'

She reached under the sunbed and found her watch. 'It's five to four,' she told him.

'Five minutes here or there isn't bad.' He laughed. 'The clock in reception must be slow. It was five to four when I walked out here.'

She made a face at him.

'Come on,' he said, 'Let me rub the cream on for you.'

'It's OK,' she told him. 'I think I'll join Selina for some tea.'

'Why don't you join me for a beer?' he asked.

She said nothing.

'The girls won't be back for an hour, their lesson has just started. The boys will be at least as long.'

'Selina is on her own,' protested Gemma.

'Sometimes Selina likes to be on her own,' said Sam.

Gemma glanced at him. Was he telling the truth or was this some ruse to get her to have a drink with him? Not that he had to resort to ruses to ask her for a drink. She sighed.

'Honestly,' he said as though reading her mind. 'She likes a little time to herself sometimes. Time to think, to grieve, you know.'

'Still?' asked Gemma.

'It was a great shock to her when Frank died,' said Sam. 'And a year isn't such a long time, after all. I was with her just before I came here. She's fine but she asked me to leave her alone.'

One drink wouldn't do any harm, thought Gemma, once Keelin didn't know about it. Keelin considered Sam, or Bru as she still called him, to be her personal property. She spent ages sitting beside him at the pool talking to him. Gemma desperately wanted to know what they were talking about but she was afraid to ask. When she took the children out in the evenings, Keelin would chatter on about Bru and how intelligent he was and how much he listened to her and took her seriously, and Gemma just worried more and more. She raised the subject with her once, asking her light-heartedly what she saw in Sam. Keelin had looked pityingly at her. 'He's an intelligent man,' she told Gemma. 'But he's fun to be with.'

'Do you – are you . . . ?'

'What?'

'Well, he's a lot older than you,' said Gemma.

'For heaven's sake, Mum!' Keelin's tone was exasperated. 'He's not my boyfriend or anything. He's nearly as old as you!'

But she still worried. While the children wanted to spend every evening with the Fergusons, Gemma had been firm about both families spending time on their own. 'We're on holiday, they're on holiday,' she told Keelin and Ronan. 'We don't have to be in each other's pockets all the time. You see the Fergusons enough all day.' And they saw far too much of Sam as he walked around in his Day-Glo shorts, his stomach firm and taut, his arms and legs strong and muscular. Half the women around the pool nudged each other every time he walked by.

'So?' He looked inquiringly at her.

A beer would be nice, she thought. She smiled suddenly. She was on holiday too. 'OK.'

'Great!'

He waited while she pulled a lime-green T-shirt over her head and slid into her black shorts. She held in her stomach as she pulled the shorts over the swimsuit. If she didn't join a gym she'd definitely buy one of those ab machines. She couldn't go through the rest of her life with a pot belly. She just hadn't tried hard enough to get rid of it before.

She folded her blue and white checked towel and left it and her book on the sunbed. She'd almost finished *The Company She Keeps*. She sincerely hoped that Kira O'Brien would get it all in the end. The man, the money and the company. Gemma thought it was about time that women had it all.

'Come on, then.' Sam ushered her ahead of him. His hand touched her back. She tried to ignore the frisson of electricity that shot through her. This is a holiday thing, she told herself. This has happened to you before. It happened in Torremolinos with Jack Martin who you never saw again. It happened in Majorca with that English bloke. It's the sun and the sand and the feeling of freedom. It's not for real.

'Would you like to walk a bit first?' asked Sam. 'I thought we could go to Rui's bar.'

'If you like,' said Gemma.

They walked down to the beach. The sea was calm today, bright blue against the pale sand. Although the beach was crowded further along, this patch was quiet. Sam didn't speak and Gemma didn't feel the need to talk. They walked in companionable silence along the water's edge.

'Reminds me of – who were they – Burt Lancaster and Deborah Kerr, was it, in *From Here to Eternity*,' said Sam.

'I never saw *From Here to Eternity*,' said Gemma. 'My mum liked it, though.'

Sam laughed. 'Great beach scene between Burt and Deborah, but no point in talking about it if you haven't seen it. I like old movies,' he added. 'Most of the women had much better roles than they have now. Katharine Hepburn, for example. Or Bette Davis. Much stronger than Julia Roberts or Cameron Diaz.'

'Possibly,' Gemma agreed.

'Oh, definitely,' said Sam.

They lapsed into silence again. Gemma enjoyed the warmth of the air, especially now that the sun wasn't at its strongest. I'm walking along a beach in Portugal with an attractive man, she told herself. On my own. As though we were – as though . . . She couldn't quite complete the thought.

Rui's bar was busy, but there was a free table on the deck. Sam shouted a greeting to Rui who brought them out a couple of beers.

'You look much better today,' he told Gemma. 'Not all wet, no?'

She smiled. 'No. And I feel much better today!'

'It was bad news for you to be here in the rain,' said Rui. 'But since that day – glorious sunshine, especially for you.'

'Thank you,' said Gemma. 'It has been wonderful.'

'And you have found a nice man in Sam.'

Gemma blushed. 'He's a very nice man.'

'I love him,' said Rui. 'As much as my own son!'

'Give it a rest, Rui,' said Sam easily.

'Oh, OK.' Rui grinned. 'I just thought I would put in the good word for you, Sam.'

Gemma giggled and propped her feet up on the edge of a wooden flower tub.

'Sorry,' said Sam. 'He gets a bit carried away sometimes.'

'I like him,' said Gemma. She sipped the beer and looked out to sea. There were still lots of people splashing about in the water. It doesn't take much to make people happy, she thought suddenly. A bit of warmth, a splash of water and that's it!

'Restful.' Sam's voice broke into her thoughts.

'Actually I was thinking how happy people were,' said Gemma.

'People generically or anyone in particular?' asked Sam.

She gestured towards the beach and sea. 'Those people,' she said. 'Carefree. Even if it's only for two weeks.'

'And what about you?' asked Sam. 'Have you been carefree this week?'

She put the glass on the table. 'Mostly,' she said carefully.

'When not?' asked Sam.

'Oh, you know. When I see you and Keelin together.'

'Gemma, we've been through this,' said Sam. 'Keelin is a nice girl. She enjoys talking to me. She – she sees me as a kind of father figure. Don't laugh at me!'

'I'm not laughing,' said Gemma seriously.

'I don't mean that she sees me like her father or anything, but I think she just likes talking things over with a man instead of getting the female point of view all the time. And she sees me as a grown-up, Gemma. Not a potential boyfriend.'

'But she gets made-up for you,' protested Gemma. 'Every evening the kids want to know if we can go out with you and Selina.'

'Have you spoken to her?' asked Sam.

'Once or twice,' admitted Gemma.

'And?'

'Oh, she pretends not to care about you,' said Gemma.

'That's because she doesn't,' Sam told her. 'There's a lot more interesting guys around here than me for her to think about.'

'I hope you're right,' said Gemma. 'I don't want her heart broken.'

'I'm sure it will be,' said Sam, 'but not by me. And I bet she'll do her fair share of heartbreaking when she's a little older. Just like I'm sure you did.'

'Not at all.' Gemma looked wistful. 'I got married too young, really.'

Sam looked at her carefully. 'And why did you divorce him?' he asked.

'Loads of reasons,' she said. 'Mainly because our priorities had changed. He became a workaholic. I became a mother. Both of us forgot why we'd married in the first place.'

'And why was that?' asked Sam.

'Sex.'

'What!' He stared at her and she laughed.

'We both fancied each other like mad,' she told him. 'But it's not enough, is it? You have to want the same things from life. I thought we did, at the start. But in the end, we didn't.'

'And what made you decide?' asked Sam. 'If you don't mind talking about it.'

Funny, she didn't mind talking to him about it. Even though she fancied him like crazy on one level, on another he was just so easy to talk to.

'I think I'd decided long before the event,' she said. 'But I heard him on the phone to a colleague of his. He was meeting her. In her house.'

'Oh,' said Sam.

'I was feeling particularly low at the time,' said Gemma. 'I'd put on tons of weight after I had Ronan and I just couldn't shift it. This colleague of David's, Bea, was a damned sylph. He made some comment to her about my size and I flipped. If I'd still loved him, I wouldn't have.'

'He sounds like a shit,' said Sam.

Gemma sighed. 'He's not really. People change, that's all.'

'So did you ever love him, do you think?'

'Oh, yes,' said Gemma firmly. 'I really and truly did love him. But he was never there, always working. And he was doing it for us, that's the worst of it. He made lots and lots of money and he thought it was enough, but it wasn't.' She clasped her hands behind her neck. 'I married him because I thought he'd want to be with me forever. But he didn't. To be honest, I don't think he was that upset when I told him I wanted a divorce.' She smiled slightly. 'Do you know, that hurt my pride more than anything. I wanted him to say that we could work it out, that he'd change, that it'd all be different. But he didn't. He told me not to be ridiculous. After a while, he tried the "it'll all be different" turn of phrase but it was too late by then.' She sighed. 'But I still wonder if I did the right thing for the kids. I know I did for me, but maybe I should have stuck it out for them.'

'Keelin wonders about that too,' said Sam.

'I know.' Gemma nodded. 'We've talked about it a lot. She asks if he'd ever come home and I tell her no. I think, in her heart of hearts, she understands, but sometimes she thinks that it would be nice to have him at home.'

'He's married again,' said Sam shortly. 'Doesn't sound like he's planning on it.'

Gemma laughed. 'I know. And so does she. Also, Sam, I lied when I said him not being too upset hurt my pride more than anything. Him getting re-married did. Funny, it took me ages to get over that.' But I am over it, she realised suddenly. I don't mind that he's got someone else. I did. But I don't any more. She was surprised to suddenly feel this way. She thought about it again, pictured him sitting beside Orla, talking to her. It didn't hurt. At all. She imagined them

208

holding hands. Him kissing Orla. Her kissing him back. Nothing. She smiled.

'What?' asked David.

She looked inquiringly at him.

'What are you smiling about?'

'Nothing,' she said. 'I'm just thinking that – that David does love the kids.'

'They're good kids.' Sam looked at her curiously. 'Ronan is so cheerful and warm-hearted. Keelin is smart. Of course he'd love them.'

'Don't break Keelin's heart,' begged Gemma. 'I know you don't think she's in love with you. But just in case.'

'Gemma, her heart isn't mine to break,' said Sam. 'And if you must know, Fiona and herself keep a list of the desirable men they've seen on the beach each day. I don't even feature on the list!'

'Promise?'

'I swear,' he said solemnly. 'Can I get you another drink?'

She hadn't realised that her glass was empty. She nodded.

'Anyway she's much more assured than I was at fourteen,' said Sam when he returned with another couple of beers. 'She's got men pegged, I can tell you. At her age, I was afraid to talk to girls!'

'They probably fancied you from afar,' said Gemma.

'The ones I liked had blokes swarming all over them,' said Sam. 'I didn't get a look in.'

Gemma frowned. 'I would have thought you'd have your fair share.'

He shook his head. 'I was too bloody academic in those days,' he told her. 'Dad made sure I studied and I did. It wasn't until I left school that I realised there really was more to life! But at fifteen I didn't go to all of the social things you're meant to go to and I got this reputation of being a swot. And nobody was interested in me.'

'Actually, I bet a whole load of girls were madly interested in you,' Gemma told him. 'All of those girls who thought that they were sensitive types and didn't have much time for clubs or whatever themselves. They probably looked at you and said, there's the man for me. Tall, dark, handsome and intellectual to boot. An absolute dream.'

'I don't think so.' He smiled. 'I had dreadful spots.'

Gemma laughed.

'You know, I've been trying to make you laugh all week,' complained Sam, 'and the only time you do, it's to mock my youthful infirmity.'

She laughed again. 'Sorry.'

'I bet you were the sort of girl who had blokes flocking around her in droves,' said Sam.

'What makes you say that?' Gemma sat up straight and pulled in her stomach again. She'd buy that ab machine as soon as she got back. It was appalling how slack her muscles were.

'You look like the sort of person who would be fun to know,' he said.

She looked at him through narrowed eyes. 'Do you mean I look like the kind of girl who'd have got her kit off?'

'No!' He looked horrified. 'I didn't mean that at all.'

'That was the kind of girl that most blokes wanted to know at my school,' Gemma said.

'You must have gone to a much more progressive school than me,' he told her. 'I meant you're attractive, Gemma. That's all.'

'Don't bullshit me.' She drank some beer.

'Why is it bullshit?' he asked.

'Look, Sam, I like you. I think that you're pretty attractive. I can understand how women are besotted by you. You're a nice bloke and you've been good to my kids. But don't make fun of me. Please.'

'Gemma, you're the most insecure person I've ever met.' Sam took her hand in his and she almost jumped out of the chair. His touch was warm and gentle. 'Why do you talk about yourself as though you're the wrong side of forty and in rapid decline? Not,' he added, 'that there's anything wrong with being forty either! One of my very best female friends is nearly fifty!'

'I don't talk about myself as though I'm in a rapid decline,' said Gemma as she wondered about Sam's nearly fifty best female friend. Who was she? What did she look like? Did he have a thing about older women?

'You do,' said Sam. 'You look in the mirror and you see all your bad points. I look at you and I see a good-looking woman, with a wonderful smile and the kind of body I dream about.'

'Oh, come on!' She slid her hand out of his. 'Let's say I'm good-looking – subjective though the call is – but the kind of body you dream about?'

'Curvy,' said Sam.

She began to laugh.

'What?' he asked.

'Ronan says it's squishy.'

He grinned. 'No, it's not. It's curvy.'

'To me, squishy means fat.'

'Gemma, no matter what yardstick you use, you're not fat! You're just right. Really, you are. I don't know why women are so obsessed with

210

looking like twigs. Selina is always going on about her bloody weight. You're perfect.'

She looked at him. 'I do like it when you say things like that.'

'I mean it,' he said. 'I really do.'

What would he be like in bed? she wondered. What would it be like to have him undo the buttons of her dress one by one until it fell onto the floor? What would it be like to slide his shirt from his shoulders? What would it be like to feel the heat of his lips on hers and the force of his body beside her. And what would it be like, she asked herself viciously, when he saw her damned Caesarean scar on her flabby stomach! He might like curvy but he sure as hell didn't mean a curvy bloody stomach!

'What are you thinking?' he asked.

'Nothing,' she said.

'It looked deep.'

She shook her head. 'Not at all.'

'Have you ever considered getting married again?'

The question was so unexpected that she nearly choked on her beer. She spluttered and coughed while Sam looked at her anxiously.

'You OK?' he asked when she'd finally composed herself.

'Fine,' she said.

'Well?'

'Well what?'

'Have you?'

She stared out to sea. She hadn't and that was the truth. She'd hardly thought about men at all since she'd left David. And she'd been young then. She could have met men but she hadn't wanted to. Hadn't felt there was any point.

'No,' she said.

'Why not?'

'Somebody once said that when a man gets a divorce, he gets it for another woman. When a woman gets a divorce, she gets it for herself.' Gemma drained her glass. 'I got the divorce for myself. It would hardly make any sense for me to jump right back into the same frying pan again, would it?'

Sam laughed. 'I suppose not.'

'And what about you?' Gemma couldn't believe she'd asked him the question. 'Have you got anyone special in your life?'

Sam heaved a deep sigh. 'Not any more. I went out with a girl for six months last year. A really nice girl. Curvy.' He grinned at Gemma. 'Smart. Sassy. And desperately dying to jump into marriage. I didn't realise it straightaway, of course. Sometimes I think that men are pretty

211

dense about things like that. But suddenly I realised that she was talking about houses and furniture and holidays abroad all the time.'

'And, after six months, you weren't ready for it?'

'I would never have been ready for it with her,' said Sam. 'Lovely and all though she was.'

'Maybe you're not a commitment sort of bloke,' said Gemma. 'If you've reached the ripe old age of thirty without being ensnared.'

'Maybe not.' He made a face. 'But Lauren didn't see it like that. She wrote to me. Rang me up. Called around to my house. It was a nightmare.'

Gemma stared at him. 'She stalked you?'

'Not quite,' said Sam. 'But she just couldn't get over it.' He shuddered. 'Turns out she had this – thing – about being married before she was thirty.'

'And how did you stop her?' asked Gemma.

'I didn't,' said Sam. 'She went abroad for a year. Something to do with work. I was never so damned grateful about anything in my life.'

'I'll bet,' said Gemma.

She didn't want to marry him. But she would give anything to go to bed with him. The thought shocked her. It had been so long since she'd felt like this that she thought that there was now something wrong with her. She thought that she'd never be able to feel that type of desire again. But, sitting beside Sam, looking at him, being close to him, it was hard not to want to sleep with him. Rather fortunate, she thought, that it would be utterly impossible since she was sharing an apartment with her two children. Anything more effective at dampening down passion than a couple of kids had yet to be invented.

'What do you do when you go home?' asked Sam.

'Do?' she asked.

'In your spare time,' he said. 'What do you do socially?'

She laughed at him. 'My social life is an arid desert,' she told him. 'When I'm not working, I'm bringing the kids places. Not so much Keelin any more, I guess, but Ronan plays football for the local under-twelves and that will have started up again by the time we get home.' She shuddered. 'I stand on the sidelines in freezing weather and shout things like "Offside, ref" when I haven't a clue what it means! And I'll tell you something, if you want to see naked pride and ambition, stand with parents at a kids' soccer match!'

Sam laughed. 'But there must be things you like doing,' he said.

'I read a lot,' said Gemma. 'My favourite time of the day is in the evening when they've gone to bed. I sit in front of the TV and I read.'

'What do you—'

'Mum! Mum! There you are!!'

She turned round at the sound of Ronan's voice. He was running along the beach waving at her.

'What?' she cried. 'What's the matter?'

'Nothing,' he gasped as he reached the bar. 'We didn't know where you were. I wanted some money to buy ice cream. Ian's mum said that you might have gone for a walk with Sam.'

'Did she?' asked Gemma. 'Why did she think that?'

'Because Sam wasn't around either. And he told her he was going to take you for a walk.' Ronan looked at her impatiently.

'I see,' said Gemma.

'I told you I'd been with Selina before I went to the pool,' said Sam.

'I know,' said Gemma.

Ronan looked from one to the other. 'Well?' he asked. 'Can I have some money, Mum? Can I?'

She picked up her bag and handed him some money.

'Thanks!' he said. 'Keelin was looking for both of you too. I'll tell her you're here, will I?'

'No,' said Gemma. 'It's OK, Ronan. We were just having a drink and we're finished now. We'll walk back with you.' She stood up.

'Great,' said Ronan. 'Hey, Bru, do you want to play volleyball in the pool? There's going to be a game later.'

'Sounds fun,' said Sam.

He followed them down the steps of the wooden deck and back along the beach.

Chapter 24

'Have you got your solutions?' asked David.

Orla looked up from her travel bag. 'Solutions?'

'For your lenses.'

'Yes.' She zipped the bag closed. 'I have everything.' She lifted the bag from the bed and carried it into the living room. David followed her.

'It's early,' he said. 'Would you like another cup of coffee before you go?'

Orla shook her head. 'No, thanks. It'll only mean I have to stop somewhere along the way and I'd rather keep driving.'

'You will take care, won't you?'

'Of course.' She pulled her navy sweatshirt over her head.

'You'll be there before anyone else.'

'Doesn't matter.' Her voice was muffled from beneath the fleecy top. 'It'll give me time to settle in. And I think they've got a swimming pool and sauna in the hotel. I'll find things to do.'

'What time is your dinner tonight?' he asked.

'Seven.'

David looked at his watch. 'It's only twelve now, Orla. Are you certain—'

'Honestly, David,' she interrupted him. 'I want to go now. I really do.' She shook her hair out of her eyes. 'It's a four-hour drive to Cork.'

'OK,' said David. 'I'll carry this to the car for you.'

'Fine,' said Orla.

She picked up her keys from the table. She was looking forward to her week's training in Cork. Even though she was sure the sessions themselves would be pretty boring, she needed to get away from the apartment and from David. It was extraordinary, she thought, how he'd suddenly become anxious about her, now that she was going away for a week on her own. They'd barely spoken to each other since

214

Friday night and now, because she was going somewhere without him, he'd become solicitous. She would've thought he'd be glad to see the back of her for a while.

She watched him place her bag into the boot of the Honda. He looked tired. All the late nights working or nipping into the pub for a drink before he came home were taking their toll. If only he'd bloody talk about it! If he'd listen to her explain why she needed to change jobs! She gritted her teeth. She didn't owe him an explanation. She'd tried to explain but he hadn't listened then so why would he listen now?

She opened the driver's door.

'Drive carefully,' said David.

'Yes,' she said. 'I will.'

He might be feeling more solicitous, she thought, as she eased the car out of the parking space, but he still didn't bother to kiss me goodbye. She swallowed the lump that had formed in her throat. A few weeks ago he wouldn't have let her go anywhere without making love to her first. Sod him, she thought, as she turned on 98FM. I'm going to enjoy being away for a while.

When he got back to the apartment David changed the sheets on the bed and straightened the duvet. Then he made himself a cup of coffee and took a doughnut from the bag that Orla had bought yesterday. He'd almost lectured her for buying the doughnuts – what was the point in paying for half a dozen when she wouldn't be around to eat them? But he'd said nothing, conscious that Orla was like a cat on a hot tin roof at the moment, and very aware that he was partly to blame for the frostiness that had sprung up between them.

But it was her fault, he thought, as he sat down at the table and gazed out over the bay. She hadn't told him about the job. She hadn't told him about meeting the sales director of Serene Life. David knew Bob Murphy quite well and he hated to think that Bob had been talking to his wife about a job and he hadn't known about it himself. He could have bumped into Bob anytime and looked a complete fool. Five days. OK, so he could allow her having to think about it for a few hours on her own, but five days! The whole idea of being married to someone, surely, was that you sat down and talked about big decisions with them? And he was the ideal person for Orla to talk to. Not only her husband, but someone who had turned down three offers from Serene Life in as many years. He would have been able to tell Orla that Bob Murphy really wanted David Hennessy but knew that he was never going to get him. He would have told her that Bob would probably pressurise her into trying to find out about his contacts and prospective clients.

He would have been able to point out that, in all probability, Serene Life were using Orla to get at him.

But she hadn't told him for five days and by that time she'd already decided to take the job. She'd pretended that she was still thinking about it, but David had seen in her eyes that she really wanted to give it a go. He'd have been happy for her to give it a go with anyone else. But not Serene Life.

He sighed and drained his coffee. Orla was so ambitious, he thought. Sometimes she seemed so much older than her twenty-four years. She'd talk about pensions and benefits and illness as though she'd experienced them all. She could deal with older people without them resenting her – he'd had a problem with older people when he'd started out. She hated it when she didn't get anything from a client. She sulked and took it personally. David was always telling her not to take it personally, to learn from the experience, but she couldn't.

He got up and leaned against the patio door. She didn't need to push herself so hard. He knew that she wanted to earn as much as he did, to contribute equally, as she put it, to the running of their home together, but he didn't want her to. It wasn't that he was so old-fashioned that he believed she should be sitting at home all day waiting for him, but he wanted to be the one who was in control of the finances. He wanted to earn more than she did so that, even when he was handing over a huge slice of his monthly income to Gemma, he would still be providing for Orla. Was it so wrong to feel like that?

Gemma had never cared who earned more. When they'd married first, she actually brought home more money than he did. Her take-home pay was derisory, but she got very generous tips from all her clients which, in their first months together, meant she was the main source of income. But once his career had taken off, once he'd strung a few good sales together, David had realised that there was a lot of money to be made in selling pensions. He set himself targets – to bring in as much as Gemma. To bring in a little more than Gemma. To bring in twice as much as Gemma. And then, finally, to earn so much that Gemma could stay at home with their baby daughter and be there for him when he came home himself.

Gemma hadn't minded that lifestyle, or so he thought. She'd been quite happy to give up work after Keelin had been born. She'd thrown herself into the whole house and mother thing and she'd been good at it. When he got home she'd have the dinner ready and start telling him about the things that had happened during the day. But he hadn't wanted to listen to her talking about Keelin's teething problems or the leaky washing machine. He'd wanted to talk about how much commission he'd just earned on selling a bells-and-whistles policy to a wealthy client. That had been so much more real to him than Gemma's trivial conversation.

And she'd nagged at him so much. Day in, day out, always complaining. He couldn't understand it when he'd provided so much for her. Especially when he'd become top salesman and had reaped the benefits of their rewards system by getting free holidays abroad for himself and Gemma. She'd enjoyed the holidays but she just didn't seem grateful enough.

Why was it, he asked himself, that no matter what he did, nobody seemed grateful enough?

Gemma had been grateful about the holiday to Portugal, though. He'd felt particularly pleased with himself when he heard the pleasure in her voice as he agreed to pay for them. She must have doubted that he would fall for the 'it's Keelin's birthday' line but he agreed with Gemma that the children should have as many opportunities as any other kids. He smiled as he recalled the surprise and elation in Gemma's voice when he'd said yes.

It hadn't been a bad marriage, he thought, as he rinsed his cup under the tap. It had just gone wrong somehow. They'd both made it go wrong, although – and Gemma had never stopped pointing this out – he'd dealt it the final blow.

What would have happened, he wondered, if she hadn't picked up the phone and heard him talking to Bea Hansen? Bea had been on his team at Gravitas at the time. She was a tiny little thing, five feet tall, weighed around seven stone, with big grey eyes and soft brown hair. Gemma had met Bea a number of times and she liked her a lot. But she hadn't believed him when he'd told her that the bantering between them meant nothing.

'You said you couldn't wait to see her!' She'd stared at him in shock. 'You said you'd make an excuse to get out of the house.'

'It wasn't like that,' he'd replied feebly.

'You said that at least in her house there was room for two people on the sofa.' She'd looked down at her nonexistent waistline and started to cry.

The thing was, she'd been wrong about Bea and him. Sure, there'd been a bit of chemistry between them. Sure, he'd liked being with his colleague. Sure, he kissed Bea once or twice on the lips, but only fleetingly and never with the promise of anything more to come. But Gemma had freaked out completely and told him that if he liked his job so much that he had to shag the women who worked with him, he could keep it. And them. No amount of apologising or explaining or being nice to her had made any difference. It was as though he'd passed a mark which Gemma had set and, having passed it, he couldn't come back.

He hadn't wanted to leave Gemma and the children. He'd wanted to work it out. But if he hadn't left Gemma he wouldn't have met Orla. And Orla was the woman he'd always dreamed of meeting.

What would have happened, though, if Gemma had said, 'All right, let's forget about Bea'? Would he still be married to her? Would he be coming home from Portugal today with his wife and two children?

He looked at his watch. They were due back sometime in the afternoon; he remembered checking the times with Gemma before they left because there'd been the question of whether or not he'd get to see them today. He hadn't seen them last Sunday because their flight had been early in the morning. He wondered whether or not Gemma had organised someone to meet them and bring them home. He picked up his Filofax and flicked through the pages. They were due in Dublin at three o'clock. Perhaps, he thought, he should go and meet them. That would be a nice surprise.

∽

It was nearer five when their flight touched down. Gemma sighed with relief because Keelin and Ronan had spent most of the time squabbling with each other. Keelin's veneer of sophistication had disappeared now that she was alone with her brother again and she wasn't trying to impress Sam McColgan, although she'd still made an effort with her hair and had robbed Gemma's Happy perfume once more. Gemma had bought another bottle at Faro airport on the way home and had given the first bottle to Keelin. 'But not to be worn to school, madam,' she'd said and then felt a warm glow of happiness when Keelin had told her that she was the greatest.

The glow of happiness had gone now. There had been something so unreal about the week in the sun. Keelin had blossomed, Ronan had worked off all of his excess energy and she'd allowed herself to relax as totally as she could.

And there'd been Sam. Every time Gemma thought of Sam she glanced at Keelin. How right had Sam been about Keelin? Did she really just enjoy talking to him because he was an adult who, she believed, understood her? Or was it just that her daughter had fallen for someone sixteen years older than her?

She remembered the first time she'd fallen for someone other than David Essex. Until she'd seen Les Freeman – a year ahead of her in school – she'd been devoted to David Essex. Posters of the tousle-headed pop star were plastered all over her bedroom wall. But when she first noticed Les Freeman, all that changed. And then, every time she saw him, her heart would tumble over in the most unnerving way. She'd lost tons of weight because food had seemed so unimportant. Well, she thought grimly, Keelin better not lose any weight over Sam McColgan. She doesn't have an ounce to spare.

'What?' Keelin glared at her as she undid her seat belt.

'Nothing,' said Gemma. 'Nothing at all.'

'Now that we're home I suppose you're going to start getting at me again,' said Keelin mulishly.

'Don't be ridiculous,' said Gemma. 'Come on, Keelin. We've had a great time. Haven't we?'

Keelin flashed her blue eyes at her mother and suddenly smiled. 'Yes, we did.' She retrieved her bag from beneath the seat in front of her. 'It was great of Dad to pay for it, wasn't it?'

'Wonderful,' said Gemma dryly.

'And it was great to meet Fiona and Ian.'

'And Bru,' said Ronan. 'Bru was brilliant, wasn't he?'

'I liked him,' said Keelin primly. 'He understood me.'

Gemma shot her an anxious look.

'Ian has invited me to his birthday party,' said Ronan. 'It's on the first of January.'

'And I'm going to keep in touch with Fiona by e-mail,' said Keelin. 'I can do it from the computer in school.'

'We'll probably never see them again,' said Gemma.

'Why not?' asked Keelin. 'They live in Wicklow. That's not so far away.'

'Great,' said Gemma unenthusiastically. She hoped that the new-found friendships would fade over the next few weeks. She really didn't want to be involved with the Fergusons any more. 'Come on,' she told her children. 'Let's go.'

Their luggage was in the first batch that appeared on the carousel. Gemma hauled the bags onto a trolley and pushed it into the arrivals area.

'I hope we get a taxi easily,' she said as she looked around the crowded terminal. 'This place just gets busier and busier!'

'Look!' Ronan grabbed her by the arm. 'Over there, Mum! It's Dad!'

'Dad?' Gemma followed his pointing finger. She stared in amazement as she saw David standing there. Her blood ran cold. Why was he there? What had happened?

Ronan rushed off towards him while Keelin followed at a more sedate pace. Gemma pushed the trolley after them.

'David,' she said as she caught up with them, 'what on earth are you doing here?'

'Waiting for you,' he said. He smiled at her. 'I thought you might like a lift home.' She looked fantastic, he thought. Her hair, glinting with auburn under the lights, was pulled back from her face. Her arms and legs were tanned to a golden brown. She wore a black shirt and stonewashed jeans and he could have sworn that she'd lost weight. And although her brow was furrowed, she didn't have the usual harassed look in her eyes.

'What made you think we needed a lift?' She smiled at him. 'I mean, it's great that you're here and everything but we were going to get a taxi.'

'Oh, I wanted to see you all,' he said as he hugged Ronan again.

Gemma frowned slightly. 'You're sure there's nothing wrong?'

'Absolutely not.'

'Well, then.' She smiled at the children. 'That's great, David, thank you.'

He took the trolley and began to push it while Keelin and Ronan walked either side of him towards the car park.

'Did you have a good time?' he asked as he paid for his ticket.

'It was brilliant,' said Ronan.

'Not the first day,' Keelin reminded him. 'It was raining.'

'Raining!' exclaimed David, 'I bet your mum wasn't too happy about that!'

'None of us were,' said Gemma.

'But then it was great. And we made friends.'

'Did you?' David led them to the car.

'Fiona and Ian,' said Ronan. 'They live in Wicklow. And their uncle. His name's Bru.'

'Bru?'

'Sam, actually,' said Gemma calmly. 'He was very nice.'

'He was great,' said Ronan. 'He played football with me every day. And tennis with the girls.'

'Quite the superman, then?' said David dryly.

'He *was* super,' said Keelin. 'He talked to me as though I had a mind of my own which is more than you ever do.'

'Keelin!' said Gemma.

'Well, he did.' Keelin's cheeks were pink. 'We talked about lots of things.'

'How old was this bloke?' David opened the car door.

'Thirty,' said Gemma.

'Thirty!' David looked at his ex-wife and his daughter. 'What were you doing hanging around with a thirty-year-old man, Keelin? You're only a child. And what were you doing letting her?' His glance at Gemma's was accusing.

'Oh, for heaven's sake!' cried Keelin. 'You're kind of letting your imagination run away with you, Dad. I told you, we just talked. Mum can vouch for that,' she added tartly, 'she kept an eye on me all the time.'

Gemma shrugged.

'Besides,' said Keelin as she got into the back seat, 'it's no big deal, is it? After all, that's only sixteen years older than me. Same as you and Orla.'

Gemma didn't know whether to laugh or cry as she watched a gamut of expressions run across David's face.

'It's completely different,' he said eventually. 'Completely.'

They fastened their seat belts as he turned the key in the ignition.

'I don't see how,' murmured Keelin.

'Keelin.' Gemma turned round in her seat and looked warningly at her daughter. 'Leave it alone. Sam was a nice guy and we all liked him.'

'He liked you too,' said Ronan suddenly.

'Pardon?' Gemma could feel a blush staining her cheeks.

'He told me. He said, "Your mum is very pretty, isn't she?"'

'He was probably joking,' said Gemma quickly.

'No he wasn't,' said Ronan. 'He just said it when you were in the pool one afternoon. You were wearing your yellow swimsuit and he said it to me.'

Gemma knew that her cheeks were scorching red. She remembered floating in the pool in her yellow swimsuit while Sam and the kids were playing football or something. Now she wished she'd been holding her stomach in at the time.

'How's Orla?' A complete change of direction in this conversation was essential.

'Fine.'

Gemma glanced at David. His jaw was set and he stared straight ahead.

'Did she mind you coming to pick us up?' she asked.

'She's away this week.' David indicated right and overtook a plodding Ford Ka.

'Where?' asked Gemma.

'On a course,' David replied. 'In Cork.'

'Why didn't you go too?' Gemma could hear the tension in his voice.

'It's an induction course,' David told her. 'Orla's changed jobs. She's working for Serene Life now.'

'Serene Life!' Gemma looked at David in astonishment. 'Bob Murphy's crowd?'

'Mmm.'

'You used to work for him when he was at Gravitas, didn't you?'

'I worked with him,' said David, 'not for him.'

Gemma acknowledged the difference with a shrug. 'So why did Orla decide to move? Better package?'

'I suppose so,' said David tautly.

Gemma sat back in the passenger seat. She recognised the signs. David had been angry with her in the past. She could see that he was very angry with Orla now. She didn't envy her. David's anger was the worst kind – slow-burning and long-lasting. In fact, thought Gemma, as she glanced at her ex-husband, she actually felt sorry for the current Mrs Hennessy.

Chapter 25

David helped them carry their cases into the house.

'It was really kind of you to meet us,' Gemma told him. 'Thanks.'

'Mum, can I go to Neville's?' asked Ronan. 'I want to show him the stuff I brought back.'

Gemma glanced at her watch. 'If you like. But be back in an hour, Ronan. No later.'

'OK,' he said. 'Thanks.'

Keelin disappeared upstairs and closed her bedroom door. The beat of her latest CD echoed around the house.

'Why don't you tell her to turn it down?' David frowned.

'Because if I do, I'm a nagging old bitch of a mother,' said Gemma. 'If I say nothing, she'll eventually turn it down herself.'

As if to lend truth to Gemma's argument, the music suddenly stopped and Keelin came downstairs again. She'd changed into a clean T-shirt and had taken the scrunchie out of her hair so that it almost hid her face. Gemma sighed. Keelin had looked so pretty with her hair tied back. Now she'd reverted to her sullen look again.

'I'm going around to Shauna's,' she told Gemma. 'I won't be long.'

'Back in an hour,' said Gemma. 'You've got school tomorrow and I want to make sure that both you and Ronan have everything organised properly.'

'I have,' said Keelin.

'An hour,' repeated Gemma.

Keelin banged the hall door behind her. Gemma and David stood looking at each other.

'I really picked you up so that I could see them,' said David blankly. 'But they're not that interested in seeing me.'

Gemma smiled sympathetically. 'They're still on a high from the holiday,' she told him. 'They want to tell their friends about it.' She walked into the kitchen and David followed her. 'Would you like some tea?' she asked.

'Coffee, if you have it,' said David.

Gemma filled the kettle and spooned some granules into a cup.

'Slice of fruit cake?' she asked.

'Sure.'

She unwrapped a loaf-sized cake from some greaseproof paper.

'Homemade?' asked David.

'I went on a baking binge before we went away,' confessed Gemma. 'The freezer's full of bread.'

'What sort of bread?' asked David. He remembered the times when he'd come home and the house had been filled with the enticing aroma of freshly baked bread.

'Tomato,' she told him. 'Onion. And saffron.'

Her tomato bread had been fantastic.

'Can I have some?' he asked.

'Pardon?'

'Some tomato bread. I always loved your tomato bread, Gemma.'

'Pity you never told me that when you lived with me.' The words came out before she could stop them and she bit her lip. She sounded mean and she hadn't intended to.

'I know,' said David. 'I'm sorry.'

'It doesn't matter.' She poured the hot water into the cup. 'And you can certainly have some bread if you like but not now because it is, I hope, frozen solid. But take some with you by all means.'

'OK,' said David. 'I will.' He sipped some coffee then took a bite of the fruit cake. 'This is lovely,' he told her.

'New recipe,' she said. 'Keelin made it.'

'Keelin baked a cake?' David looked at her in astonishment. 'I thought she was going through a kind of Iron Maiden phase.'

Gemma laughed. 'Most of the time. But occasionally she succumbs to normality. She got the recipe for this from Shauna's mum.'

David sighed. 'It's bloody difficult being a parent, isn't it?'

'Yes.' Gemma turned away from him and fished the tea bag out of her cup. 'Particularly a single parent.' She took her cup and walked past him to sit at the round dining table.

'I'm not exactly renowned for my sensitivity, am I?' asked David.

'Nope.'

'Gemma—' He broke off and looked at her as she tucked her hair back behind her ears. He remembered her doing that when he'd gone out with her first. It was driving her mad, she'd told him. It was too

224

long and the curls were part of a perm that was growing out. But he'd liked the mop of unruly curls. She'd been so pretty then, in a muddled, careless sort of way. She'd also been full of laughter and fun. She'd made him laugh too. How could it have all just slipped away?

'What?' she asked.

'Nothing.' He shook his head.

Gemma regarded him thoughtfully. He looked tired, she thought. As he'd done so often in the second year of their marriage when he'd decided that he was going to be the top salesman in Gravitas Life. He'd gone out all hours of the day and night chasing customers, meeting as many prospective clients a night as he possibly could and then coming home and writing up his notes about them before falling asleep on the sofa. She shouldn't have let him push himself so hard. He was supposed to have been a fun sort of person. He'd become an automaton instead.

'Were you really unhappy?' he asked suddenly.

She looked away from him at a spot on the wall.

'Yes,' she said eventually.

'Why?'

'Lots of reasons.' She shrugged. 'It just turned out differently to what I'd expected.'

'Didn't you ever think we could work it out?'

She laughed shortly. 'Loads of times. Every time I asked you to be home before eight and you said of course you would. Even though nine times out of ten you wouldn't get back until much later, I always hoped.'

'I was trying to build us a life, Gemma,' he said.

She shook her head. 'You were building something for you,' she told him. 'Not for us.'

'But you got so much out of it,' he objected. 'The house, the presents, the holidays . . .'

'I didn't get you,' she said. 'I married you, David, not a house.'

'So it was really bad?'

'It's in the past,' she said. 'We're older now. We've changed.'

'If you hadn't heard me talking to Bea—'

'I don't want to talk about it any more, David.' Gemma got up and brought her cup to the sink. 'It was good at the start and then it went wrong. As far as I was concerned, Bea was just a part of it.'

'And Orla?' he asked.

'Orla?' She looked at him in puzzlement. 'Orla had nothing to do with us.' She frowned and looked suspiciously at him. 'Had she?'

'Of course not,' he said vehemently. 'I didn't know Orla when I was married to you.'

Gemma shrugged. 'Well, then, I've nothing to say about Orla.' Although, she told herself, that was a lie. She really wanted to ask him what it was like living with someone who was younger than him. Someone who turned people's heads. Someone who was keen and ambitious in a way that she had never really been. And she wanted to tell him that she'd felt betrayed when he married the long-legged, flame-haired bimbo bitch.

David sighed. He wasn't sure what he'd wanted Gemma to say. That she was jealous of Orla? That was a ridiculous thing to expect. But, he realised, he did want her to feel jealous! He wanted her to envy him for having found his beautiful, younger wife. He wanted to think that there was something that he had and Gemma hadn't. He was shocked to discover that he felt like this.

'She's incredibly clever,' he said. 'I guess that's why she's gone to Serene.'

'You're not happy about it?' Gemma rinsed the cup under the tap.

'What do you mean?'

'David, don't be stupid. It's perfectly clear that there's something about her new job that bothers you. I can't imagine you want to talk to me about it, but if you do – go ahead.' She blinked in amazement as she said the words. She was suggesting that her ex-husband could share his troubles about his new wife with her! What on earth was the matter with her? She couldn't believe that she was turning into his marriage counsellor!

'It doesn't bother me,' he said. 'Well, I suppose, I'm just concerned that she's gone to Serene under false pretences.'

'False pretences?' Gemma rewrapped the fruit cake and put it in an airtight box.

'Gemma, you remember Bob Murphy! He wanted me to go to Serene when he left but I thought I'd do better at Gravitas. Which I have done. But ever since then he rings me up a couple of times a year to "talk about old times". He's made me three direct job offers and he's hinted at opportunities in Serene for me loads of times. I think he's offered Orla the job just so he can get at me.'

'Really?' she asked. 'You really believe that?'

'Of course.' David looked surprised.

'That's so bloody patronising, David. And so bloody typical of you!'

'What do you mean?'

226

'You're saying that this bloke only offered Orla a job because she's married to you. How much more insulting to her do you want to be?'

'It's the most likely reason,' David protested.

'What about the reason that she's good enough?' asked Gemma.

'Oh, Gemma—'

'As far as I remember you've always boasted to me about how fucking good she is.' Gemma was unable to keep a trace of bitterness out of her voice. 'So clever. So ambitious. So determined. And still only twenty-four. That's what you've told me on any number of occasions, David. But now that she's been offered a job with another company, you're trying to say that it's only because she's married to you. That's ridiculous.'

'I never—'

'Don't bother patronising me either,' said Gemma.

'I'm not—'

'Because I think Orla is obviously as smart and clever and ambitious as you say she is. And I don't think you should run her down in front of me.'

'I'm not—'

'You're lucky to have found her. You're lucky to have someone who loves you and who you love. You're lucky to have had a second chance, David. So don't go screwing it up.' Gemma glared at him and then, suddenly, started to cry.

David watched her, uncertain of what to do. He'd never known what to do when she cried and she'd cried an awful lot when she was married to him. Then it was usually because he'd let her down over something. He suddenly realised how often he'd let her down, how often she'd probably cried at home when he wasn't there. He hadn't meant to make her cry then and he certainly hadn't meant to make her cry now.

'Gemma,' he said awkwardly.

'I'm all right.'

He got up and walked over to her. 'What's the matter?'

'Nothing.' She rubbed at her eyes. 'I'm fine.'

'You're upset.'

The concern in his voice made the tears fall again. She tried to stop them but they spilled out over her eyes and down her cheeks to splash on the kitchen counter.

'Oh, Gemma, I'm sorry. I don't know what I've said or done but I'm sorry.'

227

He hadn't said anything to make her cry. He hadn't done anything to make her cry. She was crying for what could have been. She was crying because they were divorced and he had remarried and it was too late for them. And because no matter how many times she told herself that she'd made the right decision, sometimes she missed having him in the bed beside her.

'What's the matter, Gemma?'

'Nothing.' She wiped away the tears and sniffed. 'It must be coming back from holidays.'

'The holiday was meant to make you feel better.'

'I do.' She gave a watery smile. 'Honestly.'

He put his arm round her and hugged her gently. 'I wish it could have been different,' he said. 'I honestly do.'

⤶

Keelin sat in Shauna Fitzpatrick's bedroom. Shauna's parents had redecorated it in the last week and Shauna had picked out the pale blue paint, the matching curtains and the contrasting corn-yellow carpet. Shauna had taken down her posters of Robbie Williams and David Beckham and had replaced them with a copy of one of Monet's water lily paintings. The effect was significantly more sophisticated than the poster-covered walls that Keelin had last seen.

'I miss the posters,' Shauna confided. 'But Mum said that they'd go back on the walls over her dead body! I'm allowed to put them on the door and the wardrobe, but I don't know, Keelin. I'm not sure that I'm into Robbie Williams any more. And since David married Posh Spice and had a baby, I'm gone off him.'

'We need to find real blokes,' said Keelin.

'Oh, real blokes!' Shauna tossed her hair. 'Where would you find a decent real bloke around here? They're all spotty retards!'

Keelin nodded feelingly.

'Did you meet anyone on holiday?' asked Shauna.

'Would I be that lucky?' Keelin made a face.

'No one?'

'No,' said Keelin. 'There weren't any good-looking ones around. We saw a couple of Germans the first full day we were there and we chatted to them for a while but they were staying miles away so it was no use.'

'Pity,' said Shauna although she was relieved too. She hadn't wanted Keelin to have found anyone. When they finally started going out with blokes, they'd do it together.

'There was a man, though,' said Keelin.

Shauna stared at her. 'What sort of man?'

'Not the way you think!' Keelin giggled. 'He was the uncle of the girl I hung around with in Portugal. Dead nice, Shauna. And dead gorgeous too! But a bit on the ancient side for me – he was thirty!'

'Thirty!'

Keelin nodded. 'But, you know, he didn't seem so old. He was nice and he chatted to me like I was properly grown-up. If only he'd been a bit younger I could have fancied him myself!'

'Keelin, thirty is pushing it a bit.'

'I know,' she said. 'And even though I think so too, it suddenly occurred to me that the age gap between me and him was the same as between Orla and my dad. And it was the weirdest feeling.'

Shauna looked at her sympathetically. 'Gross,' she said.

'I mean, it could have been her and Dad,' she said. 'You know, like, years ago. I can't get my head around it, Shauna.'

'I suppose it's different when you're older,' said Shauna.

'I suppose.' Keelin sighed. 'Anyway, it wouldn't have mattered what I thought about him because he fancied my mum.'

'Keelin!'

'He did,' said Keelin. 'He was looking at her when he didn't think she'd notice. And whenever we were talking he'd always ask me about her. How she got on with my dad. How she got on with Orla. That sort of stuff.'

'Do you mind?' asked Shauna.

Keelin leaned back against the bedroom wall. 'I don't know,' she said honestly.

'Would it be good for your mum to have a boyfriend?'

'That sounds disgusting,' said Keelin. 'A boyfriend.'

'Whatever.'

'Part of me thinks it would be nice,' said Keelin. 'Part of me hates the idea. If she had to have one, Bru would be a good one for her to have, I suppose.'

'And does she fancy him?'

Keelin wrinkled her nose. 'I dunno. She acted funny with him, but not funny like she fancied him – I can't explain.'

'Will she see him again, d'you think?'

'Probably not.' Keelin leaned her head on her knees. 'I don't think she liked him as much as he liked her. It's a bit unfair, though,' she added, 'that both my mum and my dad have other people in their

229

lives and I haven't managed to scoop one boyfriend yet. Spotty retard or not!'

Shauna laughed. 'It's Alison Fogarty's birthday party in a couple of weeks. She's invited loads of people. Maybe we'll get lucky there.'

'Maybe.' Keelin's eyes brightened. 'I feel as though I need a boyfriend now, Shauna.'

'God, don't tell me you've turned into one of those man-mad maniacs.'

'It's not that bad,' said Keelin. She looked at her watch. 'I'd better go. Mum said an hour and it's a little over that now. Given that we've spent a halfway decent week I suppose I'd better not antagonise her too much! Call for me tomorrow?'

Shauna nodded. 'Quarter to nine. See you then.'

'Cheers.' Keelin got up from the floor. 'I hate the idea of going back to school. I really do!'

⤳

Keelin let herself into the house and walked into the kitchen. She was surprised to see her father still there and her mother's eyes bright with unshed tears.

'What's the matter?' she asked, unable to keep the panic out of her voice.

'Nothing,' said Gemma. 'Nothing.'

'You look upset.'

'We were just talking,' said David.

Keelin stared at them. 'Why do you have to fight? You shouldn't need to fight any more.' Her voice trembled. 'I hate you both, I really do.' She stalked out of the room and slammed the door behind her.

Gemma moved as though to follow her.

'Leave her,' said David. 'She'll be all right in a minute.'

But Gemma was horribly afraid that she wouldn't, horribly afraid that they'd managed to break the tenuous bond they'd managed to forge over the last week.

230

Chapter 26

Orla stepped out of Brown Thomas and looked around her. Cork city was less crowded than Dublin. The more leisurely pace had allowed Orla to stroll around the department store during her lunchtime break from the Serene Life induction course and do some stress-free shopping. It was nice to get out of Jury's Hotel, where they were staying and where the course was being run, and wander around the city. It was a long time since she'd been in Cork. The last time she'd visited had been in her second or third year at college when a group of them had rented a house for a long weekend. Most people had spent the weekend in a state of hazy drunkenness but Orla had worked on one of her study assignments. The weather had been glorious, she remembered, she'd managed to get sunburned sitting out in the garden of the cottage as she went through her lecture notes and sipped Ballygowan. I must have been such a bore, she thought as she recalled it. Nose in a book, always trying too hard to be the best. She couldn't help it. When you had four very competitive brothers, they brought it out in you.

'Orla!'

She spun round at the sound of her name.

'Orla O'Neill! Over here!' He was waving at her from the other side of the street. She stood and stared at him, quite unable to believe her eyes.

'Jonathan?' She mouthed the name. 'Jonathan?'

He waved again. 'Wait for me!' He spotted a break in the traffic then dodged between the oncoming cars to end up on the pavement opposite her.

'Hello, Jonathan,' she said.

'Orla O'Neill!' He smacked a kiss on the side of her cheek. 'I can't believe it's you.'

She couldn't believe it was him either. She couldn't believe she was standing beside the guy who had meant so much to her a few years

231

ago. Jonathan Pascoe, captain of the rugby team, tall, well-built, not exactly good-looking because his nose had been broken twice and he still had a scar over his right eye from a particularly vicious stamping incident on the pitch, but still undeniably attractive.

'What are you doing here?' he asked.

'Working,' she told him. 'And you?'

'The same.' He put his hands on her shoulders. 'I never expected to see you here, Orla. I thought I was hallucinating for a moment.'

'I thought you might be a hallucination myself,' she admitted. 'You're supposed to be in England.'

'Not at all.' He grinned at her. 'D'you think I could stay away that long? I was there for six months and then a great opportunity came up in Blarney so I came home.'

'Blarney?' She looked at him inquiringly. Blarney was about five miles outside Cork city. 'I didn't think you were interested in the tourist industry.'

He laughed. 'Don't worry, Orla, I'm not giving guided tours of the castle or helping folks to kiss the Blarney Stone. I'm working for an engineering company – got to use my qualifications after all.'

'Do you like it?'

'It's great,' he said. 'Good company, nice working environment, lots of people my own age.'

'And you've got a bit of a Cork accent already,' she teased.

'Ah, go on!' He pushed her playfully.

'Honestly,' she said. 'You have.'

'I suppose you pick it up,' he acknowledged. 'Though there's people from all over the place working with me. My closest colleague is actually from Denmark.'

Orla glanced at her watch.

'You're not tired of me already, girl, are you?' He rolled his eyes in mock horror. 'I wanted to ask you for a coffee. Or something stronger.'

'I have to get back,' she told him. 'My next session is at two.'

'Where are you staying?' he asked.

'Jury's.'

'I'll walk back with you. My car is parked nearby. I'm on a half-day today and I came into town to pick up some stuff for my house.'

'You've bought a house?' she asked.

He nodded. 'Near Blarney. It's lovely, Orla. Dormer bungalow, third of an acre, only built last year. It was a real bargain because the couple who lived there split up and they were anxious to sell so I got it

232

much cheaper than you'd think. It's in great nick because everything is so new.'

'Lucky you,' she said dryly.

'Yes, well, I'm sorry for them and everything but it was lucky for me.' He grinned at her. 'What about you, young Orla? What's been going on in your life?'

She didn't want to tell him. She didn't want to say that she was married with two stepchildren, one of whom was only ten years younger than her. Right now, a couple of days into the course and away from David, she didn't feel married at all.

'Orla?' He looked at her quizzically.

'Oh, sorry.' She smiled. 'I was daydreaming. I've got to give a talk next session and it suddenly came into my head.'

'You haven't changed a bit then,' he said. 'How many bloody times did we go out together and I'd be trying to have a romantic conversation with you and you'd suddenly ask me a question about careers?'

'Not often,' she said.

'Very often.'

'Was I an awful bore?' she asked.

'You were a bit intense,' said Jonathan. 'But you were never boring.'

She sighed. 'I think I must have been. I don't know how you put up with me for so long.'

'I put up with you because I loved you,' he said simply and Orla thought that her legs were going to give way beneath her.

'You never said anything about love.' Her tone was accusing.

'What was the point? You knew what you wanted and it wasn't settling down with me, was it?'

Part of her had wanted to. That was why she'd split up with him. Jonathan had made her feel like she'd never felt before. When she was with him she never wanted to be anywhere else. And yet she'd worked so hard to get her place at college. She wasn't a natural, gifted student like Abby who could turn out pages and pages of elegantly argued work at the drop of a hat. Orla had to study hard, to really work at it. And she hadn't wanted to throw it all away just because Jonathan Pascoe had made her heart beat faster and her legs feel like jelly. She'd asked her mother about it and Rosanna had told her that there were plenty of men around who'd make her feel like that. It was picking the right one at the right time that was the trick. Rosanna had encouraged her to keep studying and Orla had believed that her mother was right.

'You always wanted a career, didn't you?' asked Jonathan. 'It was more important to you than anything else.'

He hadn't seen her wedding ring. Her left hand tightened its grip round the Brown Thomas bag.

'I was too young,' she said. 'We both were.'

'And now?' asked Jonathan.

She couldn't speak. What sort of a career did she have, she asked herself, after all that studying? She was just a saleswoman. A good saleswoman, she thought fiercely. A really good saleswoman. The hotel loomed up in front of them and she turned to him. 'I have to rush. I'm late.'

'How long are you here for?' he asked.

'Not long.'

'Are your evenings free?'

She wanted to say no but she couldn't. She nodded.

'How about I pick you up at seven? We could go out somewhere.'

'Oh, I don't know, Jonathan. I—'

'Come on, Orla. It'll be fun. There's lots to catch up on.'

'Well—'

'Seven,' he said firmly. 'I'll book somewhere. I'll see you then.'

'OK,' she said.

'Fine,' said Jonathan. He kissed her briefly on the cheek and then strode ahead of her to unlock his Range Rover.

She was still shaking by the time she got back to her room and unpacked her shopping. She laid the moss-green Lainey Keogh wool suit on her bed and wondered if it was a good sign that she'd blown so much money on clothes on a day when she'd met again the first man that she'd ever loved.

She didn't do well in that afternoon's session. She was supposed to be selling a complicated policy to a family of four and she kept getting the details mixed up, much to her own annoyance and to the frustration of the session co-ordinator.

'You're really not with us this afternoon, are you, Orla?' he asked.

'I'm sorry,' she said. 'I have an awful headache. I'm finding it hard to concentrate.'

'Take something for it,' he snapped.

'I did,' she lied. 'I'll be better soon.'

She was glad when six o'clock came and the session ended. She told the rest of the group that she was going out for dinner, that a walk might clear her head. Then she went up to her room, stepped out of her clothes and under the shower.

Jonathan Pascoe. When she'd told him that it was over between them he'd said that she'd broken his heart. Which was something of an exaggeration because she'd seen him a couple of weeks later with one of the prettiest arts students in the college. He hadn't looked like a guy whose heart was broken. Until the day she saw him with Marianne Walsh, Orla had constantly wondered whether she'd done the right thing. She'd been on the point of ringing him and telling him that she'd made a terrible mistake when she'd seen them sitting on the lawn outside the library, sharing a punnet of strawberries and laughing at one of Jonathan's terrible jokes. She'd told herself that she'd done the right thing, that there was more to life than someone who made you laugh when you were feeling down, who made you tingle all over when he kissed you, who was good to be with. She told herself that she was far too young to get entangled with anyone at that point in her life.

Which was bloody ironic, she thought, as she stepped out of the shower and wrapped a towel round her, since it hadn't taken her that long to get entangled with David Hennessy.

She bit her lip. At the time she'd first met Jonathan, David and Gemma had still been married. David had gone home every night and climbed into bed beside Gemma. When she'd been lying in bed with Jonathan, David had been lying in bed with Gemma. Even if things hadn't been perfect between them, she was sure he'd sometimes put his arm round Gemma and gather her to him in exactly the same way as he now did with her. And he'd kiss Gemma gently on the face and throat like he did with her. And then his hands would slide along Gemma's thighs as they did with her. And he'd probably told Gemma he loved her while he was doing it.

She shook her head. She shouldn't be thinking like this. It was stupid.

The moss-green Lainey Keogh suited her. It brought out the golden-red in her hair and the almost imperceptible colour in her cheeks. It emphasised the slimness of her frame and made her look effortlessly elegant. She sprayed herself with Contradiction and walked downstairs to the lobby. It was exactly seven o'clock.

Jonathan Pascoe was waiting for her. He wore a dark-green suit, cream shirt and green tie.

'Snap,' he said as she walked up to him. 'We're obviously on the same wavelength colourwise!'

'Obviously,' she said.

'But it looks much better on you,' he told her. 'You look lovely.'

235

He still hadn't spotted the ring. Despite the fact that the sleeves of the loosely knitted jacket almost reached her fingertips, she thought it was the first thing that he'd notice. She'd toyed with the idea of leaving it behind but rejected it almost at once. Whatever was going on between herself and David now, they were still married. And she did love him. She just didn't like him very much at the moment.

'I thought we'd go to the Arbutus Lodge,' said Jonathan. 'It's got great views over the city and the food is wonderful. I'm sure you'll like it.'

'OK,' she said. 'Whatever you think.'

She followed him into the car park and got into the Range Rover.

'Why on earth are you driving this?' she asked.

'Company car.' He grinned at her. 'I sometimes have to go on-site, you know, and usually it's somewhere mucky. I like this.'

'Show-off.' But her tone was amused.

He drove in silence across town to the restaurant. As he'd promised, the views over the city were spectacular. She looked out of the window at the network of orange and white lights below them and murmured her appreciation.

'I knew you'd like it,' he said. 'It's your sort of thing, Orla.'

'And how do you know what my sort of thing is?' she asked.

'I always knew,' he said seriously.

A waiter approached the table and handed them the menus.

'I have to tell you something,' she said to Jonathan.

He raised an eyebrow inquiringly.

'I – well, the truth is, Jonathan, I'm married.'

He regarded her thoughtfully.

'I should have said it before now.'

'Why didn't you?' His eyes darted to her left hand which she'd placed on the table. The diamond engagement ring glittered in the light.

'I don't know.'

He looked from her ring finger to her eyes. 'I'd heard.'

'Really?'

'From Martin. You met Martin a while ago, didn't you? I keep in touch with him.'

'Oh.'

'So, you see, I knew already.'

'Then you should have said something,' she snapped.

'Why?' he asked.

She was silent for a moment. 'I don't know.'

The waiter returned and smiled at them. 'Are you ready to order?' he asked.

'I am,' said Jonathan. 'I know what I want already. The mussels, please, and the Dover sole.'

Orla scanned the menu. 'I'll have the Caesar salad and I'll have the sole too,' she said.

'Thank you.' The waiter took their menus. 'And to drink?'

'A bottle of the '95 Australian Chardonnay,' said Jonathan. 'We both like it.'

'Certainly.'

Jonathan looked at Orla. 'You still do like Australian Chardonnay, don't you?'

She bit her lip. 'Of course.'

'So, Orla. Tell me all about your marriage. Tell me why it was OK to marry someone else when you wouldn't even consider having a long-term relationship with me. Tell me what it's like to be married. And why you accepted my invitation to dinner.'

'I accepted your invitation to dinner because you made it,' she said tartly. 'It wasn't for any ulterior motive so don't bloody flatter yourself.' She looked down at the table while she composed herself again.

'Fair enough,' said Jonathan calmly. 'If a bloke is insane enough to ask a woman to dinner he always runs the risk that she'll actually accept.'

'You didn't have to ask,' she said. 'And you could have called me to cancel. I wouldn't have cared.'

'But I would,' he said. 'I wanted to see you again.'

She said nothing but twisted her engagement ring round on her finger.

'Tell me about it,' he said, his tone conciliatory. 'Come on, Orla, I'm sorry I've been ratty with you.'

She looked up at him again. His eyes were soft.

'Come on,' he said. 'I won't be nasty, I promise.'

'You were never nasty,' she said. 'Not to me, anyway.'

'I wasn't nasty to anyone.' His voice was light. 'You know me, Orla. Pascoe the pacifist.'

Her smile wobbled but she took a deep breath. 'I met him at work,' she said. 'His name's David Hennessy.'

'You work for some insurance company, don't you?'

'I've just changed jobs,' she told him, 'that's why I'm down here. A week's course before I start. I was with Gravitas when I met David. He was giving the course there and we clicked straightaway.'

Jonathan looked at her. 'But getting married, Orla. Wasn't that a rather drastic step?'

She shrugged. 'We loved each other. I know it sounds mad, considering what I'd always said at college, but I was crazy about him, and he was crazy about me.'

'Was?' asked Jonathan.

'Is,' she amended.

'Martin says he's older than you.'

'So are you,' she said smartly.

He laughed. 'I asked for that. Much older, is what Martin said.'

'Martin never did learn to keep his big mouth shut, did he?'

'Nope,' said Jonathan.

'Yes, David's older than me. He's forty.'

Jonathan whistled under his breath.

'Don't be like that,' she said sharply. 'Forty's not so old.'

'I know,' said Jonathan. 'There are people in the rugby club down here who are forty. Not playing, most of them, but they're in the club.'

'Sod off,' she said. 'As it happens, David is very fit.'

'For his age,' said Jonathan.

'Don't.' She tried hard to keep the tremor out of her voice.

'I'm sorry,' he said. 'I'm just envious of the man.'

The waiter returned and placed their starters in front of them. David tasted the wine and nodded that it was OK. Orla looked at the perfectly presented Caesar salad and didn't feel in the slightest bit hungry.

'So why did you marry him?' asked Jonathan. 'Why didn't you just go out with him?'

'I did go out with him,' she said. 'Then I married him.'

'I'm not doing this very well, am I?' He looked ruefully at her.

'I married David because I love him very much,' said Orla. 'I wanted to marry him, Jonathan. I really did.'

'Didn't you ever think about me?' he asked.

'Pardon?'

'I was crazy about you, Orla.' He sucked at a mussel and she made a face.

'And then you went out with Marianne Walsh,' she reminded him. 'And after that,' she closed her eyes, 'as far as I remember, there was Jean Willis, Clodagh Bennett, Sara-Jane Lawlor and Rhona McAdams. There might have been more, but I can't remember.'

'Don't you see,' he grinned at her, 'they were just taking my mind off things.'

238

She laughed suddenly and so did he. The atmosphere between them lightened immediately. She picked up her fork and began to poke at the salad.

'Tell me about him,' demanded Jonathan. 'What has he got that I haven't?'

'I don't know,' said Orla. 'We just seemed to fit, that's all.'

'That's the second time you've talked about your relationship in the past tense,' said Jonathan. 'Do I gather that, perhaps, all is not perfect?'

'When is anything perfect?' she asked lightly. 'I'm married to him and I love him.' I think, she added to herself. Though sitting here with Jonathan I can't help remembering how I once felt about him.

She remembered his kiss. The first time. They'd gone to Mao's for noodles and beer and afterwards they'd walked to Trinity, hand in hand. She'd been wearing high heels and couldn't keep her balance on the cobblestones of the quadrangle. He'd carried her, then suddenly let her down again and kissed her. He'd tasted of garlic and beer but so had she so neither of them minded.

'What are you thinking?' he asked.

'I'm remembering when you kissed me,' she told him.

'Garlic,' he said.

'And beer.'

They both laughed.

'It wasn't exactly romantic, was it?' Jonathan smiled.

'Oh, I thought it was pretty OK.'

The waiter cleared away the dishes. Orla had eaten a quarter of the salad.

'Did you ever think of me?' asked Jonathan. 'Afterwards?'

'Oh, for heaven's sake.' She looked at him impatiently. 'Jonathan, you know that I cared a lot about you. But I wasn't ready to settle down and, besides, how many boyfriends had I had? Two, three? I was a late developer, you know! I needed to spread my wings a bit.'

'You could have come back,' he said.

She shook her head. 'I changed.'

'Not that much,' he told her. 'You're still as gorgeous as ever.'

She wished he wouldn't say things like that. She wished that she'd listened to the voice in her head that – as she was closing the hotel bedroom door behind her – told her that dinner with Jonathan Pascoe was not a good idea.

'Anyway,' she said, 'your heart mended quickly enough. You found other people and I found David.'

'I don't mind the fact that you found someone,' said Jonathan. 'I'm just surprised that you married him.'

'It seemed like a good idea at the time,' said Orla flatly.

'Seemed?'

She shrugged. 'We had a row. Over me taking this job. He's being childish about it.'

Jonathan laughed. 'I'm glad to know that a forty-year-old man can still be childish.'

'Men can be childish until they're senile,' snapped Orla. 'I've got four brothers, remember? I'm very well equipped to know exactly how childish men can be.'

'So with all that experience you still couldn't stop having a row with him?'

She grimaced. 'No. It was really stupid.'

'His fault, I suppose?' Jonathan raised an eyebrow.

'Naturally,' said Orla. 'He didn't want me to take the job.'

'Why?'

She was silent while the waiter placed their main courses in front of them.

'Well?' asked Jonathan, when they'd been served with a selection of vegetables to go with the fish.

'I'm not sure.' She squeezed lemon over her sole. 'I told him it was because he wanted me under this thumb, but I'm not convinced that's the reason. I think he just didn't like the idea that I could get a better job myself.'

'Maybe he was afraid of younger men eyeing you up,' said Jonathan. 'After all, he probably couldn't believe his luck when you said you'd marry him.'

'Why?' she asked.

'Come on, Orla, no offence or anything, but if the bloke got to forty without tying the knot . . .'

'What on earth makes you think he's never been married before?' asked Orla.

'You mean he was?'

She nodded. 'And he has two kids.'

'Orla!'

She said nothing.

'How old are the kids?' asked Jonathan.

'Keelin is fourteen, Ronan is eleven.'

'You're joking!'

'Why should I be joking?'

240

He put his knife and fork on the plate. 'I don't know. It's just – hard as it was for me to imagine you as a married woman, picturing you as a married woman with two stepkids is almost impossible.'

'They don't live with us,' said Orla. 'They live with his ex-wife.'

'And how do you get on with the ex?' asked Jonathan.

'I hardly ever see her,' said Orla. 'Whenever the kids come over, David picks them up. I've met her a couple of times, but I usually just speak to her on the phone.'

'And what does she look like?'

'You know, Jonathan, you're the most awfully gossipy sort of person,' complained Orla. 'You're not like a bloke at all. You're not supposed to be interested in what my husband's ex-wife looks like. That's the sort of thing I talk about with Abby.'

'Abby.' Jonathan smiled. 'Lovely girl. Has she hitched up with anyone?'

'No,' said Orla. 'Fancy your chances?'

He grinned. 'Not from here. I haven't been in Dublin in months.'

'Do you like it down here?' she asked.

'It's lovely,' he told her. 'Nice countryside, nice people, good job – I'd hate to go back.'

Part of her was relieved to hear him say it. She'd had visions of him turning up on her doorstep, pleading to be let in. Although, she told herself, that was terribly presumptuous of her. He might have loved her once, but that really didn't mean he cared now. Probably tonight was just one of those 'for old time's sake' dinners where he thought that there was a remote chance he could get her into bed. She took a large sip of her Chardonnay. He'd been bloody fantastic in bed.

'Remembering again?' he asked.

She shook her head. 'No.'

He sat back in his chair and gazed thoughtfully at her. She looked thinner than he remembered, and there were dark circles under her eyes. But she was still as beautiful as ever, with her stunning red hair, her dark-blue eyes and her Celtic complexion. He'd been crazy about her but he knew that she'd been right to break it off. In a frenzy of lust and passion he might just have married her himself and that would have been a terrible mistake because she hadn't loved him. At least now she was the only one who seemed to have made a mistake.

Orla looked out of the huge picture window at the city below. She couldn't believe that she was sitting here with Jonathan, remembering times past and wishing, no matter how faintly, that she was single again and free to put her arms round his neck as she used to and kiss him on

241

the mouth the way she used to. She bit the inside of her lip. Why was she thinking like this? She hadn't loved Jonathan half as much as she loved David. She hadn't felt the same connection with him at all. And yet somehow she couldn't help feeling that now, over five years later, it might have been very different.

'I have to get back,' she said.

'Back? Already?'

'We start early in the morning. I have loads of stuff to read up on. I really must get back.'

'Orla, you're a grown woman. You don't have to rush back like a schoolgirl.' His tone was amused.

'I'm not rushing back like a schoolgirl,' she objected. 'I have work to do, Jonathan, that's all.'

'Ah, the work ethic reasserts itself,' he said wryly. 'Just as it always did.'

She blushed. She knew what he was referring to. The night that they'd first made love they'd lain together, cuddled beneath his duvet, until she'd suddenly shot out of bed and told him that she had to go because she had an assignment to finish. She'd got the highest mark ever for her assignment but Jonathan had been hurt by her sudden departure.

'Really, Jonathan. I should go.'

'Have a coffee at least,' he said.

She nodded and Jonathan ordered coffees. He was still attractive, she thought, as she looked at him in the soft light of the restaurant. Still attractive and interesting and available.

And she was none of those things. Well, she was still attractive, there was no point in false modesty. She'd never be stunningly beautiful but she knew that she looked good. But interesting – she wondered if she'd ever really been interesting. She'd always been so damned hardworking and so bloody studious. Interesting wasn't exactly the right word. And she certainly wasn't available. She might be going through a particularly sticky patch with David right now but there had to be some way that she could make things all right again. She thought back to their wonderful honeymoon in the Caribbean and how they'd made love every single night and how much time they'd spent with each other – and never once, she told herself, never once had they hankered to be back at work and selling goddamned pension policies to goddamned clients.

They drank their coffees in silence. When they'd finished, Jonathan asked for the bill.

'Let me.' Orla pulled the silver salver with the pale blue docket towards her.

'Don't be stupid, Orla.' Jonathan reached out to take it from her. His hand closed over hers. She felt the warmth of his skin and she shivered. He slid his fingers between her own. 'It's nice to be with you again,' he said.

She couldn't speak. His touch was familiar and unfamiliar. She stared at him.

'You still care about me, don't you?' he said.

She pulled her hand away from him. 'I care about lots of people,' she said. 'And I'd prefer to pay for dinner.'

'Let me pay,' said Jonathan. 'I asked you, after all.'

She sighed.

'Don't worry,' he said dryly, 'I'll drop you back to your hotel and I won't even attempt to sneak a goodnight kiss from you.'

He kept his word. And she didn't know whether to feel relieved or insulted.

Chapter 27

Gemma looked through her appointments for the day. Fridays were always busy and today was no exception – half a dozen cut and blow-drys, two permanent colours, one repair job on a home colour that had gone drastically wrong and, she groaned, Tessa O'Dwyer's highlights. Tessa had a magnificent mark of wheat-coloured hair which needed the highlights to give it movement and vitality. But they took forever to do and while she was doing them Gemma had to listen to whatever drama was currently besetting Tessa. There always was a drama. Tessa was unable to live her life any other way. Gemma had told Sam the truth when she'd said that hairdressers were amateur psychologists. There was something about sitting in front of a hairdresser that made most women unburden themselves, and Tessa unburdened herself more than most. Last month it had been the story of her night of passion with her attractive colleague. They'd spent the night in the very modern Morrison Hotel and had spent over two hundred quid on champagne. Gemma sighed. No chance of a night of passion at the Morrison for her! The phone rang and she reached out to answer it.

'Curlers,' she said.

'Hi, Gemma.'

'Liz! How are things?'

'OK,' said her sister. 'I was wondering if you're busy today.'

'Up to my neck,' said Gemma. 'I'm booked up all day.'

'I need your help,' said Liz.

'Not again,' said Gemma.

'On a hair matter,' Liz told her. 'It's your speciality, after all.'

'What do you want to know?'

'It's not what I want to know, it's what I want you to do.'

'What?' asked Gemma suspiciously.

'I need you to do it for me tonight,' said Liz.

'Tonight!'

'Gemma, it's not like you're Nicky Clarke or anything,' said Liz crossly. 'There's no need to say tonight like I'm asking the utterly impossible.'

'You almost are,' Gemma said. 'Honestly, Liz, I'm really busy. What do you need?'

'I want you to plait it for me.'

'Plait it!' Gemma made a face at the receiver. 'You can plait it yourself.'

'But not that lovely little French plait you do where you put the flower in it as well,' wheedled Liz. 'You know how well it looks on me, you say so yourself.'

'Liz, it's hardly long enough to be plaited,' said Gemma. 'And if you hadn't rushed off to that amateur you went to the last time—'

'You hairdressers are all the same.' Liz sounded aggrieved. 'Where did you get this done the last time? It certainly wasn't here! I needed a trim, Gem, and I went to the salon next door. It's not a crime.'

'I never said it was.' Gemma laughed. 'But she gave you more than a trim!'

'Yes, well, I know it wasn't great,' admitted Liz. 'But I was in a hurry and I needed it done quickly.'

'You should plan it better,' said Gemma.

'OK,' Liz said. 'I know. I admit it. I'm a hair slob. But I want to plan it this evening, Gem. Come on, you can help me, can't you?'

'Oh, I suppose so.' Gemma sighed as she looked at her list again. 'But please get here by six, I'd like to get home to the kids at a halfway reasonable hour.'

'I'll go over as soon as I finish work,' promised Liz. 'And it only takes you a few minutes.'

'I wish,' said Gemma. 'Anyway, why the hurry? What do you need this for?'

'I'm going out with Ross tonight,' said Liz. 'He asked me yesterday. It's a family thing.'

'A family thing!'

'His sister's birthday. Her thirtieth. She's having a meal in Fisherman's Wharf. Her husband, and another brother and sister. They're all bringing their respective spouses or partners. Ross asked me.'

'Bloody short notice,' said Gemma.

'He wasn't sure I'd come,' Liz told her.

'It's still short notice.'

'He probably didn't know whether to ask or not,' admitted Liz. 'After all, we don't know each other that well and maybe he thought that asking me to his sister's party was a little over the top.'

245

'Maybe his sister thought asking you to her party was a little over the top,' suggested Gemma.

'Possibly,' Liz agreed. 'But I want to go, Gem. I really do. And I know that in the past if some guy asked me to his sister's party I'd look at him as though he was cracked, but this time I don't care. I want to be with him.'

'You do have it bad,' said Gemma flatly.

'I know.' Liz laughed shortly. 'It's never happened to me before, Gemma, never. And it's so bloody wonderful that I can hardly believe it.'

'Enjoy it while it lasts,' said Gemma. 'You'll come down to earth soon enough.'

'Maybe.' Liz sighed. 'But right now I'm perched on cloud nine.'

'I'll see you later then.' Gemma couldn't stand the conversation any longer.

'Sure,' said Liz. 'Thanks, Gemma.'

'Don't mention it,' said Gemma wryly and hung up.

⌒

Orla replaced the telephone and lay down on her bed. There was no answer from the phone in the apartment and she couldn't get through to David's mobile. If he'd been home she would've told him she was leaving straight away. Now she didn't know what to do.

She closed her eyes. She'd spoken to David every evening on the phone but their conversations and been terse and difficult. Especially the night of her dinner with Jonathan. The phone had rung just as she entered the bedroom and she'd been bright and brittle with David, chattering away in a manner most unlike her. He, by contrast, had been cool. He'd rung earlier, he said. Where had she been?

Why was it that the simplest question annoyed her? Admittedly this time because she'd been to dinner with an ex-boyfriend and it had stirred up some deeply forgotten memories but, even still, David's questions seemed to have unspoken anger. He wasn't to know where she'd been, after all. He was quizzing her as though she was in some way owned by him. As far as he was concerned she was at her week's induction course and there was no need for him to question her at all.

I want to get it back, she thought miserably, as she turned onto her side. I want to get back the feelings I had for him. The sense

246

of perfection that was there before. Surely it was real, not something I imagined existed?

She opened her eyes and looked at her watch. It was three o'clock. She should go for a swim and a sauna. Relax. Chill out. Get ready to be the person he wanted her to be when she went home.

The ringing of the phone startled her. She reached out and picked up the receiver.

'Hello,' she said cautiously.

'Hi.'

'Jonathan.' Her voice was a croak.

'You said you were going back today.'

'I – am.'

'The desk told me that you hadn't checked out. That you'd kept the room until tomorrow.'

'The course finished at lunchtime,' she said. 'I planned to go home today.'

'But you haven't checked out,' he repeated.

'No,' she said. 'I haven't.'

'Why?'

'Because I wasn't sure whether or not to hang around. A few people decided to stay. I thought I might too. It's good team-work.'

'Ugh, Orla, I hate that word.'

'What word?'

'Teamwork. It's such bullshit. Nobody really works as a team. It's all individual.'

'Maybe in engineering it is,' she said waspishly.

He laughed. 'We're more team players than anyone else.'

'Then cut the crap,' she told him.

'That's my girl.' He laughed. 'Always defensive.'

'I'm not always defensive,' she said.

'No. Sometimes you go on the attack.'

She was silent.

'If you're hanging around I wondered whether or not you'd like to come to dinner again.'

'I'll probably have dinner with the Serene Life people.'

'You must be sick of them by now,' he told her. 'Come on, Orla. Have a break.'

'Oh, I'll probably just go home,' she said.

'When?'

'Later.'

'If you're going you should go now,' he told her. 'You shouldn't drive on your own late at night.'

'Don't be ridiculous,' she snapped. 'If I go it'll be in a couple of hours and I'll be home before ten.'

'I worry about you,' he said.

'Not you too.'

'Pardon?'

'David is forever saying that. I worry about you. I want to look after you. I'm concerned. Why do you all feel you have to care about me? I can look after myself.'

'Don't you think it's rather touching that we all want to look after you?'

'No,' said Orla. 'It's a pain in the fucking neck.' She hung up.

Why couldn't they leave her alone? Why couldn't she have a little peace and quiet?

⤳

David looked through his Filofax. He'd deliberately kept his schedule light because Orla was coming home today. He wanted to be there when she got in, to welcome her and tell her how much he loved her. He'd missed her terribly this last week. He hadn't been able to say the things he'd wanted to over the phone. She'd seemed remote and distracted and said that the course was tiring. He was sure that it was. When she got home he'd apologise to her. He'd been wrong to let his annoyance and his concerns about her new job spill over into the way he talked to her. She was very sensitive about her work and she hated the idea that he might be in some way patronising her. And he knew that but he'd still acted stupidly. Worst of all, he'd tried to punish her by ignoring her at her going-away drinks and spending half the night talking to that stupid tart, Avril Grady. He couldn't stand Avril, as Orla should have known only too well. How is it, he wondered, that you can find yourself in a situation which has spun out of your control before you realised what was happening?

Which, of course, reminded him of Gemma. He closed his eyes when he thought of Gemma crying in the kitchen and how he'd felt when he put his arms round her and held her to him. It was as though fifteen years had suddenly peeled away and he was holding Gemma as he'd held her when he'd first been married to her and when he'd loved her so much. Thank God Keelin had come in, he thought with relief, because in the mood he'd been in he could have done something really stupid like kiss Gemma and that would have been a disaster for everyone. Although, he thought wryly, Gemma wouldn't have let him kiss her. Would she?

She'd looked so different when he'd picked them up from the airport. Pretty and animated in a way he'd once associated with her but had long since forgotten. And that had made him want to protect her and care for her all over again.

He snapped the Filofax shut. What sort of person was he, he asked himself, that his emotions could flip-flop all over the place like this? He knew that he loved Orla. But he couldn't help having the nagging doubt that if he truly loved her as much as he believed, he wouldn't have wanted to put his arms round Gemma.

He sighed. And the other nagging and deeply disturbing thought was that he'd once loved Gemma very much. Or at least, he'd thought he had. What if he only thought he loved Orla too? What if he was the sort of bloke who hadn't really got the faintest idea of what love really meant? What if he just thought with his dick and not his head? Because, in both cases, it was the outward appearance of the girls that had first sparked his interest. Gemma, with her happy-go-lucky, careless look which was young and vibrant and reminded him of being on the beach in Australia. Orla, years later, looking so different but so eminently desirable in her stern-cut trouser suit and her scraped back hair but with a body that spoke of hidden treats beneath the external packaging.

He closed his eyes. He felt as though he was going crazy.

༄

The phone was ringing as Keelin and Shauna walked in the front door. Keelin dropped her bag in the hallway and picked it up.

'Hi,' she said.

'Keelin, it's me.'

'Yes, Mum.'

'I'll be a little late in this evening. Liz is coming in after work to get her hair done. I'm sorry, I'll be back as early as I can.'

'That's OK,' said Keelin.

'There's mushroom pie in the freezer,' Gemma told her, 'you can defrost some for dinner if you like. Ronan is with Neville's mum this afternoon. He should be home by six.'

'OK,' said Keelin again.

'Is everything all right?' asked Gemma. 'I'm sorry I'll be late but—'

'It's fine,' said Keelin impatiently. 'It doesn't matter.'

'I like being there when you—'

'I said it's fine,' said Keelin again. 'See you later.' She hung up and went into the living room. Shauna was curled up on the sofa, flicking through a copy of *Just Seventeen*.

'The bloke on page twelve is gorgeous,' said Keelin as she sat down beside her friend.

⌒

David looked at his watch. Three o'clock. He wondered whether or not Orla had left for home by now. He looked at the computer screen in front of him and at the blank spaces which he hadn't filled with appointments so that he'd be home at the same time as her. He wasn't sure exactly what he'd say. He'd practised a few things. Like, 'I think we've been going through a rocky patch. But everything will be OK.' Or, 'Have I been a bit ratty with you lately, Orla? I'm sorry. I didn't mean to.' But they all sounded trite and insincere. He was almost certain he remembered using similar phrases to Gemma once and the thought terrified him. He didn't want to be the sort of bloke who treated women badly. He didn't think he was that sort of bloke. He mightn't always get things right, but his intentions were good. Weren't they? He went into the kitchen and opened a bottle of Rioja. It wasn't his favourite wine but Orla liked it. She'd appreciate him opening it and letting it breathe. He'd just finished pulling out the cork when the phone began to ring.

'Hello,' he said.

'Hi, David.' Orla's voice was faint, as though she was out of range on her mobile.

'Orla? Where are you?'

'I'm still in Cork,' she said.

'Still in Cork?' he echoed. 'I thought you were coming home tonight.'

'Probably coming home tonight,' she corrected him. 'It's just that a group of people decided to stay and I thought, well, it's only one more night so I thought I'd stay.'

'But—' He gritted his teeth.

'I'll be back tomorrow.'

'What time tomorrow?'

'Early,' she told him. 'I'll leave directly after breakfast.'

'I thought you'd be home tonight,' he said tightly. 'I made sure that I wasn't meeting anyone because I thought you'd be home tonight.'

250

'I'm sorry,' she said. 'I really am. It's – well, there's a lot of people staying and I didn't want to be the only one. You understand?'

He exhaled slowly. 'I understand.'

'I'll see you tomorrow,' she said.

'Yes. Sure. Tomorrow.' He replaced the receiver and stared across the empty living room. Why wasn't she coming home? Did she want to stay away so much? He closed his eyes. Did he want her to stay away?

When he opened them again he was conscious that there was something different about room. It took him a few minutes to realise that the sculpture of the African woman was missing. He frowned. He hadn't moved it, he knew he hadn't. It couldn't have gone far. It wasn't as though there was a lot of spare room in the apartment.

He went into the bedroom although he knew it couldn't be there. It was too big not to be noticed. He would have noticed if it was in his wardrobe. But he opened it anyway and peered inside, feeling silly. Then he opened Orla's wardrobe. Her perfume rushed to greet him, a mingling of Issey Myake and Calvin Klein. He breathed in the scent of her, suddenly missing her very much. He touched the sleeve of her silver-grey business suit then withdrew it and closed the door abruptly. If it was still in the apartment, the only place the sculpture could be was in the tiny storage area at the end of the hallway. But he'd opened the door of it recently, surely he would have seen the sculpture if that's where it was.

The first thing he saw when he opened the door was his golf bag, tilted to one side. Behind it was a bundle of coats, too many for the small rack that he'd hung on the wall when he'd first moved in. The vacuum cleaner, his kitbag full of old sailing gear and Orla's tennis racquet were all piled in there too. And so was the African woman. He stared at it, unable to believe that it had been there and he hadn't noticed. Orla had obviously moved it, but when? He shook his head. And why?

Well, he thought, she may have put it in there but he certainly wasn't going to leave it there. He pushed the bags and coats out of the way, then carried the sculpture back into the living room.

How come he hadn't noticed that it had disappeared before now? he wondered. How long had it been since his African Queen had been relegated to the back of the storeroom?

He sat down and closed his eyes. Maybe he really *was* going crazy?

⌒

Gemma ran a comb through Liz's hair.

'You're sure you want the plait?' she asked.

'Certain,' said Liz. 'I'm going sophisticated tonight. I'm wearing my only little black dress and my pearls.'

'Which pearls?' Gemma divided her sister's hair into sections.

'The ones I bought in Majorca. Remember? The year I left school?'

Gemma screwed up her nose. 'Vaguely. Didn't you go with Jennifer Thomas and Tina Alford?'

'Yes. I haven't seen them in years.' Liz looked at Gemma in the mirror. 'Strange, isn't it? We were such great pals in school.'

'What did they do afterwards?' asked Gemma.

'Jennifer got married,' remembered Liz. 'And I have a feeling that Tina moved abroad.'

'It's such a bloody epitaph, isn't it?' Gemma began to twist Liz's hair into the plait. 'She got married. Like her life ended.'

'It's not always like that,' said Liz.

'Isn't it?'

'I hope not.' Liz smiled at her. 'Anyway, your life hasn't ended, Gemma.'

'That's because I got a bloody divorce!'

'You do all right,' said Liz. 'You've got a nice house and two kids and an ex-husband who doesn't hate you.'

'I don't know about that.' Gemma pulled at Liz's hair and her sister winced.

'What about him giving you money for the TV? That was pretty decent, wasn't it?'

'Oh, God,' sighed Gemma. 'I really have to pay him back for that. I can't keep the money, I really can't.'

'Don't be stupid,' said Liz. 'He gave it to you for a TV and you bought a TV.'

'Yes, but for a third of the price,' said Gemma. 'And he gave it to me for our main TV only Dad bought me that.'

'Isn't it great to have all these men showering money on you.' Liz laughed.

'If only I could manage the money a bit better, it might be,' said Gemma.

'You should ask David to help you.'

'Help me?' Gemma slid a clip into Liz's hair.

'Get him to look over your financial health and give you some advice. That's his job, isn't it?'

'I know,' said Gemma. 'I wanted to ask him before but I can't help feeling it would be a mistake.'

'Why?' asked Liz. 'You could talk to him like a professional.'

'He's my ex-husband,' said Gemma dryly, 'I don't think professionalism comes into it somehow.'

'It'd be free advice all the same,' said Liz. 'Why not? He might even see that he's not giving you enough money and up your payments!'

Gemma grinned. 'I can't see that happening somehow. But maybe I'll give him a call.'

'Once his new wife doesn't know about it.'

'Why should she care?'

'It's not easy being a second wife,' said Liz.

'You'd know?' Gemma looked at her in the mirror. 'You're thinking about stepping into the role?'

'Not yet.' Liz smiled. 'Maybe not at all. But I know that, even though Ross says some awful things about Jackie, there's still a bond between them.'

'Well, there's nothing between David and me,' said Gemma, clamping down on the memory of him holding her in the kitchen. 'Nothing at all.'

'Why don't you try and meet someone new?' Liz half turned in the seat.

'Don't you start.' Gemma sighed deeply and pushed Liz round again.

'Ouch!' Liz made a face at her. 'Start what?'

'On at me about meeting someone. Niamh never stops. "Get out there. Find someone else. Live a little."'

'She has a point.'

Gemma shook her head. 'I can't, Liz. I have the kids to think about.'

'Keelin's fourteen,' Liz told her. 'Pretty soon she'll be into boyfriends of her own – if she isn't already. And she'll be staying out all night and generally giving you a hard time. And next thing you know she'll have left home and you'll be on your own.'

'I'll still have Ronan,' said Gemma.

'He won't be far behind her,' said Liz. 'Ten years from now, he'll be twenty-one and you'll be wishing that you'd taken your opportunities to get out and about.'

'Rubbish,' said Gemma.

'What about the holidays?' Liz turned round in the chair to face her sister. 'I should've asked you. Didn't you meet anyone there? Holidays are always good for that.'

Gemma felt the colour rise into her cheeks. She bent down to pick a roller from the floor.

253

'Well?' asked Liz again.

'I didn't have time for meeting people on holidays,' said Gemma.

'Then why get into a flap about it when I asked?' Liz grinned at her. 'Oh, come on, Gem – not even a one-night stand?'

'Actually,' said Gemma as she worked her way to the ends of Liz's hair, 'as it happens there was nearly someone.'

'Nearly?'

'We met a family. Mother, two kids and mother's brother. Very nice people.'

'The brother?' asked Liz.

'He was nice,' said Gemma. 'But he was younger than me, Liz. And I have a horrible feeling that Keelin liked him rather too much.'

'A crush,' said Liz dismissively.

'Maybe. But I wasn't going to hop into bed with someone she had a crush on.'

'Did you want to hop into bed with him?' Liz turned round again, her eyes wide.

'I'm nearly finished! Keep still, would you?'

'Did you?' asked Liz. 'Tell me.'

'It was a holiday kind of thing,' said Gemma. 'And I didn't go to bed with him. What do you think I am? Anyway, he was too young.'

'How old was he?' asked Liz. 'Eighteen? Nineteen?'

'Thirty,' said Gemma.

'That's not too young,' protested Liz. 'Though it's certainly too old for Keelin!'

'As Keelin rather tellingly pointed out, it's the same age difference as between David and Orla.'

'She said that?'

'She most certainly did.'

'Well, well. And what did you say?'

'What could I say?' asked Gemma. 'They left the day before us. I doubt that we'll see them again. The family is from Wicklow anyway.'

'Would you like to see him again?' asked Liz. 'What was his name? What was he like?'

'Liz, it's irrelevant. I won't see him again.'

'But you liked him,' said Liz.

Gemma shrugged. 'He was a nice guy.'

'Why didn't you go for it?' asked Liz. 'Surely by now you must be tired of celibacy!'

'Liz!'

Her sister made a face. 'I certainly am. And I reckon I've had more of my share of it than you over the last few years.'

Gemma finished the plait and stepped away from her sister. 'Does that feel OK?'

'It's fine,' said Liz impatiently. 'Gemma, come on, give it a go.'

'There's nothing to give a go to,' said Gemma. 'I knew I shouldn't have said anything. You're blowing it all out of proportion.'

'Do you think so?'

'For goodness sake, Liz, give it a rest!' Gemma picked up a mirror and held it behind Liz's head. 'There. What do you think? Can Cinderella go to the ball tonight?'

'It's great.' Liz smiled at her. 'Thanks, Gem.'

'You're welcome,' said Gemma. 'Only next time try and make an appointment like everyone else. I hope you have a great time tonight.'

Liz made a face. 'I'm nervous.'

'There's no need to be,' said Gemma.

'I know. But all the same . . .'

'He asked you, didn't he?'

'Yes. At the last minute.'

'Maybe he was nervous about it.'

'And maybe he wasn't going to. Maybe the rest of them don't want me there. After all, none of them know me.'

'They will after tonight.' Gemma grinned at her sister.

'Oh, Gemma, I hope I'm doing the right thing,' said Liz.

'Of course you are.' Gemma put her arms round her sister. 'You deserve someone nice and decent, Liz. You really do.'

'So do you,' said Liz. 'Meet this bloke again. Give it a chance.'

Gemma smiled wryly. 'I already had my chance and I blew it.'

'Don't say that!'

'Have fun,' said Gemma. 'Be good.'

She was the last one left in the salon. She pushed all the chairs into position in front of the mirrors and checked that everything was neat and tidy. She stared at herself in the mirror.

The light tan suited her. She looked better than she had in ages. She felt better too. Somehow she didn't feel as though the weight of the world was planted firmly on both her shoulders.

Liz was right. She should make things happen instead of sitting back and allowing them to and then complaining because nothing ever happened the way she expected. She should organise herself better. She should sort out her finances.

She picked up the phone and dialled David's number.

255

Chapter 28

G emma was watching the TV when the doorbell rang. She got up,
adjusted her dress, glanced at her reflection in the mirror and
went to answer the door.

'Hello, David,' she said.

'Hi.'

'Thanks for coming over straightaway. You didn't need to. Any time
would have done.'

'It wasn't as though I had anything else on tonight,' said David.
'Orla won't be home until tomorrow so tonight suited me.'

'How's she getting on?' Gemma asked the question casually.

'Oh, fine,' said David. 'She doesn't say much about it – well, what
can you say really? Those courses are such a bore!'

'I'm sure she'll be glad to get home.'

If she'd liked the idea of coming home, she would have come home
tonight, thought David bleakly. She wouldn't have stayed to do her
bit of bonding or whatever she wanted to call it with her team. A few
weeks ago she would have rushed home to be with him and he would
have wanted her to rush home to be with him. But now it seemed as
though neither of them was comfortable in the other's company. It's as
much her fault as mine, he said to himself. She should have confided in
me sooner. I would have been supportive. I would have told her about
Bob Murphy and that crowd of sharks he works with.

'David?' Gemma looked at him, query in her eyes.

'Sorry, what?'

'I asked if you were going to stand here all night! Come on.'

'Sorry, I was daydreaming.' David put thoughts of his wife out of
his mind while he followed his ex-wife into the living room.

She switched on the main light to complement the lamps that had
been lighting the room. 'So that we can see what we're doing,' she
said. 'Do you want a drink, or anything?'

'Not unless you're having one.'

'I opened a bottle of Vinho Verde before you came,' she said. 'It's one I brought back from Portugal. It's light. Would you like some?'

'OK.' David opened his briefcase. 'Thanks.'

Gemma took a couple of glasses from the beech sideboard and poured the wine into them. She handed one to David who tasted it.

'Not bad,' he said.

'It was nicer there!' She laughed. 'David, thank you again for the holiday. I can't tell you how much the children enjoyed it.'

'That's OK,' he said.

'It was nice for them to make new friends too,' said Gemma.

'What about Keelin and the bloke?' asked David.

Gemma felt colour stain her cheeks. 'That was nothing,' she said.

'Are you sure?'

'Of course.'

'It's just that I'm not here to watch over her. I worry,' David told her.

She looked at him. 'Do you?'

'Of course I do.' He put his glass down on the table in front of him. 'Just because they're not with me every minute of every day, Gemma, doesn't mean I don't care about them.'

'I wish you'd cared more when you lived here,' she said.

'So do I,' said David as he took a big yellow pad out of the open briefcase.

❧

Orla turned the car into the cobbled courtyard in front of the apartment building. The space in front of their apartment was empty which meant that David was out. She bit her lip. She knew that she should have phoned him again. When she'd said earlier that she wouldn't be home she should have known that he'd make a few calls, set up a few meetings and do anything rather than spend the time on his own. Until Jonathan phoned her at the hotel, she'd actually made up her mind to come home despite what she'd told David. But after Jonathan's call she wanted to see him again, she couldn't help herself. She wanted to talk to him, to look at him, to experience the feelings that she felt for him again. So she'd phoned him back and told him that she was staying for another day.

'Brilliant!' he exclaimed. 'I'll take the rest of the day off. There's a whole series of things we can do.'

The series of things included queuing for nearly an hour to kiss the

Blarney Stone at the top of Blarney Castle to acquire the fabled gift of the gab. Orla and Jonathan had stood in a snaking line of tourists – mostly American – while a chill easterly breeze reminded them that autumn had arrived.

'Why did you choose this?' she demanded after she'd almost broken her neck trying to get into position to kiss the stone. 'I mean, it's not as if I can't talk enough as it is.'

'Oh, the gift of the gab is completely different,' Jonathan assured her. 'I kissed it the first weekend I came here. Now I know that I can talk my way out of anything.'

'Well,' she said as she righted herself again. 'I hope it'll be worth the undoubted visit to my chiropractor that'll ensue from this.'

'Have you a bad back?' he asked.

'Sometimes.' She rubbed the base of her spine. 'I think it came from carrying all those books around when we were in college.'

'Why were you so serious about it all?' He fell into step beside her as they left the grounds of the castle and walked back to his car.

'I don't know,' she answered. 'I suppose I just felt that I was there to study and so I should study, that's all. And I had the example of my brothers to follow, of course. I can't help myself.'

'Very few of us felt like that. At least, as much as you.'

She shrugged. 'It's the way I am.'

'But didn't you ever think you'd do something more interesting with your life?' he asked.

'What do you mean?' She stopped walking and turned to face him.

'Getting the job. Getting married.' He shrugged helplessly. 'It seems such a – oh, Orla, look out!' He grabbed her by the arm and pulled her onto the grass verge and out of the way of the huge tourist bus that was descending down the road at speed.

'God almighty!' Her heart thudded in her chest. 'What on earth was he thinking about! This road is too narrow to come charging along it like that. Did you get his number, Jonathan? There must be someone we can report him to. That was bloody reckless. Absolutely—'

'Orla, Orla!' He shook her gently. 'Calm down. You're OK.'

She was still shaking although she wasn't sure whether it was from anger or from the fright.

'He should be reported,' she repeated. 'Let's face it, I could have been mowed down. It was incredibly dangerous. I wonder did he have a licence at all. You know some of these guys probably just rent out a bus and pack tourists into it. They could—'

258

'Orla.' Jonathan interrupted her. 'I think kissing the Blarney Stone certainly worked with you.'

She stopped her tirade and giggled. 'I was mouthing off a bit.'

'A lot. But everything's OK now.'

'Yes,' she said. 'And thank you.'

'Thank you?'

'For rescuing me. For plucking me from the jaws of death.'

'He probably wouldn't have actually hit you,' admitted Jonathan.

'He might have.'

Jonathan smiled. 'I like to be cast in the role of saviour,' he said. He tightened his grip on her arm. 'Come on, let's get back to the car before someone else has a go at you.'

The wind was bitingly cold. In the distance, the rolling green hills had disappeared into a backdrop of mist and the sheep in the nearby meadows clustered close to the stone walls. She clambered into the Range Rover and shivered.

'You need something to warm you up,' he told her. 'We both do.'

'Turn on the heater,' she said.

'I had something a little more imaginative in mind,' said Jonathan. He switched on the ignition and revved the engine. They drove up the country road in a silence broken only by the occasional swish of the wipers across the windscreen as the mist enveloped them.

'Where are we going?' she asked.

'To warm you up,' he replied.

She glanced at him. He was concentrating on the narrow, twisting road, watchful for oncoming traffic.

'Ouch!' She lurched in her seat and bit her tongue.

'Sorry,' said Jonathan. 'Pothole. The roads are a disgrace around here. Never mind, almost there.'

'Almost where?'

He turned to glance at her. 'My place, of course.'

Jonathan's was a granite-walled bungalow with a black slate roof and old-fashioned sash windows.

'It still looks very new,' he told her as she got out of the jeep. 'But kind of sympathetic to the landscape, I think, even though the windows are actually PVC!'

'It's nice.' She stood in the gravel driveway and looked at it. 'It's homely.'

'It's a lot more homely inside,' said Jonathan. 'Come on. Let's go and warm up.'

He unlocked the front door and she followed him inside.

'Oh, Jonathan!' she exclaimed. 'It's absolutely gorgeous.'

He grinned at her. 'It is, isn't it.'

She looked at the polished floorboards and the newly-painted walls. 'Did you do this yourself?'

'Are you mad?' he asked. 'Nope. Previous owners.' He shrugged. 'I know I should feel bad that their marriage went down the toilet but it's an ill wind as they say and I've done particularly well out of their misfortune.'

'You certainly have.' Orla walked down the hallway and opened the door facing her. It led into a good-sized kitchen with a quarry-tiled floor and a huge green Aga against the wall. 'How very town and country,' she teased.

'It's not exactly how I imagined I'd end up.' He laughed. 'But the Aga's fantastic. Heats the house. Heats the meals for one. Between the Aga and the microwave I can't go wrong.'

'All you need is a golden Labrador and you'll be accepted by the neighbours.'

'And a brace of pheasant hanging in the shed.' He grinned at her. 'I don't think so somehow. I know I'm living in the country but I hate to think of where my food comes from. I like meat to look as though it's appeared by some magic design. I don't like to think of it as possibly being from the herd of cattle up the road.'

'I know what you mean,' said Orla as she watched him pour generous measures of whiskey into a couple of tumblers.

'You've probably turned into a great cook.' He handed her a glass. '*Sláinte.*'

'*Sláinte.*' She echoed the toast and sipped the whiskey. She could feel it warming every part of her body. 'I haven't, you know,' she said.

'What?'

'Turned into a great cook. I'm a terrible cook. We had some of David's friends over to dinner and I was practically institutionalised afterwards. I got myself into a terrible state. Not to mention the fact that I melted a plastic bowl full of chopped carrots beforehand.'

He laughed. 'I'd have liked to be there.'

'No you wouldn't.' She shook her head. 'The stench of burning plastic was disgusting. A pall of smoke hung around for ages afterwards. And poor old David couldn't understand why I was practically in hysterics.'

'What about his previous wife?' asked Jonathan casually. 'Was she any good in the kitchen?'

260

'Gemma.' Orla took another slug of whiskey. 'Gemma was the ultimate stay-at-home wife. Home baking, home decor, home anything – Gemma was a paragon of those virtues.'

'But they split up.'

Orla nodded. 'She was also a nag.'

'And that was the reason?' Jonathan looked surprised.

'Among other things.'

'So if you start nagging him he'll give you the boot too?'

'Sod off, Jonathan,' said Orla. She walked across the kitchen and looked out of the window. The mist had turned into rain, trickling down the glass. Although she was warmer now, she shivered again.

'I'm sorry.' Jonathan stood beside her.

'It doesn't matter.'

'Do you love him?' he asked.

She watched a bead of rain as it slid down the window. Did she love him? Of course she did. But at this particular moment? Knowing that he was annoyed with her? Knowing that he was punishing her for his annoyance in a particularly childish way? How did she feel about him right now?

'I already told you that I do.'

'Then why are you here?' asked Jonathan.

She turned to look at him. 'Because you brought me here,' she said.

Six hours later, she switched off the car ignition and gave silent thanks that she hadn't been stopped on the way home. She'd had a second whiskey at Jonathan's house and had refused the third. She'd drunk too much to drive but she hadn't cared. She'd had to leave Jonathan's. She couldn't stay.

She hadn't wanted David to be out. She'd hoped that he would be waiting for her when she got back. She wanted to have her judgement validated by seeing him as soon as she could.

But he didn't care, she thought. He'd grown tired of her just as he'd grown tired of Gemma and he hadn't even bothered to wait for her. She rubbed at her eyes then got out of the car and retrieved her bag from the boot.

Part of her clung to the hope that he actually was at home and that there was another reason for the car to be missing. But the apartment felt empty the moment she stepped inside the hall door.

She walked into the bedroom and threw her bag on the bed. Then she went back to the living room and looked around as though there might be a clue to his whereabouts. It was incredibly tidy. The cushions were plumped up, there were no old newspapers lying around and her magazines were neatly arranged in two magazine racks. 'Two,' she said out loud. He must have bought another one. The sculpture of the African lady was back in its place too. Orla smothered a smile as she imagined David lugging it out of the storage room wondering why on earth she'd put it there. She wanted to put it back but she didn't have the energy. She felt utterly exhausted.

There was an open bottle of red wine on the kitchen counter. She'd been about to make herself a cup of tea but the wine seemed much more appealing. She poured herself a drink, enjoying the satisfying sound as the liquid glugged out of the bottle. She filled the glass to the brim and carried bottle and glass into the living room.

⌇

'So what do you think?' David asked Gemma who was studying the pad in front of her.

'You make it look so simple.' She looked up and pushed her hair out of her eyes. 'Why can you make it look simple when I make it so difficult?'

He smiled at her. 'Because, my dearest Gemma, I don't spend half my salary on new dresses. Or new coats. Or new eyeshadow. Or new perfume. Or—'

'OK, OK!' She stopped him, laughing. 'I get the drift. Cut down on the mad, extravagant impulse purchases. Set myself a budget for household things. Live a sensible life.'

'You can still buy clothes,' said David. 'Only not just every day.'

'You wouldn't believe how boring my life would be if I couldn't buy clothes.' She poured the last of the wine into the glasses. 'And that's the truth, I suppose, David. I spend so much time running around doing things that buying is therapeutic.'

'It was therapy for you even before you had to spend your time running around doing things,' said David dryly.

She looked at him and smiled. 'I suppose you're right.'

He smiled back at her. She looked positively pretty tonight, he realised, with her honey-coloured skin and her soft brown hair and

262

her laughing eyes. She reminded him once again of the Gemma he'd fallen in love with. He caught his breath. He didn't want to think like this.

⌒

Orla poured herself another glass of the Rioja and looked at the clock. Where was he? she wondered. Meeting clients? After nine o'clock at night? It seemed highly unlikely. Maybe he'd gone to the pub again. She was tired of him going to the pub on the way home in the evening, even if he only had one pint. It was the idea of him sitting on his own at the bar, studying a pint like someone who had nothing better to do, that bothered her. Did he think that there was nothing better in his life? Did he prefer a glass of Guinness to being with her?

She sipped the Rioja and stared, unseeingly, at the African woman in the corner.

⌒

Gemma looked at the bottle of Vinho Verde in surprise. She hadn't realised that they'd finished it – that she'd finished it, really, because David hadn't drunk very much.

'I suppose this kind of extravagance will have to go,' she said as she held up the bottle. 'Wine in the evenings.'

'You don't have to spend a fortune on it,' David told her.

'You always did.' Gemma replaced the empty bottle on the table. 'Remember when you joined that wine club? All those tastings you went to? And all the bottles you brought home?'

'They were investments,' said David. 'That's completely different.'

Gemma made a face at him. 'I could never see the point of that,' she said. 'Why stock up on bottles of wine you can't drink? It makes no sense.'

'They become valuable,' said David.

'But what's the value?' Gemma looked at him in puzzlement. 'I buy a designer dress and it's expensive but I get pleasure out of wearing it. And people tell me it looks nice so I feel good in it. So it's an investment of sorts. But a bottle of wine that you can't drink! I find it hard to believe that you think it's better to buy wine you can't drink than a dress you can wear.'

'I'd look pretty silly in a dress,' said David, deadpan, and then both laughed.

263

He could see that she was slightly drunk. He'd only had a glass of the wine himself and she'd finished the bottle, talking and drinking at the same time in very much the way she had when they were younger. She'd been interested in what he was saying and her conversation was animated as she asked him about the policies she had and what they were worth and whether she should cash them or not.

She's not stupid. The thought came to him suddenly and surprised him. For so long he'd thought of her as silly or irresponsible but she wasn't. The questions she was asking were the ones he'd ask himself.

'You look lovely tonight.' The words were out before he could stop them.

'Pardon?' She looked at him in surprise.

'You look lovely,' he said. 'I haven't seen you looking as well in ages. The holiday obviously suited you.'

'It was relaxing,' she said. 'I recharged my batteries, I think.'

'More than that,' said David. 'You seem to have recharged everything.'

'David!' Gemma blushed.

'Seriously,' he told her. 'You seem different, Gemma. More like the Gemma I used to know.'

'Don't be silly,' she said abruptly. 'I'm certainly not the Gemma you used to know.'

'Do you ever think about it?' he asked.

'What?'

'Our marriage. Do you ever think about how good it was?'

'When I think about it,' she told him softly, 'I think that the good bits were all early on. And that you got caught up in work and I got caught up in the kids. And we forgot about being caught up in each other.'

'But don't you think that we could have changed it?' he asked.

She shrugged. 'Maybe once. But then it became too late.' She stood up. 'We've talked about this before, David. And I can't understand why you seem to want to talk about it so much now. You're married to someone else.'

'I know,' he said. 'Maybe that's what makes me remember our marriage.' He smiled at her. 'I'm sorry if it makes you uncomfortable.'

'It's OK,' she said. 'I just don't see any point in talking about it any more.' She walked out of the room and upstairs to the bath-room.

The conversation bothered her, like all conversations with David bothered her a little lately. He seemed to want to revisit the past all the time whereas she – well, she was ready to think about the future. And she couldn't understand why he was so obsessed with what had gone before when he had a future that was clearly mapped out for him now.

⤸

Orla poured the final glass of Rioja down the kitchen sink. The wine, on top of the whiskey she'd drunk earlier and the fact that she hadn't eaten very much, was making her tired. She filled the kettle and spooned instant coffee into her big green mug. She opened the bread bin. The bag of donughts she'd bought before she went on the course was at the back. He'd eaten one or two, she realised, but that was all. The bag was greasy and sticky from the melting sugar and seeping jam. She picked it up and threw it in the bin.

What does he want from me? she asked herself. What does he want and can I give it to him any more?

⤸

'Dad!' Keelin stopped in surprise as she saw her father and mother sitting side by side on the sofa.

'Hi, darling.'

'What are you doing here?' she asked.

'Keelin!' Gemma looked at her. 'That's not a very nice way to talk to your father.'

Keelin shrugged. 'He's never here. Why is he here now? It's late.'

'He was helping me to organise our finances,' said Gemma.

'Take more than one person,' retorted Keelin. 'Has he succeeded?'

'Oh, I think so.' David smiled at her. 'There's very little that can't be sorted by a little judicial planning.'

'Does this mean there'll be more pocket money?' asked Keelin tartly.

'Don't push it,' warned Gemma. 'Why don't you make yourself useful and put on the kettle?'

'Why do I always have to make myself useful?' grumbled Keelin who nevertheless went into the kitchen and did what she was told.

265

'She looks different,' remarked David as his daughter left the room.

'It's the make-up,' explained Gemma.

'She's too young for make-up!' exclaimed David. 'You shouldn't let her go out with her face covered in muck.'

'David, it's very little make-up. You didn't even realise she was wearing it.' Gemma sighed. 'I'd prefer if she didn't wear it either but I can't stop her and I'm not going to nag at her about it.'

'Has she a boyfriend?' he asked. 'I hope not, Gemma. She's only fourteen.'

'I had a boyfriend when I was fourteen,' said Gemma.

'Who?'

'None of your business,' she returned. 'Admittedly, I was fourteen and a half, but on the basis that kids grow up quicker now, she's entitled to have someone.'

David sighed. He found it hard to believe that his daughter could be interested in boys although, looking as she did now, he could see why boys might be interested in her. It was a frightening thought.

'She'll be OK, won't she?' He looked anxiously at Gemma.

'Of course she will.' Gemma smiled and hoped that she was right.

Keelin returned carrying a tray laden with tea things. She slid it onto the coffee table and sat on the floor beside them.

'Will I pour?' she asked.

'Yes,' said Gemma.

It was nice to see them together. Gemma's heart lurched suddenly as she looked at them – Keelin sitting on the floor, her back resting against the front of the sofa, beside David's legs. They were very alike, she realised. Keelin had always taken after him in looks but now, seeing the two of them so close together, Gemma suddenly realised how much she resembled her father. She'd always thought of Keelin as hers – even when she spent time with David – because she always came home to her. But, she realised, Keelin was part of both of them. No matter how much she regretted anything that had happened in the past, she could never regret Keelin. Or Ronan.

The music which signalled Sky News on the Hour alerted them to the time. David looked at his watch as though he needed to be convinced that it was eleven o'clock. 'I'd better get going,' he said.

'Why?' asked Keelin.

'It's late.'

'Not that late.'

'Late enough, young lady. Surely you should be in bed?'

266

'Oh, for God's sake!' she stared at him. 'You really do think I'm still a child, don't you?'

'I'm sure—'

'She goes up at half-ten during the week,' said Gemma firmly.

'Ronan was quite happy to go up at nine,' said David.

'He's a kid.' Keelin snorted.

'Anyway.' David got up and put his cup on the coffee table. 'I should be off. I'll see you Sunday as usual, Keelin.'

'What exciting trip had you got in mind for us?'

'I don't know.' He shrugged. 'Where would you like to go?'

'Don't care,' she said shortly.

'We'll decide then,' said David. He pulled on his jacket. 'I'll go home and get my beauty sleep now.'

'Did Orla mind you being out tonight?' asked Keelin.

David shook his head. 'She's still away.'

'Still?' Keelin looked surprised. 'I thought you said that she'd be home at the weekend.'

'It's the weekend tomorrow too,' said David.

'If I was married to someone I wouldn't spend a night away from them,' declared Keelin.

David and Gemma exchanged glances.

'I wouldn't,' repeated Keelin. 'And I bet she misses you like crazy, Dad.'

'Possibly,' said David as he got up and looked for his keys.

Gemma handed them to him and followed him to the door.

'Thanks again,' she said.

'No problem.' David opened the door. 'See you Sunday.'

'Sure,' she said.

He leaned towards her and kissed her quickly on the cheek. 'Take care.'

'You too,' she said.

She closed the door without waiting for him to drive away.

267

Chapter 29

When David turned into the parking area in front of the apartment block he was astonished to see Orla's car already there. He frowned. She'd definitely told him that she wasn't coming home tonight. He remembered the phone call quite clearly. Why had she changed her mind? He got out of his car, locked it and almost sprinted into the building.

He could hear the TV as he put his key into the latch and pushed open the door. He walked into the living room. Orla was sitting on the sofa, drinking a cup of coffee, her long legs drawn under her while she watched a late-night movie.

'Hi,' said David.

She glanced at him. 'Hi.'

'I didn't expect you home this evening,' he said.

'So I gather.'

'You said you wouldn't be home this evening.' His voice was accusatory.

She shrugged. 'I changed my mind.'

'I would have stayed here if I thought you'd be home.'

'Would you?'

'Of course,' said David.

'I hadn't noticed that my being here before made you stay home.'

'Don't be silly.' He sat down in the armchair opposite her. 'You know I'd have been here.'

'Where were you until this hour?' She put her coffee cup on the table beside her.

'I was . . .' David suddenly realised that telling her he'd spent the evening in his former wife's house probably wouldn't go down very well. But if he lied and she found out about it, things would be even worse. Orla was watching him, aware of his hesitation.

'I had to meet some clients,' he said. 'Then I popped over to Gemma's.'

'Gemma?' She looked at him in surprise. 'Why did you have to go to Gemma's?'

'Because she asked me to,' said David. 'She wanted some help with her financial planning.'

'Oh, for God's sake.' Orla's tone was disgusted. 'She can organise her own financial planning perfectly well.'

'No, she can't,' said David. 'She's absolutely hopeless with money.'

'Not from where I'm sitting,' said Orla.

'What do you mean?'

'It seems to me she does bloody well. She taps you for cash on demand – the holiday, the TV, anything for the kids – and you just give in every time.'

'It's not like that,' said David.

'What's it like?' asked Orla.

'She does her best,' he told Orla. 'It's just that she's scatty about it.'

'Give me a break,' muttered Orla. She picked up the coffee cup and drained it. 'Anyway,' she continued, 'what kept you so long? Look at the time! Surely it only takes a few minutes to scribble a cheque and walk out again?'

'I told you, I was going through her finances,' said David. 'You can't do that in five minutes, Orla.'

'How long did it take?'

'I don't see that it makes any difference,' he said.

Orla looked away. He didn't understand. She knew he didn't and she didn't expect him to. It worried her to think of him spending time in Gemma's house. Which was, no doubt, a haven of domesticity in comparison to the apartment where he'd been living on his own all week. Gemma had probably fed him her wonderfully produced homemade food and given him something to drink and pandered to his ego in a way that Orla couldn't. She twirled her solitaire diamond engagement ring round on her finger.

'Anyway, what brought you home tonight after all?' asked David. 'Don't tell me that you suddenly got disillusioned with Serene?'

'No,' she said shortly. She'd come home because she was afraid to stay away. She'd wandered around Jonathan's old-fashioned house and thought to herself that it would be a lovely place to live and she'd been horrified that she'd visualised herself living there with him. And then, as she'd been standing at the kitchen window looking out onto the rolling hills behind the house, he'd stood behind her and put his arms round her and kissed her on the neck.

She shivered as she remembered his kiss. She'd half expected it, had been ready for it, ready to reject him. But she'd turned to look at him and he'd kissed her again, on the mouth this time and she hadn't been able to help herself. She hadn't wanted to kiss him too. Hadn't believed that she would. But when his lips pressed on hers, she'd allowed herself to relax into his arms and had surrendered herself to the pleasure of it. She hadn't even pulled away when his right hand slid under her bulky Aran jumper and she'd been able to feel the warmth of his touch through the thin fabric of her sheer white blouse. She hadn't pulled away either when he'd finally lifted the Aran over her head and dropped it on the terracotta tiles of the kitchen floor. It had only been when he'd opened the buttons of her blouse, unclipped her bra and closed his hand over her breast that she'd suddenly asked herself what the hell she thought she was doing.

Jonathan had been very understanding. He'd apologised, told her that of course she needed time and space to get herself together and told her that he'd always loved her. And he'd kissed her again and told her that she'd better go now if she was going to go at all. She'd found it very difficult to leave. Being with Jonathan had reminded her of a time when things were easy and uncomplicated and when she'd always known exactly what she wanted.

'Would you like some tea?' David's voice broke into her thoughts.

She shook her head.

'I'll put on the kettle,' he said. 'I'm going to make some anyway.'

Maybe it would be like this with Jonathan too, she thought. It would be passionate and exciting at first and then it would descend into the triviality of putting on the kettle.

But Jonathan wouldn't spend evenings with his ex-wife. Orla bit her lip. What is wrong with me? she cried silently. What do I want? Why is everything so bloody, bloody difficult?

⌒

Gemma set the alarm to go off half an hour earlier on Monday morning. She'd decided, following her financial overhaul, to be even more organised in the rest of her life. An earlier start in the mornings meant that she had time to shower and get dressed before hauling Keelin and Ronan out of bed. While they were getting ready, she prepared breakfast. By the time that they were leaving for school, Gemma was ahead of schedule and was able, for the first time that she could remember, to drive across the city to the hairdressing salon without screaming at the cars in front of her to get a move on.

Niamh was surprised to see Gemma walking in the door before nine o'clock. Normally her friend arrived to work in a flurry of movement, apologising for being late while taking off her jacket and checking her appointments all at the same time. Today, Gemma was relaxed and cheerful and, Niamh noticed, had even managed to put on her make-up before arriving at work. Normally Gemma slapped on a light foundation and some lipstick at the back of the salon before greeting her first client.

'What's got into you today?' Niamh looked pointedly at the big clock on the back wall.

'What d'you mean?'

'It's only a quarter to nine,' said Niamh. 'You're here, you've already got your make-up on and you look great.'

'Thanks,' said Gemma. 'You mean most of the time I look awful?'

'You know exactly what I mean,' Niamh told her. 'In all the time I've ever known you, Gemma Garvey, you've never managed to get your foot inside the door before nine. What's happened?'

'Don't laugh,' warned Gemma as she hung her jacket on the coat stand.

'I won't.'

'David came over the other night,' Gemma explained. 'We went through all my finances. He told me ways of making savings. He gave me a lecture about being organised.' She grimaced. 'When we were married and he gave me lectures I never wanted to listen, but this time I did. Actually, he talks a lot of sense, which is a bit hard to take! But he was very nice and helpful and I thought that instead of just my finances I should take a look at my whole life.'

'Good God,' said Niamh.

'And so I did. And one of the things I decided was that I'm always late for work and that's going to change from now on.'

Niamh grinned at her. 'But I know that you're going to be late. I factor that in to everything!'

Gemma laughed. 'Not any more. You're looking at the new, methodical Gemma Garvey.'

'I give it a week,' said Niamh.

'Oh ye of little faith,' said Gemma as she took her brushes out of the steriliser and got ready for the day ahead.

⌒

Keelin sat on top of her desk, her feet on the chair beside Shauna as

271

they waited for Miss McGrath to arrive for their economics lesson. She picked at the remnants of Pearly Pink nail varnish on her thumbnails. Nail varnish was not allowed in school but Keelin had hoped that, since Pearly Pink was sugary and pale, nobody would notice. Gemma, however, had spotted it just as she was about to have breakfast and had ordered her upstairs to remove it. Keelin had objected, Gemma had insisted and they'd argued fiercely for a couple of minutes before Gemma had told Keelin that if she didn't remove it then Gemma would. Forcibly. Keelin had given in but her efforts with the remover had been perfunctory and patches of Pearly Pink remained. Those patches were driving her crazy.

'So did you like having your dad over for the evening?' asked Shauna. Keelin had told her about David's arrival to discuss the finances of the household.

'It was nice,' she admitted. 'I felt like we were a family. I know that's kind of pathetic, Shauna, but it was comforting.'

'And they're getting on better, your mum and dad?'

'That's the silly thing.' Keelin flicked her hair out of her eyes. 'Since he married Orla, he's getting on much better with Mum. I've only seen her upset once. They used to snap at each other all the time.'

'Maybe he appreciates your mum more now that he's living with someone else,' suggested Shauna.

Keelin wrinkled her nose. 'That doesn't make sense. I'd have thought that he resents any time he spends away from Orla. Although,' she conceded, 'she was at some course last week. That's why he was able to drop over.'

'How are you getting on with her?' Shauna wanted to take advantage of Keelin's sudden willingness to talk about her family. Shauna thought that Keelin kept her feelings bottled up far too much.

'OK, I suppose.' Keelin shrugged. 'I don't see her much – she seems to go to her parents' house most Sundays while we're at lunch.'

'Did you go anywhere nice yesterday?' The one advantage of having divorced parents, Shauna thought, was that you were brought out far more often than with a mother and father who still lived together. The Fitzpatricks hardly ever went out to lunch, whereas Keelin was always being taken somewhere new.

'He dragged us out to Malahide,' said Keelin. 'What a waste of time! Exchanging one place by the sea for another. We had lunch in a pub, which was OK, and then he made us walk around the marina which was bloody awful. There was a force ten gale blowing yesterday and I was freezing.'

Shauna giggled. 'I spent yesterday with Becky and Stephen and the new baby. It was fun.'

'How's Becky?' Keelin asked after Shauna's older sister who'd just had her first baby.

'She's fine,' said Shauna. 'A bit tired though and she was telling me some awful things about giving birth.' She shivered. 'It was absolutely disgusting and makes me even more certain that I never want to have kids.'

'Especially not if they turn out like Pat Lacey.' Keelin nodded across the room in the direction of one of their classmates.

'Poor Pat,' said Shauna. 'Imagine having to wake up to that face every morning!'

Keelin glanced at Pat's face, covered with acne, and offered up a prayer of thanks that the worst that had ever happened to her was an occasional spot in the middle of her forehead or chin.

'Hey, Keelin!'

She turned round as Donny Gleeson walked up to her. She knew Donny well because he lived round the corner from her and he was the one boy in the school that she'd known before she started there. He was in the same French class as her but certainly shouldn't be in Room 2 now because he did science, not economics.

'Hi, Donny. What's up?'

'I have a message for you,' he said. 'From Mark.'

'Mark?'

'Mark Dineen,' said Donny impatiently.

'Oh.'

'He wants to know if you'd like to go to Alison Fogarty's party with him.'

Alison Fogarty was also in the same class as Keelin. In a school where many of the children had wealthy parents, Alison's were one of the wealthiest. She was also one of the oldest in their year and a certain cachet was attached to being friendly with her. Keelin wasn't in her select group but Alison wanted to have the biggest party ever and she'd asked everyone in their year.

This is the first time anyone has ever invited me out – even if I was going to be there anyway! The thought danced into Keelin's head. She was conscious of Shauna sitting beside her, listening to Donny asking her about the party on behalf of a guy who wouldn't ask her himself.

'Why doesn't he ask me himself?' she asked.

'Because you ignore him all the time,' said Donny. 'He's afraid of you.'

'I'm going with Shauna,' said Keelin.

'Oh, I don't mind,' Shauna lied. 'Go with Mark if you like.'

'I couldn't do that,' said Keelin. 'I promised I'd go with you.'

'I thought we could go in a foursome,' said Donny. 'If you'd like that, Shauna?' He looked at her and Keelin suddenly saw he was nervous. He wants to go with Shauna, she realised. He fancies her!

'What do you think, Keelin?' asked her friend.

'Sounds like fun.'

'OK.' Donny beamed at both of them. 'I'll tell Mark. It'll be great!'

He managed to dodge out of the room just as the economics teacher walked in and ordered Keelin to get off the desk and to sit down properly in her chair.

⌐

Orla sat in a traffic jam in Donnybrook and seethed with rage. Why, she wondered, had they (whoever 'they' were) decided to dig a hole in the middle of the road which had reduced traffic down to an almost stationary lane of cars? She looked at her watch. She was already late for her appointment with one of the partners in a solicitor's practice in Stillorgan. She'd just come from a very unproductive meeting with Damon Higgins of Blanca Kitchens & Floors. Higgins had finally agreed to meet her and she'd been pinning her hopes on a successful meeting with him to land her first decent client for Serene. So far, she'd brought in a few individual clients but nothing spectacular. The rest of her team weren't doing much better and she was feeling very pressurised. Blanca Kitchens & Floors was to have been her big deal, the one that would get her name in lights at Serene. Even though the number of employees was low, bringing them all into a scheme would have been great. But the long-awaited meeting with the company's managing director had been a complete failure. He'd moaned about the thin margins they worked on, the competitive nature of the market and the absolute necessity for them not to provide anything more in benefits than they already did for their employees. And, as far as Damon Higgins was concerned, providing a pension scheme was a definite step too far.

Orla wished he'd told her that at the start instead of holding out the promise of business for her. And before she'd ploughed through all those brochures on fitted kitchens and natural wood flooring.

She put the car into first and moved three yards. This was utterly ridiculous, she thought. The city was impossible to get around by car and yet there was no other way of getting from Finglas to Stillorgan. She reached for her phone and dialled the number of the solicitors.

'Tom Mannion, please,' she said. 'Hi, Tom, it's Orla Hennessy. I'm sorry, I'm stuck in a traffic jam in Donnybrook. The way things are going it'll take me at least another fifteen minutes to get to you.' She winced at the lie, it was going to take a lot longer than that. Then she bit her lip as Tom Mannion told her that he was going into a meeting in half an hour. At most, she'd have fifteen minutes to make her pitch. She hung up and rubbed her forehead. She was getting the most awful headache and the back of her neck hurt too.

The line of cars moved forward another couple of feet. She was never going to make it to Mannion's office in time. She thumped the steering wheel in frustration. The phone rang.

'Hello,' she said, wondering if Tom was calling to reschedule.

'Hi, there.'

Orla moistened her suddenly dry lips. 'Jonathan?'

'Who else?'

'Where are you ringing from?' she asked.

'Home,' he replied.

She pictured him in the huge kitchen with the terracotta floors and the green Aga. 'What are you doing there? Shouldn't you be at work?'

'I do a lot of work from home,' he told her. 'I was sitting at my desk thinking about a problem I'm having with a venting duct and I suddenly thought of you.'

'I remind you of a venting duct?'

He laughed. 'Of course not. But I was looking at the drawing and trying really hard to figure out what I should be doing and I thought that what I really should be doing is holding you in my arms.'

'Jonathan!'

'Have you a problem with that?' he asked.

'Of course I have,' she snapped. 'I'm married, Jonathan.'

'You're miserable,' he said.

The cars moved forward again. Orla was slow putting the Honda into gear and the driver behind her rewarded her by blasting the horn at her.

'Oh, keep your hair on!' she yelled.

'What?' asked Jonathan.

'Not you,' she said. 'I'm in the car at the moment, sitting in a traffic jam in Donnybrook village, late for a meeting and being hassled by the dickhead in the car behind me.'

'That's the problem with living in the city,' he said. 'Just imagine, Orla, if you were here with me, the only thing you'd have to worry about is the flock of sheep on the land next door.'

She was silent.

'I miss you,' he said.

275

'Jonathan, I know I gave you my number but I never really thought you'd ring.'

'Shouldn't have given me the number if you didn't want me to ring,' said Jonathan teasingly.

Orla's heart was racing. The idea of being with Jonathan now was very appealing. The thought of him holding her in his arms as he'd done so recently, of him kissing her neck, her face, her lips – she closed her eyes as she thought of him kissing her lips. The driver behind blasted the horn again. She opened her eyes and moved forward all of a foot.

'Orla?'

'Jonathan, I can't be with you and that's that.'

'Are you happy?' he asked.

'Not right now,' she said tartly. 'Right now I'm suffering from restrained road rage. I've just come from a crappy meeting, I'm late for another one and I'm not happy at all.'

'I meant with the Ancient Mariner.'

'Don't call him that!' He'd christened David with the nickname after she'd told him that her husband enjoyed sailing.

'I love you,' said Jonathan. 'I always have and I always will.'

'You're being stupid.' Orla wiped her sweating palms on the edge of the driver's seat.

'I'm telling you the truth.'

Orla said nothing.

'Do you want me to hang up?'

'No,' she said. 'You might as well talk to me. I'm going nowhere fast.'

'I've had lots of girlfriends,' said Jonathan. 'You know that already. But I've never felt half of what I feel for you with any of them.'

Orla bit her lip.

'I couldn't believe it when Marty told me you'd married. I really couldn't. I said, not Orla. Orla hasn't time to get married. Orla wants to do something with her life.'

'Getting married isn't something?' she interrupted.

'Not for you.'

She put the car into gear. This time she managed to travel about ten yards.

'Orla, if you really and truly love him I won't do anything to rock the boat. You know I won't. But if you're not happy, you owe it to yourself to do something about it. Before you waste your life.'

'I'm not wasting my life,' she said. She was level with the hole in the road now. The next time the traffic moved, she'd get by it and the road ahead was clear. She might make it in time for her meeting with Tom Mannion yet.

'I wouldn't have tried to get in touch if I hadn't met you,' said Jonathan. 'It just seemed as though it was fate or something.'

'Cut the crap,' she said acidly. 'You don't believe in fate. As I remember we had a very heated discussion about that a few years ago.' One which had involved lots of drink and in ending up in bed together. Orla wished she hadn't remembered that.

Jonathan chuckled. He'd clearly remembered it too.

'I like talking to you,' he said.

'Well, this conversation is coming to an end now,' she told him as she put the car into first gear yet again and, this time, drove round the hole. 'I've just gone by the traffic obstruction, I'm booting out to a meeting, I can't talk to you any more, Jonathan.'

'Do you love me?' he asked.

She speeded up. 'No,' she said.

'Do you care about me?'

She moved into the fast lane. 'Of course.'

'Will you phone me?'

'I don't think so.'

'Why?' asked Jonathan.

'Because I don't think it would be a good idea,' she said.

'We're old friends,' he told her.

'We're old lovers,' she said acidly. 'And that's something completely different. If you want to meet old friends, give Abby a call. I'm sure she'd love to hear from you. I think she always fancied you herself!'

'Oh, Orla, you're being silly.'

'I'm not.' She changed lanes again, moving to the inside to overtake a Fiat which was driving far too slowly in the outside lane. 'Look, Jonathan, I've got to go. I'm busy.'

'OK,' he said. 'Just remember that I'm here if you need me.'

'I'll remember,' she said as she accelerated past yet another car.

She arrived at Mannion & Battiste a couple of minutes later.

'I'm so sorry,' said the receptionist. 'But Tom told me to tell you that he had to leave for his meeting. He suggests you call again to reschedule.'

Orla clenched her teeth and closed her eyes. She felt like crying with frustration.

'OK,' she said finally. 'Tell him I'm sorry to have missed him.'

She turned on her heel and walked out of the office. It was only when she was driving back toward the city that she realised that she should have asked the receptionist if she had adequate life cover herself.

Chapter 30

Gemma hadn't seen Liz since her sister's date with Ross Harrington. Liz had phoned her to tell her that it had gone really well, that she seemed to get on with everyone, that Ross had been absolutely great. Gemma had listened to the besotted tone in her sister's voice and thought that maybe Liz really had met the right man this time. It would be somewhat ironic, she thought, if that man turned out to be a divorced bloke with custody of the children. She wondered what Frances thought of Liz's relationship. She couldn't help thinking that her mother would absolutely freak out at the idea of Liz acquiring a ready-made family and a husband whose wife had left him.

I wonder how I'd feel if David had actually left me, she thought, as she hauled the vacuum cleaner out from beneath the stairs to begin her Sunday housekeeping. If it hadn't been me who'd initiated the whole thing. I don't think I could have stood it if he'd just walked out.

She looked at her watch. David should be here shortly to pick up the kids. When she was younger Keelin had loved to go out with her father but she was objecting to it more and more these days. Today she'd complained that she had homework to do. Gemma found herself in a quandary about Keelin's unusual interest in doing homework. She wanted to encourage her daughter's studies but she couldn't help feeling that Keelin would simply wait for David and Ronan to go out before disappearing to meet Shauna Fitzpatrick.

She went upstairs and tapped on Keelin's door.

'Come in,' said her daughter.

Gemma pushed the door open and went inside. Keelin was sitting at her desk, her maths book open in front of her.

'How are you getting on?' asked Gemma.

'Oh, all right.' Keelin sighed. 'Maths is not my thing.'

'It wasn't mine either,' admitted Gemma.

'I like languages,' said Keelin. 'I'm OK at French and German and Spanish. I'm not too bad at English and Irish. I stumble around at geography but I get reasonable marks for it. But maths – I'll never be any good at maths.'

'My best subject was home economics,' said Gemma. 'Though it was the cooking and food science part I was good at. Not the household management.'

Keelin smiled at her. 'But now Dad has sorted that out.'

'If I can stick to his plan,' said Gemma.

'I liked having him here,' Keelin said. 'It was nice.'

'I know,' said Gemma.

Keelin frowned. 'Do you ever think you shouldn't have got a divorce?'

Gemma considered her answer carefully. 'No,' she told Keelin. 'Sometimes I miss having your dad around, but that's just because it's hard being on your own. At first I thought I'd made a mistake divorcing him because it's so difficult to go through with it. But it was the right thing to do, Keelin, even though it might not always seem like that.' And the fact that he got married again and I didn't still doesn't mean it was a mistake, she thought, even if sometimes I've felt that way.

'I thought that one day he'd come back,' Keelin confided. 'That he'd realise he missed us.'

Gemma shook her head. 'That'll never happen, Keelin. I don't want it to happen.'

'I know,' said Keelin, 'but it's nice to imagine it, sometimes.'

'Are you going to go out with Dad this afternoon?' asked Gemma.

Keelin sighed. 'Do I have to?'

'It's part of the custody agreement,' said Gemma.

'But surely I should be able to say what I want to do.'

'I'll talk to your dad about it,' said Gemma. 'But I'd like it if you went out with him today. Unless you really have loads of homework.'

'Why?' asked Keelin. 'What exciting things have you planned for our absence?'

'Washing your clothes.' Gemma ruffled Keelin's hair. 'Cleaning the bathroom. Vacuuming the house. Wonderful domestic sort of things.'

Keelin grinned and closed her books. 'Oh, OK. I've finished this anyway. I'll be a dutiful daughter.'

'That'll be a first,' said Gemma and kissed her on the head.

⌐

David was late. It was after one o'clock before he arrived.

'Sorry,' he said as Gemma answered the door. 'I couldn't help it.' He didn't say that he was late because Orla had wanted to talk. To sit down and discuss things properly, she'd said, and he told her that he'd like nothing more than to talk to her but not today. Today he was seeing his children. She'd looked unhappy. He felt guilty. And then the traffic had been awful for Sunday.

'There's something I wanted to ask you,' he said to Gemma as he followed her into the kitchen.

'What?'

'It's my parent's golden wedding anniversary next month. They'd like you and the children to come to their celebration.'

'Oh.'

'Gemma, you know that you've always got on with them. They adore the kids and they'd really like all of you to be there.'

'Will Orla be there?' asked Gemma.

'What do you think?' David shrugged. 'Of course she'll be there, Gemma. And I understand if you don't want to come but I know that Mum and Dad want you to, and so do I.'

'Why didn't Patsy or Brian ask me themselves?' asked Gemma.

'They were afraid you might say no,' said David. 'I told Mum I might be able to persuade you.'

'And how did you think you could do that?' asked Gemma. 'Tie my hands behind my back and march me there?'

'No!'

She laughed. It was strange, she thought, how she laughed so much more with David these days. 'It was a joke, David.'

'Oh.'

She sighed. 'It's difficult. Being there with Orla. I know I should be able to cope with it and yet—'

'You don't have to talk to her,' said David.

'I know.'

'And she's more likely to be intimidated by you than you are by her.'

'What on earth makes you think that?' asked Gemma.

'Oh, come on, Gem. You're older than her. More mature. You can cope better.'

'I beg your pardon?' Gemma stared at him. 'I'm the person who had to call you in to look over her finances, remember? Coping is not exactly my thing.'

'Gemma, you cope really well,' said David. 'I know I've always been dismissive of how you deal with money, but there's more to life than that. You bring up the kids, you work, you look after the house – there's a lot of coping there, Gemma.'

280

'Not really,' she said.

He took her hand and held it between both of his. 'Honestly,' he told her. 'I usen't to appreciate you. That's all.'

'You're being silly.' But she smiled at him.

'So will you come?' he asked.

'When?'

'Their anniversary is on the twenty-ninth but that's a Thursday. They're having the party on the Friday.'

'Where?'

'At home,' said David.

Gemma made a face. Patsy and Brian lived in a big, detached house in Templeogue. It was a good house for parties, she'd been at quite a few in the time that she was married to David, but she would have preferred if the party wasn't in their house. It would be stepping back into the past and she was trying to look to the future.

'Oh, OK,' she said unenthusiastically, 'only I want a proper invite. I don't want to arrive and for people not to know that we're coming.'

'They're not sending out invites.' David laughed at her. 'It's informal, Gemma. Just family and friends.'

'And ex-wives,' she said dryly.

⤷

David had looked terrible, thought Gemma, as she watched him walk to the car with the children. He had shadows under his eyes and his smile when the kids had come downstairs to greet him had been forced. Gemma wanted to ask him what the matter was but she was afraid of interfering. It was probably just a difficult account. There had been numerous times in their marriage when he'd been tired and ratty because he was struggling to get business or because he'd missed an important client. He'd looked then the way he looked now. Gemma was surprised at how sorry she felt for him. It seemed to her that the last thing he probably wanted to do that day was to take Ronan and Keelin to the bowling alley or to the movies or wherever it was they were going. He hadn't taken them back to the apartment for lunch since the first time when Orla had dished up bolognese sauce to Keelin.

Gemma smiled wryly. She actually even felt a little sorry for Orla who had probably tried too hard to get things right. I'm going soft in my old age, she told herself as she hauled the vacuum cleaner out from the cupboard beneath the stairs. Feeling sorry for the flame-haired,

281

long-legged, bimbo bitch is certainly not part of my agenda. She switched on the machine and begun to clean around the house. She sang as she worked – although Frances insisted that Gemma was completely tone deaf she enjoyed singing with the hum of the cleaner to drown out her voice.

'Th-i-i-i-ngs– can only get better!' she warbled as she snaked across the living room towards the hallway, pulling the cleaner behind her. When she sang, she always sang songs from her clubbing years and she had a soft spot for little Howard Jones.

She jumped in shock as she realised that there was a shadow across the floor which meant that there was somebody at the door. How long had they been there? she wondered as she switched off the vacuum cleaner. Hopefully, the noise actually had drowned out the sound of her voice. She opened the hall door.

'Oh!' She stared in surprise.

'Oh?' asked Sam McColgan. 'Is that all the welcome I get?'

'No,' she said slowly as she looked at him, taking in the fact that he'd had his hair cut short and spiky since she'd last seen him. It made him look even younger. 'No, of course not. How are you?'

'Fine,' he said. 'And you?'

'I'm fine too.' She was grateful that she hadn't changed into her scruffy jeans for cleaning the house as she so often did but was still wearing the simple loose black dress she'd worn for David's arrival. It was an old dress, worn specially to emphasise the fact that she was taking a more serious approach to her life. She'd wanted to look sensible and responsible and she knew that the black dress was ideal for that. Because of its flattering cut it had the added advantage of not making her look fat either.

'You look well,' said Sam. 'Still holding on to the tan, I see.'

Gemma smiled. 'I go brown quite easily and hang on to it for ages too. It's desperately unfashionable though.'

'Looks healthy,' said Sam.

'Thanks.'

They stood staring at each other. She had to drag her eyes away from his face.

'Am I interrupting something?' he asked finally. 'Are you busy?'

'Oh, no,' she replied. 'Just cleaning.' She groaned internally. It sounded so suburban and boring and middle-aged! She should have said that she was meditating.

'I thought I heard the vacuum cleaner,' said Sam. 'I had to ring the doorbell a couple of times.'

'Sorry.'

He shrugged. 'No problem.'

'I didn't actually hear the doorbell,' Gemma explained. 'I saw your shadow in the hallway.'

'I don't want to bother you if you're busy—'

'No. It's no bother.'

'In that case,' he smiled at her, 'is there the slightest chance that I could come in?'

'Oh. Yes. Sure.' She opened the door a little wider. 'Don't trip over the vacuum,' she warned. 'You can go into the kitchen. It's straight ahead.'

Sam stepped over the hose and walked into the kitchen-cum-dining room. It was a comfortable room, he thought, as he looked around. A room which reflected the lives of the people that lived in the house. The cooker was a serious stainless-steel piece of work built into pale beech units. The walls were covered with tiny framed photographs of Keelin and Ronan. A selection of colourful magnets was stuck to the tall fridge in the corner of the room and a mound of freshly washed clothes was piled on the worktop.

'Sorry about these.' Gemma followed him into the kitchen and gathered the clothes into her arms.

'It's fine, Gemma,' he said. 'Don't bother moving things.'

'Would you like a drink?' she asked as she deposited the clothes in a basket in the corner of the room. She pushed her lacy white Wonderbra beneath Ronan's multicoloured T-shirt.

'Beer would be nice.' He sat down.

Gemma took a can of Budweiser out of the fridge and handed it to him.

'Thanks,' he said. He looked at her. 'Not having anything your-self?'

'I'm not thirsty,' she said.

He pulled the ring on the can and took a mouthful of beer. Gemma sat on one of the high stools beside the breakfast bar.

'That's not fair,' said Sam.

'What?'

'Sitting there. Higher than me. Makes me feel like one of your kids.'

She smiled slightly. 'Sorry.'

'I thought you might be pleased to see me.' Sam raised one of his dark eyebrows inquiringly.

'Well, sure I am,' said Gemma. 'Only why are you here? I haven't heard

283

anything from you since we got back from holidays – not that I expected to,' she added hastily. 'But why have you turned up now?'

'I wanted to see you again,' said Sam. 'I didn't get in touch before now because I was plucking up my courage.'

'Don't be ridiculous.' Gemma's tone was abrupt.

'Why shouldn't I have to pluck up courage?' asked Sam. 'You gave me a hard enough time in Portugal but not as hard as you would have given me if I'd met you here.'

'I didn't give you a hard time,' she protested.

'You didn't make it easy,' he told her. 'God knows, I practically had to beg you to come for a drink with me.'

Gemma said nothing.

'I wanted to ring you almost as soon as I got home,' said Sam. 'But I thought it would be better to wait.'

'Don't be silly.'

'You know, you'd think it was you who worked in college, not me.' He grinned at her. 'You have a way of talking to me that makes me feel like a two-year-old.'

She smiled. 'Maybe it's because I'm a mother.'

'That too, I suppose.'

'Sam, it was nice of you to call around and everything, but I've got lots to do today.'

'Cleaning the house?' He looked at her. 'Come on, Gemma! I can think of better things.'

'Like what?'

'I came to ask you to lunch,' he said.

'Lunch.'

'Yes,' said Sam. 'Lunch.'

'Why didn't you simply phone me?' she asked. 'And how did you know where I lived?'

'I knew where you lived because the kids exchanged addresses,' he told her. 'And if you thought for one minute I'd phone and be fobbed off by some excuse, you don't know me very well.'

'You could have bumped into David,' she said. 'Or the children.'

He shook his head. 'No, I couldn't.'

'It's his day to see them,' said Gemma.

'I know.' Sam got up and left his half-finished can of beer on the counter. 'You told me about it. Picks them up between twelve and one every Sunday.'

'He was late today.'

'Yes,' said Sam dryly, 'I noticed.'

Gemma suddenly realised that her heart was racing. 'You were outside?'

'Of course,' he said. 'Then I had to wait to be sure they'd gone. I didn't want them suddenly coming back because Ronan had forgotten something.'

She smiled tentatively.

'So, how about it?' he asked.

'Where?' she asked.

'I don't mind.' He grinned. 'Wherever you like, Gemma.'

'I don't know anywhere for lunch,' she said.

'Then allow me to choose,' said Sam.

She picked at her fingernail. 'I don't know if I can,' she said.

'Why not?'

'I've so much to do.'

'Like cleaning the house?'

'Yes,' she said.

'Leave it.' He made a face at her. 'Forget it. You don't have to do it today.'

'Oh, but I do,' said Gemma. 'You don't seem to realise that I'm working to an absolutely inviolable time schedule here! It's all planned. The kids need stuff ironed for school tomorrow. If I don't vacuum the house now it won't get done this week—'

'Gemma, Gemma!' he interrupted her. 'Life's too short, you know.'

'It's not,' she said. 'Things have to get done. I've got a plan. It's all organised.'

He looked at her. He thought that there might be tears in her eyes but he couldn't be certain because she had the most luminous eyes he'd ever seen. He'd expected her to object to lunch and he'd anticipated all her arguments. But he hadn't expected her to cry.

'Gemma,' he said gently, 'you can do those things any time.'

'No, I can't,' she told him. 'Don't you understand? I have to have everything organised exactly right so that the whole week runs smoothly.'

'Why?' he asked.

She stared at him. 'Because otherwise the kids will get in a tizzy and I'll be the one running around trying to find things and we'll argue and they'll throw tantrums – Sam, it's all very well you being some kind of easy-going bloke who doesn't mind living in the squalor of his apartment but I'm different. I was the person who's best exam result was in home economics. I'm good at running the house – at cooking and washing and cleaning. I can't help it. It's the way I am.'

285

'What makes you think I live in squalor?' he asked.

She blushed. 'I'm sorry, that was awful. There's no reason. I'm doing a bit of male stereotyping, I guess. When I met David first, he was the messiest, untidiest person I knew. It took me a year to teach him how to use the washing machine. Of course he changed,' she added. 'The more successful he became at work, the more pathologically tidy he got at home.'

'I'm not David,' said Sam quietly.

The words hung in the air between them. Gemma bit her lip.

'No,' she said eventually. 'You're not. In some ways you're quite like him Sam. But in others, you're completely different.'

'I don't know David,' said Sam. 'But I'd rather think that I wasn't like him in any respect.'

He was very different, thought Gemma. David would never have talked like this to her when she first knew him.

'I don't know what you're like, Sam,' she said.

'I want to give you the opportunity to find out.'

She looked around at the jumble of clothes in the washing basket and the pile of already washed clothes waiting to be ironed.

'Besides,' said Sam lightly. 'You didn't worry too much about cooking and cleaning on holidays.'

'That was different!' she told him. 'But it's not the real me, Sam. You might have liked me a lot in Portugal but you liked the holiday Gemma not the real Gemma.'

'And there's a big difference?'

She sighed. Was there? She'd had fun on holidays, despite the fact that she was in a state of constant terror about Keelin and constant lust over Sam. Funny, she didn't feel the same degree of lust for him now that he was sitting in front of her, dressed in charcoal-grey jeans and a plain Nike top, but he was still very attractive. Even with short hair. The cut, she thought as she appraised it, wasn't at all bad. It suited him although he'd looked great with long hair. She smiled as she remembered him running up the beach, his T-shirt soaking wet and his hair plastered to his head. A fisherman. God, she thought, she'd been completely carried away by the moment! He didn't remind her of the old pictures of David this time either. He was just another man, though it was hard to disguise his almost boyish good looks. But he was less like someone you'd throw your life away on now. Less desirable.

Actually, Gemma allowed herself, he was just as desirable. To say anything else was kidding herself.

'Gemma, I like you. I thought we got on.'

'Got on?' She sighed. 'We weren't together long enough to get on.'

'And whose fault was that?' asked Sam. 'I tried everything!'

'Oh, Sam. I did like you. I still like you. But this is stupid.'

'Why?' He got up and stood beside her. 'Why is it stupid?'

'We're different people,' said Gemma. 'You're young and single. You live on your own. I'm the mother of two kids, for heaven's sake!'

'And you think that prevents us from getting on?' His brown eyes searched her face.

'Not entirely,' she conceded. 'But you've got a different life to lead, Sam.'

'Gemma, you're being ridiculous,' said Sam. 'I like you. You like me. That's as far as we've got. I'm only asking you to lunch, you know!'

'But you might ask me again.'

'That probably was the idea.' He grinned at her. 'We move on from just liking to liking a lot. But we can't do that on an empty stomach.'

'It's the kids,' said Gemma despairingly. 'Who knows how they'll react if I start to go out with you. Keelin especially.'

'Gemma, I'm surrounded by hormonally challenged kids every day of the week,' said Sam. 'I know a lot about kids. In Wicklow, I used to help with the under-tens soccer team! And as for Keelin, you're using her to hide behind.'

'I'm not!'

'Every time I try to get closer to you, you use Keelin as a barrier. How she might feel. How she might react.'

'She's my daughter,' said Gemma. 'I care about her more than anything.'

'I understand.' Sam nodded. 'I absolutely understand, Gemma. But she's her own person and you've got to give her credit for that.'

'I do,' said Gemma defensively.

'It was hard for her to come to terms with your divorce,' said Sam. 'And even harder for her to accept that David married Orla. But she's trying, Gemma.'

'Well, if she's finding it hard to come to terms with David and Orla, she's going to find it even tougher to think of you and me having a relationship,' Gemma told him.

'Who said anything about a relationship?' Sam smiled at her. 'All I'm doing is asking you to lunch.'

She wanted to go with him. She knew she did.

'Why is it so difficult for you?' asked Sam. 'What's stopping you?'

'I don't know.' This is crazy, she told herself. He wants you to go to lunch with him. And you want to go. But you keep finding excuses not to. Why?

He watched her as she tried to keep her face expressionless. But he could see the doubts and uncertainties racing across it as if she spoke them aloud.

'You've punished yourself enough,' he told her.

'Punished myself?' she looked at him. 'What do you mean punished myself?'

'It seems obvious to me that you think you should be punished for the break-up of your marriage,' he said. 'By not having a life of your own, Gemma.'

'I do have a life of my own,' she retorted. 'I go to work. I meet other people. I . . .' She stopped and swallowed hard.

'There's more to life.' Sam wanted to take her by the hand but he was afraid of terrorising her even more. He was surprised at how much he wanted to hold her, to protect her. He'd been astonished at how much he'd been attracted to her on holidays and how shocked he'd been when he realised that she was a mother of two children. He could see that she wasn't a starry-eyed teenager, but he still hadn't pegged her as a divorced woman with two kids. And she was so lovely to look at. He liked the way her eyes sparkled, the way her hair curled endearingly around her face, the way she smiled when she was happy. From the moment he'd set eyes on her, when she was wet and shivering, he'd been attracted to her.

'It was my fault,' she said.

'What was?' asked Sam.

'The divorce.'

'Your fault?' Sam stared at her. 'I thought you asked him to leave because he was never there. Because you grew into different people. That's what you told me, Gemma.'

She bent her head and looked at her feet. 'I didn't really have to throw him out,' she said quietly. 'Sure, he was always late home. Sure, I thought he might be having a fling with Bea Hansen, from his office. But he wasn't beating me up. He was good to the kids. He brought home lots of money. It was just that I thought it would be different. And when it wasn't, I made him leave.'

'You were unhappy,' said Sam.

'Yes,' she said. 'But I put how I felt above everyone else. I should have stuck with it but I didn't.'

'Gemma, you're being really hard on yourself.' Sam rested his hand lightly on her shoulder.

'I could have tried more,' she said. 'I wanted to punish him, Sam,

288

for the fact that I didn't see him and I wasn't happy. But maybe I've ended up punishing the kids even more. That's why I'm so worried about Keelin. OK, so she's not madly in love with you. But what matters is that she needed someone like you. She talked more to you than she ever has to me. Or to her dad. And surely that can't be right.'

'You're getting it all out of proportion, Gemma,' said Sam. 'And, despite what magazines might say about teenagers confiding in their parents, I can't help thinking that their parents are usually the last people that they want to confide in at all.'

Gemma laughed shakily. 'I feel a terrible failure,' she told him.

'You're not,' he said. 'Really you're not.'

She slid off the stool and walked out of the kitchen. She didn't want to cry in front of him. But she felt like crying and she didn't know why. There was something about him that made her feel as though he would protect her. Comfort her. But she didn't want to let him.

Sam pushed open the living-room door.

'I'm sorry,' he said. 'I seem to have the worst possible effect on you. I make you unhappy and I wanted it to be just the opposite. I wanted to ask you to lunch. I wanted you to enjoy yourself with me.'

Gemma looked at him. She hadn't lied when she said he reminded her of the David she'd once known. In many ways he pushed all the same buttons as David once had. When he wasn't in his gentle, caring mode, he was handsome, articulate and amusing – all those things she'd loved about David. But those attributes hadn't been enough to keep their marriage together. She'd wanted more than David could give her and, in the end, there was no way out. But maybe there should have been. Maybe they could have tried harder and she could have avoided the pain of parting. Nobody told you that about divorce. Nobody said how gut-wrenchingly awful it was to divide up your life and your home and your feelings. Even when it was something you knew you wanted, it was hard.

The idea of ever going through a divorce again had put her off marriage more than anything else! But David had got over it. David had got married. David had found the flame-haired, bimbo bitch. David obviously wasn't too worried about another divorce.

Niamh would be disappointed if she didn't go. She'd told Niamh about Sam in a dismissive manner so that her friend wouldn't think that she had been in the slightest bit attracted to him. But Niamh had looked at her in her particularly appraising way and asked whether or not she'd see him again. When she had shrugged, Niamh had laughed and winked knowingly at her. She could almost hear Niamh asking her what on earth she was waiting for, how often did available, attractive men come around? Especially at her age.

Gemma shivered. Over the last couple of months she'd lost that terrible feeling of being old and washed out. She'd been feeling better about life, more content with how things had turned out. She'd even started to come to terms with David's marriage.

But if she went out with someone herself . . . she couldn't get her head around the idea of going out with someone. It seemed so long since she'd done it. She was out of practice. Portugal had been different. Anything could happen on holidays. But in the cool, grey light of an autumn day in Dublin things were much more complicated. How would she feel when he didn't call her again? How would she get over that? Or, worse, if they went out for a few dates and then he decided that he wasn't interested any more. People would laugh at her. Gemma Garvey thought a good-looking bloke found her attractive. What an idiot!

And what would Keelin say? She knew, deep down, that Sam was right about Keelin. She'd liked him but that's all it was. And he was right, too, about her using Keelin as an excuse. But that didn't mean that Keelin would be very happy with the idea of her going out with Sam. What if Keelin hated the idea? What would she do then?

Sam watched her thoughtfully. 'Is it such a big decision?' he asked. 'Because if I'm causing you all this soul-searching, I'm sorry. Maybe you're right, Gemma. Maybe I'm making a big mistake.'

She turned to look at him. When she thought about it, he looked nothing like the younger David. David had been taller. His hair blacker and, of course, David's eyes had been blue. David also had a more impatient look than Sam, who was standing easily by the wall, his hands in the pockets of his jeans as he looked at her. She wanted to go out with him! The idea of lunch with someone was so enticing. She wanted to forget about the washing and the cleaning and the vacuuming and do something mad and crazy. As if, she told herself, Sunday lunch could be either mad or crazy.

'I'll go.' Sam took his hands out of his pockets. 'I made a mistake, Gemma. I don't want to cause you any hassle.'

'And just as I'd decided that lunch was an option,' she said, a cautious smile creeping across her face.

∽

They went to Elephant and Castle, the clattering, noisy and cheerful

290

restaurant in Temple Bar. They sat in a seat at the window and Sam ordered spicy chicken wings between them.

'They're nice and hot,' he told her. 'Absolutely gorgeous. I eat here a lot and the wings are my favourite.'

'Fine by me.' Gemma pulled her cream-coloured cashmere cardigan more tightly around her.

'Cold?' asked Sam.

'No.' She shook her head. She'd decided, just as they were about to leave the house, that the black dress probably looked too drab on her. So she'd rushed upstairs to fetch the soft cashmere cardigan with the pearl buttons just to lighten it up a little. But she hadn't had time to put on any jewellery or even touch up her lipstick. She was on a lunch date with a man for the first time in five years and she wasn't even wearing lipstick!

At least I'm wearing my nicest underwear, she thought, even if by default. She was wearing the matching La Perla set that she'd bought herself for her thirty-fifth birthday. The wispy black bra and briefs had decimated the available balance on her credit card. The only reason that she'd worn them today was that all her other black bras were in the wash and Gemma would never have dreamt of wearing any other colour beneath a black dress. And once she was wearing the bra, she had to wear the matching briefs. Not that she intended to give Sam McColgan the slightest opportunity to see her underwear, of course, but wearing the decent stuff gave her confidence!

'What have you been doing with yourself since the holiday?' asked Sam. He nibbled at the chicken and flecks of orange sauce splashed his forehead.

'Nothing much,' said Gemma. 'You?'

'The start of a new term is always busy.' He wiped the sauce from his forehead and took another wing. 'I've been working away at lecture schedules and admissions and all that sort of thing.'

'It must be interesting,' she said.

'It can be. And the first term is always the most interesting because you've got all the new students.' He grinned at her. 'They come in having been the top dogs at school and suddenly find themselves completely unsure of what's going on. It's a great education in life.'

'What did you really want to do?' she asked.

'Sorry?'

'If you hadn't gone into admin. If you hadn't studied commerce.'

'To be honest, I wanted to do maths,' he told her.

'Maths?' She looked at him in surprise.

He nodded. 'It was my favourite subject. That's why Dad used to nag me all the time. He thought anyone who could understand the course was a genius.'

'So why didn't you?' she asked.

'Because I really wasn't good enough,' he told her. 'And I was too lazy. I would have had to work extra hard to keep up with the people who had real talent. And that wasn't what I wanted.'

'Are you good at sums?' she asked.

'Sums?'

'You know, adding, subtracting, dividing, multiplying. Or are you good at all that "let x equal y" stuff?'

He laughed. 'Both.'

'OK.' She sat back on the bench seat. 'Four hundred and six multiplied by eighty-five.'

'Thirty-four thousand five hundred and ten.'

'Eight thousand and three divided by twenty-seven.'

'Two hundred and ninety-six. Point four.'

'You'd be a handy man to bring around the supermarket,' she told him. 'Save me bringing a calculator.'

'I'm utterly useless in a supermarket,' he said. 'I buy absolute rubbish all the time. And I certainly wouldn't dream of bringing a calculator with me. What for?'

'I check the prices,' she told him. 'I have a budget.'

'Is money very tight?' he asked. 'Do you struggle, Gemma?'

'When I got divorced first I read loads of things about it,' she said. 'One of them was that the standard of living for women can drop by up to seventy-five per cent.'

'You're joking!'

'It was an American book,' she said. 'So it might be completely wrong. The thing is, the kids take up a huge amount of money and I'm particularly bad at managing it. I'm brilliant at everything else – well, you've seen my cleaning obsession already! But David came around to the house recently and went through my finances and advised me. I'm not actually as badly off as I thought, but I do have a horrible habit of blowing money on nonsense. The calculator is to keep me on track.'

'I'm quite sensible with money,' said Sam.

'You don't look it,' she told him.

'Why not?'

'I think sensible money people should look like David. You know – suits, neat hair, shiny shoes.'

Sam laughed. 'He doesn't look like that all the time, surely? In fact, he didn't look like it today. I saw him, remember?'

292

'Today he was wearing his neat polo shirt and his chinos. They're his casual clothes. Even when David's being casual he looks neat.'

'That really bothers you, doesn't it? That he turned from a slob into a neat person?'

She smiled faintly. 'A little.'

'And that's when it all started to go wrong.'

'That wasn't why, though.' She took a sip of water. 'Look, Sam, can we stop talking about David? I can't believe I'm sitting here with you talking about my ex-husband.'

He smiled at her. 'I don't want to talk about him either. I was trying to be sensitive.'

'Sensitive?'

'You know. Get in touch with your feelings, that sort of thing.' She stared at him and he laughed. 'You look great when you're trying to decide whether to be annoyed or not.'

She tried not to smile but she couldn't help it.

'And you have the loveliest smile.'

'Don't say that.'

'It's true. Look, aren't you going to eat any of these?' He pushed the bowl of wings towards her.

'Of course.' Gemma took a wing and nibbled at it. The truth was that she wasn't very hungry. Sitting opposite Sam was making her heart flutter in the kind of way that made eating difficult.

'Have you missed me?' asked Sam.

Gemma laughed. 'No!'

'Thanks.' He looked ruefully at her. 'Ask a stupid question . . .'

'I miss being on holiday,' she told him. 'I miss the sound of the sea and the feel of the sand beneath my feet.'

'Gemma, you live a couple of hundred yards from the sea,' objected Sam.

'It's not the same,' she said. 'Besides, when you walk to the seafront from my house, the first things you actually see are the pigeon house smokestacks and the port dock's equipment. It's not exactly scenic, you know.'

'Better than the view from my apartment,' said Sam.

'What's that?' asked Gemma.

'The wall of the apartment opposite,' he told her.

'Where do you live?' she asked.

'Glasnevin,' he said. 'Handy for the university and much closer than Wicklow.'

'How is Selina?' asked Gemma.

'She's great.' Sam dipped the last wing in the sour cream. 'She's been in such a good mood since the holidays! The kids are happier too.'

'I liked her.'

'She liked you.'

'I should ring her, perhaps.'

'She'd like that.'

The waitress came and took away the empty bowl. Gemma had eaten two wings while Sam demolished the remainder, talking and eating with a facility that amazed Gemma.

The first time she'd gone somewhere to eat with David, he'd taken her to the Bad Ass Café, less than a hundred yards away from where they were now. She'd had her first pizza calzone, the folded up pizza, with David. She hadn't known what it was and had ordered it simply to find out. I don't do that any more, she thought suddenly. I ask if I'm not sure what something is. They'd gone to a pub afterwards but she couldn't remember which one. Then she'd taken the last bus home. But not before David had leaned her up against a wall in one of the side streets and kissed her like she'd never been kissed before.

'You OK?' Sam broke the silence.

'Yes, fine.'

'You're thinking,' he said.

'Nothing important. That your hair looks nice like that.'

He smiled. 'I thought of calling in to you to get it done but then I decided you might not appreciate me doing that.'

'It suits you.'

'I always grow it in the summer and cut it for term time. And this is it in its casual incarnation. You wouldn't recognise me if you saw me in college.'

'Would you like something else to eat?' Sam broke into her thoughts. 'You haven't had much so far. Don't think I hadn't noticed that I was practically single-handed in my demolition of the chicken wings.'

She smiled and shook her head.

'How about some dessert?'

She looked at the menu. The desserts sounded sinful. The yoghurt with honey and nuts was probably one of the least decadent. But still, no doubt, guaranteed to plant lots of pounds on her hips. It was great to be sitting here with such temptations in front of her and not to feel hungry.

'The yoghurt is nice,' Sam suggested.

'Just coffee,' she said.

'Cappuccino?'

294

'OK.'

Sam signalled to the waitress. He gave Gemma a last chance to order dessert but she shook her head. Food didn't seem important. Being with him was more important. Listening to him. Getting to know him. Liking him. And he was very likeable. Too good to be true, she thought bleakly. A good-looking man who's nice to know. There's probably a deep, dark secret in his background somewhere.

'Why did you invite me to lunch?' she asked abruptly when the waitress had left.

'Because I wanted to see you again,' Sam told her.

'Why?'

'Why not?'

She pushed her hair behind her ears and leaned forward. 'Look, Sam, I don't want to appear as though – as though I'm fishing for compliments or anything but you could have anyone you liked. Why me?'

Sam leaned towards her and she moved away. 'I like you,' he said.

'You like me?'

'Of course.' He smiled. 'When we met at Rui's you were soaked to the skin and you looked so miserable! I wanted to put my arms around you and warm you up there and then.'

'That's silly.'

'No it's not! And then you talked to me.' He leaned his head to one side. 'You're a good listener, Gemma. You listened to me like I was a real person. I know you said it was a hairdresser thing, and maybe it was, but you listened to me!'

'You're nice to listen to,' she said.

'I don't usually spout off about my dad the first time I meet a woman,' said Sam. 'But I felt as though I'd known you forever, Gemma. It was easy to talk to you.'

'You were right.' She laughed and her smile lit up her face. 'It's the hairdresser thing.'

'It was more than that,' he said. 'I felt as though we clicked.'

She wanted to believe that they'd clicked. But she wasn't ready to take his word for it. 'Maybe.'

The waitress brought the coffees. Gemma spooned the froth off the top of her cup and swallowed it.

'Why do people do that?' asked Sam.

'I've absolutely no idea.' She licked the spoon and put it on the side of the saucer.

The restaurant was crowded now. Gemma hadn't noticed how packed it was. How every table was full and how the noise level had soared. She felt as though she was in a little bubble with Sam, that everyone was distanced from them, unable to reach them.

'Oh my God!' Suddenly she bent down beneath the level of the table, hiding herself from view.

'Gemma! What's the matter?' Sam leaned towards her. 'What are you doing?'

'It's them,' she hissed. 'They're looking for a table. They'll see us.'

'Who?' he asked.

'David! And the children. Don't turn round, Sam, please.'

Sam ignored her pleas and glanced over his shoulder. He recognised Keelin instantly, although her back was to him and she didn't notice him.

'Don't worry,' he murmured to Gemma who was practically stretched out on the bench opposite him. 'There aren't any free tables.'

'They might wait.' She groaned. 'I should have thought that they could come here. Ronan likes it.'

'Well, unless he's prepared to wait, he won't get anything to eat,' said Sam. 'And, knowing your son, I don't think he'll want to wait.'

Sam was right. As he spoke, the Hennesseys turned and walked out of the restaurant.

'You can come out now,' said Sam as they walked down Fleet Street. 'They've gone.'

Gemma sat up and ran her fingers through her tousled hair. Sam laughed.

'What?' she demanded.

'Oh, Gemma! You spend so much time worrying that you're an elderly, creaking mother of two. And you've just behaved like a teenager out with someone that her mother disapproves of!'

She giggled, she couldn't help it. 'They could have seen us,' she told him.

'So what?'

'Oh, Sam, you can't say that.'

'I admit,' he agreed, 'it wouldn't exactly have been part of my game plan.'

'It would have been a nightmare,' said Gemma.

'But they didn't see us and so it doesn't matter.' Sam grinned at her. 'You really did look funny down there, Gemma.'

'OK, OK.'

They both started to laugh. And then Sam reached over the table and caught hold of Gemma's hand. He twined his fingers round hers while they laughed together.

Chapter 31

When Sam stopped his four-year-old Citroën outside the house, Gemma looked around to see if anyone she knew was in sight.

'What's the matter?' asked Sam.

She shook her head. 'Nothing.'

'Why the furtive glances?'

'No reason.' She turned to him. 'I'd better get inside. Thanks for a wonderful lunch.'

'Do I get invited in?' he asked.

'Not this time.'

He smiled at her. 'Scared?'

'No!' Her tone was sharper than she'd intended.

'Certain?'

'Of course,' she said more calmly. 'I just want to finish the cleaning before David and the children get home.'

'Romance is alive and flourishing in Sandymount,' he said.

'Sorry.' She looked at him apologetically. 'That sounded awful, didn't it?'

He nodded.

'Another time, Sam.'

'So there will be another time?' His eyes were serious although his tone was light.

'If you want,' she said.

'Oh, I want,' said Sam. He touched her on the cheek with the tips of his fingers. 'I sincerely want.'

His touch was gentle, barely there. She wanted to lean against him, to bury her head in his strong, dependable shoulders. Strong, yes, she told herself as she steadied her racing heart. Dependable – who knows?

'I'd better go,' she said.

'I'll call you,' said Sam. 'How would next Sunday suit?'

'Call me.' She opened the car door and slid out. 'We'll talk about it.'

297

'Take care,' he said.

'You too.'

When she got indoors she rushed up the stairs and looked at herself in the bathroom mirror. Her cheeks were flushed and her eyes were bright. And it was hard to keep the smile from her face.

She raced around the house with the vacuum cleaner, ignoring the carpet under the beds or behind the sofa. She piled the laundry into the washing machine, at the last minute remembering that Ronan's navy socks were not run-proof and managing to stop the machine before the cycle had begun. God is on my side, she thought, as she fished out the filthy socks. On a normal day I wouldn't have noticed and there would have been a crisis when I discovered that Keelin's school blouses had turned a delicate shade of grey. But it wasn't a normal day. It was a wonderful day. She hadn't wanted it to be a wonderful day, but it was.

She held her hand to her face and covered the spot where Sam had touched her. So stupid, she told herself, to have almost fainted at the tenderness of his touch. So utterly silly to imagine that the imprint of his fingers were burned into her cheeks. But so wonderful to remember the moment.

～

David and the children arrived back just as she was unloading the washing from the machine. She was glad that they'd caught her in the act of doing something very motherly and dull.

'Have a good day?' she asked.

'Not bad,' replied Keelin. 'Dad took us shopping. He bought me a new sweatshirt! Then we went to lunch. We went to the Sports Café.'

'A new sweatshirt! That was nice of him.'

'It was,' said Keelin.

'And how about the Sports Café? Did you enjoy it?'

'Brilliant,' said Ronan. 'They have a racing car there. I sat in it.'

'Good,' said Gemma. 'Any chance you could remove your foot from the sheet, please?'

'Sorry.' Ronan stepped off the edge of the sheet she was trying to fold.

'What did you do today?' asked David. 'Anything interesting?'

Gemma bent over the laundry basket so that he couldn't see the colour of her cheeks. 'What would I be doing that you'd find interesting?' she asked.

'I don't know,' said David.

'Well then.' She straightened up again and brushed her hair from her eyes.

'Maybe you should come out with us next Sunday,' he suggested. 'Make a foursome of it.'

She stared at him. 'I don't think Orla would be very pleased about that!'

'She wouldn't mind.'

Gemma looked at Keelin and Ronan who were both leaning against the wall watching them.

'Haven't you two got something better to be doing?' she demanded.

'No,' said Keelin.

'Well, bring this lot upstairs then,' ordered Gemma as she thrust the basket of clothes at her. 'And, Ronan, wash your face. It's filthy.'

Keelin reluctantly took the basket and left the room, Ronan tagging along behind her.

'You shouldn't say things like that,' Gemma told David when they'd gone. 'It makes them think the wrong thing.'

'Wrong thing?'

She shrugged. 'That we're still a family.'

'We are,' said David.

'We're not,' said Gemma. She leaned against the kitchen counter. 'And I don't want to go out with you and the children, David. We had lots of opportunities to do that in the past and we didn't take them.'

'Ah,' he said. 'Putting the boot in, Gemma.'

'Not at all,' she said firmly. 'Telling it like it is.'

He looked at her in surprise. She'd never used that tone of voice with him before. He was used to hearing Gemma sounding forlorn. Or pleading. Or hopeless. Or angry. But never completely in control of a situation. Yet today, there was something different about her. Even how she looked, he realised. Her eyes were sparkling. Her cheeks were pink. Each time he saw her these days she was looking better than ever. Not so long ago, she'd looked perpetually tired. But today – today she looked really fantastic. Today she looked like the sort of woman a bloke would like to take out. The sort of woman you'd want to know was waiting for you at home.

⤙

Orla jumped as she heard David's key in the lock. She swept the photographs into a big pile on the biscuit-coloured rug.

'You're late.' She looked up as he walked into the room.

'Not very.'

'Would you like some coffee?'

He shook his head. 'What are you doing?'

'Going through some old stuff.'

He sat down in the armchair opposite her. 'Old photos?'

She shrugged. 'Clearing things out.'

'Why?'

'Oh, getting rid of clutter.'

'Old photos aren't clutter,' said David. 'They're interesting. And I've never seen any old photos of you.'

'You don't want to.'

'Yes, I do,' he said.

She shrugged again. 'They're all people you don't know.'

He picked up a photograph and looked at it. Orla, her friend Abby Johnson and two other girls that he didn't recognise were standing under the archway at Trinity College. Their arms were linked and they were laughing. Orla's hair was even longer than now and it fell around her face in a cloud of red curls.

Another photograph. This time of Orla in an oyster-white evening dress, a silver chain round her throat and a man in a tuxedo beside her.

'Trinity Ball,' she said succinctly. She just about remembered it. She'd been more drunk that night than she'd ever been in her life before. But she'd waited until Jonathan had disappeared somewhere before she threw up into a litter bin.

David skimmed through the photos. The same people appeared in most of them, always smiling, always happy. And Orla's smile had been the widest of them all.

'You enjoyed college,' he said.

'Yes.'

'Do you still see many of these people?' he asked.

'Abby, of course,' she said.

'And the others?'

'That's Valerie. Remember I went to her engagement party?'

David nodded. 'And the men?'

'Jonathan,' she said. 'I went out with him for a while.' She kept her voice steady, even as he glanced at her. 'And that's Martin. Abby went out with him. And those blokes – they're Stephen and Graham and Sean. They were fun. Always doing mad things.' She laughed shortly. 'I suppose most of them still are.'

'Why do you think that?'

'Why shouldn't they be?' she asked. 'They're probably still living in gangs together, renting places, going on the piss every night and eating rubbish.'

'Would you prefer that?' asked David.

'To what?'

'To living with me?'

Orla felt tears well up in her eyes. Ten minutes ago she would have preferred it. Ten minutes ago she was thinking about how she'd wasted the best years of her life by being old before her time. Her mad years had been the ones she'd spent renting an apartment with Abby. And even then she hadn't been mad enough. When it wasn't studying, it was working. She'd always put something ahead of having fun.

'Orla?' David looked at her. 'You wanted to talk earlier. I couldn't. What about now?'

She couldn't talk to him now. She couldn't talk to him knowing that she'd been thinking of Jonathan Pascoe and how much she missed him. If she talked to David now, she'd only say things that she might regret. She needed to get her thoughts in order first.

She shook her head. 'Not now.'

David looked at her for a moment. 'OK,' he said, 'but don't expect me to hang around waiting for you.'

⌒

Everybody pretended that team meetings at Serene Life were friendly affairs. The newest member of a team would make coffee and the team leader brought biscuits. Meetings were held, not in the intimidating boardroom, but in one of the smaller meeting rooms nearby. Naturally team meetings were not in the slightest bit friendly. How could they be when the different people picked over each other's clients, wondered about their failures, were falsely fulsome in their praise for successes and all the time calculated what the effect on their commission figures would be? Team meetings were the same no matter where you worked, but Orla had never dreaded the meetings at Gravitas Life in the same way as she dreaded the meetings at Serene.

She looked at her watch. Eight fifty-five. The meeting started at nine. She felt sick to her stomach at the thought of listening to her team telling her how well they were doing and waiting for her major contribution. Which wasn't going to come. Which was never going to come by the look of things. She was almost at the limit of her self-belief. She didn't know how she could recapture the confidence that had seen her reach number four in one of the most competitive life assurance companies in the country. If she could do it then, she asked herself despairingly, why the hell couldn't she do it now?

Of course, as the team leader, nobody would get at her. Not at the meeting. They'd know, of course, that she was doing badly. But it didn't matter to them. Her job was to motivate them, to back up their ideas, to keep tabs on what they were doing. Her team wouldn't be upset that she was getting nowhere. But Bob Murphy certainly would.

She was the last to arrive in the room. The fluorescent light flickered irritatingly overhead. She would have liked to switch it off but the sky outside was grey and the room was dark.

She cleared her throat in the slightly nervous way that she always did before a meeting. Although she didn't know it, it was her air of vulnerability that quite often closed sales for her. People couldn't believe that the attractive, red-haired girl with the shy smile could possibly sell them a dud.

'Good morning,' she said. 'Welcome to another week.'

The four members of her team grunted.

'Last week wasn't one of our strongest.' She cleared her throat again. 'Maeve did well – closed three good sales which brought in above-target revenue. Congratulations, Maeve.'

Maeve Burnett, a middle-aged woman who'd come late to life and pensions, was a consistently good producer. She nodded in acknowledgement of Orla's praise.

'Sean, you had a heavy schedule but you didn't close a deal. Any reasons?'

'Not really.' Sean leaned back in his chair and gazed out of the window. 'I thought I was doing everything right but obviously not.'

'Is there anything I can help you with?' asked Orla.

Sean grinned. 'I doubt that very much.'

Orla felt herself flush, but said nothing. 'Declan, on target as always. Of course, an extra sale would mean a lot to you personally in additional commission. And don't forget, a little more would bring you in line for the weekend in the Sheen Falls.'

Orla would have loved to go to the elegant Sheen Falls Hotel in Kenmare herself. She'd never been there but David had, and had painted a picture of somewhere peaceful and restful where you were cosseted from the moment you crossed the threshold. Serene Life were paying for the top five commission earners that month to spend a weekend there. A few months ago Orla would have been up to the challenge. Right now she needed a miracle just to hang on to her job. Since she wasn't producing much income herself, she was dependant on her team to do it for her. She hated the idea.

'Finally, Greg. Greg, you've had a terrible week. What's the matter?'

'I couldn't be bothered,' said Greg. 'I'm fed up with the whole lark. Sure, I'm selling something people probably need. But it's not exactly a glamour existence, is it? And I just can't get excited about where I am on some company graph.'

Orla looked at him and he yawned. 'Would you like to talk to me privately?' she asked. 'I'm not sure that you want to continue in this vein at the meeting.'

'Whatever.' Greg yawned again.

'OK,' said Orla. 'Let's remind ourselves of our targets. Everyone needs to sell two policies this week. Of course, anything more will be extra money in the bank for you! And nudges you up to the weekend away. Wouldn't you like to spend a weekend in the lovely Sheen Falls? I know I would!'

'What chances?' muttered Greg. Sean, who was sitting beside him, snorted with laughter.

Orla bit her lip. She couldn't keep control of her group if they had no respect for her. And how could they have any respect for her when she was so utterly useless? She cleared her throat again. 'Right,' she said. 'Promos, ideas. Anyone got anything? Maeve, what's your strategy for the week ahead?'

'I'm giving a talk to a couple of schools in my area,' said Maeve. 'It's part of their Business Organisation and Civics curriculum. So I'll be bringing lots of handouts with me. I'll make sure the kids bring them home.'

'Excellent,' said Orla. 'Anyone else?'

'I've sent flyers to the rowing club near me,' said Declan. 'And I'm going there tomorrow evening to meet with people.'

'Great,' said Orla.

'I've got a full week of prospecting ahead,' said Sean.

'You had that last week but it didn't work out,' Orla told him. 'Are you approaching them in the wrong way? Is there some other problem?'

'I don't know,' he said. 'What do you think?'

'Perhaps we could go through your presentation,' said Orla.

'Tomorrow,' said Sean. 'I have an appointment in half an hour.'

303

'Whenever you like,' Orla said. 'Don't forget, everyone, the more you sell, the more you earn. I'm sure there's lots of luxuries that you want in your lives – and if you sell more, you'll get them! Serene is a great company. Everyone here has an excellent salary. But it's not exactly the kind of salary that'll keep you in designer gear and fast cars. So get out there and sell!' Even to herself, her words sounded hollow. She didn't feel as though she believed them any more.

When the meeting was over, she spoke to Greg. 'You'll have to shape up, Greg. Bob is getting on my case about the revenue that this team is producing. You sold nothing last week, one policy the week before. It's not good enough.'

'If everyone on the team pulled their weight,' said Greg, 'my performance wouldn't make much difference.'

'It would,' said Orla, even though she felt sick. 'Each individual matters on a team. You know that, Greg. It's the team's overall contribution that counts.'

'Maybe I'm fed up being on a team,' said Greg. 'Maybe I'd prefer to work on my own.'

'It's easier with a team,' Orla told him. 'We can all motivate each other.'

'And who motivates you?' he asked.

'I admit,' she said, keeping her voice as even as she could, 'that my own personal contribution to the overall team income isn't as good as it could be. But that's my problem, Greg, not yours.'

'So if you don't bring home the bacon, it's only you that suffers, but if I don't, you suffer too, don't you? And that's the problem! You're having a shit time and you need us to bolster your shit figures.'

'Greg, it isn't necessary to talk like that.'

'Yeah, well.' Greg shrugged. 'I'm getting tired of it anyway. I'm twenty-three years old, Orla. I want more out of my life than persuading people that they need serious illness cover.'

'And what's that?' she asked.

'Three of my mates are talking about taking some time out and trekking through India. I thought I'd go with them.'

'Oh.' Orla looked at him in surprise. She hadn't expected that. 'Have you made up your mind about it?'

'Not yet,' said Greg. 'But don't be surprised if I'm not here by next week.'

'Let me know as soon as you've made up your mind,' she said. 'Please.'

'Sure.' Greg got up from the edge of the table where he'd been leaning. 'You should do it yourself, Orla. Might chill you out a bit.'

'Thanks,' she said. 'I'll keep it in mind.'

Maybe she should, she thought. Maybe she should forget about everything and simply disappear. Hop on a flight to London. Take a cheap seat to anywhere in the world. Wake up on the other side of the globe. With hepatitis, she told herself. Or malaria. Or at least a very nasty reaction to a mosquito bite.

She walked into her small cubicle. The message waiting light was flashing on her phone. She hoped it was someone returning one of her calls. But it wasn't. It was Bob Murphy. He wanted to see her.

Orla felt herself begin to shake. She didn't want to see him. She didn't want to listen to him telling her how terrible she was. She wanted to curl up in a corner and go to sleep.

⌒

'And I said to him, if you think I'm interested in listening to one more of your lies you have another damn think coming.' Joan Clarke looked at Gemma in the mirror as Gemma snipped at the ends of Joan's hair.

'I thought you got on with him,' said Gemma mildly. She steadied Joan's head with her left hand.

'Oh, come on, Gemma love. I'm forty years old. I don't have time to just "get on" with someone. No, it's all or nothing now.'

Gemma laughed. 'Don't you think, maybe, they're more trouble than they're worth?'

'Easily.' Joan smiled at her. 'I don't know why we bother with men at all. Overgrown children, most of them. But there's nothing quite like being with one all the same, is there?'

No, thought Gemma. There wasn't anything quite like being with one. She still hadn't got over her lunch date with Sam McColgan. When she closed her eyes she could be there again, in the bustle and the noise and the sizzling, spicy aromas of the Elephant and Castle, but cocooned in her own private world with Sam. And she could remember the way he smiled at her and the way his eyes softened when he looked at her. She could remember the touch of his fingers on her cheeks and the hammer blow of desire that had suddenly hit her.

'Gemma?' Joan looked at her. 'Are you feeling all right?'

'Sure, Joan.'

'Because you've gone into a trance.' Joan's eyes were wide and curious. 'Gemma, don't tell me—'

'Don't tell you what?' She put down her scissors and picked up a hair dryer.

'Before you switch that damn thing on!' Joan turned to look at her. 'Gemma, have you found someone?'

'What on earth would make you think that?' Gemma turned the dryer to cool.

'You have!' Joan's face was gleeful. 'Oh, Gemma, you have!'

'Don't be crazy.' But Gemma's face was pink as she began to dry Joan's hair.

⌐

'Sit down, Orla.' Bob Murphy waved at the seat in front of his desk.

Orla sat down gingerly and waited while he filled in a form in a green folder in front of him. Bob's office was quiet. She could hear the muted sounds of the phones ringing and the hum of conversation outside, but in here it was peaceful. His desk was almost empty. Bob liked to have a clear desk, he'd told her that before. Besides the folder, there was a desk tidy containing half a dozen pens, a couple of pencils and a yellow highlighter. There was an in-tray which was half full – or half empty depending on your point of view – a desk telephone and a mobile telephone, his laptop computer and a photograph of his wife, Marie, and their two children. He had two daughters. The eldest was a year older than Keelin.

'Well, Orla.' He put down his pen and looked at her. 'Things are not exactly going according to plan, are they?'

She swallowed. She was afraid that she was going to cry. She hated the way she was always on the brink of tears these days. She'd never been like this before.

'What's the matter?' he asked. 'Why aren't you bringing in business?'

She shook her head and fought to keep her voice under control. 'I just seem to be having a run of bad luck,' she said.

'There's bad luck and bad luck,' he told her. He picked up a print-out of her sales since she'd joined the company. It was a short print-out. 'This is not good, Orla.'

'I know.'

'What are you doing about it?'

'I've put together a new presentation,' she said. 'I've got quite a good list of prospects for the rest of the week. I think I can get it together.'

'What about the ones you were hopeful about? That kitchen company? The computer company?'

Damon Higgins! She still felt angry when she thought of how much of her time he'd wasted.

'The kitchen company is a washout,' she told him. 'And if Damon Higgins is anything to go by, they'll probably be in receivership before any of them get to pensionable age! But I'm seeing Tim Dunne who's the MD of the computer crowd on Friday. Plus, I've set up some meetings with the people in that new industrial estate near Foxrock.'

'Which is the problem?' asked Bob. 'Setting up the meetings or closing the sale?'

'I – I'm not sure,' she said.

'If you like I'll come with you on a few. See where you're going wrong. It could be something simple, Orla. It happens to the best of us from time to time.'

'It's never happened to me before,' she said.

'Is everything OK at home?' asked Bob. 'David all right, is he?'

'David's fine,' said Orla.

'He's not putting pressure on you? Not giving you a hard time?'

'What do you mean?'

'Is he trying to set you up?' asked Bob. 'I know David. He isn't squeezing prospects out of you, is he?'

'Of course not!' Orla was angry.

'Just checking. Of course, if you're having trouble, you could always check out a few of his.'

'I couldn't.'

Bob grinned. 'Had to say it, Orla.'

'We're professional,' she said. 'We don't rob each other's business.'

'I hope not,' said Bob. 'I wouldn't like to think David was nobbling clients who were rightfully yours.'

'He's not.' And how you'd laugh, thought Orla, if you realised that there's no chance of David robbing any of my clients because we don't even talk long enough for him to find out who they are.

'OK,' said Bob. 'You've got a month to pick it up, Orla. Then we'll talk again.'

She heard the warning in his voice. She swallowed hard and walked out of the room.

Chapter 32

Keelin looked fantastic. Gemma had to admit that her daughter had a knack with make-up. She wasn't heavy-handed with it as she'd been herself when first she'd practised with Body Shop or Cover Girl. Keelin didn't make the mistake of thinking that more was better. She'd put on a very light foundation, some blusher and a smoky-grey shadow over her eyes. Her hair was loose but neatly brushed so that when it fell over her face it looked as though it was by design, not by accident. She was wearing her black Levi's, black boots and a black T-shirt. Once again, she looked considerably older than fourteen.

'I wish I knew this Alison Fogarty person,' said Gemma as Keelin sat in the living room and waited for Shauna, Donny and Mark Dineen to call. 'And I certainly wish I knew more about this bloke you're going with.'

For the first time in her life she understood why Frances had always asked her a thousand questions before she went out. She'd tried to ask as few as possible and to do it in a light-hearted way so that Keelin wouldn't feel that she was checking up on her too much. But you had to ask, she told herself, you were responsible. And despite the fact that since her lunch date with Sam McColgan she'd decided that she was not on life's scrapheap, the idea of Keelin having a date was enough to make her feel middle-aged all over again.

'He's not "this bloke",' said Keelin. 'His name's Mark. And he's OK. I wouldn't go with him otherwise.'

'Well, don't let yourself get stuck anywhere alone with him,' said Gemma.

'Mum!' Keelin looked at her angrily.

'I'm just trying—'

'Have a bit of faith,' said Keelin. 'I'm not stupid.'

Gemma sighed. 'It's just that you're my only daughter,' she said. 'I want to protect you.'

'Smother me,' said Keelin as the doorbell rang. 'That's them. I'll get it.'

Gemma followed her into the hall. She smiled at Shauna and at the two boys with her. She knew Donny, of course. But she didn't recognise Mark Dineen. She looked at him carefully, trying to identify any possible character traits that would make him unsuitable for her daughter. But he was an ordinary-looking guy with freckles. Not attractive, thought Gemma. Keelin could probably get someone a lot more attractive if she wanted.

'You're certain that your dad is going to pick you up, Shauna?' asked Gemma anxiously.

'Of course he is,' said Shauna. 'And I have his phone with me so that if there's a problem I can call him.'

'That's a good idea,' said Gemma. 'Keelin, take this with you.' She handed the mobile to her daughter.

'I'll be fine, Mum,' said Keelin. 'I don't need a phone if Shauna has one.'

'But just in case you need me,' said Gemma.

'I won't need you.'

'Just in case,' said Gemma again and Keelin sighed heavily but took the phone from her anyway.

The party was in Alison's house, which eased Gemma's mind a little. Gemma had phoned Mrs Fogarty to find out about it. Alison's mother sounded a nice, easy-going woman who told Gemma that it was a birthday party, that Alison was fifteen and that both herself and her husband would be in the house. 'Although we've got a granny flat attached,' she told Gemma, 'and that's where we'll be. We won't interfere.'

Gemma wasn't sure she liked the sound of that. She thought interfering might be essential.

Just because you were a rule-breaking fourteen-year-old yourself doesn't mean your daughter will turn out the same way, she told herself. Keelin is sensible. Keelin won't get into any trouble.

Frances had probably thought the same about her and Liz, thought Gemma, as she closed the door behind them. Frances had probably assumed that all her lectures on boys being only after one thing had been heeded by both her daughters. She'd fondly believed that Gemma and Liz had gone to parties and dances and had sipped lemonade and had kept their distance from the frenzied hands of the hormonally-challenged guys that swarmed around them.

If only she knew! Gemma had been fifteen when she'd first drunk a pint of cider and wobbled around the road on her high-heeled shoes afterwards. She'd been fifteen and a half when Lorcan Smith had shoved his hand up her jumper and squeezed her left breast until she squealed in pain. She'd lasted until eighteen before she lost her virginity to Declan Monaghan, one of her first clients at the hairdressing salon. He'd sat down in front of her, she'd run her fingers through his hair – it had set the pattern for the rest of her life!

Eighteen is probably an ancient age to loose your virginity these days, thought Gemma. She wondered if she'd be able to think of anything except the party until Keelin arrived home.

⤺

It was half past twelve when she heard her key in the door. Gemma had gone up to bed because she wanted Keelin to believe that she hadn't spent the whole night worrying about her. Frances had always stayed up until she got home and that had driven Gemma crazy. She'd look at her watch, sigh and mutter that some people didn't seem to understand that night-time was for sleeping.

Gemma switched off her bedside lamp and closed her eyes. She heard the fridge door open and close. She heard Keelin turn off the light downstairs. She heard her footsteps on the stairs.

The footsteps paused outside her bedroom door.

'Goodnight, Mum,' said Keelin.

Gemma opened her eyes. 'Did you have a good time?' she asked.

'Yes,' said Keelin. 'It was great.'

'Anything you want to tell me?'

'Your bedroom faces onto the front of the house,' said Keelin. 'I could see that your light was on as I walked up the path.'

'Oh,' said Gemma. She heard Keelin giggle.

'Goodnight,' said her daughter.

'Goodnight,' said Gemma. She rolled over on her side and, secure in the knowledge that Keelin was safely home, she fell into a deep and peaceful sleep.

⤺

Orla was wide awake. She hadn't come close to falling asleep. At two o'clock she slid out of the bed, leaving David buried under the duvet. She grabbed her dressing gown and wrapped it round her.

She poured herself a glass of wine and curled up in the armchair nearest the window. David always closed the curtains in the evenings but Orla leaned over and pulled the cord to open them. If this was my apartment, she thought, just mine, not David's, I'd always have the curtains open so that I could look out over the sea. It was a clear night and the light of the full moon rippled on the swell of the ink-black water. She sipped the wine and sighed deeply.

Where the hell was she going with her life? she asked herself. What did she want? What mattered to her? She thought, briefly, of her chilling conversation with Bob Murphy earlier in the week and wondered whether or not she should be thinking about her marriage or thinking about her job.

If I hadn't taken the job, she thought as she gazed out of the window, I wouldn't have had a row with David. I wouldn't have gone to Cork. I wouldn't have met Jonathan Pascoe again. God above, she moaned to herself, on her first trip away from her husband what were the chances, statistically speaking, of her running into the one man in the world that she'd had a meaningful relationship with? And the worst part of it was that she really couldn't tell anyone how she felt. Her mother would sigh and deliberately not say I told you so. Abby would try to comfort her but point out that she had warned Orla that she'd recommended living with David before she'd married him. And, Orla thought miserably, Abby would also tell her that marrying someone older than her had made things more difficult. Finally, Abby would definitely tell her that she'd always believed that Orla and Jonathan were made for each other. That was the kind of junk thing that Abby would say. Orla was sure of it.

She finished the wine in a couple of gulps. What if Marty told Abby that Orla had met Jonathan? The thought suddenly came to her and made her grow hot with worry. Jonathan could easily phone his friend and tell him that he'd met Orla. And he'd hardly be able to resist telling him that he'd almost had her into bed with him. She bit her lip. She'd wanted to go to bed with him, she really had. Which confused her more than ever. Had she felt like that because she really cared about Jonathan? Or was it simply to spite David? And if it was to spite David, then what sort of awful person was she?

She poured herself another glass of wine and wondered if he'd notice that she wasn't in bed beside him. He was a heavy sleeper, though, and he'd probably just roll into the empty space in the bed, delighted that there was more room for him to spread his arms and legs. She was forever waking up to find his arm lying over her head, or his knee pressed against the small of her back.

311

But it would be nice if he woke up, she thought. If he realised she wasn't there and he hurried out to find out what was wrong with her. She imagined him coming into the living room and seeing her here in the armchair and suddenly everything between them being OK again as he lifted her up in his arms and told her that he loved her.

She snorted gently. She was too tall and too heavy for him to lift. Gemma was a better height although, she told herself smugly, Gemma was probably heavier. Blobby Gemma. Who'd be at the golden wedding anniversary.

She tightened her grip round the stem of the glass. David had told her about the anniversary celebrations and, just as she was thinking that maybe it was a good thing for her to meet his relatives again, he'd added that Gemma and the children would be there. She hadn't been able to say anything. What could she say? That she didn't want to be in the same room as his former wife? That the occasional moments when she saw his children were more than enough? He seemed to think that it shouldn't bother her, that she should be able to regard Gemma as just an old girlfriend of his. But how could she think of the woman like that? How did other second wives manage to behave civilly to the first? Was there an etiquette book you could buy? Chapter One, she thought, how to insult by being polite. Chapter Two where to stick the knife.

She shivered. David had told her that his family all loved Gemma. Mainly because she'd had two children, Orla guessed. David had one sister, a year younger than him, who'd never married. His parents absolutely adored their grandchildren. He'd told his mother not to expect any from Orla and she'd laughingly agreed but, she thought now, what if she changed her mind? How would he feel about that?

She wished she wasn't thinking of her own mother and the dire warnings she'd given her about second families and men not wanting to go through the whole baby routine all over again. She had told her mother that she didn't want to go through it herself but what if, one day, she did? She didn't want a child now but she might in a few years' time and David would be even less likely to want one then. If she was still married to David in a few years' time.

⤻

Keelin picked up the phone just as it started to ring. She was waiting for a call from Mark Dineen. It was the first time a guy had told her he'd call and, although she'd always sworn that she'd be cool about it when it happened, she was like a cat on a hot tin roof as she waited for the phone to ring. She looked at her watch. It was seven o'clock on Saturday evening. He'd told her he'd call between half six and half seven.

'Hello,' she said as she picked up the receiver.

There was a moment's silence and then a voice said, 'Hello, Keelin.'

'Bru?' she said hesitantly. 'Is that you?'

'Yes. How are you, Keelin?'

'I'm fine.'

'How's school?' he asked.

'Oh, OK,' she replied. 'Boring, really.'

'Surely not?'

'Come on, Bru,' she said. 'It's a long time since you were in the classroom!'

He laughed. 'I guess you're right.' He cleared his throat. 'Keelin, I was actually looking for Gemma. Is she there?'

'Why?' asked Keelin.

'I wanted to talk to her,' said Sam.

'About anything in particular?'

'Keelin!' Sam laughed. 'Give me a break!'

'She's not in,' said Keelin firmly. 'It's late-night closing at the hair salon so she won't be home until eight.'

'And you're on your own?' asked Sam.

'Fat chance,' Keelin snorted. 'Gran is here. I don't need her here, of course, but she's here all the same.'

'Does she come over every Saturday?' asked Sam.

'No,' answered Keelin. 'Mum doesn't work late every Saturday. Niamh just asked her today. So she insisted Gran should come around. It's ridiculous,' she continued in a higher pitch, 'to think that an old lady should be forced to come here just because my mother doesn't trust me not to throttle Ronan.'

Sam laughed. 'Is that really why your gran is there? To prevent murder?'

Keelin laughed too, if a little reluctantly. 'Sort of. Mum doesn't like spending all day away from us. So she gets Gran to come around and check things out. It's not as if I need her here, of course, it's more for Ronan's sake.'

'I understand,' said Sam.

'Because if I go out or anything, there's nobody to look after him and he is only eleven.'

'Never trust an eleven-year-old boy,' said Sam.

'Never trust one at any age.'

'That sounds very mature,' Sam told her.

'I know. I'm practising.'

He laughed. 'Will you tell your mum I phoned?'

'Yes,' said Keelin.

'Tell her I'll call again,' said Sam.

'OK.'

'It was nice talking to you, Keelin.'

'Bru?'

'Yes?'

'Do you prefer to be called Bru or Sam?'

'I don't mind,' he answered. 'I respond to both. Like a schizophrenic dog.'

Keelin laughed. 'What will I say to Mum that you called about?'

'Nothing special,' he said.

'Are you going to ask her out?'

'What makes you think that?'

'Oh, Bru!'

'Come on, Keelin.' But Sam was laughing too. 'Cut me a little slack.'

'I like you,' she said. 'But I love my dad.'

'I know,' said Sam. 'And that will never change.'

'I'll tell her you called.'

'Thanks, Keelin. It was nice talking to you.'

'You too,' she said and replaced the receiver.

She walked back into the living room. Frances Garvey was sitting in Keelin's favourite armchair. Frances always came into the house and took over, Keelin thought, as she flopped onto the sofa. She came in and looked around and disapproved of just about everything.

'Who was that?' asked her grandmother.

'A bloke,' said Keelin.

'A boy?' asked Frances. 'Were you talking to a boy?'

'More like a man, actually.' Keelin picked up the newspaper.

'What did he want?' asked Frances.

'To talk to Mum.'

'Who was he?'

Keelin shrugged. She opened the newspaper and hid her face behind it. It was none of Gran's business and she couldn't help feeling that Frances wouldn't approve of Bru. Keelin wasn't entirely sure that she approved of him either – at least not as a companion for Gemma. It had been so obvious that he'd fancied her, a realisation that had stunned

314

Keelin at first because she just couldn't imagine anyone fancying her mother! And yet, as she watched Gemma and Selina sitting talking at the bar one evening, she'd suddenly realised that Gemma was really quite pretty. Not in a gorgeous, in-your-face kind of way, and certainly not in a very modern kind of way – like Orla – but in a gentler, softer way. Keelin had been startled to think that her mother could look so attractive. So it shouldn't have been all that surprising that Bru had been interested in her, but it was still difficult to accept that he might. And since Keelin and Mark had spent over five hours in each other's company the previous night, Keelin now felt qualified to think about lust.

She wondered how Gemma felt about Bru. She'd been cool with him on holidays, never encouraging him, always just a little bit distant. She hadn't given any indication of fancying him back. Keelin turned over a page of the newspaper. It was a bit much, she thought, to have to worry about your parents' love lives when you were only just starting to worry about your own.

The phone rang again. She was out of the chair in an instant.

⌐

Orla and Abby were in Thomas Read's. The pub was crowded with people but the two girls had arrived early and had found themselves a decent niche beside the window where they could watch people scurrying by in the cold, autumn wind that was blowing up Dame Street.

'I wish I was somewhere hot.' Abby shivered involuntarily as a woman outside battled against the elements. 'I really resent not having gone on holiday this year.'

'I'm sorry I couldn't go with you,' said Orla.

'You were too busy.' Abby sipped her Irish coffee appreciatively. 'You were on honeymoon.'

It seemed like another lifetime, thought Orla. She found it hard to believe that somewhere in the world was an island where the sun was shining, where lazy blue waves broke gently onto soft white sand and where people never seemed to argue with each other. Her honeymoon had been the best time of her life, she realised. It had been two perfect weeks.

'Every time I mention your honeymoon you go off into a dream world,' said Abby dryly. 'It makes me feel as though I should have one myself.'

315

Orla glanced at her. 'Thinking of it?'

'Don't be utterly ridiculous.' Abby took another sip of her drink. 'I haven't even got a man in my life, much less a honeymoon.'

'What about Marty?' asked Orla. 'Haven't you seen him?'

Abby shrugged. 'We've been for a couple of drinks,' she said. 'But nothing more than that.'

'I thought you looked pretty happy with him at Valerie's party,' said Orla.

'I like him,' admitted Abby. 'But he's my past, Orla. He reminds me of the person I was, not the person I want to be. I've grown out of him.'

'How deep,' muttered Orla.

'Sorry?'

'Nothing.' Orla sighed. 'I didn't think people were something you grew out of. I thought everyone grew together.'

Abby laughed. 'I suppose you're right. Only Marty was always a bit on the juvenile side. That's why we split up. He couldn't take anything seriously.'

'I thought that was why Jonathan and I split up,' said Orla. 'As I recall, everyone told me that I took myself far too seriously then. Including you. And Jonathan.'

'You did!' Abby smiled at her friend. 'It's simply that they didn't take anything seriously enough.'

'But Marty's changed, hasn't he?' asked Orla. 'He's written a book.'

'Sure,' said Abby. 'A seriously weird book, Orla! Have you read it?'

'No.' Orla shook her head. 'But surely he got a huge advance for it?'

'Are you cracked?' asked Abby. 'It's not exactly mainstream, Orla. His publishers told him he'll be lucky to make a grand out of it.'

'Who published it?'

'I've no idea. He didn't say.'

'So how does he pay the bills?' asked Orla.

'He works for a courier company,' said Abby. 'He has a motorbike and he terrorises old ladies in cars by speeding up the inside lane and cutting in front of them.'

'Sounds like Marty,' agreed Orla. She poured the rest of her tonic into her vodka. 'Does he have life insurance? Or a pension plan?'

'Oh, for goodness sake, Orla!' Abby looked exasperated. 'Don't you ever stop?'

316

'It's important,' said Orla. 'For him.'

'And not for you?'

Orla grimaced. Following her meeting with Bob she'd been out every day with prospective clients. She'd managed to sell two policies this week but they were both pretty small. She wasn't very confident that her figures would be good enough at the end of the month for Bob to want to keep her. The thought made her shudder.

'Are you all right?' Abby's concerned voice broke in on her thoughts.

She nodded. 'I'm sorry. I was thinking about work.'

'Orla, we're supposed to be out for some relaxation. Not for you to think about work.'

'I can't help it.' Orla rubbed her eyes. 'I'm having a nightmare at the moment.'

'Are you?'

She nodded. 'I just can't seem to close a deal. I can't seem to meet the right people. Everything I touch is turning to dust.'

'It can't be that bad!'

'It is,' said Orla vehemently. 'I ring up, make appointments, go to see people and they blow me away! That never happened to me before. So I come back to the office and discover that everyone else on the team is doing great. At least, this week they are. Last week you might as well have sent us looking for snowballs in the Sahara for all the good we were.'

Abby laughed.

'It's true,' said Orla dismally. 'If I don't get my act together they'll fire me.'

'Why is it suddenly so difficult?' asked Abby. 'I thought you were good at all this high-pressure selling stuff. I bloody well bought a policy from you, didn't I? And I don't even have the money to pay for it.'

'Are you struggling?' asked Orla. 'I can change the structure . . . oh, I can't. It's a Gravitas policy.'

'At the time you said they were the best,' her friend reminded her.

'I sold you a really good one,' said Orla. 'Don't worry about it, Abby.'

'I'm not,' said Abby. 'I don't worry about things like this. I only worry about not having a holiday this year!'

Orla smiled weakly at her.

Abby was silent for a moment. 'Is everything OK?' she asked finally.

'OK?' Orla looked at her in surprise.

'Yes,' said Abby. 'Look, Orla, you don't seem awfully happy to me.

317

I know I might be talking complete rubbish and I'm sorry if I seem to be rushing to some stupid conclusion, but I can't help thinking that something's really bothering you. And maybe it's coming out in your work.' She looked Orla steadily in the eye.

'And you're going to be my armchair psychiatrist?' asked Orla.

'Don't be silly.' Abby drained her glass. The trouble with Irish coffee was that once it cooled down it was revolting. But those early sips were divine. 'We always used to share things,' said Abby. 'Come on, Orla. What's the matter?'

She wasn't going to tell her. She couldn't admit to her friend – close and all though they were – that she'd been right all along and that her marriage to David was turning into a fiasco.

'Nothing's the matter,' she told Abby. 'The work thing is getting to me, that's all.'

'Can't David help?' asked Abby. 'After all, according to you he's Ireland's top policy seller. Surely he's got a few tips for you?'

'I don't need David's tips,' said Orla tightly. 'I can manage myself.'

'I'm sure you can,' said Abby. 'But wouldn't it be nice if—'

'I said I can manage myself.' Orla drained her drink. 'Come on, Abby. I feel like getting blitzed. Want another?'

⤶

The wind was so strong that Gemma could feel it buffeting the car as she drove across the East-link. An icy blast whipped around her when she rolled down the window and tossed the toll into the basket. She rolled up the window as quickly as she could.

She was tired. Niamh had rung her last night to see if she could work all day today and Gemma had agreed. But she was exhausted after nearly twelve hours on her feet. Some hairdressers used a high stool to sit on as they cut a client's hair but Gemma preferred to stand. Suffering for her craft, she'd called it when she'd started out, but today it just felt like pure stupidity. And her back was absolutely breaking. She shifted into a more comfortable position in the driver's seat.

As soon as Frances left, Gemma was going to run a hot bath and soak in it for an hour. She glanced at the package on the passenger seat beside her. She'd bought a bottle of Estée Lauder bath oil which, she hoped, would do all the things to her skin that the bottle promised. She'd also bought a regenerating face mask. She wasn't quite sure what the face mask would regenerate but she was prepared to give it a try. She'd felt the usual twinge of guilt as she lashed out the money on

318

ridiculously expensive products that she could have got for a quarter of the price at Tesco's. But it wouldn't be the same, she told herself as she tried to justify the expense. At least this way she'd know that she'd really made an effort. Besides, she'd earned the price of the bath oil in tips today. So she wasn't really wasting money. She could afford to treat herself. Probably.

⌐

The smell of furniture polish hit her the moment she opened the front door. She gritted her teeth. Every single time that Frances came over she did something around the house. She cleaned windows, or washed every piece of crockery, or polished their meagre pieces of silver despite the fact that Gemma did all these things regularly herself. No matter how many times she told her mother not to bother, Frances ignored her. Frances was obsessed with cleaning, thought Gemma. She couldn't remember a time in her childhood when every surface in the house wasn't dusted, when every floor wasn't washed, when anything left lying around wasn't put away. It had driven them crazy as children but it had rubbed off in some ways too. Gemma knew that she was a good housekeeper which made her mother's behaviour even more irritating. She sighed, composed her face into a smile and pushed open the living-room door.

Frances was sitting in the armchair nearest the TV. Keelin's armchair, noted Gemma.

'Hi.' She dropped her bags on to the sofa. 'How did you get on today?'

'I polished the hall floor,' said Frances. 'Honestly, Gemma, you should look after it better. It didn't look as though it had seen a cloth in months.'

'That's because of Ronan,' said Gemma, as calmly as she could. 'He walks muck and dirt into it and no matter what I do it ends up scruffy.'

'He's in his room at the moment,' said Frances. 'His friend Neville is with him. I had to insist that they came in when it started to rain, they were playing some kind of rugby game and getting absolutely filthy. They're playing with the computer now.'

'And Keelin?'

'She's in her room too.' Frances pursed her lips – a sign, Gemma knew, that there was more she wanted to say but was holding back. Well, thought Gemma, she wasn't going to give Frances the oppor-

319

tunity to complain about Keelin. She took off her jacket and deliberately threw it on to the sofa over the bags.

'Why don't you put things away properly?' asked Frances. 'You're
going to have to put them away sooner or later, why don't you do
it now?'

'Because I'm tired.' Gemma flopped into the other armchair. 'It
was a hard day at the salon today. And it's nice to come home and
sit down.'

'If you'd stayed married to David—'

'Please, Mum, don't start all that again. I'm fed up listening to it.
It was five years ago. David is married again. Let's drop it, shall
we?'

'That's the way you'd like it, isn't it?' There were two pink spots on
Frances's cheeks. 'If you don't talk about it then it doesn't matter. And
you can always go shopping to make yourself feel better anyway.'

'Rubbish!' Gemma sat up straight, really annoyed. 'And, if I did
think like that, where do you suppose I learned it from?'

'What do you mean?'

'Oh, come on,' said Gemma. 'I was brought up by you, wasn't I?
You were never a great one for talking, were you? I don't remember
any heart-to-heart conversations when I was younger. Well, not with
me, anyway. You had quite a few with Michael.'

'Don't talk nonsense.'

'I'm not,' said Gemma. 'I'm just saying that you never gave a toss
about me or Liz. The only person you bloody cared about was Michael.
And you're happy that my marriage fell apart – it justifies your belief
that I'm a useless incompetent. You're probably quite pleased that Liz
had the baby too – you always thought she was flighty! But good old
Michael and his perfect bloody family are living proof that you did
something right.' She heard the quiver in her voice at the end of the
sentence. She bit the inside of her lip, not wanting her mother to realise
how upset she was.

'I never believed you were stupid until today,' said Frances sharply.
'But I was wrong. You know perfectly well that I love you all
equally.'

'Bullshit!' retorted Gemma.

'There's no need to descend to that level,' said Frances. 'If you
can't argue with me without swearing then you're less educated than
I thought.'

'Oh, for God's sake!' Gemma got up from the armchair and walked
across the room. She took a bottle of gin from the sideboard and

filled a crystal glass with the clear liquid. Then she added some Slimline Tonic.

'Drinking will help,' said Frances bitingly.

'Yes,' said Gemma. 'It will. It'll help me get over the fact that my own mother thinks I'm a stupid, incompetent woman who couldn't hang on to my husband and can't manage my home!'

Frances said nothing. Gemma's eyes glittered with unshed tears. She was not, she told herself, absolutely not going to cry in front of her mother. She hadn't cried in front of Frances since she was twelve years old and had been told that girls of her age shouldn't cry. Which she hadn't believed then and didn't believe now. There were plenty of things to cry about in life. And a lot of times you felt much, much better for it. But not in front of Frances.

'You could start managing your home by putting the shopping away,' said Frances. 'If there's frozen food in there it'll melt all over the sofa.'

'Haven't you got it yet?' demanded Gemma. 'I'm not stupid! Of course there isn't anything frozen. Do you think I don't know that it would melt? How dense do you think I am?'

'Right now?' asked Frances.

Gemma took a large mouthful of her drink. 'Look,' she said. 'I married the wrong man and it didn't work out. You didn't like him when I married him but ever since I divorced him you go on and on as though he was God's bloody gift to me. Well, he wasn't. You were right about him at the start – which should make you feel good. But he's married to someone else now and he's not coming back and – believe it or not – I don't care. I'm glad. I don't love him. I haven't loved him for a long time. And I'm doing a hell of a lot better without him. Even though that means sometimes I don't put my shopping away immediately. Or don't polish my floors. As if—' she drained her gin and tonic, 'as if it matters whether they smell of pine fucking forests or not!!'

'Gemma!'

'What?'

'I told you there was no need to swear.'

There was a hint of hysteria in Gemma's laugh. 'That's all that matters to you, isn't it? How things look? Not how they actually are? You'd have been perfectly happy for me to be utterly miserable with David once we'd stayed together. And you'd have been perfectly happy for Liz to marry anyone just so that she wouldn't end up being an unmarried mother.'

321

'That's not true.'

'Isn't it?'

'Of course not.' Frances got up out of the armchair. 'And if you think like that then I'm going home. I won't stay where I'm not wanted. Or, at least, where I'm not wanted now. I was wanted earlier, of course, when you were working. It's OK for me to be here when you need me, isn't it? But once I've outstayed my usefulness, I've outstayed my welcome!'

Gemma rubbed her temples. 'I'm sorry. I didn't mean to—'

'You did mean to,' said Frances. 'You meant every word.'

'It's just—' Gemma swallowed. 'You always criticise me. I don't need you to tell me where I'm going wrong. I just need you to love me all the same. You don't.'

'How can you say that?' demanded Frances. 'You know perfectly well that I love you. You and Liz and Michael.'

'But you love Michael the most.'

'Oh, grow up, Gemma.' Frances draped her silk scarf around her neck. 'I love all my children equally.'

'Well it sure doesn't seem like it,' said Gemma.

'I can't believe I'm hearing this,' retorted Frances. 'After all I've done for you!'

'Oh, all what?' snapped Gemma. 'All the times you've told me I shouldn't have married David? All the times you told me I should have stayed with him? All the times you've cleaned out my cupboards and told me that they were hygienic now? All the times you've waved Mr Sheen around my house when I haven't asked you to?'

'You ungrateful little wretch!' Frances almost spat the words at her daughter.

Gemma winced. The two women watched each other silently.

'I'll go,' said Frances tightly.

'Don't.' Gemma felt that if her mother walked out the door now they might never set foot in each others' houses again.

'You want me to stay so that you can insult me some more?'

'No,' said Gemma. 'I don't. But I don't think you should drive home when you're mad at me.'

'I'm not mad at you,' said Frances. 'I'm disappointed in you.'

'You were always disappointed in me,' said Gemma bitterly, suddenly overcome. 'And maybe you've a right to be. I messed up my life, after all. And I guess I *am* ungrateful. You came here today and looked after Keelin and Ronan and I should be grateful to you. I'm sorry.'

322

'I'm disappointed that things weren't better for you,' said Frances carefully. 'I'm not really disappointed *in* you, Gemma. That was the wrong thing to say. And I don't want you to feel obliged to be grateful either. I want to feel as though you're not simply putting up with me, wishing I was someone else looking after your children.'

'I don't wish that,' Gemma told her.

'Don't you?'

'No!' Gemma shook her head. 'I trust you with them. I know that they'll be OK with you.'

'And you know that I love them?' asked Frances.

'Of course.' Frances did love them, Gemma thought. Although she suspected her mother loved Michael's children more.

'I don't love anyone more than anyone else,' said Frances, as though reading her thoughts. 'Not Thomas or Polly, or Suzy, or Keelin or Ronan. They're all my grandchildren and I love them all equally. As I loved my children equally.'

Gemma grimaced.

Frances sighed. 'I'm sorry if you don't believe me,' she said. 'The thing is, I'd expected Michael to cause me trouble. A boy – I knew nothing about bringing up boys! I thought it would be cider parties in the field behind the house, and fights and goodness knows what else. But he was so academic. I was really proud of him when he got that college place in England. And then he met Debbie and it all seemed to fall into place for him.'

'And then they had Thomas and Polly and became Mr and Mrs Middle-England,' said Gemma.

Frances smiled faintly. 'I suppose so.'

'And lived happily ever after.'

'Because he doesn't look for the same kind of challenges as you,' said Frances. 'Because he doesn't fight for things to be better all the time. Or different all the time. Because he's happy and accepting and because he knows what he wants from life.'

'I thought I knew what I wanted from life,' said Gemma. 'I thought it was David.'

'I knew it wasn't David,' said Frances. 'But, once you'd married him, I thought you should have tried harder.'

'I did try!' cried Gemma. 'You don't know how hard I tried.'

'I suppose I don't,' said Frances. 'It just seemed to me that you were so crazy about him that it couldn't have all changed. I remember it, you know. The day you came home and talked and talked about him. How good-looking he was. How sexy.' She made a face.

'I didn't say sexy,' Gemma told her.

'Actually what you said was that he was a sex-machine,' said Frances dryly.

Gemma blushed. 'I hadn't, obviously, had any experience of him at that point.'

'You mean he wasn't a sex-machine?'

'Mum!' Gemma stared at her. 'Was that a joke?'

Frances shrugged. 'Sort of.'

Gemma couldn't hide her surprise. Frances never joked. In fact, it was a standing joke between Liz and herself that their mother didn't even know what a joke was.

'Sex-machine or not,' she said eventually, 'he wasn't the right man to be my husband. Which was sad.' She rubbed the side of her nose. 'I didn't want it to end in divorce. I really didn't. But I was going crazy and I knew that things weren't going to get better.'

'I wanted to help you,' said Frances. 'I wanted to tell you that it would be OK. But you wouldn't let me.'

'You told me it would work itself out,' Gemma reminded her. 'You told me to stick with it.'

'I thought it was the right thing, at the time,' said Frances. She ran her fingers through her hair. 'I guess I was wrong.'

'I wish you'd been right,' said Gemma.

'I didn't want you to have to stand on your own two feet,' said Frances. 'I wanted you and Liz to have jobs that you like but then get married—'

'—And live happily ever after,' finished Gemma. 'Oh, Mum, it'd be nice if life was like that, but it's not.'

'I know,' said Frances. 'And I'm probably a fool, Gemma, for thinking that it should be.'

'You're not a fool.' Gemma's tone was vehement. 'I want exactly the same for Keelin. I suppose one day I'll be screaming at her over some bloke.'

'Oh, yes.' Frances remembered suddenly. 'A bloke phoned today. She said it was a man, actually.'

'For Keelin?' asked Gemma. 'What man?'

'She wouldn't say,' said Frances.

'Was it Mark?' asked Gemma. 'She went to a party with a guy called Mark. Not exactly God's gift, but she seems to like him.'

'I don't know,' said Frances. 'When I asked was it a boy she snapped that it was a man.'

Gemma grinned. Typical of Keelin to antagonise Frances. She

324

wondered why it was that her mother rubbed both of them up the wrong way. Although, she had to admit, right now she felt closer to Frances than in a very long time.

'I never screamed at you.' Frances returned to their original conversation.

'What?'

'Over boys. I never screamed at you. Even though sometimes I felt like it.'

'OK.' Gemma grinned. 'I'll concede that. You were far too ladylike to scream.'

'I don't think you need to yell at children,' said Frances. 'I tried to be the kind of mother that didn't yell.'

'You never needed to,' Gemma told her. 'Your voice was enough. I've tried it on Keelin myself sometimes, but it never works. I don't think I've got the pitch quite right.'

Frances smiled wryly. 'The trouble is only just beginning with Keelin,' she said. 'I hope you fare better with her than I did with you.'

'Oh, I suppose she'll hate me,' said Gemma. 'But, deep down, I hope she'll always love me.'

'I *do* love you, Gemma.' Frances gazed at her daughter. 'I know we don't see eye-to-eye over a lot of things, but I'll always love you.'

'I love you too,' said Gemma. 'But I need to know that my life is my life and you won't always tell me that I should have done things better.'

Frances was silent for a moment, then nodded. 'I simply wanted the best for you,' she said. 'You and Liz. And when I thought you weren't getting the best, or giving yourselves the best, I suppose I blamed you instead of – of supporting you. I thought that would help you see how much it mattered.'

'Really?' Gemma asked.

'Yes,' said Frances. 'Do you think I read all of the wrong books about bringing up children?'

Gemma sighed. 'I don't think there are any right books about children,' she said. 'Keelin and Ronan drive me to distraction most of the time. Keelin now, especially. She's suddenly got this interest in boys, when she dresses up she looks about seventeen – it terrifies me.'

'Exactly!' Frances's eyes lit up. 'Exactly, Gemma. That's what happened when you went out to the disco for the first time. Remember? You were thirteen years old and you shouldn't have even been let in to the place! But you swore to me that thirteen was fine, that it was for teenagers. Then

325

you went upstairs and when you came back down again you looked at least eighteen.'

Gemma remembered. She'd worn a skin-tight white dress, ridiculously high-heeled white sandals, and had sprayed her hair so that it stood up on her head like Blondie's. She'd been a great fan of Blondie. Still was.

'I had a good time,' she told her mother.

'That was what I was afraid of,' said Frances.

'Not that good a time!' Gemma looked shocked. 'I might have looked older but I was still only thirteen.'

'It was because you looked older . . .' Frances sighed. 'I was always terrified for you, Gemma, you were so vibrant and headstrong, always ready to try anything.'

'I wasn't stupid,' said Gemma. 'Not all the time.'

'You were independent,' Frances said. 'Both you and Liz. And, after Michael, it was hard to cope with it.'

'You should be pleased that we were independent,' said Gemma. 'And proud. We've managed to stand on our own two feet no matter what.'

'I know,' said Frances. 'I am proud of you.'

'Really?'

'Of course,' said Frances fiercely. 'Of course I am. Maybe I don't show it but I think you've done really well on your own. I only wish you didn't have to be. That's all, Gemma. Truly.'

Gemma still didn't want to cry in front of Frances. She blinked hard so that the tears wouldn't fall. 'Thanks,' she said.

'You don't have to thank me for loving you,' said Frances. 'I've always loved you. And if I didn't show it the right way, I'm sorry.'

'Well, if I didn't realise it, I'm sorry too.' Gemma sniffed.

Frances put her arm around Gemma's shoulders. It was the closest she'd come to giving her daughter a hug in years.

'OK,' she said, eventually. 'Now I really must get home. I set the oven timer before I came out and your father's dinner will be ready soon.'

'Thanks for coming over.' Gemma's voice wobbled.

'No trouble,' said Frances briskly. 'Give me a call if you need me next week.'

'I will,' said Gemma.

'Take care.' Frances pulled on her coat and left.

When her mother was gone, Gemma hung up her coat and brought her bath oil and face mask upstairs. That must be the biggest row I've had with her in ages, she thought, as she pinned her hair back from her face. And the deepest conversation. We actually dealt with issues. Despite the shouting, it was really quite grown-up!

Usually dealing with her mother made her feel as though she was about sixteen again. She always felt that, with Frances, criticism was only just below the surface. And she'd always supposed that the criticism was because Frances didn't love her. Not because she did. Yet she hadn't felt that way this evening. She'd seen Frances as another adult, possibly for the first time in her life. It was pretty odd to think that it was only now that she considered herself to be an adult in the company of her mother!

But that wasn't Frances's fault. Because, thought Gemma, as she rubbed the apricot-scented mask on to her face, despite sometimes getting depressed about being thirty-five, despite sometimes thinking that her life was over before it had started, despite having had meetings with lawyers, for goodness sake, she'd never actually managed to feel properly grown-up.

She was the divorced mother of two children and sometimes she didn't feel any more qualified for life than she had when she actually was sixteen. The world was full of people living their grown-up lives and doing grown-up things. And she was only now beginning to feel that she might actually be part of it.

Chapter 33

'I don't want to go.' Keelin stood with her hands on her hips staring defiantly at Gemma who was stacking the breakfast things in the dishwasher.

'Look, Keelin, it's the only time he gets to see you,' said Gemma pleadingly. 'How do you think he'll feel when you say you don't want to go out?'

'Why should he care?' asked Keelin. 'He's probably just as bored as us traipsing around.'

'That's not fair,' said Gemma. 'I thought you understood, Keelin.'

'I'm fed up understanding.' Keelin's bottom lip trembled. 'I don't want to be dragged to another restaurant and another bowling alley, or art gallery or whatever he thinks might be a worthwhile excursion just because he has access. I'm not a commodity, you know.' She tossed her hair back and looked at Gemma with a challenge in her eyes.

'How about if he simply brings you back to the apartment?' asked Gemma. 'That's not being dragged around.'

'No,' said Keelin.

'Why not?' Gemma was becoming exasperated. 'What else are you planning to do with the day? And don't say study because I won't believe it.'

'I want to go out with Mark,' said Keelin.

'Oh,' said Gemma. She scratched the side of her head. She could understand perfectly why Keelin didn't want to go out with David if she was going out with her boyfriend instead. In the matter of dads versus boyfriends, dads were always going to lose out. She could also understand how wearing it was to be brought out by someone all the time.

'Dad'll be disappointed,' Gemma told Keelin.

'Well, he can't always have everything the way he wants,' said Keelin mutinously.

'He doesn't always have everything the way he wants,' said Gemma.

'Yes, he does.' Keelin sat on the kitchen worktop and swung her long legs back and forth. 'He has us and he has Orla.' She looked at her mother thoughtfully.

'What?' asked Gemma.

'It's funny with Orla,' said Keelin.

'In what way?'

'I don't know exactly.' Keelin shrugged. 'It's an odd kind of relationship.'

Gemma rinsed out the teapot then turned to look at Keelin. 'What on earth makes you say that?'

'They hardly spend any time together,' she said. 'I asked Dad about his day. He's at work all the time. So's Orla. And he takes us out on Sundays. The only day they can possibly be together is Saturday.'

'People live their lives in different ways.' Gemma was intrigued by Keelin's insight into David's marriage. 'They're probably happy that way.'

'I wouldn't be,' said Keelin.

'You never know,' said Gemma. 'Sometimes you don't want the other person to be around all the time.'

'What about Bru?' asked Keelin. 'Speaking about relationships.'

Gemma felt herself blush. 'Bru?'

'Did you ring him back?' She'd told Gemma that he'd phoned late last night and Gemma had thanked her for telling her and kept on reading her hairdressing magazine. Keelin had wanted to ask more but Gemma's face warned her not to.

'Yes,' said Gemma. It had been nearly midnight when she'd called. She'd wanted to wait until Keelin was asleep. They'd talked for almost an hour. About silly things.

She hadn't wanted to hang up.

'What did he want?' Keelin asked.

'To see me sometime.' Gemma felt terrible about keeping things from Keelin. But she hadn't told her daughter about lunch with Sam McColgan and she wasn't going to. Not unless she went out with him again.

'I like him,' said Keelin. 'But he's not Dad.'

'Of course not!' Gemma hugged her. 'Of course not,' she repeated.

'So are you going to go out with him?'

'How would you feel about it?' asked Gemma.

Keelin shrugged. 'Odd,' she admitted. She smiled slightly at Gemma. 'It was strange to see him look at you on holiday, Mum. Fiona and me laughed at it but I felt funny all the same. He's in love with you.'

'Don't be silly.' Gemma put a washing tablet into the dishwasher and filled the rinsing compartment with rinse-aid.

Keelin picked at her nails.

'You should put nail guard on over the varnish,' said Gemma. 'It'll stop it from chipping.'

'Do you love him?'

'No,' replied Gemma firmly. 'But I like him.'

'So do I.'

'I know,' said Gemma. 'I thought, maybe, you kind of loved him yourself.'

'Mum!' Keelin looked at her. 'That's gross. He's much older than me.'

'You said yourself that it's the same difference between David and Orla,' said Gemma.

'Yeah. And their relationship is on the rocks.'

'Keelin, it isn't.'

'Want to bet?' Keelin sighed. 'What is it with grown-ups?' she asked. 'You'd think that you'd manage to sort it all out by now, wouldn't you? But you're as bad as any of us.'

Gemma laughed. 'That's what makes life so interesting,' she said. 'You never learn it all. And,' she added, 'I only decided that last night.'

Keelin smiled. 'I don't know if I want you to go out with Bru,' she said. 'I like him. But I don't know if—'

'Keelin, don't worry,' said Gemma.

'How can I help worrying?' asked Keelin in a tone which was a mirror of the one Gemma often used herself. 'You have my heart scalded!'

And both of them smiled.

⮌

David arrived at half past twelve. He still looked exhausted, thought Gemma as he came into the house. And the flecks of grey that had been sprinkled through his hair had suddenly become more and more evident. He smiled at her as he walked into the kitchen.

'Nice smell.'

'Casserole,' she told him.

'Pity you have to eat it alone.'

'I don't mind,' she said. 'Anyway, it's one of the things I freeze.'

'Is there enough for all of us?' asked David.

Gemma furrowed her brow. 'What do you mean?'

'What if I stay for dinner today? Would you have enough?'

330

'I . . .' Gemma was at a loss.

'If it's too much trouble then it doesn't matter,' said David. 'But I know the kids are tired of traipsing around town. It was fine when they were smaller and they liked being brought out by me. But now Keelin's bored out of her mind. She said that last time. I know I should have said something earlier but I thought that, perhaps, if I had lunch here then we could chat and she could do her own thing afterwards.'

'But – what about Orla?' asked Gemma.

'She doesn't mind,' said David. 'She goes to her mother for Sunday lunch now.'

'The food won't be ready for another hour.' Gemma glanced at the oven timer.

Keelin interrupted them by dancing into the kitchen, earphones in her ears. 'Hi, Dad.'

Keelin was wearing her usual black jeans and – her only concession to colour – her red lycra T-shirt. But she looked different today. It wasn't her clothes, David realised. It was something about Keelin herself. Her eyes were bright and her usual frown had disappeared. She looked pretty. In fact, he thought as he studied her more closely, she looked pretty gorgeous. How did I manage that? he wondered. She's my daughter. She's part of me. And she's beautiful. His heart lurched.

'Hi,' he said. 'How would you like to stay in for lunch today?'

'Stay in?' She switched off her Walkman.

'Have lunch here?'

Keelin glanced at Gemma who said nothing.

'Suits me,' she said. 'But it means we'll have eaten one of this week's dinners too. Mum always makes too much on Sundays so she doesn't have to cook when she's working late.'

'How organised of you,' murmured David.

'I don't need you to sort out every aspect of my life,' said Gemma tartly.

He laughed. Why did he assume, Gemma asked herself, that she had nothing better to do on Sundays than to hang around and wait for him to bring the kids back home? He hadn't asked her if she was busy, if there was a reason he couldn't stay to lunch. He hadn't even seemed to think it might inconvenience her. As far as he was concerned, she was still just there to cook for him!

'I wouldn't impose,' he said, breaking in on her thoughts. 'But Keelin told me you do all the cleaning on Sundays. I thought that, after lunch, I could do the cleaning for you.'

'You!' She looked at him in complete astonishment.

331

'Why not?' he asked. 'I know how to turn on the vacuum.'

'David, you were always too busy to clean,' Gemma protested.

'Too busy to smell the roses,' said David. 'But I'm going to start now.'

Gemma couldn't think of a reason to say no. She felt sorry for David who was probably as tired of taking out the children as they were of going out. She shrugged helplessly and David immediately offered to start the cleaning. She let him get on with it while she rummaged in the freezer and found some fruit which she could use to make a dessert.

She had to admit that Sunday lunch with David and the children was fun. David didn't nag at her, criticise her and generally make her feel useless as he once had. He praised her cooking, asked how things were going at the hairdresser's and was generally easier to get on with than she ever remembered. He started reminiscing too, telling stories of the first few months of their marriage while Keelin listened with interest and Ronan demolished the remains of the forest fruit pavlova that Gemma had hurriedly put together.

'Remember the first holiday I got from Gravitas?' asked David. 'The weekend in Amsterdam?'

Gemma nodded. She'd liked Amsterdam with its quaint canal-side streets and high doll-like houses. They'd hired bicycles and cycled around the city, managing to get confused in the semi-circles of Herengracht, Keizersgracht and Prinsengracht. It was only when Gemma had spotted a particularly decorative hook outside one of the houses that they'd managed to get their bearings.

'What was the hook for?' asked Keelin.

'To get furniture into the house,' Gemma explained. 'The Dutch used to be taxed on the frontage of the house. That's why they built them tall and thin. But it makes it impossible to get furniture to the top so that's why they have the hooks.'

'Cool,' said Keelin.

'And then we went to the coffee shop,' David reminded her.

'Oh, yes.' And Gemma flashed a grin at him because she'd had one of the cookies that were laced with cannabis and she'd been utterly spaced for the rest of the evening. She didn't want to tell Keelin about the cookies. She'd never have any control over her again if her daughter knew that Gemma had wandered around Amsterdam high as a kite and preaching peace and love to all and sundry.

At exactly three o'clock Mark Dineen called for Keelin. Gemma smiled at him and invited him in but he shook his head and said that he'd wait outside. She didn't try to change his mind. Keelin clattered down the stairs, kissed Gemma lightly on the cheek and said that she'd be back later.

'By teatime,' said Gemma.

'Mum!'

'If you want to do anything else, phone me. I'm expecting you back by six. That's three hours, Keelin. You'll be all talked out in three hours.'

Keelin made a face but nodded.

David turned to Gemma and sighed. 'She's grown up,' he said. 'I didn't realise it before but she's not a child any more.'

'Oh, she is,' said Gemma firmly. 'But she's a child who has finally discovered the opposite sex. It doesn't make her grown-up. Just growing up.'

'It frightens me,' David told her. 'It makes me feel old.'

Gemma laughed. 'I've felt like that ever since she started to talk and said no! I suddenly realised that she was a real person who had likes and dislikes of her own.'

'I guess it's more difficult for me,' said David. 'I don't see them every day.'

'Oh, David, you see them a lot.'

'It's not the same.' He grimaced. 'I thought it didn't matter but, you know, it probably does.'

'I don't suppose that having divorced parents is the ideal for any child.' Gemma walked back into the living room and David followed her. 'But at least we've been kind of civilised about it. That must count for something.'

'Can I go out?' Ronan burst into the room. 'I want to go to Neville's.'

Gemma glanced at David. 'Sure,' he said. 'But be back when your mother tells you.'

'Teatime,' she said.

'OK.' Ronan beamed. 'See you later. 'Bye, Dad.'

The house seemed unnaturally quiet when he'd left.

'You didn't exactly get to see much of them today, though,' remarked Gemma.

'But it was better,' David told her. 'They were more relaxed and, to be honest, so was I. Thanks, Gem.'

'You're welcome.' She got up. 'I'm going to put on some more coffee. Do you want a cup?'

'Love one,' he said.

He liked this house, he thought, as he sat in the armchair while she made the coffee. There was something restful about it. It wasn't as designed as the apartment, of course. The suite of furniture was more battered than his and there were unmistakable signs of child occupation all around the place. He'd almost broken his neck by tripping over

333

Ronan's football boots at the top of the stairs. But it was a relaxed home, a comfortable home. He closed his eyes.

Gemma was astonished to find him sleeping when she returned with the coffee, his head lolling to one side, his mouth half open so that he was snoring gently. She put the coffee down beside him but he didn't wake up. She sat down and opened the newspaper. Happy families, she thought wryly, as she turned to the TV listings.

~

It was five o'clock when Orla arrived back at the apartment. Sunday lunch with her mother had turned into something of a routine. She'd leave for her parents' house at the same time as David left to get his children. Once or twice he'd brought them back at the apartment and she'd arrived home to find them there. Keelin had been as cool and dismissive as ever while Ronan smiled at her and said hello but without really noticing who she was. And those times David had smiled at her too but she knew that he was wishing that she hadn't come home so early. So the last few weeks she'd taken to arriving back at the apartment much later. But today both Rosanna and Gerry O'Neill were suffering from bad head colds and Orla knew that they just wanted to be left alone. They weren't hungry so she'd had a salmon cutlet in the kitchen by herself while her parents snoozed in front of the TV. When they eventually woke up she'd asked if there was anything she could do for them and Rosanna had told her, very firmly, that she could just go home. Be there when David gets back, Rosanna had said.

In all the Sundays that Orla called around, her mother had never asked her about the state of her marriage. Orla had been sure that one day Rosanna would ask why she never spent a Sunday with David and the children and she'd practised her answer over and over so that it came out easily. 'I see enough of him during the week! Besides, it's good for him to have time alone with his children.' She was able to say it lightly, putting the emphasis on the right words, making it sound as though she didn't care.

And I don't care, she told herself as she opened the door to the empty apartment. I don't care what he does any more. I'm past caring.

She sat on the sofa and pulled her legs up under her until she could rest her head on her knees. She had a headache and her eyes hurt. She felt utterly exhausted. Every moment when she wasn't actually doing anything, she starting thinking about her marriage until she was really afraid that she was heading for a nervous breakdown. And when she wasn't thinking about David and herself, she was thinking about her job

334

and how it had turned into a complete and utter nightmare. She'd break into a sweat then, as she'd think about the rest of the month and how she needed to bring in clients every day and how she wasn't managing to do that. And she wondered how she'd cope when David left her because she'd never get another job in the pensions industry. And she hadn't the faintest idea what else she could do.

She could move to Cork. The thought pushed its way into her head more and more frequently these days. She could move to Cork and live with Jonathan who really and truly loved her. Jonathan who understood her ambition. Jonathan who'd known her when she was fun to know and who wanted to make life fun for her again. If only he was here, in Dublin, she thought. She could see him, talk to him, make a choice.

'As though I have a choice,' she said out loud. 'As though I can just walk away from everything.'

But why not? Why stay in something that was making her so miserable and making David even more miserable? She had the rest of her life ahead of her. And David? Two divorces wouldn't look too good on his CV! She laughed mirthlessly. She was considering divorce and she hadn't even been married a year. She was the girl who despised the celebrity columns in magazines where two-bit actresses divorced their husbands 'of three months', citing irreconcilable differences. Whenever she read things like that she always wondered what on earth was wrong with these women. Why had they married men whom they so clearly didn't know? Or why didn't they bother to give things a chance? Sometimes, though, the person you married turned out to be a different person to the one you thought he was.

Sometimes, you didn't need to give things a chance. You knew.

⤸

The sound of the phone ringing woke David up. He looked around in bewilderment for a moment as he rubbed his aching neck. It took him a few seconds to realise where he was. He looked at his watch. Five o'clock. He'd have to get home soon, to the unwelcoming apartment and to Orla's accusing face. He was dreading going home.

Gemma's voice was muffled through the closed door but he could make out what she was saying. Her tone was happy, almost excited. 'No, it doesn't matter,' he heard her say. 'I can wait . . . If I can, you can,' she said, after a pause.

A brief silence, and then she laughed. 'David's here. No! Of course I didn't expect him to stay.'

David leaned towards the door so that he could hear more clearly. Had his staying for lunch messed up her Sunday? She hadn't objected. And what else had she got to do?

She laughed again. It was a long time, David thought, since he'd heard Gemma laugh like that.

'OK,' she said. 'But if you don't call me, I'll call you.'

Who was she talking to? Liz? Frances? He snorted. Gemma would never laugh like that talking to Frances. She and her mother were two very different people.

Gemma opened the door and walked in. 'Hi,' she said. 'Did I wake you?'

He shook his head. 'I'd just woken anyway. Who was on the phone?'

'David!' She made a face at him. 'None of your business.'

'Sorry. Habit.'

'Would you like some tea or coffee before you go?' she asked.

Was this a way of just getting rid of him? Was she tired of having him in the house? 'No,' he said. 'It's OK.'

'Fine,' she said.

He got up. 'I take it I've outstayed my welcome.'

'Not at all,' she said. 'But you've other people in your life too, haven't you? I'm sure Orla will be pleased if you get home early.'

'I'm sure she will,' said David dryly as he put on his jacket.

Chapter 34

When Brian and Patsy Hennessy had first moved into their house in Templeogue it had been in the depths of the country. Patsy's mother, who'd lived in Clanbrassil Street, within walking distance of the city centre, had been shocked to discover that her daughter was now living in a house with a large garden backing onto a field full of cows. Patsy's mother was a city woman through and through. She'd never quite come to terms with Patsy's move to the country where she could walk out of her front gate and pick blackberries from the huge bushes either side of the house. But, of course, Templeogue was no longer in the country. It was now part of the city, a desirable suburb where houses which had been built long after Patsy and Brian moved there had rooms half the size and no gardens to speak of. When they were smaller, the children had loved playing in the grandparents' garden.

After the divorce, Gemma's relationship with her in-laws remained friendly. Patsy often phoned her for a chat – usually about Keelin and Ronan, although Patsy would ask about Gemma too. She wasn't a demonstrative woman but Gemma had always found her easier to talk to than Frances. She never felt as though Patsy had judged her in the same way as Frances had. Even though she was trying very hard to understand Frances a little better.

She exhaled slowly as the taxi drew up outside the house. She wasn't looking forward to this evening. She must have been mad to agree to come.

The house was ablaze with light. Even the cherry blossom tree in the front garden was decked with coloured fairy lights which swayed in the evening breeze. There were wind chimes in the garden too – Gemma wondered how long it would be before one of the neighbours lost patience with their irritating tinkle and pulled them up.

'Come on,' she said to the children. 'Are you ready? Got the present?'

'Of course I've got the present,' said Keelin who was carrying the gold-framed photograph of herself and Ronan. 'You asked us that a hundred times before we left.'

'Sorry,' said Gemma.

Keelin opened the car door and shivered in the cool night air. She was wearing a dress, one that Gemma had bought for her last Thursday when they went late-night shopping together. The dress was red velvet, off the shoulder, with a neckline which was lower than Keelin thought her mother would allow. It showed off her still faintly tanned skin and, with her hair caught back from her face with two red clips, Keelin looked very elegant.

'Think about it, Mum,' she said when Gemma sighed over the fact that her daughter looked so sophisticated, 'some of those young supermodels are only thirteen! By comparison I look like a kid.'

'Some kid,' said Gemma as she took in the make-up, the eyeshadow and the cleavage that was definitely more pronounced than it had been during the summer.

'I wish I could've worn my jeans,' complained Ronan who was pulling at the jacket of his suit. 'Granny doesn't mind me in jeans, you know.'

'I know,' said Gemma. 'But I wanted us all to look good tonight.' So that nobody can say I haven't looked after them. So that nobody can think that I don't do a good job. So that I can feel confident and assured in the bosom of David's family and in front of David's wife.

She paid the taxi driver and followed the children up the garden path.

'Gemma!' Patsy opened the door and held out her arms to embrace her. 'It's lovely to see you again.'

'And you too, Patsy.' Gemma kissed the older woman on the cheek. 'You look fantastic!'

'Thank you,' said Patsy. 'I spent all day at the beauty salon to look like this. If I smile too much it might all fall apart. Keelin, my goodness, you look absolutely wonderful. Quite grown-up! I can hardly believe it.'

Keelin blushed. 'Thanks, Granny,' she said.

'You make me feel positively ancient,' said Patsy. 'And you too, Ronan. What a smart suit.'

'I wanted to wear jeans,' said Ronan.

Patsy smiled at him. 'Next time.' She put her arm round Gemma's waist. 'Come on in,' she said. 'There's a good crowd here already.'

Gemma had deliberately chosen to arrive late. She didn't want to hang around a half-empty room and make awkward conversation, particularly if David was there.

She followed Patsy into the living room. The double doors between living and dining rooms had been opened, giving plenty of space for the throng who'd gathered there. Both rooms had been redecorated since Gemma's last visit. The old Navan carpet had been replaced by wooden floorboards. Gemma looked at them more closely and realised that they were probably the original floorboards, sanded and polished. Brian had doubtless done the job himself – unlike David, he was an avid DIY enthusiast.

Gemma recognised some of Patsy's neighbours, and some distant relatives standing around in groups. Her eyes scanned the room for David and Orla. She didn't see them but she caught the eye of David's sister, Livvy.

'Hi, Gemma.' Livvy smiled at her.

'Hi, Liv. How are you keeping?'

'Oh, fine,' replied Livvy. 'And you?'

'Fine,' echoed Gemma.

'Gemma, darling, here's a glass of champagne!' Patsy thrust the flute glass into Gemma's hand. 'And what about Keelin? Is she allowed?'

'One glass,' said Gemma.

Keelin followed Patsy to the bar which they'd set up at one end of the room, leaving Gemma and Livvy together.

'I didn't expect to see you here,' said Livvy.

'I didn't expect to be invited.'

'I was surprised when I heard you had been. No offence.'

Gemma had never been particularly comfortable with David's sister. Livvy was a year older than her and she'd always made Gemma feel inadequate. Gemma was in awe of the fact that Livvy had a string of qualifications to her name and was engaged in some kind of complex scientific research in UCD. Gemma had never felt able enough to talk to Livvy about her work and Livvy had never ever asked about Gemma's hairdressing abilities. She could do with a good cut, thought Gemma, as she appraised the other woman's locks. It was far too heavy on top and that fringe was too long. Maybe it was meant to give Livvy a girlish look but it only succeeded in making her appear gawky. Of course Livvy had never much bothered with her appearance, always insisting that the mind was more important than the body.

'Is David here?' asked Gemma.

'Why?' asked Livvy.

'I just wondered.'

'Not here yet,' answered Livvy. 'Maybe he wants to make a dramatic entrance with your replacement.'

They were all probably thinking that, Gemma mused. Maybe they were all wondering what would happen when David and Orla showed up. Perhaps they were secretly hoping for fireworks when old and new wives met each other. Patsy and Brian would be hoping, of course, that it would all be terribly civilised but the fun for everyone else would be if it wasn't. She smiled to herself. It wouldn't be a problem for her. Given she was so secure in the knowledge she'd made the right decision about her divorce. Secure in the knowledge that David's remarriage hadn't the power to hurt her any more. And certainly secure in the knowledge that, even if she and Sam weren't an official item (as yet she'd only seen him once since lunch, for a couple of drinks after Thursday's late-night opening at the salon), he made her feel as good as any 24-year-old, flame-haired bimbo bitch. And she didn't even think of her as a bitch any more.

'Do you like her?' Livvy broke the silence.

'Pardon?' Gemma glanced at David's sister again.

'Orla. What d'you think of her?'

'Nothing.' Gemma shrugged. 'I hardly know her.'

'You must see her, surely?'

'Why?' asked Gemma.

'When you're dropping the kids over – times like that.'

'David picks the children up,' said Gemma. 'I've only met Orla a couple of times. I haven't been in his apartment since they married.' She had hated the apartment anyway. It was too modern, too chic, too stylish for her. And it would be a nightmare to live in with kids. She remembered thinking that she'd been around children too long when she'd thought that. The apartment was an interior designer's dream, after all.

'I haven't seen much of her either,' said Livvy.

'You don't see much of David.' Gemma sipped at her champagne. It was making her light-headed because she hadn't eaten anything all day. She'd rushed home from the salon, dived under the shower and got dressed again all in half an hour. She hadn't had time to eat anything at home, and she rarely had more than a cup of tea and a scone when she was working.

'No.' Livvy pushed her heavy hair out of her eyes. 'My brother and I are not exactly close. And, of course, since he married the red-headed hooker he hasn't had time for anyone else.'

'Hardly a hooker,' said Gemma mildly, though she liked the fact that Livvy apparently had as little time for her successor as she'd had for her.

'She hooked him good and proper.' Livvy grinned at her joke.

'I think he hooked her,' said Gemma.

340

'I always thought he'd stay married to you,' said Livvy. 'I thought you two worked well together.'

'We didn't,' said Gemma shortly.

'You were a better match,' Livvy observed. 'With this one, he's always wondering if she's going to leave him. Or do better than him.'

'Not really?'

Livvy nodded. 'You know, he really just wanted another version of you, Gemma.'

'Oh, come on!'

'Honestly. I don't suppose he seriously thought that Orla would give up work when she married him, but I think he saw himself as being the man of the house once again. You know David, Gemma. Loves to be in charge of things. Only he's finding it more difficult this time.'

'How do you know?' asked Gemma.

Livvy tapped the side of her nose. 'Sisterly intuition.'

Gemma was surprised. She didn't think Livvy had ever had any sisterly intuition about David.

'Gemma! How lovely to see you!' Brian Hennessy, a burly, older version of David, appeared at her shoulder and put his arms round her.

'And you, Brian.' Gemma turned to him and kissed him.

'You look lovely,' he said. 'I think you grow more attractive with every passing day.'

'I love you, Brian.' Gemma smiled at him. 'I always did.'

He laughed and hugged her. 'Glad you could make it tonight.'

'Oh, I'm glad to be here,' she said.

'We didn't know whether to ask you or not.'

'It could be a little awkward,' conceded Gemma. 'But I haven't seen David or Orla yet.' She said their names easily.

'David rang to say they were delayed,' said Brian. 'Something to do with Orla getting home late from work.'

⤿

David and Orla were caught in a two-mile tailback in Dundrum village. There'd been an accident at the traffic lights and, as yet, the two cars hadn't been moved.

Orla could feel David's anger as he fumed silently beside her. She avoided looking at him, knowing that if she hadn't been half an hour late in getting home they wouldn't be stuck here now. She'd been getting out of the shower when the taxi arrived and David had asked him to wait for fifteen minutes. The driver said that he couldn't – he had another fare.

341

He told David that he'd have to re-book the taxi through central control. Even though she couldn't see him, Orla could feel David's anger crackle through the house.

Naturally, the re-booked taxi was even later and David was incandescent with rage as he peered over the apartment balcony waiting for it. He'd drive himself, he told Orla who was checking to see that her stockings were straight. He told her in such a way that she knew his evening had been ruined. She knew that David hadn't wanted to drive to Patsy and Brian's. He'd been looking forward to an evening of food and drink. Then, as they'd been about to get into David's BMW, the taxi showed up.

David had muttered something which she didn't quite hear but which she knew apportioned the blame to her. Why was it, she wondered, that every little thing that happened these days was somebody's fault? Her fault for being late. His fault for insisting on waiting for the taxi. Her fault for using all the hot water. His fault for forgetting to switch on the immersion heater.

And now, she thought, as she leaned back in the hard seat of the taxi, they'd be in a house full of his relatives who barely knew her but who all knew his bloody perfect ex-wife. And whose fault did they think the break-up of his marriage was?

⤶

Gemma locked the bathroom door and looked at herself in the mirror. She retouched her blusher and her lipstick and sprayed some more Happy behind her ears. If only it was one of those aromatherapy perfumes that did what they promised! Being happy would have been nice. Quite suddenly she was nervous about meeting David and Orla. The feeling had come to her unexpectedly, as she stood talking to David's cousin Andrew and his wife, Grainne. Grainne told Gemma how well she was looking tonight.

'Although,' she added, 'under the circumstances I suppose you felt you had to pull out all the stops.'

'What do you mean?' asked Gemma.

'Come on, Gem!' Grainne smiled at her. 'David and the new Mrs Hennessy! I haven't seen her since the wedding, but she was damned gorgeous at that.'

'Thanks, Grainne,' said Gemma.

'You were lovely at your wedding too,' said Andrew and Gemma smiled gratefully at him.

'How do you get on with her?' asked Grainne.

Gemma wished fervently that people would stop asking her how she got on with Orla. How the hell did they think she got on with her, for heaven's sake! She made a noncommittal reply and headed for the bathroom.

She looked at herself in the mirror again and pulled at a strand of hair to tease it gently across her forehead. She looked quite good tonight, she realised. Her skin was clear, her eyes bright and her lilac Ben de Lisi dress was perfect. She'd ached to buy something new to wear but, having spent money on Keelin, she simply couldn't afford anything new herself. So she'd taken out all the evening dresses in her wardrobe, none of which she'd worn in the past five years. She was surprised, and very pleased, to discover that both the Ben de Lisi and the Frank Usher still fitted her. They must have been pretty loose-fitting when she'd bought them! Nevertheless it was gratifying to be able to pull up the zips with only a little effort and it gave her a self-satisfied glow to know that the ridiculous sums she'd spent on them had turned into – as she'd told David at the time – an investment!

She tightened the butterflies on her black pearl earrings and adjusted the matching pearl necklace. She took a deep breath. They'd be here soon and she was ready.

She'd just reached the top of the stairs when Patsy Hennessy opened the front door. Gemma wasn't able to turn back quickly enough to avoid David's surprised look as he saw her standing there.

Orla followed him into the house. She, too, saw Gemma on the stairway. She bit her lip as she looked at David's ex-wife. Blobby Gemma looked wonderful, thought Orla. The dress she was wearing flattered her figure and the colour suited her skin. Gemma's hair had been skilfully pulled back from her face and secured by a clasp which exactly matched the dress. And the heavy black pearl jewellery she was wearing looked dramatically sophisticated. Orla immediately felt young and silly in her short black cocktail dress with the shoestring straps. Her hair, flowing loose around her shoulders, was too informal. She also wished that she'd worn something a little more interesting than a plain gold chain round her neck. It had looked simple and elegant earlier. Against Gemma's pearls, though, Orla was convinced it looked childish.

'Hello, David.' Gemma kept her voice as even as she could. It was harder than she'd thought. Her heart was thudding in her chest. She wanted to appear completely in control of the situation but she wasn't sure that she could be.

'Hi, Gem.' He caught her by the shoulders and kissed her lightly on the lips. 'You look wonderful tonight.'

'Thanks.' She turned to Orla. 'Hello,' she said.

The bimbo bitch looked great, thought Gemma. She'd have given anything to be able to wear the sheer slip of black material that was posing as a dress and that showed off the younger girl's lithe body to such advantage. And her legs, encased in black stockings with a diamanté design up the side, seemed to go on for ever and ever.

'Hello, Gemma. It's a long time since we've met.'

'I suppose we're not likely to meet very often.'

'I suppose not.' Why does she make me feel like this? wondered Orla. She's not as pretty as me. She looked great on the stairs but she's older than me. She has some little wrinkles around her eyes. And she's fatter than me, even though you can't really see her stomach in that dress.

'Have you been inside yet?' asked David.

'Oh, yes,' replied Gemma. 'The kids are in there, doubtless raiding the food. I was talking to Livvy earlier.'

'Livvy,' said David dissmissively. 'I bet she was a riot.'

'She's all right.' Gemma defended her ex-sister-in-law for the first time in her life.

'Will we move in?' asked Orla. 'It seems a bit daft to stand here.'

David nodded. He and Orla walked ahead of Gemma.

Her bum wouldn't look big in anything, thought Gemma gloomily as she watched the younger girl. And I'd never be able to wear shoes with heels like those. Not with my feet, always tired from standing all day!

⤙

'I don't know if we should have asked her.' Patsy and Brian stood beside each other and looked at Gemma as she chatted to one of their neighbours. Patsy leaned her head on Brian's shoulder as she spoke.

'It would have been odd if we hadn't,' said Brian.

'Not that odd,' said Patsy. 'Surely people don't ask the other wife along to most parties?'

'I've no idea.' Brian shrugged. 'It's a whole new ball game to me.'

Patsy sighed. 'I wish divorce had never been introduced in this country.'

'It would have been worse if they'd stayed together, I suppose,' said Brian.

'Would it?' Patsy looked up at him. 'Maybe if they hadn't been able to get divorced, they would have worked it out.'

'That's David's new wife.' Livvy nodded in Orla's direction while she stood beside Joanne McCullough, Brian and Patsy's next-door neighbour. 'She's pretty, isn't she?'

'She's good-looking all right,' said Joanne. 'How on earth did David manage to land her?'

'Oh, my brother's not so bad himself,' Livvy said. 'At least, the girls in school always thought so. They used to throw themselves at him.'

'She looks terribly young,' said Joanne.

'Twenty-four.'

Joanne sighed. 'I remember twenty-four! Not terribly well, but I do remember it.'

'I remember it myself,' said Livvy. 'And I'm damn glad I wasn't married at that age.'

'It's terribly civilised.' Joanne scanned the room for Gemma. 'If Richie and I split up, there isn't a hope in hell that I'd stay in the same room as him, let alone his new model.'

'I'm sure it's all a pretence,' said Livvy. 'Gemma probably wants to scratch Orla's eyes out.'

'The way Orla's looking, I think it might be the other way around.' Joanne had found Gemma by following Orla's gaze. David's ex-wife was at the other end of the room chatting to Patsy's sister Ellen. Gemma was laughing, her head slightly to one side, her body relaxed. By contrast, Orla was alone, standing ramrod straight against the wall.

'Maybe I'd better rescue her,' said Livvy. 'Just in case she's thinking of doing any damage.'

⌐

'We got Gran and Granddad a photograph,' Ronan told David as they stood side by side. 'It's of me and Keelin. Mum dragged us into a studio to get it done properly. I don't know why Gran and Granddad would want a photo, but Mum thought they'd like it.'

David smiled at him. 'They want things to remember you by.'

'They don't need to remember me,' said Ronan. 'They can see me any time they like.'

David put his arm round his son and hugged him just as Keelin arrived beside them holding a full glass of champagne.

'I hope you're not drinking that stuff,' said David.

345

'Mum said I could.'

'She said one glass,' Ronan told her.

'Gran topped it up,' confided Keelin. 'She said it was OK.'

David sighed. 'I'm trying to bring you up to be a decent, clean-living young lady and you're guzzling champagne!'

'Better than guzzling rotgut,' said Keelin cheerfully.

David couldn't think of anything to say to that. He watched her sip her drink and wondered, once again, when exactly she'd turned from being a child into a young adult. For the first time in his life he felt his age.

⁓

'Want a top up?' Livvy walked up to David's wife and waved a bottle of wine in front of her.

'Thanks.' Orla nodded.

'Having fun?' asked Livvy as she poured ice-cold Sancerre into Orla's glass. Brian and Patsy had left the wine in the back garden to keep it cool. Now, with the temperature plummeting, it was too cold.

'It's a good party.' Orla was noncommittal.

'Oh, go on!' Livvy grinned. 'You know quite well everyone's intrigued about you and Gemma. I can't help thinking that Mum and Dad invited both of you just to give it that extra little buzz.'

'Not really?' said Orla.

'Maybe not really,' Livvy admitted, 'but it's the sort of waspish thing mum would do. She always likes a bit of drama.'

'I've no intention of creating any drama,' said Orla sharply.

'I'm sure you haven't,' said Livvy. 'So, tell me, how's love's young dream?'

Orla felt herself flush. 'I wouldn't call us love's young dream,' she said.

'Why?' asked Livvy. 'David fell head over heels in love with you. And you're young. He probably thinks he's dreaming!'

'I doubt that very much,' said Orla.

'You know, Mum tried to dissuade him from marrying you,' Livvy said. 'She told him that you'd change more than him. That he'd already decided what he wanted from life but that you hadn't. She didn't think it was fair on you.'

'Neither set of parents was too happy, as far as I recall,' said Orla. 'Mine tried to stop me too.'

'So why did you marry him?' asked Livvy. 'If it's not too cheeky a question.'

346

'It is a bit.' Orla pushed her hair behind her ears.

'Fair enough,' said Livvy cheerfully. 'I don't talk to David myself very much. It's not that we don't get on but we just have very different views on life. We started off the same – relaxed, easy-going – like our parents. But David got bitten by the commerce bug and I could never quite connect with him after that.'

'I didn't think you were exactly the relaxed type,' said Orla. 'What about your research?'

'That's my life,' said Livvy simply. 'And I don't get paid a fortune for it. But I don't care! That's the difference between David and me. He values every second of his time in monetary terms.' She smiled at Orla. 'Well, probably not every second. Maybe I'm being a little unkind. But money means so much to him.'

'Why do you think that is?' asked Orla.

'I dunno.' Livvy pondered the question. 'He was always a competitive sort of bloke, though. It usen't to be about money, of course, it was sports – he played every sport you could think of and he always wanted to win. Maybe when he stopped doing that he just transferred it all to his job.'

'He's generous with it.' Orla thought about the flowers he'd bought. The times he'd brought her away. The jewellery. The underwear – when they first started going out together he used to buy her an incredible amount of underwear. He hadn't bought her anything in ages.

'Are you all right?' Livvy looked at her curiously.

'Fine,' said Orla. 'I'm fine. It was just a rush getting out this evening. And the traffic was awful.'

'No wonder David looked in a temper when you arrived.' Livvy laughed. 'He still thinks that you should be able to get round Dublin in fifteen minutes. He's forgotten that the city's changed in the last ten years!'

⌒

Gemma was pouring herself another glass of champagne when Andrew kissed her on the back of the neck and almost made her spill the drink.

'If that had gone all over the table I'd have hit you,' she said. But her smile took the annoyance out of her words. She liked Andrew.

'You're looking ravishing tonight,' he told her. 'You're quite the talk of the party.'

'Don't be silly.' She blushed.

'Oh, but I'm not,' he told her. 'The blokes are giving points to you and Orla. You're on top at the moment.'

'Andrew, that's outrageous!' She glared at him. 'You're not really, are you?' she added.

'Absolutely,' he assured her. 'For general sexiness and personality.'

'I hope you're making this up,' she told him, at the same time feeling flattered that, even in something as juvenile and stupid as this that she might really be outscoring Orla.

'Cross my heart and hope to die,' he said solemnly.

'You deserve to be shot,' she told him. 'Has anyone ever told you that it's very politically incorrect to treat women like prizes in a raffle?'

He laughed. 'I thought you'd be pleased.'

'I – oh, go away, Andrew,' she said. 'Or I'll do something stupid like pour my drink over you.'

'I gave you top marks for the dress,' he told her. 'You look fabulous in it, Gemma.'

'Go away,' she said again, although her tone was mild. 'Or I'll tell David what you're up to.'

'Now I'm worried!' Andrew grinned at her before grabbing a can of beer and disappearing into the crowd.

꙳

Orla couldn't remember the name of the woman who'd spent the last fifteen minutes telling her what a wonderful woman Gemma was. If she was that fucking wonderful, Orla thought savagely, David would never have left her. Why was it that they all seemed to like her so much? She hadn't made him happy, had she? She'd thrown him out of the house, hadn't she? Orla watched as Gemma laughed and joked with some of David's relatives. Stupid bitch, she thought. I bet none of them really like her. They're just being polite. As Gemma walked away from the bar, Orla strode towards it. She needed another drink and she needed it now.

꙳

'Why are you all by yourself?' Keelin stood beside Orla.

Orla blinked at her a couple of times. Three glasses of wine in quick succession had made her light-headed.

'I don't know many people,' she said.

'Dad should introduce you,' Keelin told her. 'He's not great at the social niceties though.'

348

Orla grimaced. 'You don't think so?'

'Nope. Mum was always saying that. Dad does his own thing, she used to say. And he does.'

'You might be right.' Keelin was more tuned in than she'd realised, thought Orla woozily. And she was being amazingly friendly. She wondered why.

'Don't you visit Gran and Granddad often?' asked the younger girl. 'We used to come here a lot when Mum and Dad were married.'

'I haven't been here since before your dad and I got married,' said Orla. 'I don't think they like me very much.'

'Why?' asked Keelin.

'Because I married him,' said Orla. 'Maybe they thought he'd get back with your mum.'

Keelin sighed. 'I thought that too,' she said.

'And is that what you want?' Orla wasn't sure she wanted to hear the answer.

'I don't know,' said Keelin. 'Sometimes. But sometimes not.' She looked at Orla quizzically. 'Do you love him?'

'Pardon?'

'My dad. Do you love him?' asked Keelin.

'I married him.' Orla didn't think she should be talking to Keelin like this. She was David's daughter and she was only a kid for all that she looked incredibly sophisticated tonight. 'I suppose I must love him if I married him.'

'But he's so old. And you're so pretty.' Keelin smiled at her. 'I know I wasn't very nice to you at first, Orla, but I honestly couldn't believe that you were going out with Dad. It seemed – well, disgusting I suppose.'

Orla twirled one of her red curls around her little finger. 'And do you still think it's disgusting?'

Keelin frowned. 'Sometimes,' she admitted. 'But if you love each other maybe it doesn't matter.'

'It's an interesting way of putting it,' said Orla.

'Mum doesn't love him anymore,' said Keelin.

Orla looked across the room to where she'd last seen David. He wasn't there. Neither was Gemma. 'Perhaps,' she said. 'But perhaps your Dad still loves her.'

Keelin wasn't listening to her. The mobile phone in her hand-bag, which she'd insisted on bringing, had started to ring. And she knew that the only person who'd be ringing was Mark Dineen. She slipped out of the room and upstairs where she could talk to him in peace.

'You OK?' David suddenly appeared beside her.

Orla nodded.

'Have enough to drink?'

'Of course,' she said.

'Why are you on your own?' he asked. 'Why aren't you mingling with people?'

'David, I don't know anyone to mingle with,' said Orla. 'Why don't we mingle together?'

He heaved a sigh. 'Who do you want to meet?'

'You don't have to make it seem like a chore.'

'It's not a chore,' he said shortly. 'Come on, Orla. Let's talk to Mum and Dad.'

Orla slipped her arm round his waist. I'm his wife, she said to herself. And they'd better believe it.

⤳

Gemma felt her throat constrict as she watched them talking to Patsy and Brian. Orla was leaning against David, using his body as support. She's had too much to drink, thought Gemma, recognising the pose. It was probably quite hard for her to be here tonight, among people she didn't really know very well. Gemma felt a sudden surge of pity and then dismissed it. Orla had everything she wanted, she thought. The flipside was a night like tonight. She walked past the four of them, holding her stomach in and her shoulders high. Orla might be married to David, and she, Gemma, might have no interest in him anymore, but she wanted to look as desirable and attractive as she ever had. Just so he'd know that she wasn't ready for the scrap heap yet. And so's Orla would know it too.

⤳

She walked out into the relative quiet of the back garden. The sky was black but it was impossible to see the stars through the white and yellow glow of the city lights. She remembered when she'd first come out here with David they'd stood in this garden and looked up at the star-studded sky. He'd pointed out constellations to her – Orion, with his three-starred belt, and Cassiopeia, the beautifully named W-shaped collection of stars. She craned her neck backwards but she couldn't make

350

any of them out tonight. She'd loved him then, she really and truly had. She'd believed that it would work out, that she'd be with him forever.

She shivered and rubbed her shoulders. It was cold out here but she needed some time on her own. It wasn't easy to watch Orla being with David, no matter how her feelings for him had changed. It was a territorial thing, she told herself. Even though she no longer wanted to be with him it was hard to see someone else stepping into her shoes.

She wished that Sam McColgan was here with her to put his arms round her and tell her that he loved her. And she laughed at herself for being naïve. He's not going to make declarations of undying love, she told herself. That's for Keelin and Mark! Not for adults. And yet, she thought, she wanted him to. Since she'd gone out with him it was as though her whole life had changed. She tried to tell herself that it was childish to feel like this but if it was childish to feel a fizzing excitement about life again, then it was a damn nice way to feel. It was the way David had first made her feel.

⌒

Gemma came in from the garden just as David decided to get another few bottles of wine.

'Oops!' She stepped back as the kitchen door swung open.

'Gemma, sorry!' David stared at her. 'What on earth are you doing out here? It's freezing.'

'I just came out for a breath of air,' she told him. 'It's stifling inside.'

'Good party, though,' said David.

'Yes.'

'Keelin looks spectacular.'

'Doesn't she.' Gemma smiled. 'She spent hours getting ready. I thought we wouldn't get here until past midnight, she took so long.'

'Well, the effect is certainly stunning. I just hope this bloke she's seeing appreciates her. And keeps his filthy mitts off her,' he added darkly.

'Oh, Mark seems nice enough,' said Gemma mildly. 'And she's mad about him, which is great.'

David looked at her curiously. 'Why is that great? I thought it'd be better for her not to be mad about anyone just yet.'

'She needs to learn about it all,' said Gemma. 'Fourteen is fine.'

'It's just that I can remember what I was like myself at fourteen,' said David. 'I don't like to think of how spotty blokes might be imagining my daughter.'

Gemma laughed. 'Isn't that the terror of all fathers?'

351

'I suppose so.' David laughed too. 'I remember one girl, Antoinette Galvin her name was, she was a right cracker and I was crazy about her.'

'You never mentioned her before,' said Gemma.

'It was when I was fifteen,' said David. 'She was fourteen. She was fabulous, Gem, an absolute—'

'I get the picture,' Gemma interrupted.

'I had all these great dreams about her,' David told her.

'David, I don't want to hear about what sort of dreams you had,' said Gemma.

'Then one day I saw her with her mother,' said David. 'And I immediately decided she wasn't the girl for me. Mrs Galvin was a hag.'

'David!'

'Well, she was,' he said defensively.

'And the moral of the story is?'

'If it's true that girls grow up to be their mothers, then I'm still worried about Keelin. You look great tonight, Gemma.'

'For heaven's sake!' She looked at him. 'That's a long-winded way of paying me a compliment.'

'I don't know how I'm meant to be with you anymore,' he said. 'It's so strange, we've lived together, slept together, had two kids – and yet we're supposed to be just polite.'

'Hey, don't knock it.' Gemma grinned. 'Just polite is a great achievement in the divorce stakes, you know.'

He sighed. 'Maybe.'

'Anyway, if you have kids with Orla, then you'll really have to worry about them,' said Gemma.

'We won't have kids,' said David.

'Are you sure?'

'Absolutely.'

'She might want them,' said Gemma.

He shook his head.

Gemma rubbed her shoulders again.

'Are you coming back inside?' asked David. 'Or do you want to freeze to death out here?'

'I'm coming back in,' said Gemma. 'And you should take most of the wine inside too, otherwise you'll be handing out wine ice-pops before too long.'

Orla saw them coming in together. She gritted her teeth. What the hell were they doing outside? It was all very well for Gemma to stroll back into the house as though she hadn't a care in the world and for David to follow her, laden with bottles of wine, but why were they out there together in the first place? He was her bloody husband, not Gemma's. She was his ex-wife. Ex, she said to herself. But you'd never guess it the way they were laughing and joking. Never mind what he insisted about how civilised the split had been. That was a load of crap. First wives shouldn't be friendly with their ex-husbands. It just wasn't right.

⌒

Brian made a speech about how happy he was to be celebrating fifty years of marriage to Patsy.

'She was only a slip of a thing when I married her,' he told the assembled family, 'and I was surprised she went through with it. But glad, of course, because it was the best thing that ever happened to me. And I'm glad you're all here to share this time with us.'

Everyone clapped and raised their glasses. Gemma realised, ruefully, that the likelihood of her ever celebrating a golden wedding anniversary with anyone was pretty remote. I'd probably be too gaga to understand what was going on even if I lived that long, she thought, and laughed out loud.

'Are you all right, Gemma?' asked Brian Hennessy.

She grinned at him. 'I know I'm talking to myself. But it's not a sign of senility, I promise you.'

'I hope not.' He grinned back at her. 'Otherwise I'm in deep shit.' He took her by the hand. 'Come on. Let's have a dance.'

⌒

'Dance with me.' Orla touched David's arm, interrupting his conversation with Andrew.

'In a minute,' he said.

'Oh, fire ahead.' Andrew smiled at him. 'If you don't dance with her, David, I certainly will.'

David took Orla's hand and put his arm round her. She rested her head on his shoulder and closed her eyes. If she didn't think about anything, she told herself, she could pretend it was like before. She could imagine, perhaps, that they were dancing as they'd danced on their wedding day, when she'd been the only woman in the world for him and when she'd loved him beyond question. But she couldn't think of nothing. She thought of Jonathan Pascoe and his arms round her and of how he'd wanted her so much. And how she'd sensed that want and need and desire in him and how she'd felt it too.

The Bangles were asking her if this feeling was an 'Eternal Flame'. She shivered.

'Are you all right?' asked David.

'Yes,' she whispered.

⤳

Andrew Hennessy had taken it upon himself to act as DJ for the rest of the night.

'A little less of this smoochy stuff!' he cried. 'A little more action!' Patsy smiled as he put on a Glenn Miller CD.

'In the mood anyone?' She grabbed Ronan by the hand and started to dance.

'She'd better be careful she doesn't give herself a heart attack,' murmured Livvy who was standing beside her brother.

'She's as fit as a fiddle,' said David. 'I just wish I had half her energy.'

'I would have thought you'd need twice it, what with little Miss Legs and Boobs,' said Livvy.

David glanced at her. 'You're talking about my wife, I take it.'

'Who else.' Livvy grinned. 'All the old men are following her around the room, David. I didn't realise how gorgeous she was. It's all that natural beauty look. Makes them think she's a young, virginal creature they have to protect. But, of course, they have to get past you first, which is half the fun.'

'Don't be so utterly ridiculous,' snapped David.

'About what?' asked Livvy. 'Them stalking her or you protecting her?'

He said nothing.

'Is everything all right?' Livvy asked after a pause.

'Of course.'

'You aren't regretting jumping into the marriage boat again, are you?'

'What makes you say that?' asked David.

'I'm your sister,' she said. 'I know you, David. The chase is everything, isn't it? Having is something quite, quite different.'

'Oh, grow up Livvy,' he snorted and he went to get another can of beer.

Orla knew that she'd had too much to drink. She wasn't drunk – not falling down drunk, not staggering round the place drunk – but she knew that if she sat down somewhere quiet she'd just fall asleep. Her feet were killing her, too, in her high-heeled stilettos. She leaned against the wall and watched Keelin and David dancing together. She'd been shocked at how grown-up Keelin looked tonight and how attractive she was with her black hair, dark eyes and sallow skin set off to perfection by the red dress.

And she is my stepdaughter of sorts, thought Orla. But if we went into a pub together, people would probably think that we were sisters. Had Gemma looked like that once? But Gemma was altogether fairer, less dramatic in appearance. Gemma was a comfortable-looking woman, attractive without being threatening. More attractive tonight, though, than Orla had ever seen her. She could understand how David might have fallen for a younger Gemma, with firmer boobs, finer features and – as he'd once told her – a body like a rake.

'Hello, Orla.' Gemma decided that she couldn't put it off forever. She had to speak to David's wife. She was conscious that, out of their peripheral vision, almost everybody in the room was watching them and wondering what they'd say to each other. Quite possibly nothing! The thought struck Gemma as she approached Orla. The younger girl could simply walk away. But she didn't.

Orla stood up a little straighter, although it made her feet hurt even more.

'Hello, Gemma.'

'Enjoying the party?'

'Sure.' Orla shrugged. 'It's not exactly my thing, but it's OK.'

What would be her thing? wondered Gemma. All-night raves?

'Patsy looks great, doesn't she?'

'She's a good-looking woman,' agreed Orla.

'Maybe that's where David gets it from.'

Orla raised her eyebrows.

'I always thought he was very good-looking,' said Gemma. 'Especially when I first met him.' She smiled at the memory. 'Long hair, good body – couldn't help myself.' The thought of Sam McColgan suddenly pushed itself into her head. Another long-haired, good-body person. She bit her lip. Was she really going to walk down that particular road again? She wished she could stop thinking about Sam as though he was a fixture in her life. As though he was someone she could even contemplate marrying. She'd made a mess of one marriage, she told herself, by thinking of David exactly the same way before she'd really got to know him. The thing about life, she told herself, is that you only think you learn from your mistakes. In fact you make the same ones over and over again.

Orla noticed Gemma's sudden hesitation. She still loves him, she thought frantically. She'd like to get him back. And maybe David wants to go back. She felt sick.

'Excuse me,' she said. 'I need to go to the bathroom!' She pushed passed Gemma and hurried out of the room.

Gemma stared after her. She'd wanted to be friendly. She'd tried to make the first move. If the silly bimbo cow didn't want to reciprocate, it was her problem, not mine, thought Gemma. She looked around the crowded room where everyone was studiously avoiding her glance. Sod them all, she thought. I don't need to know them any more. I don't need to care.

↩

Orla sat on the bathroom floor. Her body was trembling and the taste of bile in her mouth made her feel wretched. Why did I marry him? she asked herself. Why did I believe all that bullshit about him loving me more than anyone else in the world? Why did I believe him when he said it was all over with Gemma? It isn't all over. It was never all over. She still loves him and he still loves her and I've been the biggest fool in the world.

↩

Gemma tapped Andrew Hennessy on the shoulder.

'Time for a dance,' she told him.

He grinned at her. 'OK. But if I'm going to dance with you I want smoochy music. Hang on.' He changed the CD to Whitney Houston singing 'Saving All My Love For You'. 'Right, Gemma. Let's do it.'

She leaned her head on his shoulder. He was nice, she thought, sleepily. All of David's family were nice. It was a pity David himself hadn't been nicer.

'Excuse me.' She looked up. David was beside them. 'I think this one is ours.'

Andrew looked from one to the other. David smiled at him. 'It's our song,' he explained.

356

Gemma transferred her hold from Andrew to David. 'It's not really our song,' she told him. 'We don't have a song.'

'It's the closest we'd get, though,' David said. 'Remember Dollymount?'

She nodded. Shortly after they'd started going out together, David had taken her to the Bull Wall in Dollymount – a notorious spot for lovemaking on the backseat of a car.

He'd borrowed Brian's car and there was no question of making love on the backseat of the Fiat Mirafiori. They'd gone for a walk along the beach instead. They'd stood at the edge of the water and allowed the water to lap against their bare feet and Gemma had shrieked that it was bloody freezing. And then David had carried her into the sand dunes and they'd made love for the first time.

It had been wonderful, if slightly uncomfortable. Gemma remembered being stabbed in the cheek by a stem of tall, pipe-like grass just as David entered her, so that she'd squealed in pain. And he'd stopped and looked at her and asked her was everything all right. She'd said that it was, that she'd been hurt by the grass, not him, that he was the perfect fit for her. And he'd laughed and begun to move inside her so that she suddenly forgot about the grass, and about the chill of the night and lost herself to the pleasure of David. He'd been a good lover that night. He took his time, asked her if it was OK for her, touched her in all the places that she liked to be touched. It had been instinctive with him and she'd decided, there and then, that he was the only man in the world for her. She'd wanted to stay huddled in the sand dune with him forever.

Later, when they got back to the car, David had turned the radio on and Whitney was singing her heart out. He'd smiled and told Gemma that was how he felt about her and it had been perfection.

'Do you remember?' asked David.

'Of course I do,' she whispered.

'I loved you then,' he said. 'I really did.'

'I know,' she said. 'I loved you too.'

She could feel the thud of his heart, just as she'd felt it then. I still have power over him, she thought suddenly. I can still make him want me. She tightened her hold on him and felt him pull her closer to him.

Eat your heart out, bimbo bitch, she thought.

357

Chapter 35

O rla closed the bathroom door behind her. She still felt sick but she knew that she wasn't actually going to be sick again. Her legs were trembling, though, and she was finding it hard to keep her balance. She wanted to go home. She'd had enough of Brian and Patsy's damned party. She'd had enough of watching people watching her and more than enough of feeling as though she was in a losing competition with blobby-but-sexy Gemma.

She walked into the living room and felt her head spin. They were wrapped round each other. There was no other way to describe it. Gemma's arms circled David's neck and his hands were at the base of her back. He was holding her tightly to him and she was allowing him to hold her. They were smiling at each other. And, although nobody else seemed to be paying them a blind bit of notice, Orla could see that nobody in their right mind would think that they were a divorced couple.

⌐

He still fancies me, thought Gemma. He still fancies me and, even though I don't fancy him any more, it's bloody good to know.

She's still sexy, thought David. I'd forgotten how sexy she could be.

I *won't* lower myself to make a scene, thought Orla, as she walked unsteadily across the room.

The music ended just as she reached them. David kissed Gemma on the cheek and she squeezed his hand. Then she saw Orla and moved away from him.

'We're going,' said Orla.

'What?' David looked at her.

'We're going,' she repeated.

'It's early yet,' he objected. 'Nobody else is going.'

'We are,' she said firmly. 'It's three in the morning. I'm tired. We're going.'

'She's right,' said Gemma. 'I think I'll go myself.'

'So you should, you blobby bitch,' snapped Orla.

'Orla!' David's tone was horrified.

'Enjoy it did you?' she asked him, the words spilling out. 'Enjoy wrapping yourself round your ex-wife while I was watching? And you?' She glared at Gemma. 'I suppose you're just grateful for a bit of male company, even if he is someone else's husband!'

'Orla, for goodness sake, keep your voice down,' said David. 'And I wasn't – I don't know where you got the idea—'

'It was nothing, Orla,' said Gemma. 'Honestly.'

'Don't make me laugh,' snarled Orla. 'You fat old blobby cow!'

'Orla, you're tired,' Gemma said soothingly.

'You're drunk,' snapped David.

'I'm fine,' said Orla. 'Abso-fucking-lutely fine.'

The air crackled between them. David looked around the room. The guests were chatting to each other, studiously avoiding the developing scene.

'David, Orla, there's a taxi outside.' Livvy walked up the them. 'I was going to take it but maybe you'd like it instead.'

'Good idea, Livvy,' he said. 'Thanks.'

'Trying to get rid of me?' asked Orla.

'You're tired,' said Livvy.

'I'm fine,' said Orla. 'And where are you going, blobby?' She looked at Gemma.

'I'm going to get my children and leave,' said Gemma. 'Fortunately they haven't seen you make a show of yourself.' She walked away.

'Come on, Orla.' David took her by the arm which she wrenched away from him. 'Come on,' he repeated. 'You're right. We should leave.'

This time she followed him.

↶

David paid the taxi driver then strode up the steps to the apartment. Orla had to hurry to keep up with him although by now she could hardly walk in the high-heeled shoes. He opened the apartment door and walked straight into the bedroom. He took off his jacket and hung it neatly in the wardrobe. Orla watched him.

'Oh for God's sake!' she finally burst out. 'Why don't you just shout at me and get it over and done with.'

'Shout at you?' His voice was even. 'Why should I shout at you?'

'For getting angry. For making us leave,' she said.

'I certainly didn't want to go.' He loosened his tie and opened the top button of his shirt. 'But you didn't exactly leave us with much choice.'

'I know you didn't want to leave,' she spat. 'It was quite obvious that you didn't want to leave. You were having much too good a time exactly where you were, practically having it off with Gemma in front of me. You bastard!'

David eased his shoes from his feet. He sighed and looked up at her. 'Don't be absolutely ludicrous,' he said.

'Don't be absolutely ludicrous.' She mimicked the tone, one which she imagined he must have used when the children were small. Patronising. Dismissive. Arrogant.

He got up and went into the bathroom. She heard the splash of water in the sink and the sound of him cleaning his teeth. She sat on the spot vacated by him and tried to control the trembling in her body. He flushed the toilet and emerged from the bathroom again.

'You made a mockery of me tonight,' she said. 'You ignored me. You laughed at me. You spent the whole time panting after your ex-wife. And then you practically made love to her in front of everyone!'

'Orla, when I married you I married you because of your brains. I didn't realise that you only had them out on loan at the time.'

'You shit.' She clenched her teeth. 'How dare you talk to me like that.'

'It's true,' he said.

'I suppose that Gemma – the woman you said had all the intellectual power of a beanbag – is smarter than me? That's why you spent so much time with her, is it?'

'I didn't spend "so much time" with her, as you put it,' said David. 'I was polite to her. I danced with her. She was there and I had to acknowledge her, which I did. Now stop behaving like a bloody child and come to bed.'

'Why?' she demanded. 'So that you can roll over with your back to me and think of her?'

'For God's sake, Orla!'

'Because that's what it's all at, isn't it? You never stopped loving her. She was the one that threw you out. You pretended that everything was fine because you couldn't stand the idea that someone less brilliant than

360

you couldn't live with you any more. So you set up this life as a work-obsessed man whose wife didn't understand him. But she understood you only too bloody well, didn't she? She knows exactly what buttons to press on you, David Hennessy! "Oh, David, helpless little me, I can't manage my money. Can you help?" "Oh, David, the poor, poor children need a holiday. I wouldn't ask, of course, but they so desperately need to get away." And then, tonight, she tarts herself up to the nines and swans around in front of you so that you can't help wondering why you ever left her. Don't think I don't know what's going on, David.'

'Orla, you need your head examined,' David told her.

'Do I?' she snapped. 'Maybe I do. Maybe I need to find out why I thought you loved me in the first place.'

'That might be a good question to ask.'

Orla bit her lip. 'You're so right! But you always knew with Gemma, didn't you? It was her "bubbly nature", that's what you told me. And the way she always asked your advice. And – obviously – the way she wrapped her fucking body around you!'

'That's enough, Orla.'

'No, it's not enough.' Orla could feel the rage coursing through her. 'It's not enough. It'll never be enough. Even on our fucking honeymoon you were buying her bloody presents. God, how stupid could I have been? I was blinded by the fact that you seemed so much more mature than anyone else I'd ever known. I allowed you to buy her things. I must have been out of my mind.'

'You're certainly out of it now,' said David.

'You think?' Orla opened the wardrobe door and began to pull David's clothes off the hangers. 'You really think that, do you? Well, let's see how out of my mind I am. I think you still love Gemma and you want to be with her. I'll make it easy for you, will I? Go back to her, David. I'm sure she'll be so happy to discover that you really care. Maybe she worked the best scam in the history of the world to get her man back. Divorce him. Brilliant!'

'Stop it, Orla.'

'No!' she cried. 'I won't. I think it's time I took a stand. My stand is that you should go back to the blobby bitch and see how much you like it.' She pulled a suitcase from beneath the bed. David watched her, his arms folded.

'You're being more childish than I could ever have imagined,' he said.

'Go ahead, patronise me. I don't give a shit!' She tore his trousers off the hangers.

361

'Orla, you've had too much to drink and you're behaving like an adolescent.'

'I suppose if I were Keelin you'd slap me!'

'Very possibly,' said David dryly.

'Well, that'd be abuse.' Orla pushed the clothes into the suitcase and tugged at the zip.

'You're ruining my things,' said David. 'You can bloody pay for them to be pressed again.'

'I don't think so.' Orla lifted the half-closed case. 'This should be enough to keep you going.'

'Orla, stop being so melodramatic. I know life hasn't been great but you're being so incredibly stupid I can hardly believe my eyes.'

'Believe them.' She carried the case into the living room. 'Believe them!' She called back to him.

David took a deep breath and counted to ten. He walked into the living room in time to see her step onto the balcony with the suitcase.

'For God's sake, Orla!' he cried.

'I told you, there's plenty of stuff here to keep you going. I'm sure she'll be only too pleased to take you in tonight! She's probably hot for it after your escapades on the dance floor.'

'Orla!'

David couldn't make it in time to stop Orla from heaving the case over the wrought-iron balcony and throwing it down into the flowerbeds below. A couple of shirts fluttered out of the opening as it fell.

'You stupid, stupid, bitch!'

She shrugged and pushed past him.

'If that's the way you want it,' said David.

'Yes,' she said.

'Fine.' He went back into the bedroom and emerged a few minutes later fully dressed. He said nothing to Orla, just walked out of the apartment and slammed the door behind him.

'Good!' she said as the door closed.

Then she burst into uncontrollable tears.

⤺

David got into the car, switched on the ignition and drove along the coast road. He drove carefully, conscious that he shouldn't be driving at all, wary of being stopped by the cops. Getting busted for drunk driving would just about be the icing on the cake, he thought, as he glided to

362

a very gradual halt at the traffic lights. If he got done for drunk driving that'd be the end of his career, the end of everything. And all because of that stupid, stupid cow. God, he couldn't believe how she'd carried on. And for what? A dance with Gemma, some polite conversation with her, nothing more. Orla was obviously out of her mind.

He yawned and felt the car slip away to the left. He opened his eyes wide and pressed the button to roll down the window. A blast of cold night air was what he needed to stay awake. Not that he should be awake, of course. Right now he should be in bed asleep. But she was in his bed, in his apartment. He should have gone back up and thrown her out! He'd been too shocked, not thinking properly. He shook his head. Maybe he should go back.

He was too tired to go back. He was closer to Gemma's house than the apartment now and he didn't want to risk returning to Dun Laoghaire. He'd been lucky so far, light traffic and no cops. Better not push it.

He drew up at the kerb outside Gemma's and looked at his watch. The numbers were blurred but it was after five. He suddenly thought that maybe she wasn't there, maybe she was still at the party. Once he and Orla had gone Gemma might have decided to stay. That would be just perfect, he thought as he walked up the pathway. Gemma having fun at his parents' party while he'd been thrown out of his own apartment by his wife.

He rang the bell.

Gemma heard the ringing but she wasn't sure where it was coming from. She struggled to open eyes that felt as though they were sewn together.

'Mum!' Keelin was shaking her. 'Mum, there's someone at the door.'

Gemma sat up and looked at her daughter. 'What?'

'Someone at the door,' said Keelin.

'Who?'

'I don't know.' Keelin's face was worried. 'I didn't look out.'

Gemma threw back the duvet and shivered in the cool air. She padded over to the window and peered out. She saw David's car outside the gate. Her heart lurched. She could only think that something terrible must have happened.

'I think it's your father.' She turned to Keelin. 'Stay here.'

'Why?' Keelin followed her. 'I want to come downstairs.'

Gemma grabbed her dressing gown. 'Stay here,' she said again.

She turned off the house alarm and unlatched the door. David was leaning against the side of the porch, his eyes half-closed.

'David!' she hissed. 'What the hell are you doing here? What's wrong?'

He blinked a couple of times. 'I had to come here,' he said. 'There was nowhere else.'

'What on earth are you talking about?' She stared at him.

'She threw my stuff out,' he said. 'Silly bitch.'

'What?' Gemma shivered again. 'You'd better come in.' She allowed David to step into the hallway. Keelin was hanging over the banister, looking down.

'Keelin, go back to bed,' said Gemma.

'Why is Dad here?' asked Keelin. 'What's the matter?'

'Is anything the matter?' Gemma asked David. 'Is there anything that affects the children?'

He shook his head.

'We'll talk about it in the morning,' she told Keelin. 'Go on, back to bed. Now.'

Keelin knew when she was beaten. She went back to her bedroom.

Gemma led David into the living room and turned on the gas fire. He flopped down on the sofa.

'David!' She glared at him. 'Don't you dare go to sleep! I want to know why you're here. What you want. Why you even think I should have let you into my house in the first place.'

David leaned forward, and rubbed his face with his hands.

'I'm sorry,' he said. 'Maybe I shouldn't have come. But she told me to come and I just did. I should have gone back and argued but I didn't have the energy, Gemma.'

'Who told you to come?' asked Gemma. 'Orla? Why would she tell you that? What happened, David?'

He looked up at her. 'She's lost it completely,' he said. 'She said that I humiliated her tonight. That I was having it off with you on the dance floor. That everyone was laughing at her. And she threw a complete fit when we got home. She started ripping my clothes off hangers and shoving them into a suitcase and then she threw it out of the window.'

'She what!' Gemma stifled a giggle at the thought of David's suits flying through the night air.

'I left the case in the car.'

Gemma bit her lip. 'Why did she behave like this, David? Surely she wasn't jealous of us dancing together?' She swallowed hard as she remembered the way she'd danced with David. Deliberately smoochy while she smiled and laughed with him and tried to prove that she was a mature but sexy woman who knew what her ex-husband liked. 'What would she have to be jealous about!'

David shrugged helplessly.

Gemma kneeled down beside the fire and held her hands out in front of it. 'Let me make some tea,' she said. 'I'm tired and I'm cold and you probably are too. I'll make some tea and then you can tell me about it.'

David nodded and leaned back on the sofa. Gemma went into the kitchen and filled the kettle. She was utterly bewildered by the turn of events. She couldn't quite believe that David was sitting in her house at – oh, God, half past five in the morning – and telling her that Orla had thrown him out. I have to be dreaming, she thought as she took a couple of mugs out of the cupboard. This is some weird hallucination as a result of mixing wine, gin and bloody Malibu!

And yet, she thought as she leaned against the worktop, Keelin had suspected that everything wasn't perfect. And so had Livvy. And she had deliberately danced in a provocative way with David just to piss Orla off. Well, it looked like she'd got more than she bargained for.

'Mum.' Keelin's voice was a whisper.

Gemma spun round. 'I thought I told you to go back to bed,' she said.

'I know,' said Keelin. 'But – but why's he here, Mum? What's happened?'

'I don't know.' Gemma sighed. 'It looks like he had a row with Orla.'

'Oh, wow!' Keelin breathed out slowly. 'And he's come back to us, Mum.'

'He may be in the living room but he's not staying,' said Gemma firmly.

'But, Mum—'

'Keelin, I don't know exactly what the problem is but I'm damned if I'm going to have him here. I'm his ex-wife, you know. We're divorced.'

'But what if he divorced Orla? And you got back together with him?' Keelin looked at Gemma. 'You might love each other again, Mum.'

Gemma tried to keep her emotions under control. She knew how much Keelin would have loved for them to be together again but she also knew how many times she'd told her that it was impossible.

'Keelin, he's married to Orla now. And if they've had a row, that's very sad. But it doesn't mean we're getting back together. There was plenty of time for that before he ever met Orla, you know.'

365

'I know,' said Keelin despondently. 'I just thought that this time it might be different.'

'Oh, Keelin.' Gemma put her arm round her. 'I'm sorry. It can't be. It really can't.'

'I love you both.' Keelin rubbed her eyes. 'I really do. I want everyone to be happy, Mum. That's all.'

'I know.' Gemma hugged her even tighter. 'I know.'

She took a couple of tea bags out of the bright yellow canister and dropped them into the teapot. She poured boiling water over them and slowly stirred the pot. Her head was spinning, from the alcohol and from David's almost incoherent ramblings about Orla. She can't really have thrown his stuff out of the window, thought Gemma, as she took two red mugs from the cupboard. He must be making that up. She poured the tea into the mugs and carried them into the living room. David was leaning back in the sofa and his eyes were closed again.

'Tea,' she said sharply and he immediately sat up straight.

'Thanks.' He took a mug and curled his hands round it.

'You'd better tell me what exactly is going on,' said Gemma. 'I'm confused.'

'You're confused!' David snorted. 'Not half as much as me, Gemma. I've done everything for her, everything! And this is how she treats me.'

'What have you done for her?' asked Gemma.

'I gave her a job, for starters.'

'Oh, come on, David. You told me all about that. You trained her, that's all.'

'I marked them on the training course,' said David. 'I gave her a brilliant score.'

'Did she deserve it?' Gemma raised her eyebrows.

'Of course she did,' said David. 'But that's not the point. I made very positive comments about her. I got her on a good team. I helped her to do well.'

'And, of course, you married her,' said Gemma dryly.

'Yes.' David looked at her defiantly. 'I married her.'

'Because you loved her?'

He sighed. 'Because I thought I loved her.'

'And now?'

He put the mug of barely tasted tea on the coffee table in front of them. 'Oh, God, Gemma – I just don't know any more.'

He looked dreadful, thought Gemma. Over the past weeks she'd watched him move from looking tired to exhausted and to distracted but she'd never seen him look so totally despondent in her life before. She saw the lines on his forehead and the wrinkles around his eyes. It wasn't an old face. But it was the face of a man who was forty.

'So what do you want?' asked Gemma. 'Why did you come here?'

David looked up at her. His eyes were bloodshot. 'I don't really know,' he said. 'She yelled at me to come back to you and I just did.'

Gemma sighed. If he'd come back to her as quickly in the past – she shook her head. It was too late to have those kind of thoughts now.

'What's gone wrong between Orla and you?' she asked.

'She said I humiliated her. She didn't like us dancing together.'

Gemma grimaced. 'I don't blame her. I was being silly with you, David.'

'She said you wrapped your body around me.'

'It was stupid,' said Gemma. 'I was showing off.'

'Were you?'

'Yes,' she said flatly. 'I should have had more sense.'

'I was surprised,' he said, 'at how sexy you were.'

'Yes, well, I shouldn't have been.' She rubbed her arms. 'But last night was just one night. It wouldn't have mattered if things were OK. So what went wrong before that?'

He groaned. 'Everything, Gemma. Just everything. The last while we've done nothing but argue. It all started when she took the Serene job.'

'But I thought you'd sorted that,' said Gemma in surprise. 'I remember you told me about it and how you – patronisingly, I think I said at the time – thought that she'd only got the job because Bob Murphy really wanted you. Surely you talked to her about it?'

'Not really,' he said. 'I was too annoyed at her. And after she came back from her damned course in Cork she was quite, quite different. I couldn't talk to her. The one time I offered, she didn't want to talk to me. You know me, Gemma, I hate scenes at the best of times. So it just kind of drifted . . .' He shrugged helplessly.

'But David, you were so crazy about her.' Gemma finished her tea and pulled her dressing gown more tightly round her. 'Every bloody time you picked up the kids you never wasted an opportunity to tell me how crazy you were about her. And how brilliant she was. Do you mean that you never really loved her at all?'

'I don't know!' David sounded despairing. 'I thought I did but it's been so hard lately, Gemma. And in the last few weeks whenever I've been here, it's seemed so peaceful in comparison to home. I haven't wanted to leave.'

367

Gemma toyed with the belt of her gown. 'Don't talk crap,' she said. 'You're romanticising things here just because they're not working out the way you thought with Orla. You're looking back at the good times we had and comparing them to now, and forgetting absolutely everything else.'

'No,' he said. 'It's not like that. I know we had a terrible time, especially towards the end. I keep thinking, maybe it's me. I married two women and I've made both of them so unhappy. What's wrong with me, Gemma?'

'Stop being so melodramatic,' she said. 'If you've fallen out of love with Orla then you need to talk to her about it. If you haven't, then you definitely need to talk about it. But either way, David, it's her you should be talking to tonight. Not me.'

'You don't love me any more, do you?' he asked.

'David, why do you think I divorced you?'

'You can still love someone and not be able to live with them,' said David.

'No you can't,' said Gemma.

'I can't talk to her tonight.' David sighed and leaned back in the sofa. 'She threw me out. That's rich, isn't it! It's my damn apartment and she threw me out.'

'You kind of make a habit of getting thrown out, don't you?'

He looked at Gemma ruefully. 'What is it about me?' he asked. 'What am I doing wrong?'

Gemma smiled at him. 'You're just a man, David. You do everything wrong!'

'Very funny,' he said.

'You think of yourself too much,' she told him. 'How things affect you. How you feel. It all goes back to the job with Serene, doesn't it? How you got mad at her because she didn't tell you about it and I bet you froze her out. Wouldn't talk to her. Gave her the silent treatment.'

David stared at her.

'David, every single time we argued that's what you did. And, after a while, I couldn't stand it any more. If something was wrong, the onus was always on me to try and put it right. To apologise. To appease. To cheer you up. And I got fed up with it. It seems that Orla has too, except it hasn't taken her very long.'

'I'm not like that,' said David.

'I'm tired.' Gemma was suddenly overcome with exhaustion. 'I really don't want to sit up all night talking to you about your marriage, David. I want to go back to bed.'

'I can't go home,' said David. 'Not tonight. And I really shouldn't drive, Gemma. I was lucky not to get stopped on the way here.'

'You can sleep on the sofa,' she told him.

'Thank you.'

'I'll bring you some blankets.' She got up and took the mugs back into the kitchen. She emptied David's unfinished tea down the sink, rinsed the mugs and left them on the drainer. Then she went upstairs and brought some blankets back down to him.

'I appreciate this,' he said.

'Just tonight,' she told him. 'Sort it out tomorrow.' She yawned and rubbed the back of her neck. 'Goodnight, David.'

'Goodnight, Gemma,' he said.

⌒

Orla shivered. She hated being in the bed on her own. She pulled the duvet more closely around her and wished that she could fall asleep. But she couldn't. All she could think about was David and his face as she'd thrown his stuff over the balcony. He'd been horrified and amazed and stunned and furious. She'd seen all of those emotions in his expressions. And, she supposed, there'd been disgust with her too. Did she love him any more? she wondered. She must, if she'd got so mad at him tonight. But maybe that was merely fury at his behaviour with Gemma.

Bloody blobby Gemma! Who'd looked so charming and elegant and at ease with everyone and everything. And who'd been so outrageous in the way she'd laughed, joked and danced with David. Orla had been an emotional wreck walking through the front door with him. But the evening hadn't taken a breath out of Gemma. No problem to her.

She rolled over.

And what about Jonathan Pascoe? She hadn't spoken to him in the last week even though he'd left two messages on her mobile phone. But she hadn't wanted to talk to him and listen to him telling her what a mess she'd made of her life and how she'd be better off without David.

Maybe I'd be better off with nobody, she thought. Maybe I'm just meant to be on my own. An independent career woman, like I always wanted.

Except, she thought, as she turned over yet again, that my career is down the pan too. She closed her eyes more tightly. She wasn't going to think about it any more. She needed to sleep. Things might be clearer in the morning.

Chapter 36

B ut she couldn't sleep. She tried everything – counting sheep, self-hypnosis, emptying her mind – but sleep wouldn't come. Every time she tried not to think, a whirlpool of thoughts and memories raged around her head. Even the sheep-counting ended in disaster. Instead of them leaping over the fences and bounding into the distance, Orla's sheep piled up into an undignified heap on top of each other.

At seven o'clock she could stand it no longer. She got up, made herself some coffee and had a shower. She didn't feel much better after the shower. Her eyes were still heavy and her body felt leaden, as though her very bones were exhausted. She pulled on her fleecy jogging pants, her sweatshirt, her charcoal-grey Aran jumper and her walking boots. She wrapped a woollen scarf round her neck and pulled her hat over her head. Then she let herself out of the apartment and walked to the coast.

It was freezing. She could feel the cold try to pierce its way through her layers of wool and cotton. She walked parallel to the railway tracks, past the ferry terminal and the yacht clubs and then along the pier. There was nobody else around in the gloom of the morning. It was windy along the pier and, though the harbour was relatively calm, on the other side of the wall angry foam-capped waves threw themselves onto the rocks before falling back into the sea.

Orla wrapped her arms round her body. What am I doing here? she asked herself. It's cold, it's dark and it's lonely. But it hadn't been lonely during the summer when she'd strolled here hand in hand with David while he told her stories of his Laser racing and threatened to get a sailboard again. She remembered laughing at the thought of him dressed in a body-hugging wet suit, skimming the surface of the bay. He'd been quite affronted by her laughter and she'd put her arms round him and pulled him closer to her and she'd kissed him, passionately, in full view of everyone else who'd been promenading along the pier that day.

Suddenly she wanted him to be with her again. She wanted the closeness of him, the comfort of him, the knowledge that he loved her.

If this was a movie, she thought, I'd turn round and he'd be at the beginning of the pier and he'd be holding a bunch of roses. I'd turn round and see him there and we'd stand still and look at each other for a moment. Then I'd run to him and he'd gather me into his arms and everything would be all right again.

The image was so powerful that she almost believed in it. She stared across the harbour, unwilling to look back and realise that it was only her imagination, that David was probably enjoying breakfast in Gemma's as she, Orla, froze her butt off on Dun Laoghaire pier.

She glanced at her watch. On a Sunday morning it was highly likely that neither Gemma nor David were even out of bed yet. She closed her eyes at the thought that they might have shared the same bed, that they might, even now, be in the same bed.

Eventually, she turned round.

There was no David, no bunch of roses in the distance. The pier was deserted. She'd known, of course, that he wouldn't be there. It hadn't stopped her hoping that he would.

⌒

Ronan got out of bed and pulled on a sweatshirt over his Manchester United pyjamas. He trotted downstairs and into the kitchen to make himself some breakfast. He'd listened for the sounds of Gemma clattering around but there'd been only silence and he realised that she was probably still asleep. He knew that it had been very late when they got home – she'd had to wake him in his grandparents' house and he'd fallen asleep again in the taxi on the way home. But now he was wide awake and hungry.

He climbed onto a three-legged stool and took his personal breakfast bowl – red with three white stripes round the rim – out of the cupboard. He filled the bowl with Coco-Pops and poured milk over them. He grabbed a spoon from the rack on the worktop then walked into the living room.

He almost dropped the bowl when he saw David lying on the sofa. A splash of brown milk and cereal spilled onto the coffee table as he put the bowl down and shook his father by the shoulder.

David groaned and pulled the blanket more tightly around him.

371

'Dad!' Ronan's voice was urgent. 'Dad, wake up!'

Eventually David opened his eyes. He blinked in surprise to see his son standing in front of him and then remembered where he was and why he was here.

'Morning,' he said as he reached up and tousled Ronan's already tousled hair.

'Hi.' Ronan sat on the sofa beside him. 'What are you doing here, Dad?'

'I stayed here last night,' said David.

'I can see that.' Ronan looked at him scornfully. 'I mean, that's obvious, isn't it? But why, Dad?'

David sighed. He really didn't know how to answer the question.

'Did you have a row?' asked Ronan. 'Did you and Orla fight?'

He didn't want to admit to it. Not to his eleven-year-old son who was looking at him in a worldly-wise way that quite astonished David.

'We had a bit of an argument,' he admitted eventually.

'Gosh.' Ronan grinned at him. 'So you came home to us.'

'Only for last night,' said David hastily. 'That's all, Ronan. Only for last night.'

'Weren't you cold down here?' asked Ronan. 'The heat only comes on at nine o'clock.' They both glanced at the gold carriage clock on the mantelpiece which told them that it was five to nine. Our third Christmas together, David remembered. A present from Frances and Gerry.

'I wasn't cold.' David sat up. 'Your mum gave me lots of blankets.'

'And you slept in your shirt,' observed Ronan.

'Yes. Well. Not something I'd recommend.' David smiled at his son.

'She'd never let me sleep in my shirt,' said Ronan. 'Not that I'd want to. I hate shirts.'

'Me too,' said David.

Ronan looked at his bowl of Coco-Pops. The chocolate had almost completely dissolved by now and the milk was dark brown. 'Would you like some?' he asked David.

'No thanks.' David shook his head and wished that he hadn't. The headache which he'd been trying to pretend didn't exist was now bouncing around his skull and the idea of food made him want to throw up. He wondered exactly how many cans of lager and glasses of wine he'd drunk last night. He had a horrible feeling that it had been far too many. But he'd been having fun in an uncomfortable

372

sort of way. The party had been a good one, lots of distant friends and relatives, whom he hadn't seen in ages, had been there and there'd been a definite edge knowing that both Gemma and Orla were there too.

What on earth is the matter with me, he asked himself, that I could get a buzz about seeing my ex-wife and my current wife at a party? Most blokes would go nuts if they knew the women were on the same street, let alone in the same room. But me – I found it exciting! Now he simply felt worn out.

'Will I tell Mum you're awake?' asked Ronan who'd been shovelling breakfast cereal down his throat. 'She'll probably want to say good morning.'

'I doubt it.' David winced as he swung his legs over the edge of the sofa and narrowly missed breaking one on the coffee table. 'I'm sure she isn't too pleased with me for turning up at all.'

'She says that you're hopeless.' Ronan looked at his father. 'She says that you're a great worker but you're absolutely hopeless.'

'Charming,' murmured David.

'That too,' agreed Ronan. 'We were talking about you on holiday.'

'Oh.' He clamped down on the feeling of wanting to be sick. If there was one thing he needed to show his son, it was that real men didn't throw up after a night's drinking.

'She said you were good to us.' Ronan cuddled up beside his father. 'She said that you'd paid for our holiday and that she'd only had to suggest it and you'd agreed. She said that you'd bought the TV – well, actually, you bought me a TV, Dad, Granddad bought that one.'

'Did he now?'

'Only you're not supposed to know that,' Ronan confided. 'Mum didn't want to tell you because she was afraid you'd get narky with her.'

'Why?'

'I dunno.' He dismissed the thought.

'OK,' said David. 'So what else did she say about me?'

'Not much.' Ronan frowned. 'That you were a good father.'

David felt the hot sting of tears in his eyes. Gemma had never told him he was a good father. As far as he could remember, she'd yelled at him that he was a useless father. He never remembered his children's birthdays, she used to shout. He expected her to do all the present-buying at Christmas. He wanted all the comforts of a family

373

and none of the responsibilities. Not once had she told him to his face that he was a good father.

He hadn't been a good husband, though. Quite suddenly he knew what she meant when she said he was never there. He never had been. Not for times like this. Not for just sitting beside his kids. He loved them, of course he did, but he'd never really considered that they'd talk about him, have an opinion on him. And that their opinion was coloured by what Gemma would say about him. It was just as well, he thought, that the bitterness that she'd doubtless felt when they split up hadn't been passed on to the children.

'Is Orla mad at you?' asked Ronan.

'I rather think she is,' said David.

'Why?'

'Oh, silly things.' David shrugged.

'She looked lovely last night,' Ronan said. 'I liked the spangly things on her tights.'

'Ronan!'

'They were great.'

'You're not meant to fancy my wife!' David laughed.

'I don't fancy her.' Ronan made a face and they both laughed together.

Keelin heard the sound of their laughter in her bedroom. She'd woken a couple of minutes earlier when the central heating had switched itself on and she'd lain under her duvet listening to the hum of voices from the living room directly below her. She realised at once that it was her father and Ronan. She wanted to go downstairs and see what was going on but she was reluctant to do it.

The laughter changed her mind. She got up and pulled on her sugar-pink dressing gown, tying it firmly round her waist. She brushed her hair before going downstairs.

'Good morning,' she said as she walked into the living room.

'Hi.' David smiled at her. 'How are you feeling this morning?'

'I'm fine,' said Keelin. 'A lot better than you, I think.'

'Why?' asked David.

'You look awful,' she said frankly. 'You're eyes are bloodshot and your hair is sticking up and you've slept in your shirt!'

'I know,' said David wryly. 'I need to shower and change.'

'Do you have a change of clothes?' asked Keelin.

David said nothing. His half-full, half-closed suitcase was still on the back seat of his car.

374

'How long do you expect to stay here?' Keelin looked inquiringly at him.

'Not long,' he said.

'Why did you come?'

'They had a row,' said Ronan.

'You and Orla?'

'Who else?' David looked at her.

'So you came back here?'

He sighed. 'I'd had a lot to drink. Call it a homing instinct.'

'Your homing instinct should have made you stay with her,' said Keelin. 'You married her, didn't you?'

'Give me a break,' said David.

'You can't run back here if you have a row with her,' Keelin told him. 'That's just silly.'

'I know,' he said.

'It'd be different if you and Mum were getting back together again,' she said. 'That's something else all together.'

'Would you like that?' asked David. 'Would it make you happy?'

Keelin bit the corner of her nail and looked at her father. She'd wished so often that he'd come back, that he and Gemma would live together again. And Gemma had told her so many times that it just wasn't possible. But here he was. He'd spent the night with them.

But not with Gemma. David had spent the night on the sofa with the old blankets for warmth. She'd often imagined him staying with them but she hadn't expected it to be like this. And yet, she thought, it could never be any other way. David had married Orla. Gemma had grown away from David. They'd both made new lives and things could never be the way Keelin had once wanted them to be.

'Keelin?' He looked at her. 'Do you want me to come home?'

'It isn't your home,' she said, hardly believing that the words were coming out of her mouth. 'It was different before. This is our place. Me and Mum and Ronan.'

'I see,' said David.

'It's not that I don't love you.' Keelin pushed Ronan out of the way and put her arm round her father's shoulder. 'I do. And I wanted you to come back more than anything. But it's changed, hasn't it? You've got Orla and things are different.'

'You both seem very fond of Orla all of a sudden,' David said dryly.

Keelin sighed. 'I hated her at first,' she admitted. 'And you wanted me to like her so much that I definitely wasn't going to. But she's nice, Dad. We talked last night. She was friendly.'

'Was she?' David looked at her in surprise.

'What did you row about?' asked Keelin. 'I knew she wasn't very happy at the party. Was it about you and Mum?'

'Why should we row about that?'

'Oh, Dad!' Keelin stared at him in exasperation. 'You and Mum were having much more fun than Orla! You both knew everyone. Poor Orla didn't. And she kept thinking people were looking at her.'

'I'm sure they were,' said David. 'She looked lovely, Ronan said so!'

'Of course she did,' said Keelin. 'But you were following Mum around all night.'

'No I wasn't!'

'Cop on, Dad.' Keelin got up from the sofa. 'You were. Now would you like a cup of coffee or anything? I need something before I collapse.'

⌒

It was nearly an hour later before Gemma woke up. She'd been quite unable to sleep after she'd left David, practically comatose, on the sofa but eventually she'd flaked out. The various sounds of people using the shower and banging doors had been filtering through to her consciousness for a while now but she'd resolutely refused to wake up. She was exhausted. And then she remembered David and shot out of bed. She pulled on her cotton trousers and long-sleeved T-shirt and went downstairs.

David and the children were in the kitchen. Keelin was showing him how to use their washing machine.

'Being helpful around the home?' asked Gemma as she walked into the room.

'I can do this,' said David. 'I've lived on my own for long enough.'

'I never said you couldn't.' Gemma sat on one of the high stools at the breakfast counter. 'How are you this morning?'

'Better,' he said. Then he grinned at her. 'Well, barely keeping it together, to tell you the truth.'

Gemma glanced at the children. 'Can you leave Dad and me on our own for a bit?' she asked.

'Sure.' Keelin dragged Ronan out of the room with her. 'I want to phone Mark anyway.'

'She's so grown-up I'm at a loss to know what to say to her,' said David.

'I know.' Gemma got up and filled the kettle. 'It's a pity the rest of us aren't.'

'Are you getting at me?' asked David.

'What do you think?' She took a loaf of brown bread from the bread bin and cut a slice. 'Want some?'

'No thanks,' he said. 'Food wouldn't be a good idea right now.'

'Would you like some coffee?' she asked.

'Tea, if you wouldn't mind,' said David.

Gemma spread some butter and marmalade onto the bread. Then she made David a cup of tea and coffee for herself. She sat on the stool again. 'What the hell was last night all about?' she asked. 'In fact, what the hell is this morning about? Why haven't you left by now?'

'I couldn't just walk out,' said David. 'Besides, I'm still sobering up. If I was breathalysed now I'd fail.'

'Have you called Orla?' asked Gemma.

'Not yet,' said David.

'Oh, for heaven's sake!'

'Gemma.' He reached out and put his hand on her arm. She stiffened. 'Relax,' he said. 'I'm not going to do anything to you.'

'Sorry.' She took a sip of coffee. 'I need my morning caffeine.'

'You always did,' he said. 'You were quite unsociable until after you'd had your coffee.'

'David, I'm not in the mood for gentle reminiscences.'

'Neither am I,' he said. 'I tried them with the kids and they pretty much told me where to get off.'

'They did?'

'Keelin told me to cop on.'

Gemma smiled faintly.

He rubbed the back of his neck. 'You've brought them up well, Gem.'

'Thanks,' she said shortly.

'I mean it,' he said. 'I've always admired you for that.'

Gemma said nothing.

'In fact, I admired you a lot more after we got divorced than while we were married. I know that's ridiculous and stupid and unfair but that's the way it was.'

'I married you for the wrong reasons,' said Gemma.

'What?' He looked at her in surprise.

'I married you because I wanted to be married. Especially to someone like you – someone who'd been around the world and had fun. I wanted to have a house of my own and I wanted my mother to envy me. And those were the reasons.'

'Gemma!'

'I loved you too, David. But I was too young and too silly to have married you.'

He looked shocked.

'Don't think it makes me happy to realise that I was as much of a fool as you,' she said. 'And don't think I'm proud of the fact that I resented you marrying Orla.'

'You resented it?'

'Of course,' said Gemma. 'For heaven's sake, David, you married a gorgeous, young, clever woman. How the hell did you think that would make me feel?'

David picked up a spoon and tapped it gently against the side of his mug. 'I suppose I knew how it would make you feel,' he admitted. 'I suppose that was part of it.'

'David!'

'Oh, not all of it,' he said hastily. 'But when I was thinking about marrying her – and I married her for loads of reasons, Gemma, honestly – I also thought that it would hurt you and I wanted to hurt you.'

She said nothing.

'Because you were the one who asked me for a divorce and I was shattered by that. It was you, Gemma. You ended it.'

'I had to.'

'I know.'

She refilled his cup. 'And now?' she asked. 'What about you and Orla now?'

'I don't know,' he said honestly. 'What I do know, Gemma, is that I care about her a lot. And I love her independence and her way of doing things and the fact that she never asks me about anything, she just gets stuck in and does it herself.'

'The complete opposite of me when we were married,' said Gemma.

'Well, yes,' said David. 'And then she changed jobs. Without asking my advice.'

'So she did the things you wanted – she was independent and gutsy and you got annoyed with her.'

David said nothing.

'Why was it such a big deal?' asked Gemma.

'Because I realised that I wanted her to ask me about things and rely on my opinion and – and defer to me, I guess.'

'Oh, David!'

'In fact I wanted her to be more like you, Gemma.'

'Even though you married her because she was different.'

'I know.' He sighed deeply. 'You know, I think I really need professional help.'

'Maybe you do,' said Gemma.

'You were supposed to tell me not to be silly,' David said.

Gemma smiled. 'I know.'

'The kids said that they felt sorry for her last night.' David tapped the mug with his spoon again.

'Don't do that,' said Gemma. 'It's something you do when you're bothered and it always drove me insane.'

'Really?'

'Yes, really.'

'They said I spent too much time with you and not enough time with her.'

'You did,' said Gemma.

'I don't know why,' said David.

Gemma looked him straight in the eye. 'Of course you know why,' she said. 'You wanted to make her jealous. And I wanted to let you.'

'I didn't. You didn't.'

'You're lying to yourself,' she said. 'You did. And I'm just as much to blame. I feel pretty rotten, to be honest.'

'Am I that bad?' he asked despairingly. 'I mean, Gemma, am I utterly useless? Is it just me? Is any of it her fault?'

'I don't know!' Gemma cried. She sighed. 'Sorry, David. I'm tired and I'm not thinking straight any more. Why don't you ring her? Apologise to her. Get on with it.'

'I'm not sure I want to,' he said.

'Why?' She looked at him thoughtfully. 'Is it really over between you, David? Already?'

'I'm not sure we can salvage it,' he said.

'David, if you can't, then I'm truly sorry.' Gemma slid off the stool. 'But you have to try. I think, maybe, we didn't try enough and we should have. You don't want to make the same mistake again. Think about it. I'm going to have a shower and get dressed.'

He sat at the counter after she left the room. He wished he'd been a better husband to her. And a better father. And now he wished he'd been a better husband to Orla. He sighed. Had he simply been bowled over by the way she looked? Was that all it was, in the end? It couldn't have been, he thought. We had fun together. We like the same things. He closed his eyes. Thinking was making his head hurt even more.

He was still sitting at the counter when Gemma came downstairs again. She was dressed in slate-grey trousers over which she wore a pale-pink angora jumper. She'd taken some time with her make-up today because she, too, had a hangover. Only, she thought, as she came down the stairs, mothers don't have time for hangovers.

The phone rang as she walked into the kitchen. She turned to answer it but was beaten by Keelin who'd jumped up at the first ring.

'Oh, hi,' she said. 'Yes. She's here. Do you want to talk to her?' She held out the receiver to Gemma. 'It's for you,' she said. 'It's Bru.'

'Thanks.' Gemma flushed slightly as she took the phone. Keelin winked at her and suddenly both of them began to giggle. David looked at them in surprise.

'Hello,' she said.

'What's so funny?' asked Sam.

'Nothing,' she said. 'How are you?' She was very conscious of David's gaze.

'I'm fine. How are you? How was the party?'

'I'm hungover,' said Gemma. 'And the party was – interesting.'

'What d'you mean, interesting?'

'Just that.'

'Do you want to have lunch today?' asked Sam.

'I can't,' she told him. 'David's not able to look after the kids and I didn't make any other arrangements.'

'How about later?' asked Sam.

'I can't go out today,' Gemma told him. 'I really can't.'

'Why don't I come over?' suggested Sam. 'I could bring some food with me, save you having to bother.'

Gemma wanted to see him again. She was surprised at how strong the desire was.

'OK,' she said. 'What time?'

'Now?'

'Not just yet,' said Gemma. 'I've things to sort out. This evening?'

'Gemma! That's hours away. How about this afternoon? Four o'clock?'

'OK.' She felt the warmth of his voice caress her. 'This afternoon.'

'OK,' said Sam. 'See you later, Gemma.'

'Who was that?' asked David as she hung up.

'A friend,' she told him.

'Who?' he asked again.

'David!' She opened the fridge and took out a carton of apple juice. She was desperately dehydrated. 'It's none of your business.'

'Are you seeing someone, Gemma?'

'It's nothing much.' She poured the juice into a long glass.

'Why didn't you tell me before now?' he asked.

She shrugged and said nothing.

'Is it serious?' asked David.

'Don't be silly.'

'I can't believe it.' He stared at her. 'You've got a boyfriend!'

'Don't say that.' She finished the juice and put the glass on the counter. 'It sounds so banal. He's a friend, that's all.'

'How long have you known him?'

'David, please!'

He looked at her thoughtfully. Her cheeks were pink under the sheen of her make-up and her eyes sparkled and her face was alight with vitality. So this was why she was looking so good these days, he realised. There was a man in Gemma's life and he made her feel good.

'It's time I was off,' he said abruptly. He went into the living room and took his jacket from the armchair where he'd left it. He said goodbye to Keelin who was removing her nail varnish and Ronan who looked up perfunctorily from the TV.

'See you next week,' said Keelin. 'Give my love to Orla. I hope you make it up properly.'

'Thanks,' said David. He walked into the hallway. Gemma stood there.

'Work it out this time, David,' she said as she opened the hall door for him.

'And you?' he asked. 'Have you worked it out?'

'I don't have anything to work out yet,' she said. 'But you have.'

'Maybe.' He kissed her on both cheeks. 'Thanks for letting me stay last night.'

'You're welcome,' she said and closed the door behind him.

Chapter 37

O rla couldn't stand being in the apartment on her own. It had never felt like her place and now she felt like an intruder. She couldn't believe that David hadn't come back. In fact she couldn't believe that he'd meekly walked out of his own apartment and driven off into the night. She supposed he hadn't had much option – at the very least he'd wanted to retrieve the clothes that she'd unceremoniously dumped over the balcony.

I must have been out of my mind, she thought. That's not the sort of thing I do. That's the sort of thing dramatic people do and I'm not a dramatic person. I'm just an ordinary woman.

Woman! She snorted. She'd behaved like a child. But, she thought, as she sat on the edge of the double bed, right now she felt like a child. It didn't seem real. It didn't seem as though this was her life. She felt as if she were observing someone else, watching someone else make a mess of things, not her.

Damn it! Orla gritted her teeth. She was supposed to be the assured one. She was the one with the career. The one who didn't need to have David hanging around the house all the time. She was the one with the long, long legs and the curling mass of red-gold hair. So why was it that she felt so young and unsophisticated and so bloody childish now? And why couldn't she stop thinking and thinking about last night?

At least the kids had been nice to her. Keelin, particularly, had been friendlier than Orla could ever remember.

Maybe it was because they knew. The thought struck her like an arrow. Maybe it was because they knew that David didn't love her any more and because they were confident that he'd be back home soon. So they could afford to be nice to her.

She felt as though she was losing her mind. Snatches of the evening kept exploding in her memory – David's appraising look at Gemma as she'd walked down the stairs (how, Orla wondered fiercely, had the bitch known when to make her appearance?); David and Gemma walking back into the house after being alone in the garden together (she'd wanted to go out and see what they were doing but at least she'd had enough pride not to); Gemma smiling up at him as they danced together later on. Then that horrible moment when she'd walked up to them and called Gemma a blobby bitch. And Lizzy rushing to smooth things over and hustle them out of the house . . . Orla groaned as she relived it again.

She didn't know what to do. But she couldn't stay here and simply wait for him to come home.

Eventually, she decided to see Abby. Maybe Abby would have some words of comfort for her although, if she knew Abby, her friend would simply tell her to cut her losses and start again.

But I really don't want to.

The realisation stunned Orla. She'd spent the last few weeks wondering how she could possibly have ever loved David, wondering exactly what it was she was feeling for him, wondering where the shared moments had gone. And just now, when she'd least expected it, she'd remembered what it was like when he loved her and she remembered how it was when she loved him. She remembered waking up beside him and sliding her body close to his. Not for sex, just because she wanted to be close to him. She remembered how they would communicate without speaking, how, in a crowded room, their eyes would meet and they'd both know exactly what the other was thinking. She remembered the closeness of driving places with him when neither of them spoke but they didn't need to say anything. When the silence between them had been a shared pleasure rather than an icy barrier.

And she wondered whose fault it was that it had gone.

She picked up her keys. It was still early, Abby would no doubt be sleeping and wouldn't be too happy about being woken up on a Sunday morning, but Orla knew that her friend would comfort her. She was glad that she'd already told her mother she wouldn't be over for lunch today. Rosanna's response had only partially surprised her. 'It's about time you and David spent a Sunday alone,' Rosanna had said. 'And you can cook for him at last.'

If only Rosanna knew. Orla felt tired as she got into her car. It was as though the energy had drained out of her. It was physically exhausting just to switch on the ignition.

She buzzed Abby's apartment three times before she heard her friend's voice on the intercom.

'Who is it?' asked Abby.

'It's me.' Orla realised her voice was a croak. 'Orla.'

'Orla!' There was astonishment and, Orla thought, almost panic in Abby's tone. 'What's the matter?'

'Let me in, Abby. It's freezing out here.'

'Yes. Of course. Sure.'

The door clicked open and Orla didn't bother with the lift but walked up the stairs to the apartment she'd once shared with Abby.

Her friend stood at the door, wearing a red sweatshirt and a pair of ancient, faded jogging pants which were now baggy at the knees. She looked hassled, thought Orla.

'Hi,' said Abby.

'Hello.' Orla smiled wanly at her. 'Can I come in?'

'Sure.'

Orla was disappointed in Abby's welcome. She knew that Abby seldom got up before noon on Sundays, but she badly wanted someone to be nice to her and Abby was treating her as though she was intruding.

'Late night?' Orla glanced around the tiny living room. There were half a dozen empty beer cans on the table as well as an empty wine bottle and the remains of a takeaway meal.

'Kind of.' Abby grimaced. 'Let me clean up this mess.'

'No, don't.' Orla shook her head. 'It reminds me of how it was when I lived here. It's fine, Abby, honestly.' She sat down on the edge of the bright orange sofa.

'So, what's up?' asked Abby.

Orla swallowed the lump that had suddenly appeared in her throat. 'I threw David's clothes out of the window last night.'

'Pardon?' Abby looked at her in astonishment.

'I threw David's stuff out of the window. We had a row.'

'A row?'

Orla sat back on the sofa. 'It was the anniversary party. Remember I told you about it? What I didn't say was that Gemma was going to be there and that I was dreading it. We had a row before we went because I was late home. Then we get to the damned party and the first person we see is Gemma and she looked fabulous. David thought so too. He danced with her. You should have seen them! Oh, Abby, I've been having a rotten time with him lately.'

Suddenly it all spilled out. How his work meant more to him than anything. How he'd been so mad at her for taking the job at Serene. How it had turned into a disaster area for her. How he'd picked Gemma and the children up from the airport after their holiday – Keelin had told her about that one day, enjoying the look of

384

discomfiture on Orla's face. How he'd spent hours going through his former wife's financial affairs. How she'd felt alienated. Unloved. Unwanted. And then she told Abby about Jonathan Pascoe and how she'd almost gone to bed with him.

'It would have been so easy to, Abby,' she said miserably. 'He wanted me and I wanted someone to love me. And when I didn't I regretted it. Especially as that was the night I came home and found out that David had been at Gemma's, going through her bloody finances! Doing more than that, I bet. I wondered why I hadn't let Jonathan tear the clothes off me and why I hadn't made love to him there on the floor of his damned rustic kitchen!'

'And why didn't you?'

Orla whirled round at the sound of his voice. She looked at him in disbelief for a moment and, once again, experienced the sensation that she was only an observer in her own life.

'Jonathan.' Her mouth formed his name.

'Hi, Orla.' He was wearing a T-shirt and jeans but his feet were bare. He looked relaxed and comfortable. And, Orla realised, he'd been to bed with Abby. She recognised it in the way he stood in front of her, in the horrified look on Abby's face and the languor in his eyes.

'What are you doing here?' She looked from Jonathan to Abby and back to Jonathan again.

'I came up to town yesterday,' said Jonathan. 'I rang you, Orla. I left a message on your mobile.'

'I didn't look at my messages,' she said. 'I was busy yesterday.'

'So I gathered.'

'And you came here, to Abby.'

'It's not what you think, Orla.' Abby looked miserable. 'It's not. Honestly. Jonathan and I, we – well, it was just—'

'I came to talk to Abby,' said Jonathan. 'I wanted the inside track on your life with the Ancient Mariner.'

'Don't call him that,' said Orla fiercely.

'And Abby and I just got to talking about old times. We had a few drinks and . . .'

'It was my fault,' said Abby. 'I was feeling lonely and down and Jonathan was there.'

'You specialise in it, obviously.' Orla looked at him bitterly. 'Catch a girl when she's not at her best, mutter a few sweet nothings into her ear and wait for her to fall into bed with you.'

'Oh, come on, Orla,' said Jonathan. 'You're being unfair. You didn't fall into bed with me, did you?'

385

'No,' she said slowly. 'I didn't.'

'I didn't either,' said Abby. 'I wanted to go to bed with him. It wasn't just that he was there and took advantage of me, Orla. I needed to go to bed with someone and I took advantage of him.'

'Oh, please!' Orla looked at her friend. 'Do you think I care much one way or the other?'

'Don't you?' asked Jonathan.

'I care that two people who I thought were my friends hopped into bed with each other,' said Orla. 'But it hasn't broken my heart, if that's what you think, Jonathan.'

'Orla, I wouldn't hurt you for the world.' Abby's eyes were pleading. 'It was one of those things. It seemed right at the time. I don't love Jonathan or anything. It meant nothing to either of us.'

Orla rubbed her eyes. 'Sure.'

'I'm sorry, Orla,' said Jonathan. 'I wouldn't hurt you for the world either. But we were talking about you and Abby said that you really love the – your husband – and that I was out of my mind if I thought you'd be interested in me and that you were going through a bad patch at the moment but that she knew everything would work itself out.'

'Oh, really.' Orla couldn't keep the irony out of her voice.

'Really,' said Jonathan. 'And I knew that she was right, Orla. You didn't want to be with me in Cork. You insisted on driving home to him, even though it was late and even though the weather was poor. You love him, not me.'

'So on that basis you thought it'd be OK to sleep with Abby.'

'Orla, it was sex, nothing else,' pleaded Abby. 'Don't blame Jonathan.'

'I'm not blaming anyone,' said Orla. 'Jonathan seems quite certain in his own mind that I'm madly in love with my husband so there's no need for you to keep making excuses for sleeping together. I'm married. You're both single. Where's the problem?'

'When you put it like that, there shouldn't be,' said Abby. 'But there is, isn't there?'

'Did you want to sleep with her before?' Orla turned to Jonathan. 'When we were in college?'

'No,' he said. 'Until we split up you were the only girl I was interested in.'

Orla sighed. 'I don't even know why I asked. It doesn't make any difference, does it?'

'No,' said Jonathan again. 'It doesn't. What I feel for you, or felt for you, is irrelevant compared to what you feel for David.'

'Are you going to leave him?' asked Abby. 'Is that why you came over?'

Orla shook her head. 'I don't know what I'm going to do,' she replied. 'I'm so bloody confused I feel as though I'm on a roller-coaster. Sometimes I think that I love David and he loves me. Sometimes I think that I love him and he hates me. Sometimes I think that I hate him and he loves me. My life is a mess!'

'And if you left him?' Jonathan's tone was neutral. 'Would you expect to go out with me?'

'Don't flatter yourself, Pascoe,' she snapped.

'What do you want to do?' asked Abby.

'I want to sleep,' said Orla. 'I'm tired. I'm hungover and I want to sleep.'

'You can use Janet's room if you like,' said Abby. 'She's gone back to Cavan for the weekend. She wouldn't mind.'

'No thanks.' Orla got up. 'I understand about you sleeping together,' she said tiredly. 'It happens. It's not a problem.' She picked up her bag. 'I've got to go.'

'Orla, you're exhausted. You should stay for a while.' Abby put her arm round her friend's shoulder. 'Have a rest. Flake out in Janet's room.'

Orla shook her head. 'It's OK,' she said. 'I'm not that tired really. I only think I am.'

'Orla.' Jonathan stood beside her. 'I—'

'Go away, Jonathan,' she said. 'I need to be on my own.' She walked out of the apartment and closed the door behind her.

Jonathan and Abby stared at each other.

'What a cock-up,' said Jonathan. 'I couldn't believe it when I heard you telling her to come up.'

'I couldn't tell her not to,' said Abby. 'I was kind of hoping you'd stay discreetly in the bedroom, though.'

'She'd have found out sooner or later.' Jonathan shrugged. 'Better sooner.'

'Do you love her?' asked Abby.

'I don't know.' Jonathan smiled wryly. 'I always wanted to protect her. From the moment I saw her I thought she was beautiful and desirable and, despite how damn severe she could be, I thought she needed to be protected. And when I met her in Cork she looked so unhappy that I wanted to protect her all over again. It seemed right somehow.'

'And last night?' asked Abby. 'The mistake. With me?'

'You thought it was a mistake too,' he said. 'You said so.'

'I know,' said Abby.

'I'd better go,' said Jonathan. 'I'll get dressed.'

He went into the bedroom. Abby sat on the orange sofa, her knees curled up. Why is it, she wondered, that people do incredibly stupid things, even knowing that they're incredibly stupid? And what were the chances of her getting the opportunity to do something incredibly stupid with Jonathan again?

Orla slid into the driver's seat and rested her head on the steering wheel of the car. Jonathan and Abby. She didn't know whether she should feel betrayed or not. Her best friend and the man she'd once loved. Could still love, for all she knew. She didn't trust herself any more. She didn't know what she was supposed to feel. Right now, she didn't feel anything at all.

She started the car and began to drive. She wasn't thinking about where she was going, she was driving automatically, signalling at turns, stopping at traffic lights. She turned on the CD and played Robbie Williams loud to keep herself awake.

She didn't know how she'd arrived at Gemma's house. She hadn't meant to come here. At least, she didn't think she'd meant to come here. But she'd wanted to find David and she'd told him to go to Gemma last night and she was pretty sure that was what he'd done.

You're a real sucker for punishment, she thought as she pressed the doorbell. Seeing two lovers with two different women on the same day.

It was only when she heard footsteps inside the house that she realised David's car wasn't parked outside. That he might not be here after all.

She didn't have time to run away although the thought rushed through her head. The door opened and Gemma was standing in front of her, a shocked expression on her face.

'Hi,' said Orla.

Gemma stared at her. 'Hello.'

'Can I come in?'

'Sure.' Gemma opened the door wider and Orla stepped inside.

'Come into the kitchen,' said Gemma. 'Ronan's in the living room. Keelin has gone out.'

Orla felt light-headed as she followed the other woman. The sense of unreality she'd had earlier was even stronger now.

'Sit down,' said Gemma. 'Would you like something to drink?'

Orla shook her head.

'Juice? Or tea? Something stronger?'

'No thanks,' said Orla. She didn't want to shake her head again. She felt as though it might fall off if she did.

Gemma sat down opposite her. She wasn't sure what to say.

Then Orla started to cry. Tears rolled down her cheeks and onto the polished wood of the dining table. Gemma reached behind her and grabbed some tissues from the box on the shelf. She handed them wordlessly to Orla who sniffed and scrubbed at her eyes.

'Where is he?' Orla finally forced the words out.

'I don't know,' said Gemma.

'Was he here? Last night?'

Gemma was silent. She didn't know whether it was better to say yes or no.

'Yes,' she said eventually. There was no point in lying.

'Why did you come to the party?' Orla finally forced the words out. 'Why did you come and make him feel that you were really the one?'

'He doesn't think I'm the one,' said Gemma. 'I was once but I'm not any more.'

'He still loves you.' Orla looked up. Her eyes were red, her face blotchy. 'He still loves you and it's destroying our marriage.'

'He doesn't love me. He probably never did.'

'Oh, come on!' Orla was angry. 'What was last night all about? Laughing together. Talking together. Dancing.'

Gemma bit her lip.

'You're so perfect in his eyes. Gemma kept the house so well. Gemma was a great cook. Gemma was great with the children.' Orla's tone was bitter.

'Oh, don't be ridiculous.' The words were harsher than Gemma had intended. Orla flinched. 'I was good at all those things but it didn't make him come home to me at night. It wasn't enough. It might have been if we'd worked at it harder, but in the end, it wasn't.'

Orla said nothing.

'He came here last night and he stayed the night. But on the sofa, Orla.'

'You danced with him. I had to do something about it. You humiliated me.'

389

'I know,' said Gemma. 'I'm sorry. I shouldn't have. I was being stupid myself, Orla. Trying to prove that I could be just as sexy as you.'

Orla looked astonished. 'You looked great and you know you do. You made things worse between us. You wanted to make things worse between us.'

'Orla, I – maybe temporarily,' admitted Gemma. 'But believe me, David loves you. I know he does. He told me himself.' If anyone had told me a few months ago that I'd be telling David's wife not to worry that he loved her, I'd have sent them straight into therapy, thought Gemma.

'No he doesn't,' said Orla.

Gemma sighed. 'I think you're wrong.'

'Why should you care?'

'Because I want him to be happy,' she said. She got up and took the carton of apple juice out of the fridge again. I do want him to be happy, she realised, as she poured herself a glass. I really do. And I want Orla to be happy too. 'Would you like some now?' She looked at Orla who nodded. I don't care that he married her. I did care, I really did, but I don't any more. And even if Sam and I don't work out, it doesn't matter. I still don't care. I'm glad he's found someone.

'He was pissed as a newt when he arrived here last night,' said Gemma. 'I didn't realise he'd been drinking that much.'

'I thought he might crash,' admitted Orla. 'I saw him drive off and I was terrified. I kept thinking that someone would phone to tell me he'd wrapped himself around a lamp-post somewhere.'

'He didn't crash,' said Gemma. 'He was somewhat the worse for wear when he arrived, but he didn't crash on the way.'

'And what did he say?'

Gemma grinned. 'That you'd thrown his stuff out of the apartment window.'

Orla smiled faintly.

'I liked that, Orla. I thought it was great!'

'It was stupid,' said Orla.

'Oh, I don't know,' Gemma mused. 'I bet you got great satisfaction out of it.'

'At the time,' admitted Orla.

'Once, when I had a row with him, I put his favourite jumper in the washing machine,' said Gemma. 'On a hot cycle. It came out about two inches by two inches. He freaked. I told him that I'd been so upset I hadn't realised what I was doing.'

Orla's laugh was shaky.

'He's not a bad person,' said Gemma. 'He's just – he likes to be in charge, Orla. He thinks he doesn't but he does. He likes showing off and generally being top dog and I suppose you could always trace it back to his childhood or something but maybe it's just that that's the kind of person he is.'

'I thought we had so much in common,' said Orla. 'But, later, I thought he just wanted you all over again.'

'It's not easy,' said Gemma. 'You think you know someone but you only ever know part of them. And you think you'll die when someone leaves you, but you put the pieces back together again. And you think you can't talk about things, but you can.'

'With David!' A flash of spirit returned to Orla's eyes. 'It's like talking to a brick wall!'

'I know,' said Gemma. 'God knows, I tried often enough.'

'It's the way his face kind of shuts down,' said Orla, 'as if he's filtering you out of his mind.'

'And he stares at a spot past your head,' said Gemma.

'And then his eyes narrow.'

'And his nostrils flare a little.'

'And he looks at you as though you were about six years old!'

The two women smiled at each other.

'He spent the night on the sofa,' repeated Gemma.

'But he didn't come home.' Orla's voice trembled.

'He will,' said Gemma.

Orla sighed. 'I hated you, you know.'

'Why?'

'Because you married him first. Because you were always there.'

'I hated you too,' said Gemma.

Orla blinked. 'Me?'

'Come on, Orla.' Gemma grinned. 'You're younger than me, you're thinner than me and you can wear something that resembles a black silk hanky at a party and look great.'

'I wanted to stab you last night,' said Orla, 'because I thought you looked sophisticated and I looked like a kid.'

'We don't have to like each other,' said Gemma. 'We don't have to get on. But there's no need to hate each other.'

'I know,' said Orla as the doorbell rang.

'Mum! Mum!' Ronan rushed into the room. 'Guess who's here!! Oh.' He stopped as he saw Orla. 'Hi, Orla. Where's Dad? Are you still fighting?'

391

Gemma and Orla stood up as Sam McColgan followed Ronan into the room. Gemma rubbed the bridge of her nose. She was too tired for all this human drama in one day.

'Ronan, Orla will be going home soon. Would you like to show Sam your new Playstation game?'

'It's great, Sam,' said Ronan. 'You're trapped in a cave and there's all sorts of witches and spells and stuff. I bet you I can beat you.'

'I bet you can too. I'll be with you in a second, Ro.' He handed the bunch of flowers he was holding to Gemma. 'I'm terribly sorry,' he said. 'I didn't think. I wanted to surprise you by coming early.'

'It's OK,' she said.

'No, it's not. I am sorry, Gemma.'

'Sam, this is Orla. Orla, this is Sam.'

'Hi.' Orla held out her hand and Sam shook it.

'Nice to meet you,' said Sam. He looked from Gemma to Orla. 'I'll go inside, Gemma.'

Gemma and Orla looked at each other.

'Is he . . . ?'

'A friend,' said Gemma hastily. 'A good friend.'

'David never told me.'

'David didn't know. He does now.'

'You really don't want him back?'

'I really don't,' said Gemma. 'And, Orla, it's not a case of what I want. He really doesn't want to come back. He might moan and groan and talk about old times but it's a load of rubbish. We lived apart for a long time before he met you. It's not a question of you or me.'

'Maybe not,' said Orla.

'Absolutely not,' said Gemma.

'I don't know whether I love him or not any more myself.' Orla wrapped her arms round her body. 'Sometimes I do and then sometimes I – it's just not cut and dried, is it?'

'I wish,' said Gemma.

'And it's not cut and dried with you and Sam?'

'I don't want it to be. Not yet.' Gemma smiled. 'I rushed into things with David. And though part of me is still rushing, I'm going to take it easy with Sam.'

'The kids know him?'

'We met on holidays,' explained Gemma.

'I'd better go,' said Orla. 'Leave you to it.'

Gemma smiled at her. 'Good luck with David,' she said.

'Thanks.' Orla exhaled slowly. 'I think I'm going to need it.'

Chapter 38

David parked his car near the Martello tower and got out. He wanted to work out what he was going to say to Orla. He wanted to have it clear in his head so that they could talk about things like rational adults instead of the spiteful, childish people they'd become. But maybe it was too late for rational talk. Maybe, once again, he'd managed to destroy a relationship without even realising that he was doing it. I'm selfish, he thought, as he watched the seagulls wheel and swoop in the grey skies overhead. I want things my way all the time. Gemma was right about that. I don't mean to be, but I am. And maybe she's right about the job too. Maybe I don't need to chase success quite so much. Maybe, he thought, as he kicked a black pebble, perfectly rounded by years of erosion, maybe I don't need to prove to everyone that I'm as good as Livvy.

He thought about his younger sister. The clever one, she used to be called. He remembered the scene again. Handing his report card to his father. Brian pursing his lips and looking at David and wondering why it was that his results were all Cs and Ds while Livvy's were straight As.

'She's the clever one, I suppose,' Brian had said as she signed the report. He hadn't said anything else. He hadn't said that David was stupid or that Ds were disappointing or that David would be consigned to life's scrapheap because he wasn't the clever one. But he'd felt like a loser against Livvy's brilliance. Until the day that he'd bought the house in Dun Laoghaire while Livvy, the clever one, was still renting a shoebox studio apartment in Kilmainham. Who exactly was the clever one now? he remembered thinking.

He sighed. You think you're in control of your life, he mused, you think you know exactly why you do what you do, but in the end your bloody subconscious is working away in the background making a mess of everything!

He'd made a mess of things with Orla for sure. He couldn't

remember much about the night before but he could remember her hunted, haunted look as she'd yelled at him about Gemma. And he'd tried to tell her how stupid she was being but that had been the wrong thing to say. And now it was probably too late. Years ago he'd been certain that Gemma would relent and that they'd get back together. Now he knew that the only thing he'd learned over all that time was that he had a habit of leaving things too late.

His headache had lifted. His mouth still felt like a horse's stable and he could feel the stubble on his chin – he hadn't been able to shave this morning, Orla hadn't thrown his razor out of the window along with everything else and he hadn't had the nerve to try Gemma's Gillette for Women.

I probably look like a loser, he thought. A boring old fart walking along the seafront on his own because he's managed to lose two good women in a lifetime.

⌐

Sam heard Orla leaving and came downstairs from Ronan's room. Gemma was leaning against the wall, holding her hand to her forehead.

'Are you OK?' His voice was full of concern.

She nodded. 'Just something I could have done without today.'

'Gemma, I'm so sorry for coming around. It was thoughtless. Selfish.'

'Yes,' she said.

'There's stuff in your life that I don't know about and don't need to know about,' said Sam.

'That's what I already told you.' She walked into the living room.

He stayed where he was. It had seemed a good idea to come early, to surprise her with his bunch of flowers and his beaming smile. God, he thought, I'm such a fool. She's already split up from a bloke like that, from someone who tried to make her fit into his life. Am I really just the same sort of person?

He pushed open the door. She was sitting on the sofa, staring ahead of her.

'Do you want me to leave?' he asked.

She said nothing.

Damn, he thought. I've lost her. And it's my own stupid, stupid fault.

'Call me,' he said. 'If you want.'

394

She didn't speak.

She heard him let himself out of the house. She wanted to run after him, to tell him to come back, but she was afraid. She wanted him so much that it hurt. When he'd walked into the kitchen it was all she could do not to throw her arms round him and kiss him. But he shouldn't have come. She'd told him to come later and he'd just ignored her. As David had always ignored her. And if he thought that a few flowers might make a difference, he was sorely mistaken.

Ronan clattered downstairs.

'Is Bru gone?' he asked.

Gemma nodded.

'I thought he was staying,' said Ronan. 'I wanted to play Tomb Raider with him.'

'You spend far too much time playing those stupid games,' said Gemma harshly.

'I like them.' Ronan was defensive. 'You like them too! And Bru—'

'I suppose he's great at them,' said Gemma.

'No.' Ronan laughed. 'He fell of the cliff at the very start.'

Gemma held out her arms and Ronan sat down beside her. She hugged him fiercely until he begged her to stop.

⟆

Orla heard the key in the apartment door and felt her stomach turn over. He'd come back. To get his clothes? Or to be with her? She picked up a magazine and sat down in the corner armchair. She needed to be cool. Relaxed.

He looked rotten, she thought, as he walked through the door. His hair was windswept, his eyes bloodshot and his face unshaven. She glanced back at the magazine.

'Hi,' he said.

'Hello.'

'How are you feeling?' he asked.

She dropped the magazine on the sofa beside her.

'I'm fine.'

He dropped his suitcase on the floor and sat down opposite her. 'I don't think I got everything,' he said.

'Sorry?' she looked at him in surprise.

'All my clothes. I'm pretty sure that a pair of boxer shorts ended up on the balcony of the apartment below us.'

'I doubt it.'

'Honestly,' he told her. 'The silk pair.'

'No.'

'I saw them go out the window but I didn't get them on the ground.'

'Oh, well,' she said, 'if they have landed on somebody else's balcony I suppose they'll be too embarrassed to give them back.'

'I sincerely hope they don't know they're mine,' said David. 'You knew the Mastersons are in the apartment below us. Considering they're both in they're eighties, I can't think it'd do either of them any good to have my boxers on their balcony.'

'Oh, I don't know,' said Orla. 'He might have a use for them.'

They looked at each other.

'That was some row last night,' said David.

'Yes.' She bit her lip.

'I've had my fair share,' he told her. 'Gemma and I had a few beauties in our day. But she never threw my clothes out of the window.'

'I'm not Gemma,' said Orla.

David smiled ruefully. 'I know.'

'I went to see her today.' Orla shifted in the armchair.

'What!'

'I went to see her. Or maybe I went to see you. I thought you might be there.'

'I went there,' he said slowly. 'You told me to and that's exactly what I did. But I didn't sleep with her.'

'Would you have?' asked Orla.

'What do you mean?'

'If she'd let you. Would you have slept with her?'

He rubbed his hand over his unshaven face. 'I don't know,' he said. 'If I did, it would have been to hurt you and not because I wanted to be with her. And so I'm very glad she didn't even give me the chance.'

'How honest of you,' murmured Orla.

'What did you and Gemma talk about?' he asked.

'You mostly,' she said.

'And what did she tell you? That I'm a no-good, not to be trusted, bastard?'

Orla shook her head. 'Nothing like that.'

'She didn't tell you I have a sensitive side, I suppose.'

'No,' said Orla. 'We just talked. It was worthwhile. We were honest with each other.'

'I want to be honest with you,' said David.

396

This is it, she thought. This is where we talk about it. This is where our lives are laid bare. She shivered.

'I didn't realise what I had with Gemma when I lived with her,' he said.

Orla closed her eyes. She wasn't sure she wanted to hear it.

'And I didn't realise how lucky I was that our divorce, while horrible and mucky and bad-tempered at the time, was pretty amicable in the whole history of divorces.'

She could feel tears forming behind her eyelids.

'And I certainly didn't realise how lucky I was that I found you,' he said.

She said nothing.

'Think about how lucky I was, Orla. I'm a middle-aged bloke, bit of a gut at this point in my life, grey hair, need reading glasses, divorced, two kids – I'm a mess, Orla, and yet I meet you and fall in love with you and you marry me.'

She bit her lip.

'And instead of being glad that I found you I treat you like you're my damn housekeeper.'

'Only sometimes,' Orla croaked.

'I don't understand myself.' David looked into her wide hazel eyes. 'I married you because I didn't think I could live without you and then I seemed to do everything I could to make you dislike me. And I really don't know why.'

'You wanted me to be her,' said Orla.

'Her?'

'Gemma.'

'No,' said David forcefully. 'I never wanted you to be Gemma.'

'I think you did.' Orla twisted a curl round her little finger. 'I think you thought that by marrying me you were getting another chance with Gemma. Only this time you'd get it right.'

'Orla, I swear to you I never for a second thought you were another Gemma.'

She sighed. 'You expected me to keep the house like she did. You wanted me to be at home whenever you were. You thought I should consult you about everything.'

'Like the job,' he said.

'I felt as though you didn't take my career seriously at all,' she told him. 'For as long as I was working in Gravitas with you, you could keep an eye on me. It was just an extension of our lives at home. Once I struck out on my own it was different.'

He flexed his fingers thoughtfully. Everyone said exactly the same about his reaction to the job.

'I admit I behaved like a shit,' he said. 'I'm sorry.'

She bit her lip. 'It doesn't make it any better that you might have been right.'

'Right?'

'I hate the job,' she said. 'I've been useless at it from the day I started!'

'You couldn't be,' he told her. 'You're a good salesperson, Orla. I've seen you working. People trust you. Think about Sara Benton!'

'Not any more,' she said. 'I've had the worst time of my life with Serene. Bob Murphy has given me a month to bring in some business before he lets me go. I've sold a few crappy little policies that someone straight out of school could sell. I've messed up two corporate accounts. It's a bloody nightmare!' She covered her face with her hands.

'Oh, Orla.' He sat beside her and put his arm round her.

'I don't want your sympathy,' she said. 'I don't want you telling me it'll be all right when I know that you're really pleased that it's been all wrong.'

He pulled her hands from her face. 'I'm not pleased,' he said. 'Why should I be pleased? OK, I don't like Bob Murphy, never have. But I love you, Orla, and I don't want anything rotten to happen to you – even with Serene. And you're right, I did feel as though I was losing some kind of control over you when you decided to move. And I felt – oh, hurt, I suppose, when you didn't tell me about the job sooner. But I behaved like a child and I'm sorry.'

'It's a bit late to be sorry,' she said.

Gemma had said that. He remembered her standing in the kitchen, wearing a green and white striped apron, looking at him with a wounded expression. He couldn't recall whether it was before or after they'd started to talk about a divorce but it had been one of many arguments at the time. He couldn't remember, either, what he was supposed to feel sorry about. But he knew that it had been too late. He'd heard the finality in Gemma's voice. And then he lashed out at her. Told her that she was a stupid bitch, that she wanted everything her own way, that she didn't give him credit for anything.

He looked at Orla. Her eyes were defiant.

'I know,' he said. 'But I'm sorry anyway.'

She started to cry then, big salty tears that slid down her cheeks and dropped into her lap.

'Orla, I love you,' said David fiercely. 'I didn't realise how much until today. And if I've been stupid enough to lose you, than maybe I deserve it. But I don't want to lose you. I really and truly don't.'

'You treat me like a child,' she said.

'Sometimes,' he admitted. 'I know. I don't mean to but I do anyway.'

'What about Gemma?' she asked.

'What about her?'

'Do you love her? Despite everything?'

'I don't love Gemma,' said David. 'I care about Gemma. That's completely different. And, to be honest, I admire her. I thought she'd be utterly useless without a bloke around the house. I expected her to fall to pieces. But she's managed to keep things going, to bring up the kids, to live her life.' He held Orla closely to him. 'Last night – I guess I wanted to be nasty to you. Things had been so rotten between us and, well, the opportunity to hurt you was there and I took it.'

'She looked great,' said Orla. 'And you looked right with her.'

'Orla, people walk around in shock because someone as gorgeous as you married me. Andy said it to me. Dad said it to me. Nobody can believe that you love me. If you do any more.'

'It's funny,' said Orla. 'But when I first went out with you I counted the hours till I saw you again. Nobody ever made me feel like you. And I felt like that every single day until we got home from our honeymoon and you switched into super-salesman mode and suddenly I didn't seem to matter to you any more. Except whenever I went out. Then you'd do everything you could to keep me home.'

'I'm an idiot,' said David. 'I wanted to prove how brilliant I was. That I could bring in the big accounts and that I could keep up payments to Gemma and provide for us too. Not only that, that I could bring in lots of money for us too.'

'But I work,' said Orla. 'There wasn't any need for you to feel that way.'

'I'm an old-fashioned sort of bloke,' said David wryly. 'I felt that I had to.'

His arm was still round her. She was comforted by it. She took a deep breath. 'You're not the only idiot,' she said.

'Oh?'

'I have to tell you something.'

She told him about Jonathan Pascoe. She told him about going back to his house in Blarney. About drinking whiskey with him. She didn't tell him about Jonathan's hand on her breast or the desire that he'd awoken in her. There were some things that she really didn't think David would want to know. But she needed to tell him about Jonathan.

When she finished, he looked at her in amazement.

'I never even thought,' he said. 'Never.'

'I believed that you and Gemma were getting back together,' said Orla. 'I wanted to pay you back.'

David sighed. 'Isn't it amazing how much goes on in people's lives that you just don't know? We were living together and I didn't know.'

'I'm sorry,' said Orla.

'Fair enough, I suppose,' he said. 'You suspect me of having it off with my ex-wife so you go to dinner with your ex-boyfriend.'

'I just didn't want you to feel as though you were shouldering all the blame,' said Orla. 'Besides, my ex-boyfriend has since been to bed with my, possibly, ex-best friend.'

He looked at her in disbelief.

'I went to see Abby this morning. Jonathan came up to Dublin last night. He wanted to meet me, apparently, but got sidetracked by Abby.'

David was astonished. 'Did she tell you about it?' he asked. 'What is it with women? How can they tell each other this intimate stuff so bloody easily?'

'I'm sure she would have told me,' Orla said. 'But she didn't have to. He was still there.'

'Oh.' David smiled at her suddenly. 'OK,' he said. 'I can't exactly top that but I nearly can. I think Gemma has a new boyfriend.'

Orla looked at him. 'I know,' she said. 'I met him.'

'What!' David stared at her.

'She was shocked when he turned up. I could see that. He said something about surprising her. He'd brought flowers.'

'She likes flowers,' said David. 'When I was in the doghouse with her I used to bring them home.'

'I don't think he was in the doghouse.'

'What's he like?' asked David.

Orla considered for a moment. 'Pretty attractive,' she said.

'Are you just saying that to make me feel bad, or is it true?'

'He's pretty attractive,' she said again.

'More attractive than me?' his voice held mock incredulity.

'Afraid so.' The corner of her mouth began to twitch. Then they both began to laugh. Shakily at first, then more and more. David gathered Orla to him and she rested her head on his chest.

'So,' he said, as their laughter subsided. 'It looks as though we're stuck with each other. Our ex's have gone off and done new things. We've been dumped. What do you think?'

'I don't want to be second best, David,' she said.

'You're not,' he told her. 'You'll never be second best. I love you. I might have lost sight of it for a while, but you make me feel like no one else ever did. Not Gemma. Not anyone.'

'Perhaps,' she said.

'Maybe we went into it thinking that everything would fall into place too easily,' he said. 'It's corny, I know, but we both had to make changes and I've never been good at making changes. But I don't want to lose you, Orla. I don't. Even if it means putting up with your habit of flinging my clothes out of the window.'

'I'm sorry about that,' she said. 'I wanted to do something spectacular.'

'You did,' he said.

'I was so angry,' she said. 'With you, with me, with everything.'

'And now?' he said.

'I'm exhausted.'

'Want to go to bed?' he asked.

'I'd fall asleep,' she told him. 'I couldn't sleep last night.'

'You see.' He grinned at her. 'We're just an old married couple at heart. We crawl into bed and fall asleep.'

She kissed him on the lips. He kissed her on the neck. Their eyes met. They didn't bother going as far as the bed.

⌐

Gemma was alone in the house at four o'clock when the phone rang. She let it ring for a moment, then she picked up the receiver.

'Hello,' she said.

'I'm sorry,' said Sam.

'Stop saying you're sorry.'

'I'm not sure what else to say.'

'I don't want to be pushed around,' said Gemma. 'I like you, but I don't want to be pushed around.'

'I won't,' he said. 'I do stupid things sometimes. Today was stupid.'

'It wasn't stupid,' she said. 'But it was the wrong time. You said it already. I've stuff in my life, Sam, and I've got to deal with it on my own.'

'Can I call around?' he asked.

'Yes,' she said. 'When will you be here?'

'Now,' said Sam as he rang the doorbell and switched off his mobile phone.

Gemma couldn't help smiling as she opened the door.

Sam's brown eyes gazed at her.

'Come in,' she said.

'I'm not going to apologize again,' said Sam. 'You're right. It gets devalued if you do it too often.'

'Sam, you're the first man I've had any kind of relationship with since David. I'm a bit rusty in the "when to get annoyed" department.'

'Forgiven?' he asked.

'Sort of,' said Gemma.

'Do you want to tell me about it?' asked Sam.

'I don't know.'

She didn't know whether or not she wanted to let him into the nooks and crannies of her relationship with David and David's relationship with Orla and all the bits and pieces that floated around her life. Until now they'd only spoken of her divorce as something that had happened and her marriage to David as something that was over. But, Gemma realised, there are parts of your life that are never really over. They become less important, part of the overall patchwork quilt that makes up your experiences, but they're always there all the same. You couldn't simply close the door and pretend that they'd never existed.

'I behaved badly last night.' They'd walked into the living room and now Gemma sat on the sofa and held one of the cushions.

'How?' asked Sam.

'I flirted with David.'

'Oh.'

'I didn't mean it as first,' said Gemma. 'But then I did.'

'Why?'

'Because I could.' Gemma was shamefaced. 'The opportunity was there and I took it. I shouldn't have done, but I did.'

'And?'

'And Orla threw a wobbler when they got home. It wasn't the only thing she threw.' Gemma smiled faintly. 'She threw his clothes out of the apartment.'

'Wow!'

'And told him to come home to me, which he did.'

'I see.' Sam got up from the sofa where he'd sat beside her and walked across the room to the window.

'He stayed the night,' said Gemma.

'I see,' said Sam.

'On the sofa.'

Sam turned to look at her. 'Why?'

'Why d'you think?' she asked. 'We're divorced, Sam. I flirted with him, he had a row with his wife, he was pissed as a newt when he came here.' She sighed. 'We don't love each other any more but he turned up on the doorstep and I couldn't throw him out.'

'Why did you flirt with him, as you so charmingly put it?'

'Because I'm a bitch,' said Gemma. 'I looked good last night, Sam. I could see how surprised David was that I looked so good. And, because I don't care about him any more, I was able to smile and laugh and generally behave in a much more seductive way than you can when you actually do love someone! And I . . .' she paused, 'I wanted to inflict some pain on Orla. Which was the most horrible thing in the world to do, but I couldn't help myself.'

'Why did you want to do that?'

'Because I might have looked good but she was younger and more lovely and because she was the one who'd married David.'

'But you don't love David.'

Gemma threw the cushion to the end of the sofa. 'Of course I don't,' she said impatiently. 'I'm just a horrible person, Sam, that's all. I had the chance to be nasty to someone and I was.'

'That doesn't make you horrible,' said Sam.

'Yes it does.'

'And when I came earlier? What did Orla want?'

'She was gutted after the row with David. She thought he'd still be here.'

'It's like one of those Russian tragedy plays,' said Sam. 'All this dark emotion bubbling under the surface.'

'Don't mock me,' said Gemma.

'I'm not.' Sam came and sat beside her again. 'And I don't blame you for flirting with danger last night.'

'I blame me,' said Gemma. 'I'm a cow.'

'Let's recap,' said Sam. 'Orla and David love each other although they've been going through a rough patch. You helped the rough patch along last night. Cue massive row between married couple. Who are now, possibly, making it up in the way most couples like to make up massive rows.'

Gemma looked up from her nails which she'd been examining closely. 'You think?'

'Gemma, Gemma, of course! What adds more spice to a marriage than a good bust-up and reconciliation?'

She sighed. 'I had those with David,' she said. 'But they were just bust-ups. We never had the reconciliations.'

'Maybe it'll be different this time,' Sam told her. 'It's a different marriage, Gemma.'

She picked at her thumbnail. 'I still feel partly to blame.'

'Perhaps you helped,' said Sam. 'If they were having a bit of a rough time and you brought it all to a head, perhaps you helped. And if you didn't,' he added, 'then you only speeded up the inevitable.'

'Maybe.'

'Gemma, you can't live their lives for them.'

'I know.' She bit her lip. 'I really do want it to work for them. A few months ago I don't know if I did or not. But now I do.'

'And for yourself?' asked Sam.

'Damn!' she said. 'I've broken my nail.'

'Gemma?'

She bit the jagged edge of the nail.

'What do you want, Gemma?' asked Sam.

She looked at him. His brown eyes returned her look unwaveringly. She moved towards him and suddenly she was in his arms and he was kissing her with an intensity that scorched her lips and fired her body.

Then she heard the key in the door and they just managed to be sitting at the opposite ends of the sofa before Keelin walked into the room.

Chapter 39

'Keelin! Can you come and do up my zip!' Gemma called to her daughter who responded by clattering up the stairs and pushing open the door of her mother's room.

'I thought this dress fitted you,' said Keelin as she tugged at the zip.

'It does,' retorted Gemma. 'It's just difficult to pull up, that's all. It pulls down easily enough.'

'There you are!' Keelin finally managed to zip up the dress and stood back to look at her mother. 'You look great, Mum. You really do.'

Gemma smiled. 'Thanks.'

She was wearing the Ben de Lisi again, this time for Liz and Ross's engagement dinner. They'd hired a private dining room in the very upmarket Merrion Hotel and Gemma had wanted to look her absolute best. She'd toyed with the idea of a new dress, but everyone had told her how stunning she'd looked at Brian and Patsy's anniversary when she'd worn the lilac dress before, so she'd virtuously abandoned the idea of spending money on a new one.

Liz had been shocked when Gemma told her that she had a perfectly good dress she intended to wear. They'd gone into town together to buy Liz something new and sexy and Liz had assumed that Gemma would be spending money too.

'I can't believe you're passing up the opportunity to buy something,' said Liz. 'You never did before!'

'I'm a different person to the one I was before,' Gemma had told her. 'And I have the ideal dress at home. But, for you,' she looked at the deep red sheath that Liz was modelling, 'that's perfect!'

Liz and Ross were getting married in three months. Liz had muttered that getting engaged, let alone having a dinner to celebrate it, was probably a bit mad, but Ross was insistent.

'It'll be fun,' Gemma assured her. 'Oh, look, Liz – that bag! Isn't it just dinky? You have to buy it!'

Gemma hadn't escaped from the shopping expedition entirely

unscathed. She'd bought a pair of incredibly expensive stockings. Liz had raised her eyebrows at the purchase and Gemma had winked lasciviously at her sister.

'We're as bad as we ever were in our teens,' observed Liz as they left the shop.

'No man is safe!' Gemma grinned at her.

She studied her reflection in the cheval mirror. Keelin was right. She looked great. She looked confident and happy and her curves were in all the right places.

'I'll do,' she said.

'Oh, Mum!' Keelin grinned at her. 'You know you look knock-out tonight. Sam will be completely bowled over!'

Gemma smiled. Tonight was the night that Sam would run the gauntlet of her family. The night he would meet Gerry and Frances for the first time. He'd met Liz already – they both liked each other enormously.

'Have you got your stuff packed?' Gemma looked at the clock. 'Dad and Orla will be here soon.'

'Yes, yes.' Keelin sighed. 'I've been ready for ages.'

'And Ronan?' asked Gemma.

'I repacked his bag,' Keelin told her. 'He'd put in three T-shirts and no underwear.'

Gemma laughed. The children were spending the weekend with David and his wife who were bringing them away to a surprise location.

'Actually it's just to the Nuremore Hotel,' David had confided to Gemma. 'It's not too long a drive and there'll be plenty for them to do. There's a leisure centre so the weather won't matter.'

'Will you be able to cope?' asked Gemma.

'Um, probably not,' David said cheerfully. 'But we'll have a go.'

The doorbell rang and Keelin clattered back down the stairs to answer it.

'Hi, Dad!' She gave her father a kiss on the cheek. 'Hello, Orla. I like your hair like that.'

'Thanks.' Orla smiled at her. 'It feels really odd, though, Keelin.'

'It looks great,' said Keelin. 'I have to admit that Mum isn't bad with the scissors. I'm thinking of letting her cut mine some day.'

'I like yours long,' said David. 'When you're not hiding behind it, that is.'

'Hi, there.' Gemma came downstairs.

She's good at coming down stairs, thought Orla. She kind of slinks down them in a terribly sexy way. I wonder if she knows that she's doing it.

'You look great,' Orla told her. 'You did the last time you wore that dress too.'

The two women smiled at each other.

'I'm about three pounds heavier than the last time I wore this dress and it shows,' said Gemma. 'Keelin had to hang out of the zip to close it.'

'You'd never guess,' said Orla.

'Would you like tea or coffee before you go?' asked Gemma.

David shook his head. 'I'd like to get started as soon as we can.'

'Orla? How about you? Or a quick snack to keep you going?'

She shook her head. 'Thanks, Gemma, but I had a huge lunch today. I was out with a client and I'm still stuffed.'

'She landed a rather good pension scheme for her new company.' David put his arm round her and hugged her. 'It'll help with the mortgage, I suppose.'

'How's work on the new house going?' asked Gemma. 'I think you're absolutely great to buy something that needs to be practically rebuilt, Orla. I don't think I'd have the patience myself.'

'Why do you think we're going away this weekend?' Orla grinned. 'They're sanding the floors. It might be habitable by next week, or it might just be a cloud of dust.'

'At least it's bigger than the apartment,' said Gemma.

'It's different to the apartment,' Orla told her. 'And that's what's important.'

Keelin reappeared with her bag and with Ronan. 'We're ready,' she said.

'Excellent.' David lifted her bag. 'Good grief, Keelin, we're only going to be away a couple of days. What's in this?'

'Stuff,' she said.

'You women are all the same.' He heaved the shoulder strap over his shoulder. 'Any chance you can carry your own, Ronan?'

'Sure I can.'

'Be good,' said Gemma. 'Have a great time.'

'We will.' Keelin kissed her on the cheek. 'Have a good time yourself.'

'Tell Liz I said hello,' said David. 'And congratulations.'

Gemma nodded. She watched them as they walked down the path to the car. David. David's wife. And her children.

A few months ago she wouldn't have believed it possible that David and Orla would want to take the children for a weekend or that she would let them. Or even that the children would go.

It's not easy, she thought, this extended family lark. But it's something you can learn to live with.

Orla waved as she got into the car. The flame-haired bimbo bitch didn't look like a bimbo any more, courtesy of the very sleek haircut that Gemma had given her the previous week. Not that she'd ever really looked like a bimbo at all, Gemma had to admit. But it had been therapeutic to think of her like that. The new, shorter style suited Orla. You could see the shape of her face better (good bone structure, thought Gemma, wistfully) and it gave her a greater air of authority. That would be tested over the weekend anyway, with Keelin and Ronan in tow.

When they were out of view, Gemma closed the door. She poured herself a measure of Baileys and sat down to await Sam's arrival. He was due in ten minutes and he was nearly always on time.

I wonder why I end up with punctual men? she mused as she closed her eyes and revelled in the calm of the quiet house. Punctual men who have finally turned me into a punctual woman! In all the time she'd been married to David she couldn't remember being ready ten minutes before she was due to go out before.

The doorbell rang. Sam stood on the doorstep, a bunch of red roses in his arms.

'Oh, Sam, thank you!' Gemma beamed at him. 'They're absolutely gorgeous. Come in while I put them in water.'

Sam followed her into the kitchen. He watched while Gemma filled two chunky glass vases with water and deftly arranged the flowers in them.

'How do you do that?' he asked.

'What?'

'Make it look so neat. Effortless. Tidy.'

'Natural talent, I guess.' Actually she was pleased to have accomplished the task without having splashed her dress.

'They look wonderful,' he told her. 'As, of course, do you.'

She grinned. 'Flattery will get you – well, you know me! A sucker for a compliment!'

Sam put his arms round her. 'You're the most fabulous woman I've ever met, Gemma. And that's not just a compliment, it's the truth.' His face was serious as his eyes met hers.

'Thank you.'

He kissed her gently on the lips but before she could respond he held her away from him.

'I brought you something for tonight,' he said.

'I know,' Gemma said. 'And the flowers are lovely, thank you.'

'Something else, you idiot.'

She looked at him while he put his hand into his pocket and took out a long, slender box.

'I wanted to get you something,' he said. 'To let you know how I feel. I couldn't think of what might be the right thing. This is Keelin's idea.'

'Oh, God!' Gemma's eyes twinkled at him.

'I asked her what you needed,' he said. 'She said that you didn't seem to need anything any more. She said that you were almost totally self-sufficient.'

'Did she?'

'She thinks you're great, Gemma. And so do I.' He handed her the box.

Gemma opened it. The watch inside was tiny, with a silver bracelet and a diamond on its face.

'Sam!' She looked at him. 'This is – this is beautiful. And you shouldn't have. Honestly.'

'Why?' he asked.

She said nothing.

'I want you to know that I spend all of my time thinking about you, Gemma.'

'Sam, it's not like you to get soppy,' said Gemma.

He smiled at her. 'We're going to your sister's engagement party,' he said. 'Romance is in the air!'

'I'm too old for romance,' said Gemma. 'My romancing days are long over. I'm just . . . just . . .'

Her words were lost as Sam kissed her.

'We'll be late,' said Gemma, breathlessly, when finally she came up for air.

'Plenty of time,' said Sam carelessly. 'We can always blame the watch.'

She laughed. 'We have to go,' she said. 'We really do.'

'I know.' He kissed her again.

'How do you do that?' she asked.

'What?'

'Kiss like that?'

'Takes two,' said Sam.

He held her close to him as he kissed her on the lips, then on her forehead, on her cheeks, at the base of her throat. And then he was tugging on the zip of the Ben de Lisi which rippled to the floor in a stream of shimmering lilac silk.

She couldn't remember feeling like this before. As though time had stopped, as though they were one person, as though everything in the world was exactly in its allotted place.

And she knew she was ready to start living her life again.